About the Author

K ATHRYN M ILLER H AINES is an actor, mystery writer, award-winning playwright, and the artistic director of a Pittsburgh-based theater company. She is the author of *The War Against Miss Winter, The Winter of Her Discontent,* and *Winter in June.*

WHEN WINTER
RETURNS

Also by Kathryn Miller Haines

Winter in June
The Winter of Her Discontent
The War Against Miss Winter

WHEN WINTER
Returns

KATHRYN MILLER HAINES

HARPER

NEW YORK • LONDON • TORONTO • SYDNEY

HARPER

HarperCollins books may be purchased for educational, business, or sales promotional use. For information please write: Special Markets Department, HarperCollins Publishers, 10 East 53rd Street, New York, NY 10022.

FIRST HARPER PAPERBACK PUBLISHED 2010.

Library of Congress Cataloging-in-Publication Data
Haines, Kathryn Miller.
    When winter returns / Kathryn Miller Haines. — 1st ed.
        p.   cm.
    ISBN 978-0-06-157957-8
    1. Winter, Rosie (Fictitious character)—Fiction. 2. Actresses—New York (State)—New York—Fiction. 3. World War, 1939–1945—New York (State)—New York—Fiction. 4. Sabotage—New York (State)—New York—Fiction. 5. Nazis—New York (State)—New York—Fiction. 6. New York (N.Y.)—Fiction. I. Title.
PS3608.A5449W54 2010
813'.6—dc22
                                                                2009035131

10 11 12 13 14   OV/RRD   10 9 8 7 6 5 4 3 2 1

For the two men who make *my* heart sing—
Garrett and Gryphon.

Acknowledgments

Thanks to all the folks at HarperCollins who have supported Rosie over the years, including Wendy Lee whose efforts haven't gone unnoticed. And my continuing gratitude for my agent, Paul Fedorko, for all that he does.

For their priceless critiques, kudos to Beverly Pollock, Paula Martinac, David Doorley, Judy Meiksin, Sloan Macrae, Carol Mullen, F. J. Hartland, and the incomparable David White. For their advice, wisdom, and support, unending gratitude goes out to Kathleen George, Nancy Martin, Rebecca Drake, Lila Shaara, and Heather Terrell. Pittsburgh's lucky to have your talent!

Mad props to the gang at Mystery's Most Wanted, and to Deane Root and Mariana Whitmer at the Center for American Music, who should've been thanked a long time ago. You both make having a "day job" an enjoyable thing.

Words can't capture how awesome my family is (both the two-legged and four-legged members), nor how grateful I am for their support in all I've taken on this year. Thanks, guys.

Much appreciation to the owners and staff at Mystery Lovers Bookshop (Oakmont, Pennsylvania), Once Upon a Crime (Minneapolis, Minnesota), Aunt Agatha's (Ann Arbor, Michigan), and Murder By the Book (Houston, Texas).

And finally, a special hat tip to the readers who've followed Rosie from book to book, attended events, and reached out through e-mail. You're awesome, each and every one of you.

WHEN WINTER
RETURNS

CHAPTER 1

The Wrong Mr. Wright

September 1943

Home. Again.

Well, not *quite* home. My best pal Jayne and I were finally in New York after spending three months with the USO in the South Pacific, but instead of boarding a train bound for Manhattan, we were heading upstate. We'd just arrived in a little town Jayne's recently deceased fiancé, Billy DeMille, hailed from. Jayne wanted to go there before we headed home, even though the funeral had most likely already happened. She needed to see her Billy's grave, the house he grew up in, the parents he loved. Manhattan would wait. We'd been gone five months after all, what were a few days more?

To her face I cheerfully agreed with her thinking, but I yearned to be back in my own bed, to wake up without the assistance of a bugle, to take a bath someplace where the water was hot and the walls were sturdy. I wanted to catch up on our rooming house gossip, read *Variety*, and plot out which audition I'd take on next. I wanted to see my nemesis Ruby and my former feline Churchill and all those other unpleasant things that used to whittle away my nerves. Now they were all part of home to me, where mosquitoes and bottle flies, war and wounded, were things you only read about in books and newspapers. I wanted to forget how people could betray one another, how the enemy was often indistinguishable from our friends, how easily you could justify murder, how fragile we all were, how love lost didn't come back to you just because you chased it down.

But Jayne had done so much for me; it was time for me to do for her.

As we walked toward Billy's parents' address, Jayne remained silent. Since Billy's death she had grown increasingly small until I often wondered if I might be able to fit her in my pocket. The light within her seemed to have diminished, and as it faded she said less, ate less, and seemed determined to take up less space. There were mornings when I feared she'd disappeared entirely only to realize that it was just the muted sound of her breathing that had fooled me.

"Hey, you," I said to her now, knocking my elbow into hers. "Can you believe we're actually here?"

"No. It feels like a dream." Her high-pitched voice had grown thin, like an untrained soprano perpetually struggling with a high note. She smiled, though it wasn't the same. Her lips no longer seemed capable of reaching as far as they once had.

Billy's parents lived on a tree-lined street that looked like it had been ripped from *Life Magazine*. So this was the Main Street America we'd heard no longer existed. Children played in the early fall sun, skipping rope, throwing jacks, and tossing a ball back and forth with the kind of repetition that suggested small-town life had nothing to offer but monotony. In the distance a young male voice made a rat-a-tat noise, which he periodically interrupted with a cry of "Die, you Jap bastards." This was the new version of cowboys and Indians, only the kids wouldn't dare let the enemy win. If you weren't on the Allied side, your fate was already decided.

A small girl pulled a Radio Flyer down a weed-choked sidewalk. Inside it lay crushed cans that threatened to topple out of the wagon and onto the concrete. As she marched on her mission, she sang a little ditty to herself, "Mr. Hitler, you are sunk. We're gonna beat you with our junk."

Had we always been so naïve? After being abroad and seeing with my own peepers what war meant, I found it hard to believe that we thought we could change the outcome by collecting some tin and having faith that if you were right you would be victorious. It just didn't work that way.

"It's that one," said Jayne. She pointed at a house surrounded by a white picket fence. Chrysanthemums the color of a ship's rusted hull sat in a large terracotta pot near the front door. Empty milk bottles huddled on the stoop waiting to be picked up. The front windows were open and white, sheer drapes fluttered in the afternoon breeze, making it look like ghosts were at play. One of the house numbers had come free of its nail and sagged to the left as though it had tired of doing its duty after all these years. A U.S. flag proclaimed the family's patriotism, although its fervor was muted by a second flag silent and still in an upstairs window. This one had only one star. That's all it took to declare, "Our boy's not coming home."

Jayne paused where the sidewalk met the path up to the house. I couldn't tell if she was hesitating out of fear or a desire to take it all in. This could've been hers, she was probably thinking. The white picket fence, the house with its drapery ghosts, the children going merrily about their business. Would she really have wanted that life? There were times when we both thought we did, but looking at this picture of domestic bliss I couldn't help but yearn for a stiff drink, a new pulp, and the promise of a Friday night spent with the biggest band in town.

"Okay," she said after a moment had passed. "I'm ready." She marched to the front door and pushed the buzzer. A wood-burned sign announced WELCOME TO THE DEMILLES.

"Come in," called a woman whose voice was deepened by age. "I'll be with you in just a moment." Neither of us moved. This welcome was intended for someone she knew, not two city gals looking to dredge up her grief. Once she realized we'd ignored her invitation, she appeared at the door, her hands busy untying her apron. If we were strangers, we deserved a stranger's welcome. "Oh, hello," she said. "Can I help you?"

Her hair was gray at the temples and swept into a loose bun at the back of her head. A strand of oyster fruit circled her neck. She was short and stout, and so maternal in her softness that I wanted to bury my head in her bosom and take in her smell. Even when she wasn't baking, you knew she was the kind of woman who constantly smelled of sugar cookies.

"Are you Mrs. DeMille?" asked Jayne.

"Yes." The quotation marks between her eyes deepened. She was worried we were bringing more bad news.

Jayne offered her hand. "I'm Jayne Hamilton."

Mrs. DeMille wiped her own hand on the apron before returning the gesture. A splash of iodine had reddened her palm. "Nice to meet you," she said.

I offered my own mitt and introduction, and she returned the favor.

"Now what can I help you with?" she asked. There was no recognition in her eyes. And why should there be? Jayne hadn't warned her she was coming. It had taken us weeks to track down an address for Billy and by that time we were already on a ship headed for home.

"I was a friend of Billy's," said Jayne.

The woman's face softened. "Oh my. Isn't that lovely? Come in, please. I just put on some coffee."

We followed her into a living room filled with photos in mismatched frames. While she returned to the kitchen, Jayne and

I settled side by side on a mohair sofa. A framed photo of FDR watched us from above the fireplace. A needlepoint pillow depicting the flag with the words "God Bless America" rested on a round Victorian chair. Porcelain kittens fought over a porcelain ball of yarn on the side table.

"She doesn't know who I am," whispered Jayne.

"Maybe he didn't tell her about you."

"But he said he had. The night he proposed he said he was writing a letter home to tell his parents all about me."

That had been days before he'd died, when his plane was shot down in the South Pacific while trying to retaliate for an Imperial Navy attack on a U.S. ship. He wasn't the only one who'd died. We'd lost dozens of friends that day.

"Maybe she didn't get the letter yet," I said. We'd all heard awful tales of mail arriving home after telegrams reporting the deaths had. Those final letters were always breezy little notes that held no hint of the danger the writer was about to head into.

"Oh, God," Jayne moaned. "That would be terrible."

Mrs. DeMille returned with a silver tray in hand. She set it on the coffee table and poured each of us a cup of weak brown liquid that smelled of chicory. If I missed anything about the South Pacific, it was the real coffee they served the officers and those who had the privilege of dining with them.

Mrs. DeMille settled in a chair opposite us, resting her head on its doily-festooned back. "Now how did you know Billy, dear?"

I tried to picture Billy as I looked at her. I'd barely known the kid—I was so wrapped up in finding my missing-in-action ex-boyfriend when Jayne was falling in love—but it was impossible to forget those gentle brown eyes, that sweet smile, and how he blossomed every time he looked at my pal. They were made for each other—two tiny people whose hands seemed to have been carved to best fit the other's in it.

Now Jayne's hands shook as she attempted to lift her cup. Liquid splashed over the side and onto the saucer. Two more attempts yielded the same results. She gave up on drinking the coffee and, with a rattle, deposited it on a doily resting by the kittens. "I met Billy in Manhattan. At the Stage Door Canteen. And we started writing each other. We saw each other again while I was touring. Rosie and I were—well, I guess we still are—part of the USO camp shows." She swallowed and I could see a hint of the old Jayne coming back. "Then . . . um . . . right before . . . you know . . . before he . . . well, we got engaged."

Mrs. DeMille sat stock-still with her cup halfway to her mouth. "I beg your pardon?" she said.

Jayne fluttered her left hand where she still wore the silver Australian coin Billy had hammered into a ring. "I'm Billy's fiancée."

"Oh my heavens," Mrs. DeMille whispered. The cup and saucer returned to the table. Her hand traveled to her mouth and rested there while she hunted for what to say next.

A door slammed in the kitchen, though to my frayed nerves, it might as well have been a bomb.

Get a grip, I told myself. You're home now.

Heavy masculine footsteps came our way. A portly man with a head ringed in whitish gray hair appeared in the doorway. One hand held his hat; the other struggled to release the strained button on his topcoat. "Oh, I didn't know you had company."

Mrs. DeMille jumped to her feet. "This is my husband. William, this is Jayne Hamilton. And . . . ah . . . "

"Rosie Winter," I said.

"Jayne was engaged to Billy."

The hat fell to the floor and the hand ceased its mission of mercy. "Engaged?" he whispered.

Jayne nodded.

The man crossed the room in two steps and crushed her in an embrace. "I'll be darned. Billy had a secret, did he?" When he released her, his eyes twinkled with moisture. Mrs. DeMille removed a handkerchief from her bra and patted her own eyes dry before passing it on to her husband. He made quick work of it before shoving the hanky in his pocket. "Blazes, girl, what took you so long to get here?"

Jayne's face broke into a smile, the first real one I'd seen from her in months. "I came as fast as I could."

He took her in, top to tail, and shook his head. "You did. I'm sure you did."

"They're in the USO," said his wife. "That's how she met Billy."

"What were you doing in the USO?" he asked.

"I'm an actress," she said. "And a dancer."

Mr. and Mrs. DeMille locked eyes for a moment, sharing a thought the way only those who've been married for a thousand years can do.

"He loved the theater," said Mrs. DeMille. "He went to it every chance he got."

"And he was a hell of a dancer," said Mr. DeMille. "But I'm sure you know that." He led Jayne back to the sofa and, with his hands still in hers, sat beside her. "We want to hear everything about you. Don't skip a thing."

I felt incredibly out of place. As Jayne began her life story, I gestured to Mrs. DeMille that I needed to use the bathroom. She pointed toward the staircase. Upstairs, I retreated into a small salmon-tiled room. My body ached from weeks spent traveling by ship and long days traveling by train. A footed, porcelain tub took up most of the space, and I toyed with the idea of filling it with hot water and taking a long soak. They probably wouldn't notice, and even if they did, I doubted they would care. Instead, I washed my face and examined myself in the medicine cabinet mirror. The yellow tint from the synthetic quinine we'd taken was starting to fade, as was the tan I'd managed to acquire despite being on the islands during the rainy season. Slowly, I was returning to my old self. Everything was going to be okay. We'd survived. And while Jayne was clearly worse for wear, she'd been right on insisting that she needed this trip.

I left the bathroom and explored the other doors branching

off from the hallway. The first room I encountered was a child's bedroom. School awards, sports trophies, and forgotten toys lined the walls and surfaces. I peered at the certificates and discovered Billy's name written again and again. So this was his room. He'd been a football player, an honor student, and a writer for the school paper. He liked teddy bears and toy trains and had a collection of kazoos. Did Jayne know all this? It didn't seem fair that there was so much about him that she hadn't learned and no Billy here to tell her about it.

A patchwork quilt covered the twin-sized bed and sang its siren song. God, I was so tired I was going goofy. I sat on the bed and leaned against the headboard but refused to give in to my desire to lie on it. Unrelated images darted in and out of my noodle until a single face rose to the top: Jack.

I'd done a fine job not thinking about him the whole journey home, and here was my exhausted subconscious dragging him out to toy with me. My ex-boyfriend Jack Castlegate, our whole reason for going to the South Pacific. After months of believing he was missing in action, I was told he was dead. I'd even mourned him, but then in the last act he'd reemerged, not only alive but in love with another woman—a Women's Army Corps private named Candy Abbott.

What a waste the last three months had been. If I hadn't gone to Tulagi, I wouldn't have had my heart broken. And Jayne wouldn't have fallen in love with Billy, only to lose him right after getting engaged. And I wouldn't have seen Peaches again—

Stop it, I told myself. There was no point in dwelling on what might have been. We were here now. That was all that mattered.

Beside the bed, on a night table dominated by a lamp shaped like a train engine, sat a photo of a boy in a cap and gown. "Hello, you," I said. "I'm guessing I'm not the girl you were expecting to find in your room." The boy smiled from some distant moment in time. I picked up his picture and grinned back . . . at a total stranger.

I recoiled from the photo like it was a pan fresh from the burner. "You're not Billy," I told him. I left the bed and looked for other photos and found, sitting atop the dresser, a snapshot of a boy with his parents. It was clearly Mr. and Mrs. DeMille in the image, but the boy was the same stranger who wore the cap and gown. Was this a brother? Maybe Billy was close enough to his sibling that he kept pictures of him in his bedroom. I didn't have any brothers or sisters myself so the idea seemed rational. Sort of.

I left the room and reentered the hallway. In the next room an elaborate red, white, and blue quilt was being pieced together, while a variety of sewing implements sat waiting for their next project. The final room was clearly Mr. and Mrs. DeMille's. Similar photos sat atop a dressing table, with the same boy grinning from behind the glass. Just the one boy. The one who wasn't our Billy.

Uh oh.

Maybe in their grief they'd decided to remove his pictures, the way members of some religions covered mirrors during their mourning.

I went back downstairs and rejoined them in the living room.

"Where have you been?" asked Jayne. Her voice was stronger, her posture improved. She seemed to take up twice as much space on the couch as she had when we arrived.

"Stomach trouble," I whispered.

She patted my knee sympathetically. She was back to herself, serving as my caregiver.

"We have something for you," said Mrs. DeMille. She pulled a ring from her finger and passed it to Jayne.

"Oh, I couldn't!"

She forced Jayne's hand to close over the ring. "No, dear. I always told Billy that when he met the right girl, he was to give her my mother's ring."

"But surely someone else should have it."

"There isn't anyone else. Billy was our only child and I know this is what he would've wanted."

Only child? My stomach began to cramp for real.

Jayne slid the ring onto her right hand. It was much too large, but she squeezed her fingers together to stop it from moving.

"Can I talk to you for a second?" I said. "It's kind of important."

Her forehead rippled with concern. "Okay."

I took Jayne by the hand and pulled her off the couch. "We'll be right back," I said.

I didn't make it two feet before Mr. DeMille stopped me. "Don't you two be going anywhere. We've got some celebrating to do. Get the glasses, Mother. We need to have a toast." He removed a crystal decanter containing a deep-red-colored liquid from the sideboard while Mrs. Demille pulled four tiny aperitif glasses from a cabinet.

Jayne took her seat on the couch again. I lowered myself, reluctantly, beside her.

"Seriously," I told Jayne, my voice so low I almost couldn't hear it. "I need to talk you. Now."

"Whatever it is can wait," she whispered back.

"Trust me: this can't."

"Well it's going to have to," she hissed. "Nothing is more important than this."

"What are you two going on about over there?" asked Mr. De-Mille. "Don't tell me you're teetotalers."

"No, sir," I said. "In fact, make mine a double."

Jayne elbowed me. Hard.

"Is this the house Billy grew up in?" I asked.

"Oh, yes," said Mrs. DeMille. "Born and raised."

"What's his middle name?"

"Robert," said Jayne and Mrs. DeMille simultaneously.

"It was his grandfather's name," Mr. DeMille added.

So much for that tactic. I scanned the room and the framed images I'd barely registered when we first came in. There was that boy again; only in these photos he was practically a man and wearing a white Dixie cup cap on the back of his head.

Please let there be a logical explanation for this, I prayed. Let Billy be a black sheep whose photo they banished from the house and replaced with—what? A beloved nephew? Or let him be the victim of a disfiguring accident that changed him from the boy they knew to the one Jayne loved. Or let this be a terrible dream and any second now I'm going to wake up on the train with Jayne sleeping restlessly in the bunk above me.

Each tiny cup was filled to the halfway point. Mr. DeMille passed them out and I fought the urge to down the thimble of hooch in a single swallow.

"What should we drink to?" asked Mrs. DeMille.

"To Jayne," said Mr. DeMille. "If you were good enough to be Billy's wife, you're good enough to be our daughter. You're welcome in our house anytime."

Jayne shuddered beside me. Fat tears rested in the corners of her eyes, but she didn't fight to push them away.

"To Jayne," Mrs. DeMille and I said.

We emptied our glasses and Mr. DeMille rapidly refilled them to the halfway point. If he kept this up, I was going to grab the decanter out of his hand and drain it myself. "This time, we drink to President Roosevelt. The greatest leader of the greatest nation on earth." We toasted the portrait above the fireplace and took a tipple.

Mr. DeMille filled the glasses a third time, emptying the bottle of its remaining contents.

"Are you sure we should have more?" asked his wife.

"It's not a celebration if you can see straight," he replied. "We still have to make the most important toast of all. To Billy."

Mrs. DeMille turned to face the portrait of the unfamiliar boy in the sailor suit. "To Billy."

"To Billy," I said, because it meant I got to drink.

The room stood still. The DeMilles stared at Jayne, waiting for her to join in their toast.

"Um," she said when the silence had grown uncomfortable. "Who's that?"

"That's Billy, of course," said Mr. DeMille.

"No it's not," said Jayne. She left her seat on the couch and approached the photo, just in case the thimble of booze had altered her vision. "That's definitely not my Billy."

"Of course it is," said Mrs. DeMille.

"Rosie?" said Jayne. "I'm not crazy, am I?"

"Nope."

Billy's mother gasped. Mr. DeMille took his place behind her and set his hands on her shoulders.

"Look, we must've gotten the wrong address," I said. "There must be a thousand William Robert DeMille's in the navy."

Jayne shook her head. "No. He described the house. The street. He even described the two of you."

"So maybe it's a lousy coincidence," I said.

"You didn't know Billy?" asked Mrs. DeMille.

"No, she did," I said. "Just not this one."

She groaned and slumped farther into her chair.

"I'm so sorry," said Jayne. "I don't understand what's happened."

"It's been an awfully long time," said Mr. DeMille. "Maybe you got the details mixed up."

"It was only two months ago," said Jayne.

"Two months?" said Mrs. DeMille. "That's not possible. Our Billy was killed at Pearl Harbor."

CHAPTER 2

The Old Homestead

Jayne rushed out of the house and onto the sidewalk. I tossed the DeMilles my apologies and hurried after her. She stopped at the curb like a trapped animal that didn't know which way to turn.

"I tried to tell you," I said.

She put her head against the trunk of a large oak that spanned the distance between the sidewalk and the street. Carved initials wounded the bark with the declaration that T. P. loved G. N. "I just don't understand. He described every detail. His mother's pearls. The tiny glasses they used whenever there was a celebration. Even those stupid porcelain cats she had on the end table."

"I'm sure there's an explanation for all this," I said.

"How?" She lifted her head and returned it to the trunk with more force. If she kept this up, she was going to have a nasty mark on her forehead. "This was the address Peaches gave me. It was off of Billy's military record."

Peaches was Paul Ascott, an officer in Billy's unit. He was also the one who'd told me my ex-boyfriend Jack was dead. And as an added bonus, he was the man I thought I could love only to find out I couldn't even trust him. Was this his final act of sabotage?

Not even I could believe that. Peaches was a master of good intentions ruined by bad choices. There were too many coincidences here for him to have simply passed on bad information.

The screen door whined open behind us. Mr. DeMille huffed down the walk.

"Oh, God," said Jayne. "The ring." She tore it from her finger and passed it to me. "Give it to him. I can't bear to talk to him again." She hurried down the block, ducking behind another tree like she was playing a game of hide and seek.

Mr. DeMille arrived beside me and I gave him a look that I hoped was sympathetic but probably made me look constipated. "We're so sorry," I said. "Please believe me that this is an awful mistake. We didn't mean to hurt anyone."

"No one thinks you did. The missus will be fine. It's just a shock, that's all." He looked up the street to where Jayne was doing a lousy job hiding. "When did she lose her Billy?"

"At the beginning of July. His plane was gunned down in the South Pacific. She hasn't been the same since, and she thought if she met you, it might help. And it did until . . . you know . . . we realized you weren't the right people."

He looked older than when we'd first met him. I hoped it was only seeing him outside that made him seem that way and not our visit that had aged him. "I've heard a lot of crazy things about this war, but this might be one of the craziest. I should've realized something wasn't right."

"So you lost your son at Pearl Harbor?"

He nodded. "He was a good boy. Smart. Well behaved. Never gave us a moment's trouble."

"He sounds like a right gee."

"I don't know what's worse: losing them when you know it

might happen or losing them when it never occurred to you they were in any real danger. I suppose it doesn't matter. Either way they're gone."

I thought of the untouched bedroom on the second floor. How many hours had Mr. and Mrs. DeMille sat in there, reliving his short life?

"Thanks for being so nice about all this," I said. "I know Jayne wishes like crazy that you were her Billy's parents. It would've made everything so much easier."

He nodded and started up the walk. He'd barely gone a step when he turned back to me. "I forgot why I came out here to begin with."

"Right. You probably want this back." I passed him the ring, and he looked at it like it was the last thing he expected to see sitting in his hand.

"Actually, I wanted to give you these." He removed two envelopes from his coat pocket. Their tops had been neatly slit open. "She doesn't know about them. I thought they might upset her."

"What are they?" I asked as I took them from him.

He peeked over his shoulder to verify that his wife was still in the house. "Letters from a man in New York City who claimed to be Billy's landlord. Our names were listed on his rental form as his next of kin."

I eyeballed the handwriting. A bold, masculine hand had written out Billy's name in thick, black ink. "I don't understand. Why are you showing us these? Our Billy isn't your Billy."

He poked the letters with his forefinger. "And neither is the boy this man wrote me about. He claims Billy was a tenant in June 1942."

I got where he was going. By June 1942 *his* Billy was dead. "Did you ever write him back?"

"There was no reason to. He wanted money for outstanding rent and I figured he was running some sort of con. They do that you know."

Boy was he right. It wasn't unusual for creditors to pop up after death notices ran in the paper. Not everyone saw war as a tragedy. Some believed it was an opportunity.

"So why'd you save them?"

He shrugged and a sad smile spread across his face. "I wish I knew. Part of me wanted to believe he'd made it out of Pearl Harbor alive and that the box they'd sent home was someone else. But I could never get used to the idea that our Billy would start over and never let us know he was safe. He wouldn't have done that to his mother." He pressed the letters into my hand. "Maybe I saved them for you. It seems to me if this man knew another Billy DeMille and you're looking for one, you two might want to get in contact with each other."

I thanked him for the letters, tucked them into my purse, and went in search of Jayne.

Jayne was silent the whole train journey home. I didn't tell her about the letters. Instead, I stuffed them deep into my purse where I swear I could hear them crinkle and sigh every time I shifted. We made it into Manhattan early the next afternoon. As we waited curbside for a cab, I took in a city changed. It was funny that both Tulagi and Manhattan were islands, and yet Manhattan had never seemed as isolated to me as the island in the South Pacific had. Even now fog hid the seams where land met water, traffic noises obliterated the calls of ships, and pollution disguised the saltwater scent of the air. Why hadn't I realized how separated we'd always been from the rest of the world? Just like Tulagi, this place was both paradise and the perfect target.

We pooled our money for a hired hack back to our rooming house in the village. Our driver didn't seem to understand that we weren't visitors arriving for the first time, and he spent the ride engaging in a breathless monologue about the ills of the city. LaGuardia needed to spend more time being mayor and less time playing conductor at the Met. Look what had happened in Harlem.

If he'd waited any longer to nip that in the bud, there'd have been dark meat rioting all over the city. Did we realize that Manhattan generated enough garbage in a day to feed the whole of Europe for a week? As for the Empty State Building—we were lucky the war had caused a real estate crunch or it might still be waiting for tenants. And speaking of empty: he hadn't had a good steak in years. What was Roosevelt thinking, making two meatless days a week? How were we supposed to support the war when we were too weak to support ourselves? Especially now that the war was creeping onto the home front. Did we know how many German U-boats had been spotted on the East Coast? How many factory workers had been arrested for sabotage? How easy it would be for the enemy to gain ground by poisoning our water supply or starting a forest fire? And it wasn't just the Krauts. We had to be vigilant about the Wops too. Who knew how many fascists were hiding among them? "The enemy's coming here, mark my words," he said. "And who can blame them when we're practically rolling out the red carpet?"

By the time home loomed in front of us, my stomach was in knots. The George Bernard Shaw Home for Women Pursuing Theatrical Vocations didn't look like I remembered it. The Civil War–era house hugged the street, its windows looking like the wide eyes of some weary coquette hoping a sailor would treat her to a night on the town. The mortar was missing in large chinks, the bricks stained by the refuse of industry, the wooden windows in desperate need of painting, one of the front-door panes broken but not shattered. Had it always appeared so shabby, or had my joy at living on my own, among like-minded people, blinded me to its flaws all these years? The driver helped us haul our luggage into the foyer, and we tipped him handsomely for the help. For a moment we stared at the photographs plastered on the wall. Our housemother, Belle, required everyone who'd ever been in residence to display their mugs so that visitors could see all the people who once lived here and muse on how many of them had gone on to fame and fortune, and how many had disappeared into obscurity. So far the disappointments were beating out the successes.

There were new faces—a lot of new faces. It was impossible to tell which of them had already come and gone during our absence and who was there to stay. One was our friend Zelda who we'd helped move in right before we left. Another was a girl with freckles and frizzy hair who seemed irritated that her picture was being taken. There was also a girl with large, pouty lips and a nose that seemed too small for her face. And what a face it was—perfectly symmetrical, so much so that whoever had taken her photo had made her stare dead-on at the camera. She was stunning in an uneasy kind of way—the kind of woman who shouldn't be pretty but was.

"New blood," I said to Jayne.

She shrugged, uninterested in my observation.

I put a hand on the door separating the foyer from the rest of the house. The knob wouldn't budge.

"Since when do they lock the door during the day?" I asked. I shaded my eyes and peered through the dirty glass. The sitting room was empty, but a shadow moved from the parlor to the kitchen.

I knocked on the door, wincing as the wood bit into my hand. "Hello?" I called out. "Hello?" Jayne joined me and after a solid minute of knocking and shouting, our housemother, Belle, rounded the corner and appeared before us.

"Yes?"

"It's Rosie and Jayne. We're back."

A key turned in the lock and she opened the door. A former vaudeville performer, Belle was wearing a robe lined in purple feathers and a headpiece decorated with the same. I used to find her allegiance to her old costumes endearing, but in the light of day, after weeks of travel, it now struck me as grotesque. She was a relic from another age, desperately trying to keep a foothold in the present before she too was replaced.

What was the matter with me? Clearly I needed a drink.

"What's with the security?" I asked.

"You can't be too careful these days." Her tone was short and quick, like the clatter of an Underwood typing out a Dear John letter.

"You don't seem very happy to see us," I said.

She shut the door behind us and relocked it. It was a new lock, so large and imperious you could develop your hand muscles just from looking at it. "I would be thrilled if I'd known you were coming."

"You didn't get Rosie's letter?" asked Jayne.

"Not unless it was written with invisible ink."

Panic opened one eye and surveyed the room. "Don't worry about it," I said. "We didn't expect a big to-do anyway. Should we go ahead and take our things upstairs?"

"Sure, but I don't know where you're going to put them. Your room's no longer available."

"Oh." There'd been a magician's assistant who moved in not long after we left. Zelda had written us about her, but I'd just assumed, based on the tone of the letter, that she would've been given the boot by now. And maybe she had. It was possible any of the new faces adorning the wall had taken over our old digs. "Any room will do. It's not like we expected you to hold ours."

Belle crossed her arms. "All the rooms are taken."

"Really?" Jayne's lower lip quivered, and I could sense that mine was on its way to doing the same. All I wanted was to be in my drafty, badly lit room sleeping on a bed that creaked every time I exhaled. Was that too much to ask?

Belle may not have cared about my wants, but she'd always liked Jayne. "Maybe one of the girls without roommates will let you stay with them," she said.

I rolled my eyes. I didn't want to live with someone else. I wanted to live with Jayne. "Who's got the singles these days?"

Belle picked up the house register and ran her finger down its list of names. "Ruby Priest."

Great. My archnemesis and keeper of Churchill, a cat that hated me with such intensity I could sense his venom from halfway across the world.

"Who else?"

The finger continued its journey down the page. "The only other single is taken by Ann Fremont. She's in your old room."

So we *had* been booted by a new girl. "Why don't you stick her in with Ruby and give us back our digs?"

"Absolutely not," said Belle. "In the first place, you don't decide who lives where, and for another Ruby and Ann don't get along."

I was starting to like this dame. If I was stuck with living with her, we would at least have one thing in common.

"Let's go talk to them," said Jayne. She started reluctantly toward the stairs, and I already felt my guilt multiplying. Was it really fair to stick her with Ruby? Jayne wasn't her biggest fan either, and after everything she'd been through, forcing her to live with a woman who thought empathy was a cheap cologne hardly seemed kind.

I was about to offer as much when Zelda appeared at the top of the staircase. "Rosie! Jayne! Is it really you?" She rushed the distance to us and embraced us in one giant hug. "Why didn't you tell me you were coming home?"

"There wasn't time," I said.

She led us toward the sofa. Someone had rearranged the furniture while we were gone, and the space no longer felt like a place where you'd want to linger. With its new sharp angles, the sitting area reminded me of a hospital waiting room. Like the exterior of the building, the interior had taken a beating. Cigarette burns poked through the rug, showing the wooden floor underneath it. Cobwebs clung to the lampshades. The patterns on the upholstery seemed to have been generated by stains rather than chintz.

Zelda plopped onto the sofa and patted the cushion beside her. "I want to hear everything about the tour. Who did you meet? What was the South Pacific like? Did you find Jack?"

Only an actress would prioritize her questions like that: famous people encounters came first, followed by descriptions of exotic locales. Then, if you had time, you could catch her up to speed on the whole reason why you'd gone abroad: to find your missing ex-boyfriend.

"We were on tour with Gilda DeVane. The South Pacific was wet. And yes I found Jack. He's alive, awaiting trial, and currently keeping company with another woman."

"What's he on trial for?"

"They say he's a deserter. He says he was in hiding because his commanding officer wanted him dead. And frankly, if I never hear his name again, it will be too soon."

"Oh . . . at least the South Pacific was beautiful, right?" said Zelda.

"Parts of it, sure, but so many of the islands have been destroyed by the Japanese. Even the natives have been—"

"Did you go to the beach?" asked Zelda.

"We were on an island. The whole thing's a beach."

"I bet you had a fabulous tan."

"Not exactly. We had to take quinine pills because of—"

"I hope you bought grass skirts. I heard you can get them for less than a buck over there."

My desire to tell her about our trip was rapidly fading. Where did she think we'd been? On vacation?

Jayne sat silently beside me. Zelda finally recognized that she wasn't just politely waiting for a pause in conversation. She was upset. "Are you all right, Jayne?" she asked.

She nodded as a new flood of tears started from her eyes. While she wept, I told Zelda about Billy DeMille. Not the whole story, just the part about their falling in love, planning to marry, and the Japanese attack that ruined it all.

"Oh, Jayne, I'm so, so sorry."

Jayne clung to this new wave of sympathy. When she was cried out, she excused herself and went to the powder room.

"Poor Jayne," said Zelda.

"You got that right. I don't know what to do to get her through this. Nothing is working."

"Being home will help. You'll see."

"Yeah, about that. The shepherd just told us there's no room at the inn. I don't suppose you'd be willing to put us up in your room?"

"I wish I could, but I have a roommate now, Doris Newcomer. I wrote you about her."

"The magician's assistant? I thought she was a grifter."

"She's reformed."

"How'd that happen?"

She lowered her voice. "Keep it on the QT, but a few months ago The Great Federico caught her dipping into the till. He fired her, and she realized she needed a fresh start. That's how she ended up bunking with me—she couldn't afford to room by herself any longer." I wondered if Doris knew Zelda was going around telling people about her checkered past. "Anyways, we get on famously. She's become as square as a shoebox and goes to mass four times a week. Exactly the kind of influence I need." I wasn't so sure. Zelda didn't have the best record when it came to choosing friends, but I didn't want to remind her of that.

Zelda looked toward the stairs as though she expected a line of women who wanted to room with us to be waiting up there. "Ruby still lives by herself."

"For good reason. Come on—you know she'd never take us in."

"I don't know . . . she tried to get me to bunk with her."

"Seriously? Is she on the nut?"

"Beats me. The way she framed it, she wanted to help *me* out, but I told her I already found a roomie."

This was an interesting development. If Ruby was willing to take on a roommate before, maybe she'd be willing to take one again. "Belle says there's a new girl in our room. What's the wire on her?"

"Ann? Pretty quiet. Keeps to herself."

"Actress, dancer, or singer?" It was funny how important those labels could be. Dancers were typically quiet and spent as little time at the house as possible. Singers were loud and grated on my nerves. Actresses were manageable, as long as they were a different type from me. Nobody wanted to bunk with the competition.

"Actress. Could be pretty successful, if she wanted to."

"What do you mean?" I said.

"She seems to think she's too good for theater. That's what Ruby told me anyhow."

"So what—she wants to be in pictures?"

"No. She doesn't want to act at all. This is just to 'tide her over.'" She colored those words in a way that made me think she was doing either an impersonation of Ann or an impersonation of Ruby impersonating Ann.

"And how is she tiding herself over now?"

"She just got cast in Bentley's new show."

Lawrence Bentley, Ruby's on-again, off-again playwright boyfriend. "Are Ruby and he still together?"

Zelda lowered her voice and leaned toward me. "Nope. They had a spectacular breakup during the summer. I think they're kaput for good this time. *He's* the one who called it off. Said she was too self-absorbed for her own good."

Wow. Talk about the pot calling the kettle black. Ruby must've really crossed a line. No wonder she didn't like our newest housemate. She wouldn't care for anyone keeping time with Lawrence. I said as much to Zelda.

"I'm sure that's part of it," said Zelda.

Jayne returned to the lobby and joined us. "So what's the plan?" she asked. Her nose was raw, her eyes red.

I fixed a smile on my puss. "I'm going to talk to the new girl and see if we can't work something out with her."

"What if she says no?"

"She won't," I said, because by that point I was so tired I would've demanded she take us in at gunpoint if I had to.

Jayne wrinkled her nose. "She's not going to be able to fit both of us in her room."

"I'm working on that." If Ann really was acting only to kill time, she may not be planning on staying at the Shaw House very long. And if that was the case, I might be able to put up with Ruby. A few weeks wouldn't kill me, though I couldn't guarantee either of us would survive beyond that.

I left Jayne with Zelda and took the steps two at time. Our door was closed, and I found myself longing to spend an afternoon staring at that familiar scarred piece of wood. I took a deep breath, donned my most welcoming smile, and knocked.

The woman who answered was the symmetrical gal from the photo downstairs. She was as tall as I was, with huge brown eyes and the kind of figure that could stop traffic from four blocks away. She smiled uncertainly at me with the kind of look that suggested she was used to getting bad news. Behind her the radio crackled with static.

"Hiya, I'm Rosie Winter." I offered her my hand, and she took it in a limp grip. Her nails were varnished bright red and showed signs that it was time for a touch-up. She was dressed in a hip-hugging blue dress with cutouts at the top. Through the holes in the fabric you could see milky white skin interrupted by a cluster of freckles.

I waited for her to return the introduction, but it never came.

"You must be Ann," I said.

"I must be." The radio continued crackling behind her. It wasn't just any radio—it was Jayne's.

"The knob's not very precise," I told Ann.

"What?"

"On the Philco. It looks like it's at one station, but it's really not." I approached the box. "See, if you just—"

She blocked my path. "No, it's fine. I like it there."

"Okay." So she liked listening to radio static. Interesting. "This is going to sound strange, but I used to live in this room. In fact, that was my roommate's radio." If she heard me, she didn't acknowledge it. "We just got back from doing a USO tour and we thought we'd be coming back to our old digs, but obviously things changed when we were gone."

She raised her chin. "Do you want the radio back?"

"I'd rather have the room." I paused, but she didn't respond. "The squawk box came with the joint. And obviously, the room is yours. I was just wondering if there was any chance you might take in a roommate."

"I don't think so." She looked toward the door, expecting me to leave.

"It's not me you'd be bunking with, but the dame with the radio rights. Jayne's a great gal and she's rarely here. You'd really be helping her out of a jam."

"Where are you staying?" Her thumb rubbed at the base of her naked ring finger.

"With Ruby Priest."

She lifted her head until I could see straight up her nose. "You're a friend of Ruby's?"

"No. Absolutely not. But she's the only other person with a single room."

She crossed her arms. "So why doesn't your friend stay with her?"

Damn this broad was hard. "Jayne's been through a lot the last few weeks—her fiancé was just killed—and it didn't seem fair to make her shack up with Ruby. Frankly, she's had all the bad news she can take."

She cocked her head to the right, and I steeled myself for rejection. America had changed during our absence—the cabbie had made that clear. You could no longer rely on the kindness of strangers. "Fine," she said. "You win."

I helped Jayne bring her things upstairs while Ann lingered on her bed, watching us as she smoked a cigarette. With her long slinky legs and almond-shaped eyes, she reminded me of Churchill watching his prey.

"Jayne," I said. "This is Ann. Ann, Jayne."

"I can't thank you enough for letting me stay here," said Jayne. "It was so nice of you to do that for a total stranger." As Jayne gushed over her generosity, Ann glared at me. Where was the quiet grief-stricken girl I'd promised her? I shrugged, trying to communicate that Jayne's sudden burst of gabbiness was a mystery to me, but I doubted Ann was buying what I was selling.

Unlike the rest of the house, our room had changed very little since we'd left. The beds were made, which was a rarity during our residence, but the furniture remained in its same positions and some of the items I'd left behind—including the books and slicks on the nightstand—hadn't moved.

"You've cleaned up the joint," I said.

"I had to," said Ann. "It was a real pigsty when I got here."

My jaw tightened. Maybe I *should've* put Jayne in with Ruby.

"So what do you do?" asked Jayne.

Ann left the bed and ashed her cigarette into a dish on the dresser. She had perfect posture, the kind that said she'd spent her summers at Miss Gloria Randall's School of Deportment with a teacup balanced on her head. "I'm an actress," she told Jayne. "For the time being."

"Oh, how exciting," said Jayne, as though she'd never encountered another performer before. "What are you in right now?"

"Nothing to write home about," said Ann.

"Oh come on," I said, "I heard you got a part in Lawrence Bentley's show."

She frowned at me. "Who told you that?"

She had a hint of an accent. I couldn't tell if it was a relic from another life or a souvenir from spending her career pretending to be other people. "I just heard the other girls talking. Did they get it wrong?"

"No, they're right. I would just prefer if people didn't talk about me."

I stifled a laugh. "You do realize you're living in a house full of women, right?"

"Not all women have to be busybodies just like not all men have to be soldiers. We choose these roles because we think we have to play them."

Jayne shifted uncomfortably beside me. This was stupid. I was making this woman our enemy when she was the only one who was helping us out.

"You're right," I said. "It's a dumb stereotype. Not every woman in show business is catty." Before I could put my foot in my mouth again, I offered them both a wide grin. "I'll leave you two to it. Ta, ta."

One down, one to go. Jayne had a living situation, and now it was time to get myself one. Before I could register what I was about to do, I marched over to Ruby's room and knocked on the door. A pleasant voice invited me to come in. Clearly she had no idea it was me.

I opened the door and found her at her dressing table. Even though it was well after noon, she was still wearing her robe.

"Hiya," I said. From the bed, my former cat, Churchill, opened an eye and took me in. I swear he did a double take before standing up, turning around, and re-situating himself with his back toward me.

Ruby grinned from the vanity mirror. "Rosie?"

"The one and only."

The grin sustained. "You're back?"

"That I am."

This was usually the time when she would start flinging barbs at me, either criticizing my appearance or whatever pathetic job I was currently using to fill my time. Ruby's predictability was one of the things I cherished most about her. You never questioned where you stood with her.

At least that used to be the case.

"It's so wonderful to see you," she purred. She left her roost and wrapped her arms around me. I took in the scent of My Sin perfume and waited for her hands to wrap around my jugular, but they never did. Apparently, this was affection she was doling out. "How was the USO tour? I heard about Gilda DeVane."

Maybe that was the reason for her odd reaction. Gilda DeVane, the Hollywood star, had been on tour with us. Unfortunately, she didn't make it out of the South Pacific with anything more than a memorial. Perhaps Ruby thought that being in the vicinity of a movie star had increased my own value and in turn might do something to up hers.

"It was fine," I said. "The whole Gilda thing took the luster off the trip, but until then we enjoyed ourselves. I mean as much as you can enjoy a war zone."

"What a tragic way to go. At least she was able to spend her final days making so many lives brighter."

It took everything in me not to gag. Suffice it to say, Gilda DeVane wasn't the angel everyone in the States thought her to be, though I was too tired to educate Ruby about her. "Yeah, she made lives bright all right. So what's new with you? What are you in now?"

"Oh, this and that." She traded the brush for a comb. "Did Jayne come home too?"

Maybe this wasn't Ruby. Maybe she'd been replaced by a twin with a much more pleasant disposition. "Yeah. Keep this on the QT, but she got engaged while we were abroad and the fellow was killed in action. That's why we came home early."

She left the mirror again and met me face to face. "Poor Jayne. She must be shattered."

"You can say that again." I plunged forward, hoping she'd continue doling out sympathy. "So I have a big favor to ask."

"I'm all ears."

Still no jabs. Was I going to wake up and discover this whole conversation had been a dream? "Belle managed to give up our room, and now I don't have a place to hang my hat. Any chance I can join you? It's temporary, I promise."

"What about Jayne?"

"She's bunking with the new girl."

There was a slight flicker in her face, nothing more than a muscle moving in one of her cheeks. It was enough to tell me that this was still our Ruby, though. I braced myself for her rejection.

"Jayne's staying with Ann?" Her upper lip curled into a sneer.

"Yeah."

"Why would she want to do that?"

I set my clasped hands on my knee and leaned toward her. "She doesn't have much of a choice. I'm not staying with that dame, that's for sure."

The sneer went to sleep. "Why not?"

"I don't know. There's something about her I don't like. I know that probably doesn't make sense, since I just met her."

The sneer was now a smile. "Oh no, it does. She's very—"

"Sure of herself?" I offered.

"Secretive," said Ruby. "I'm shocked she agreed to let Jayne stay with her. She never lets anyone in her room."

"I think she felt sorry for Jayne when I told her what happened to her. She certainly wasn't going to let me stay there. Not after I said you and I were friends."

Ruby's peepers widened. "You told her that?"

I looked away. This was a lie that couldn't survive eye contact. "Of course."

My gaze returned to her as she smiled at her lap. Once again, she didn't seem like the dame we'd left behind, but a weaker, less formed version of the girl she used to be. Maybe it only seemed that way because of time and distance, or perhaps my awareness of how Jayne had changed made me think everyone was diminished.

"So can I bunk with you?" I asked her.

"All right. But you sleep on the floor. The bed is mine."

I hauled my stuff up to Ruby's room and stored it in the square foot of space she generously announced was mine. While Jayne hit the sack in her former bed, I made a nest on the floor of Ruby's room. Ruby had finally gotten dressed in a green gabardine suit I hadn't seen before. It should've been a great color on her, but her skin looked washed out, despite the heavy makeup she'd applied. The suit was too large, too. I suspected she hadn't bought it that way—a lot about her had changed, including her waistline.

"Where are you headed?" I asked her.

"Rehearsal. I'm not sure when I'll be back." She left a key for me on the vanity. As she exited in a cloud of perfume and importance, I glared at Churchill. He'd taken over her canopied bed and seemed greatly amused that I'd been relegated to the floor.

"This is temporary," I told him. "So wipe that smug look off your face."

I curled into my nest and rolled around until I found a comfortable position. It took a long time to fall asleep. That was my parting souvenir from the South Pacific. After living in a jungle paradise where enemy bombs regularly woke us, and spending weeks sleeping on a rocking ship my stomach never quite acclimated to, sleep stopped coming easily to me. Where once I could collapse from a well-spent day and be unconscious before my head hit the pillow, now my mind prowled potential dangers that could be lurking outside.

Did Jayne experience the same constant fear? Probably, though it had to be different since she was back in our old room. Maybe if I'd been there with her, the familiarity would've pushed all those fears back to the Pacific, but on Ruby's floor, surrounded by Ruby's things, I found myself imagining disasters with alarming clarity. Clattering trash cans on the street below were bombs exploding into shrapnel. Shouting kids became soldiers; honking horns a warning that an air raid was in progress; a pigeon coasting past the window was a Luftwaffe plane that had managed to come inland without alerting our guard. Danger was everywhere. I had to be vigilant.

Eventually, my body accepted the uncomfortable sleeping arrangements and I fell into a deep sleep. When I finally awoke, it was dark out. I lay in confusion trying to sort out where I was. A weight sat on my chest. At first I thought it was metaphorical, but whenever I breathed, it did, too.

I poked the cat taking up real estate on my rib cage. The moonlight coming in the window caught his amber eyes. He stared at me, though I couldn't read what was going through his feline brain. Then he used my chest as a launching pad and leaped onto the bed.

I stretched and sat up. From my vantage the bed was empty. I fumbled in the near dark until I reached Ruby's bedside lamp. I clicked it on and tried to focus my eyes on her alarm clock. It was 11:00 p.m.

"Well, well, well," I told Churchill. "Does your mistress have a man? Who's the lucky fellow?" Once again, Churchill played the petulant confidante. I was starving, so I left him and crept downstairs. A rattle of dishes and silverware warned me that I wasn't the only one up. Jayne was sitting in the parlor, finishing up something she'd snatched from the kitchen pantry.

"Hiya," I said.

"Hiya, yourself," she replied. Her fork scraped across a plate. She was eating cake.

"Is there more of that?"

She nodded. I fetched myself a slice and joined her on the couch.

"How are you feeling?"

She shrugged. Was there a time limit on grief? It seemed to me that it should be relational to the amount of time you knew a person, but that was hardly fair. There were people I'd known for years whose deaths could pass without notice and those I'd known for much less time whose loss would destroy me.

"How's life with Ann?" I asked.

"Fine so far. I like her." She plowed the frosting with her fork, creating neat rows ready to be planted. "I told her all about Billy. She said that some people never feel the kind of love I had, not in their whole lives, and I was lucky I had the little time with him that I did."

Was this really the same dame I'd met earlier that day? "That was swell of her."

"And I said, that may be true, but I still wish we could've had more time together. And she said something I've never heard before, 'Time can be love's enemy.' I asked her what it meant, and she said that no matter how much you think you may love a person, time can rob you of that affection. You get tired of one another, the passion dies, maybe you even discover things about them that you don't like." A *V* formed between her eyes. "She seems very unhappy. I almost got the feeling that she wasn't talking about me but about her."

This was good. Jayne was thinking outside of herself. She was looking for a project. I took a bite of cake. It had victory frosting, a cruel concoction that involved neither butter nor sugar but a multitude of other ingredients chosen to look like the real thing. I swallowed hard to keep from gagging.

Jayne struggled to eat it, too. "I didn't realize I'd miss the food," she said. "Isn't it funny how well we ate over there? I thought it was going to be all canned rations and powdered eggs."

In the South Pacific we'd eaten our meals with the officers, which meant we got the best chow at camp. "I guess we should've appreciated it more."

"I wish I'd appreciated all of it more." Here came the tears. She seemed unwilling to pay heed to them, or perhaps they'd become such a part of her over the last few months that it didn't occur to her that she needed to acknowledge them. They were as natural as inhaling and exhaling. "I wish I could talk to him for five minutes. Just to clear up what's going on."

"I'm sure it's nothing, Jayne."

"He lied to me. Just like Peaches lied to you about Jack. Don't you wonder why?"

"I don't think it matters anymore." Peaches twisted the truth so badly that I couldn't tell up from down. And I had to believe that if someone lied about everything else there was to know about them, that meant they lied about how they felt about me, too.

"It matters to me." She abandoned eating the cake. Instead, she poked it with her fork until it was porous enough to use as a sponge. "What if Billy already had a wife? What if he had a girl like me at every port who was dumb enough to think they were going to get married someday?"

"You know he wasn't like that."

"No I don't. I don't know anything. Not even his real name."

I set my own cake aside. "If you really want to know, I think I can help." I told her about the letters Mr. DeMille had given me and how there was a good chance her Billy had been living at that Manhattan address. "The landlord might know something," I finished.

"He won't. He thinks Billy was their Billy, that's why he sent the letters to his parents."

I was surprised by her reaction. I honestly thought this might be the life preserver she needed. "But it's worth a shot, right? He could've left something behind that could help us understand who he was."

"Maybe." She seemed resolved to her misery, which was so unlike my Jayne. I, too, was filled with questions, but they weren't about who Billy was and why he was lying. I wanted to know how to get my best friend back.

"How about we go to Billy's address tomorrow and talk to the landlord?" I said.

She nodded her agreement and sunk into the sofa. For a while we sat in silence, watching as dimmed headlights swam past the front parlor windows. How many nights in the South Pacific had I longed for home? And now that I was here it seemed tarnished. This wasn't the home I'd pictured in my dreams.

"Will it ever get better?" she asked.

I didn't know how to answer her. Not long after I learned of Jack's supposed death, someone else we cared about was killed, diverting me from my grief. Who knows if it might have returned just as strong once that new tragedy had faded. It had seemed, at the time anyway, that I was ready to move on.

"It will," I said. "You have to give yourself time." She leaned against me and rested her head on my shoulder. "He loved you, Jayne. I'm certain of that."

She sighed into the night. "Does it really matter? Either way he's dead."

CHAPTER 3

Other People's Money

I woke up the next morning to discover that I'd been transported back to the Pacific and was being forced to keep company with a crew of drunken sailors who snored like . . . well, drunken sailors. As I struggled to make sense of how I'd ended up back on the other side of the world, the noise clarified itself. They weren't sailors; it was Ruby and Churchill performing a nasal duet so loud I expected to see the walls shake. I glared at the two of them, then focused my attention on the crick in my neck. No matter which way I turned, I couldn't shake it. The pain was here to stay.

I threw on some clothes and left the femme fatale and the feline to their wood sawing. Downstairs, I enjoyed some weak java and some tough pancakes while catching up on the local news. It was amazing how tepid the war seemed when you were no longer in the middle of it. While we were abroad, I rarely saw a newspaper and didn't think twice about how what we were witnessing was being reported. Back home, it was impossible not to think about the individual each casualty number represented or the bombs that were being dropped on islands we'd once frequented. I wanted the distance back. I wanted to see numbers as numbers and the names of foreign places as nothing more than a geography lesson. If the war had felt intrusive before, it had become downright personal now.

I had a feeling the distance was never going to return, though. As our cab driver had implied, in our absence the war had gotten too close for comfort. The papers were abuzz with stories about the enemy infiltrating America. Two German immigrants were on trial for being Nazi spies. Ernest Lehmitz and Erwin de Spretter had been air raid wardens in Staten Island, a position they exploited by funneling home information about how ill equipped we were for home front attacks. In their letters, read before the jury, they detailed how many ships were in the New York Harbor, where they were headed, and how many men they estimated were being transported. They even attempted to describe the cargo.

And they were hardly the only enemies at work. Thirty-one Germans had been arrested by the FBI since the beginning of September. They weren't just men—women, also, were in the group, including one who proudly announced that she prayed every night for the Reich's success. And it wasn't just the Germans we couldn't trust: a Portuguese stevedore who worked at Newark was sending maps to the Nazis. Radios were being seized from the homes of Italian and Japanese aliens. The papers warned that enemy operatives could be anywhere. No one should be trusted, especially those who hadn't already proven themselves with long and dedicated service to the U.S. government. The onus was on us to report suspicious behavior. It was our obligation as citizens to protect our country.

It was enough to make me lose my appetite. Although, to be fair, the overcooked pancakes were helping.

I replaced the news with the entertainment section. Maxwell Anderson was working on a new play, this one about the storm op-

eration in North Africa (a topic suggested to him by General Eisen-
hower himself). It sounded like a dreary idea for a show, though
supposedly John Garfield was going to be in it. Of course, dreary
or not, the war was still a big seller. Two shows with war themes
were in George Jean Nathan's just-released list of the best shows for
1942–43 (apparently, by releasing the list now, he didn't hold out
much hope that good things might happen in the remaining months
of the year). And Ruby's ex, Lawrence Bentley, was dipping into the
same pool for his inspiration; only in his case he seemed to think
that a big war demanded an equally big show. His take was going to
be *Military Men*, a splashy salute to the armed forces with a cast of
more than three hundred, composed mostly of actual soldiers. For
that reason, it wasn't expected to run long—just two weeks. After
that, it might travel to other cities and be stocked with other men,
though the core cast of real actors would remain the same.

So this was the show Ann was in. The idea intrigued me, especially since Lawrence had served several months abroad. It would
be great if someone finally figured out a way to dramatize what
was going on overseas that didn't turn the war into a party, though
it was a pity his version didn't seem to acknowledge that women,
as well as men, were serving our country. I switched the *Times* for
Variety and looked at the list of casting calls. Someone had already
been through it, circling audition notices and crossing out those
jobs they weren't right for. There were a number of auditions that
afternoon, all in Broadway houses. If Jayne and I played our cards
right, we could be employed by the end of the week.

"Morning," said Jayne. She was already dressed, though her
face wore a look that suggested it could use another forty or fifty
winks. "We didn't think you'd be up yet."

Who was this *we* she was referring to? "I didn't have much
choice. Turns out Ruby's a snorer."

"Poor Churchill." Jayne poured herself a cup of coffee and pried
one of the pancakes from the serving platter. It was so hard and stiff
that the syrup ran off it and immediately puddled on the plate.

"Poor nothing. He's picked up the offensive habit, too. How'd you sleep?"

She shrugged. "Okay I guess."

I tore the auditions listings out of *Variety*. "So I was thinking we'd go see Billy's landlord this morning and then hit a few casting calls this afternoon."

She chewed her lip. "Maybe we shouldn't."

"Jayne—"

She talked to her pancake. "I don't know that I want to know, Rosie."

"But last night you said—"

"Last night was last night."

I fought the urge to snap at her. How long was this going to go on? Was this how I acted when I thought Jack was lost? One minute enthusiastic and willing to face any challenge, and the next convinced everything in front of me was too hard to deal with?

Yeah, I guess it kind of was.

"Look," I said, keeping my voice low and measured. "I understand you're scared. I would be, too. But if we don't try to find out what's going on now, there's a good chance that whatever information is out there will be gone by the time you decide you're ready to face this. Maybe there's nothing to this landlord business, but don't you want to know for sure? At the very least it will help you sleep better."

She sighed heavily. "Okay. I'll go."

We finished breakfast and hit the pavement. On the way to the subway, I unfurled a map and tried to suss out our destination. Jayne and I paused beside a newspaper kiosk as I followed the squiggle that was Eighty-sixth Street with my finger.

I didn't like where it was heading.

"Do you know where we're going?" she asked.

"Upper East Side." I double-checked the cross street. Of all the rotten luck.

"Where on the Upper East Side?"

"Yorkville." Billy's former neighborhood had usurped Little Germany in the Lower East Side as the place where most German and Slavic immigrants settled in Manhattan. That section of East Eighty-sixth Street was home to a variety of German music halls and beer gardens, so many in fact that the locals called it the German Broadway. I hadn't been in that part of the city for years. It used to be a great place to go to enjoy some *Hofbräu* with the hausfraus, but not long after the war started, though well before the United States got involved, the pro-Nazi movement took hold and the streets became the sight of many a battle between those who were pro-Hitler and those who weren't. At the time I was young enough to foolishly believe it was their problem to work out, and so, like most everyone else who felt removed from what was happening overseas, I ignored what was going on and hoped it would resolve itself. Eventually, though, the neighborhood became emblematic of the growing threat abroad. The Nazis were here, too—or at least the people who supported them. Suddenly Yorkville didn't seem so innocuous. It was an infection that threatened to spread to the rest of the city and then far beyond that.

Frankly, I didn't like the idea of going there without being inoculated first.

Jayne didn't share my concerns. After all, if Billy had found it safe enough to live there, there was no reason why we should be hesitant to visit. Yet despite her logic, as we arrived uptown and walked along East Eighty-sixth Street, I could feel her moving closer to me. A German flag winked from a window, seeming to parody the starred flags so many other families hung to represent the boys they'd sent overseas and the ones who would never come home. German language newspapers waited in neat stacks at kiosks, their covers depicting Hitler and his minions. Were they criticizing the German efforts? Endorsing them? We had no way of knowing, and so, like everyone else, we assumed the worst because these people were foreign and different.

"This is the one," I said, as we reached the address on the letter. The apartment building was a former tenement that had been divided into at least twenty different apartments. They still bore the same dilapidated weariness the building had when it was housing new immigrants at the turn of the century. Laundry waved from clotheslines strung across the structure's courtyard. Bars skirted the street level windows to keep both the unwanted out and the residents in. Pigeons roosted on the ledges, decorating the stone facade with their droppings.

It wasn't hard to imagine what the apartments would look like. One room, maybe two. Shared bathrooms that you had to wait in line to use. Many of the apartments wouldn't have windows but would rely on an air shaft to deliver air and light. It was a bleak existence, no matter what the century.

We stepped into the building's foyer and stared at a row of mailboxes labeled with long foreign names that seemed to have twice as many consonants as they needed. Botanical print wallpaper peeled from the walls. Somewhere a radio squawked a German-language broadcast, while a turntable played an oompah band song. A strange array of scents gathered around us: liberty cabbage, sausage, onions. My stomach let out an unpatriotic growl.

"I can't imagine him living here," whispered Jayne.

"He might not have."

Someone entered the building behind us. We turned toward the sound with smiles plastered across our faces. A stooped old man appeared, a walking cane doing its darnedest to keep him vertical. At the sight of us he started. Apparently, it was unusual to see anyone in the building who didn't absolutely have to be there.

He murmured something under his breath that I took to be "Can I help you?" but which may have been a curse levied in a foreign tongue.

"Mr. Smith?" I asked. He shook his head no and pointed toward the row of mailboxes near the front door. There was one marked PROPRIETOR with the number three beside it.

The old man lumbered past us and disappeared. We sought out the apartment number and found it at the far end of the first floor. The door was open and a man sat in front of a radio with a napkin tucked into his undershirt to keep his lunch from staining the already dirty fabric. I couldn't tell what he was eating. It didn't share the same smell as the rest of the building.

"Can I help you?" His accent was so buried, only the inflection remained. I looked at Jayne, expecting her to take the lead, but she'd receded into the hallway, appointing me the mouthpiece.

"I hope so," I said. "Are you Mr. Smith?" I hadn't noted the significance of the generic moniker when we'd first read the letters, but then I hadn't realized we were headed into the bowels of the Bund either.

"*Ja*. I am Mr. Smith."

I fought the urge to mimic his speech patterns. That was the unfortunate thing about being an actress. Whenever I was around people with accents, my mouth longed to try it on for size, even though I knew if I did, it would look like I was mocking them.

I pulled the letters out of my purse and passed them to him. "My parents received these from you about our brother. His name was Billy DeMille."

He looked at the pages as though they were unfamiliar to him. Once he'd studied both front and back, recognition dawned in his peepers. "These were sent more than a year ago."

"I know." I bowed my head and wished Jayne wasn't there for this pathetic performance. "Our parents . . . losing Billy was very hard on them."

"He's dead?"

Jayne hiccuped behind me. I feared she was about to double over with tears, but instead she stepped forward. "He was killed in action last fall."

He eyeballed us carefully: me tall and brunette, Jayne tiny and blond. This wasn't a neighborhood where one assumed everyone was telling the truth. "You are both his sisters?"

"I'm adopted," I said.

"Sind Sie Deutsch?"

I shook my head.

"Are you here to pay his bill?"

"Er . . . no," I said. "Billy's dead. How do we even know he left here owing you money?"

He folded his arms across his chest, staining the downy fur with sauce. "Because I say so."

At least we knew what kind of person we were dealing with. "We were hoping to take a look at where he lived, you know, get a sense of where he was in his last days. Find out what, if anything, you might remember about him."

He raised an eyebrow. "Why do you care about my memories? Surely you have your own."

It was a fair question. If only I had an answer to it.

"It was a hardship, his leaving in the middle of the night without paying for that last month. I almost had to sell the building." He picked at his tooth and watched us steadily. So this was his game. If we wanted information, we were going to have to grease his palm.

I reached into my purse. There wasn't much there—getting us home from the South Pacific before our tour was up had required doling out most of my cabbage, and the rest needed to keep me afloat until I found work. The only thing in my wallet was a spanking new five-dollar bill that I was hoping would last me the week.

I passed him the fiver before I could think about what I was doing.

"Rosie," Jayne whispered.

I knocked elbows with her. "I know it's not much, but will this help make up for some of his debt?"

"Is that all you have?"

I showed him my empty wallet. Behind us a door opened. I turned in time to see a woman with a long braid disappear back inside the apartment next to Mr. Smith's.

Mr. Smith removed the napkin from around his neck and wiped his face. "Maybe it will be enough for the rent bill, but the storage space—he owed for that, too."

"He had a storage space?" said Jayne.

"At a dollar a week. Of course, I could not do anything with it after he left, not with all of his things in it."

"What did he keep in there?" I asked.

"It is not within my rights to go through a tenant's possessions."

Somehow I doubted he strictly followed that policy. "Could we get his stuff?" I asked. "It would mean a lot to our parents."

The eyebrow headed north again. This time Jayne opened her purse. She passed him another five clams.

"Yes," he said, as he tucked the bill into his shirt pocket. "I think that could be arranged."

We followed him out of his apartment and into the basement. There, a warren of fenced-off spaces secured with locks and chains held those possessions the upstairs inhabitants didn't have room for. It was an interesting display of lives they once had or were hoping to one day reclaim. Baby carriages did time by steamer trunks bearing stamps from their homelands. Lamp shades kept company with wardrobes bursting with out-of-season clothes (as though the poorest among us could afford to make such distinctions). The lighting was dim, the odor damp and musty.

"Did he ever have any visitors?" asked Jayne.

"It's not for me to say. I respect my tenant's privacy. Here we are." We'd landed at a small cage near the building's back wall. Something green leached through the cement and made a slow course toward the floor. Mr. Smith pulled a chain attached to his belt loop and produced a ring with so many keys on it I was surprised he didn't lean to the side from the weight of it. He found the one he was looking for and slid it into the lock. It opened with a ping that suggested it had been saving up a long time to make that noise. "His boxes are the ones to the right," he said.

There were a lot more things than I would've expected. Two cardboard boxes stricken with dry rot sat on top of a large metal footlocker.

"We can't carry all that," I said.

He started to close the gate. "Maybe you come back another day."

And pay another five bucks? "No—wait. Could we at least go through his things and see if there's anything we want? I mean if it's just his dirty laundry, there's no point in us hauling it home, right? And maybe we could let you sell whatever we don't want—for your trouble."

"Okay. You can do this." He gestured us into the cage. As soon as we were inside, the gate closed and the chain began to rattle.

"Hey, what are you doing?" I asked.

"You might steal from me. It is not only Mr. DeMille's things in there. So you go through his boxes, find what you want, show it to me, then I let you out."

He was going to lock us in here?

"How will you know when we're done?" asked Jayne.

"I come back in one hour." And with that, he closed the padlock and disappeared.

I tried not to think about the possibility of Mr. Smith never returning. Surely if he made a habit of that, there'd be a skeleton left behind to attest to his intentions. Instead, I pulled the two boxes off the footlocker and wiped its surface clean with my hand. "Have a seat," I told Jayne.

"You shouldn't have given him money."

"He wasn't going to let us in if I didn't. Besides, you're one to talk."

"This is my responsibility, not yours."

"And Jack was mine, yet you still went halfway across the world with me, didn't you?"

That shut her up. I opened the first box and began removing things and handing them to her. Shaving kit. Alarm clock. Bible.

All the basic possessions of your average transient staying at a flop-house.

"So what are we looking for?" asked Jayne.

"I don't know. Anything with a name on it, I guess." I was hoping there'd be a diary detailing the reasons behind Billy's name change, his real identity, and how there was absolutely no nefarious connection between the two. Instead, we found a framed photo depicting two men sitting side by side. I squinted in the dim basement light and tried to make out the faces. One of them could've been Billy.

"Is that him?" I asked.

"I think so," she said.

"Okay, hold onto this. It might be important."

The rest of the first box was filled with clothes. I exchanged it for the second one.

On top of the box was a stack of unopened mail, all addressed to Billy DeMille at the East Eighty-sixth Street address. I popped the blade out of the razor from the shaving kit and slit open the first envelope.

"What are you doing?" asked Jayne.

"What does it look like?"

Jayne's baby blues looked like they were about to burst a vein. "But isn't that illegal?"

"I don't think Billy's going to mind, Jayne." I pulled a piece of stationery from the envelope and unfurled it. It was blank. "That's odd." I passed her the page and went to work on the next envelope. The handwriting looked the same. There was no return address on either letter.

The paper inside this one was blank, too.

I opened the remaining envelopes and found the same strange story: blank sheets of paper.

"Why would someone do that?" asked Jayne.

"Maybe it wasn't someone. Maybe it was Billy. He could've wanted someone to think he was getting mail."

Jayne eyeballed the canceled stamps. "But most of these arrived after he'd shipped out. Besides, that's not Billy's handwriting."

"Are you sure?"

"Positive."

I bit my tongue. There was no point in reminding her that we couldn't be positive about anything having to do with Billy De-Mille, including his handwriting.

She took the stack of envelopes and fitted the blank pages back inside of them. She tucked the stack into her purse, along with the framed photo.

"You want to keep blank letters?"

"Yeah," she said. "I do."

I continued pulling things from the box. A porcelain shaving cup had been carefully wrapped in newspaper to keep it safe. I unwrapped it and was about to set it aside with the other useless things when a headline in the newspaper caught my attention.

WATERTOWN FAMILY MOURNS LOSS OF SON AT PEARL HARBOR

I nudged Jayne and joined her on the trunk. Together, we read the article describing the DeMilles' shock and grief at learning of the loss of their son. That wasn't all that was detailed. The article described their home, the neat string of pearls lining Mrs. DeMille's neck, the tiny aperitif glasses set to dry on the dining room table in anticipation of a celebration, even the ceramic kittens frozen at play, all in an effort to depict how surreal it was that a home thousands of miles from Hawaii was ripped apart by what happened at Pearl Harbor.

"This was how he got all the information," Jayne whispered.

"It looks that way."

"But why?"

I didn't have an answer for her. As she pondered the article, I continued my work. More clothes filled the box. I pulled out a trench coat and felt something stiff brush past me. The back panel of the jacket had an oblong shape in the fabric. Something had been sewn inside it. I showed Jayne my find, then carefully cut the seams with the razor blade. Five stacks of bills, each bound by a rubber band, awaited me.

"Oh my gosh," breathed Jayne. "How much is it?"

I rapidly flipped through the cabbage and tried to estimate the total. "Five grand maybe?"

"Where would he get five grand?"

The better question was, why would he leave it behind?

CHAPTER 4

Old Dame Trot and Her Comical Cat

We searched the rest of the clothing, but there was no more hidden cash, nor any clue as to why Billy became Billy. You changed your name to disassociate yourself from your past. And you left your past behind because you'd done something wrong. Had Billy been a criminal? Was he on the run from the coppers? Had he stolen the money in the trench coat, then, thinking twice about it, decided to leave his life of crime—and the spoils of his efforts—behind?

The only thing left to search was the footlocker. It was locked tight, and despite our best efforts with a hairpin, the lock proved immovable. I tried to shift the trunk to get another angle on it, but it was impossibly heavy.

"If you have money you want to hide, where would you put it?" I asked Jayne. "Inside a coat someone might steal or inside a foot-locker that's impossible to break into?"

She didn't answer, which was fine. It was a rhetorical question.

While I tried to figure out a way into the trunk, she stared at the picture of Billy and his friend. I could guess at the questions she was pondering. Who was the man in the picture? And why had Billy left the snapshot behind when it had been important enough to bring to this flophouse with him?

"All done?" Mr. Smith appeared outside the cage with his keys at the ready.

"I don't suppose you have a way into the footlocker?" I asked.

"It was not mine to open."

In other words, he couldn't jimmy the lock either. I tossed the clothes back into the box and restored things to the way they'd been when we'd first entered the cage.

"Aren't you taking anything?" asked Mr. Smith.

"Just a photo and some letters." Jayne showed him the items we'd set aside. Well, most of them. Half of the money was tucked into the back of my skirt, the other half keeping similar time with Jayne.

"How much longer are you going to keep this stuff?" I asked.

"Not long. With your permission, I will try to sell what I can, to pay for the rest of the rent."

I wanted into that trunk. Whatever was in there was important enough to keep under lock and key. Information about Billy's real identity could be in there. But there was no way we could get it back to the Shaw House. I doubted between the three of us we could drag it five feet.

And besides, what if it had something slightly more unsavory in it. Like say—a body?

"Thanks again," I said.

Jayne and I scrambled out of the cage and up the stairs before he had a chance to say anything else to us. Out on the street, we slowed our pace lest someone think we were up to something we shouldn't be.

"Thanks," said Jayne.

"For what?"

"For all of that. For making me come."

Shadows were growing long across the walkways. Leaves danced the distance between their branches and the ground. As we passed over them, they crunched beneath our weight. I caught our reflection in the window of a bakery. We weren't alone; there was a third form fast on our heels. He was a man—I was certain of that—though any distinguishing features were lost in the warped shop glass.

"Jayne?"

"Hmmm?" Somewhere, a fire was burning. The smell of leaves and other debris filled the air in a delicious medley of fall scents.

"Don't panic, but I think we've being shadowed."

She didn't panic, but she did stiffen in such a way that her awareness had to be obvious to our tail.

"We're going to turn up here," I said. "Just to see if he really is following us."

We turned up a side street and so did he. Fortunately, there was a crowd up ahead waiting in line for the butcher, so there was no chance of him catching us alone. I urged Jayne to speed up and matched my pace to hers. As soon as we cleared the crowd, we turned again and met East Eighty-sixth Street just as it left Yorkville.

Jayne grabbed me by the hand and pulled me to a street corner, where a copper was waiting with a handheld stop sign to direct traffic. I looked over my shoulder; our friend was still shadowing us, though he was far enough behind that I still couldn't make out his features. His oversized fedora wasn't helping matters.

"Excuse me," Jayne said to the flatfoot. "How do we get to Tiffany's from here?"

With a slight Irish lilt, the officer began reciting directions. Once he'd finished, Jayne pointed toward our unwanted companion and asked, "So we go that way?"

The flattie shook his head and started explaining the route again. Jayne's ruse worked. Certain he was our topic of conversation, our tail turned tail and disappeared back into Yorkville.

We thanked the cop and continued on our way. We'd only made

it a few feet when a female voice rang out, calling our names. My impulse was to keep walking, but Jayne stopped and turned back to see who it was. She quickly faced forward again, the color drained from her face.

"Well?" Now what? Had we escaped one danger only to pick up another one?

"You're not going to like this," she said.

"That's the theme of the day. Out with it."

"It's Candy Abbott."

My knees threatened to give out. Candy Abbott was the WAC who saved Jack and had been rewarded with his heart. I'd heard they were both back in New York, but I'd put that fact in the same mental compartment where I stored war atrocities and bad reviews.

"Rosie! Jayne!"

In unison, we planted smiles on our faces and turned to greet her.

"I can't believe you two are here! How strange is this?" She embraced us simultaneously. I pulled away too quickly and pretended I had to sneeze. It was weird seeing her out of her WAC uniform and in civvies. Her hair was done and her puss painted, making it even more evident that she wasn't just a good person, she was also a good-looking one.

"What are you doing here?" I said. There was a time when I considered her my friend, and she undoubtedly still considered me hers. She didn't know that I knew Jack. That was one of those little facts I'd kept to myself. If I was a good actress, I might've been able to keep up the ruse, but I could already feel myself slipping into the ticks and tricks that distinguished a bad performer from a capable one. I tucked my hair behind my ears. I laughed at inappropriate moments. I faked another sneeze.

"The fellow I was seeing in the South Pacific lives here." Was that all she was going to give us? What about his trial for going AWOL? Didn't that merit a mention? "You know, you two might know him. He's also an actor. His name is—"

She never got a chance to tell us. Another voice rang out, this one older and so colored with upper-crust history that the words seemed constructed out of lead crystal. "Candace? Oh, there you are. We do have to get moving, my dear. Our table's being held."

Reflexively, I ducked behind a mailbox. As I peered around it, I could make out Jack's mother as she waved her handkerchief Candy's way. "It was swell seeing you, but we have to go," I told Candy. And then I grabbed Jayne's arm and pulled her up the street.

We went straight to a cattle call at the Shubert Theatre at West Forty-fourth Street. Neither of us was in the mood to audition, but we also knew that the longer we waited to get out there, the harder it was going to be. The show they were casting for was a musical revival, one of my least favorite kind of gigs. According to the casting notice, they needed four actresses: someone to play a young girl, two women in their mid- to late-twenties, and someone between forty and fifty years old with a "mature voice." The line was packed with women who filled their time warming up their voices, chatting about other jobs, and sizing up the competition. There were at least a hundred skirts exactly like me, and ten of those were better dressed and hadn't spent an hour kneeling in dust in a subterranean cage. I wanted to blow, but I knew that things were unlikely to change tomorrow. I needed work, and there wasn't a reason in this world why I couldn't get this job over one of these other dames.

After an hour of waiting in line, the proctors finally deigned to see us. While I waited outside the door, Jayne took her turn. Her sweet, sad voice filled the air with a child's lament turned into a song. Jayne had been cursed with the kind of high, squeaky voice that only dogs responded to, but she could mimic a kid better than a kid could, a performance that was perfectly supported by her small stature. As I listened to her sing, I realized what the proctors were probably figuring out: she was perfect for this.

"Please let her get the job," I prayed. "She needs this."

I was called in next. As I walked across the stage, I realized I still had the bundle of cash shoved into my waistband. Or rather, the cash reminded me of its presence. While it had remained secure on the walk to the theater, it had started to slide, and it was only a matter of minutes before I gave birth to it downstage center. It was too late to do anything. To take it out now would only make it seem like I had a medical issue I should've attended to hours before.

"Hiya," I said to the two men and one woman sitting in judgment before the stage.

The woman spoke first, while I prayed that I didn't lay a $2,500 egg. "What will you be singing for us?"

I hadn't thought that far ahead. Normally, for a revival piece like this one, I would've dragged out "Tea for Two," but that song required movement, and I wasn't going anywhere if I could help it. "'How Deep Is the Ocean?'" I said.

"Lovely," she replied. "Proceed."

I did, with the sort of stiffness usually seen in mighty oaks. I could only move my upper body, since my lower was fixated on clenching my buttocks. That was okay, though; they cut me off after sixteen bars.

"Thank you," said one of the men. His tone seemed to imply that he was pleased with what he'd seen, but it was possible I was reading way too much into those two brief words. "Name?"

"Rosie Winter."

The three proctors exchanged a look. I couldn't tell if it was because they recognized my name or were amused, after my stiff performance, that I didn't have the self-respect to use a made-up moniker.

"That's all we need, Miss Winter," said the other man.

I goose-stepped out of the room and into the lobby. Jayne was waiting for me, face flushed, hair astray.

"Come with me," I told her. I led her to the ladies' room, where I removed the packets of money and shifted my girdle back into place.

"You auditioned with it in there?" she said.

"I forgot about it. Why? What did you do with yours?"

"I put it in my pocketbook."

And to think there were times when I thought I was the smarter of the two of us. "So I heard you in there," I said. "You nailed it."

"Tell them that. I got a thanks but no thanks."

I gave her a gentle push. "Get out of town."

"I wish I could. It was so strange. They seemed really excited when I started to sing, but when I was done, they asked me my name and that was that."

It must've been the voice. Perhaps they thought Jayne had been manufacturing it for the song, but when they realized her pipes really were pitched that high, they decided they couldn't sell it.

I didn't tell her that, though.

"They might've pre-cast it," I said. "Probably some producer's daughter. You know how it goes."

"Sure. Maybe."

I hooked my arm in hers and led her into the lobby and out onto West Forty-fourth Street. "Don't worry. This is only the first audition. You're bound to get something today."

I was wrong about that. We hit two other cattle calls and were turned away at the first round. Don't get me wrong: we were used to rejection, but it didn't normally come so early in the process. Typically, at least one of us was strung along and led to believe that the part was ours until the promised phone call never came. While in some ways it was a relief to have a *no* up-front, it was also baffling. Had something happened to us while we were in the South Pacific? As we learned about the reality of war, had we lost our ability to pretend?

I didn't think so. In fact, I was convinced that the USO experience had taught me to be a better performer, one who didn't need glitz and glamour to create good theater. Maybe I was kidding myself, though. Perhaps what seemed like improved skill was really another loss I'd been too busy to notice.

"I can't take another audition," said Jayne.

The air was moist and warm. I was dying for a bath. "No worries. I'm done for the day, too."

"I just don't understand what I'm doing wrong."

A sweet scent passed us by. Someone was selling pastries from a street cart, though to my nose it smelled like lush tropical flowers blooming in the jungle. As soon as it came, the scent was swallowed up by car exhaust and rotting garbage. Had the city always been this dirty? I'd once heard that there were so few flies and mosquitoes in Manhattan because of the pollution, yet somehow, in those same conditions, the cockroaches managed to thrive. "You know how this business is: one day you're up; the next day you're down. We were gone for a while. Maybe it's going to take some time for someone to want to work with us again."

"It's not like we were on vacation. We were performing. With a major movie star."

"Yeah, one who ended up dead." What time was it in Tulagi? On that side of the world it was already tomorrow. Whatever was going to happen had already occurred. "Look, maybe we aimed too high. Just because our last gig was on Broadway doesn't mean our next one will be. Tomorrow let's start out a little more humbly."

"And if that doesn't work out?"

"We can always go crawling back to the USO." Memory of that morning started drifting back to me. What had happened to our tail? Had he given up after he thought the cop had made him, or had he been following us from one disappointing audition to another?

I tried to eyeball the people around us, but they all wore the same nondescript look. No one made eye contact with me. In fact, it wasn't beyond reason that someone could attack us in broad daylight and not one of these people would stop and offer us assistance.

Had the world always been so mean?

"I say we take a hack home." I told Jayne.

"We can't afford that."

I patted my pocketbook, where I'd finally stashed my half of Billy's cash. "My wallet says otherwise."

"That's not our money to spend."

"Finders keepers."

She paused and stared into the street. "He must have a family somewhere, right? It belongs to them."

I was being silly. No one was going to attack us. Besides, Jayne was right. Until we knew who Billy was, we had no right handing out his dough. "Okay, we won't spend any of it for the time being."

We started walking toward the subway station. It was going on rush hour, and the sidewalk rapidly filled with suits and skirts hurrying to get home. A clap of thunder sounded above us. Before we could register the sound, a gush of rain fell from the sky, sending everyone running for the awnings.

"Maybe one little cab ride won't hurt," said Jayne.

I had the money in hand before she could finish the sentence.

When we got home, both Ruby and Ann were gone. We debated where the best place to store Billy's money might be. Ultimately we agreed Ruby's room was safer: she was too self-absorbed to question any new additions to her room, and she certainly wouldn't snoop through someone else's belongings.

We stashed the cash in my suitcase and slid it under the bed. Churchill watched us in fascination, no doubt contemplating how he might cause problems for me later.

The phone rang in the hallway. We both froze.

Was it the man in Yorkville? Had he tracked us home?

I willed someone else to get it so we didn't have to go through the terrifying experience of hearing someone say "I saw what you did" in Béla Lugosi's voice, but for the first time in the history of the Shaw House, no one rushed to the phone before me.

"I'll get it," I told Jayne. "Sit tight."

"Hello?" I said, in perfect imitation of every horror movie heroine I'd ever seen.

"Is Jayne there?"

We were safe. Sort of. It was Tony, Jayne's mobster ex-boyfriend.

I kept my voice altered so he couldn't identify me. "Let me check. Hold please."

I left the receiver on the table and went back to Ruby's room. I mouthed the caller's identity.

Jayne shook her head so hard that a clip-on earring left her ear and hit the wall.

"Sorry," I told Tony. "She's not here."

"Will you give her a message?"

"Absolutely."

"Tell her Tony B. called and I'd love to hear from her."

Just for kicks I made him spell his name and pretended I was taking dictation ("You say that was Tony P.? *P* like in *paranoid*?"). With that fun over, I signed off and put the blower down with a clang.

"How does he know I'm back?" said Jayne when I returned to the room.

"How does he know anything? He probably had spies on the ship and another waiting for us when we arrived in San Francisco." And maybe he had a spy watching us in Yorkville. Could our shadow have been hired by Tony? I didn't mention this possibility to Jayne. If her mood had been low before, it had sunk to basement-level now. "I could use a drink," I said. "What do we have left?"

"Nothing," said Jayne.

"Ann drank all our hooch?" Although the Shaw House was dry, we had cheesed a couple of bottles in the closet of our old room. You never knew when you might need to celebrate. Or commiserate.

"She said there wasn't anything there when she moved in. And she doesn't drink herself."

I didn't like that. Experience told me teetotalers had something to hide, making them unwilling to risk the tongue-loosening powers of booze. "Why doesn't she drink?"

"She said she doesn't like to lose control." Maybe Ruby was right. Maybe she *was* hiding something.

"Okay, next stop is the liquor store. In the meantime, how does water strike you?"

"Wet. Very, very wet."

I went to Jayne's room and retrieved our martini glasses. When I returned, I filled both with water from a pitcher Ruby kept beside her bed. For one delicious moment they glistened like real cocktails. But then, like booze on a stage set, a single taste made it clear they were there only for looks.

"Where do you sleep?" Jayne sat on the bed beside Churchill. He purred agreeably as she sank her fingers into his fur.

"On the floor."

"Oh." She set her drink on the bedside table and pulled the photo of Billy and his friend out of her purse.

"Do you want to keep that in here, too?"

"I guess." She passed it to me with a look that said she wasn't sure if she should leave it in my care. Once I had hold of it, though, she turned away and fished the letters out. "You might as well keep these too."

I pulled the pages from the envelopes, set them beside her on the bed, and joined her in looking at the photo. Now, in good lighting, there was no doubt that the picture was *our* Billy. His hair was a little bit longer, but otherwise it was definitely him.

His friend was in stark contrast to him. Whereas Billy was small and dark, his companion was lighter and gangly, towering at least three inches above Billy while seated. But despite their obvious differences, there seemed to be a physical similarity between the two.

"Could the guy with him be the real Billy DeMille?" I asked Jayne.

"I don't think so. I don't remember him being this fair."

They were seated on a wooden floor with their legs hanging down the side of some sort of platform. Heavy drapes hung in the background, along with what looked like a tree. It appeared the photo had originally been part of a group shot—a foot could be seen to the left of Billy's companion—but somebody had trimmed this faceless person from the original picture.

Wait a second—that wasn't a tree. Not a real one anyway. They were seated on a stage and that "tree" was a piece of scenery.

"Did Billy ever mention being a performer or maybe working in a stage crew somewhere?" I sipped at my water, trying to imagine it was vodka washing away this frustrating day.

She pondered the question before shaking her head. "No. He only ever asked me about my experiences."

Paper crinkled behind me. I turned just in time to see Churchill standing on the blank pages.

"Off," I said.

He cocked his head at me.

"Scram," I said. "You know what that means."

Despite the fact that he had no discernible lips, I swear he smiled. And then, with the sort of deliberate movement that only the evil can muster, he sprayed the paper with his foul scent.

I threw the water in my glass at him. He moved just in time to avoid the splash.

"I can't believe there was a moment in the South Pacific when I thought I missed him." I picked up the stack of blank pages and tried to keep the urine from dripping off the edge. Not that it mattered. Ruby's bedspread was ruined.

"Wait," said Jayne. "Look."

The topmost page, where the majority of the pee had landed, was covered in writing.

"What the—?"

"It's the urine," said Jayne. "It's making ink appear."

As we watched, a complete letter emerged where once there was none. Unfortunately, that was the extent of our enlightenment. The entire page was written in German.

CHAPTER 5

Whispering Friends

We spent the next hour cleaning Ruby's linens in the bathroom sink. We hung them to dry on the fire escape and clipped the letters to an ersatz clothesline we rigged in Ruby's room.

All of the letters were in German, all addressed to Billy, all written by someone named Johnny.

"Oh, hello." Ruby had arrived home and stood in the doorway, surveying our strange decorations. "What's that smell?"

"I don't smell anything. Jayne?"

"Nope," she said.

Ruby took in the rest of the changes we'd made in her absence. "And what happened to my bedclothes?"

"Your cat got overzealous."

She picked up Churchill and clutched him to her chest. If I'd tried to do that, he would've turned me into a pincushion. In Ruby's arms, he hung limp. "What did you do to him?"

"Nothing," I said.

"Somehow I doubt that. What's all this?" She swatted at the letters, clearly unaware that they weren't yellow because the paper came that way.

"Sorry," I said. "We're trying to dry out some mail that got caught in the downpour."

She peered closely at the pages. "Why do you have letters written in—is that German?" There was a note of tension in her voice. She knew that any letters written in that foreign tongue were bad news.

"It's for a job," I said. "It's an epistolary play. In German. We were hoping to figure out what we were reading before the audition."

Remarkably, she didn't question the lie. She looked exhausted. Her eyes were threaded with red, and her makeup showed signs of being on too long without a touch-up.

"Did you just come back from rehearsal?" asked Jayne.

"Yes. And it's been a long day."

"What are you in?"

Ruby ignored the question. "Are you two going to be at this very long?"

I could take a hint. "Just long enough to clean up." I plucked the letters from the line and made a hasty stack of them. "Jayne, you interested in grabbing a bite?"

"I would kill for some pie at Horn and Hardart's." She unraveled the makeshift clothesline and stowed it. Before Ruby had kicked off her shoes and drop kicked the cat, we were out of the room and on our way.

"She seems off," said Jayne as we headed out of the building and onto the street. "Any idea what's going on?"

"Not so far. But then Ruby's never been one to be open about her problems, has she?"

It was going on seven and I was genuinely famished. We ended up at a Horn and Hardart's four blocks away, where we pooled our nickels for a pair of egg salad sandwiches, two cups of joe, and a slice of lemon meringue pie. There was something comforting about dispensing the weak coffee from the dolphin-shaped spout. In fact, as I fed coins into the machine and reached inside the glass doors to claim our chow, the Automat felt more like home to me than the Shaw House had. I think Jayne felt it, too. With satisfied grins, we sat at a chrome and leather dinette and relished the perfect ratio of egg, onion, celery, and mayonnaise.

The place was halfway full and getting more so with every passing minute. Families huddled around tables, discussing their days. Businessmen dined alone with only newspapers as their companions. A factory worker, her hair pulled up in a snood, blew on a spoonful of soup, sending a vapor of steam dancing into the air. These people didn't seem threatening. If anything, they seemed, like us, desperate to find a port in the storm.

Eventually, we got to work and examined the letters. The strange language was peppered with words we did know—the names of places and people that stood in stark contrast to the foreign words. Newark was mentioned, and Manhattan. So was the real Billy DeMille's hometown. But the words were so far apart from one another that they lost their meaning. Until—

"Levane," I said. "Johnny Levane."

"Who's that?"

"Presumably the Johnny who wrote these letters. See?" I tapped one of the pages. "He wrote his full name with his address on this one."

The name pinged something. I swore I'd heard it before. The information tried to make it to the surface, but just when I thought I had it, it darted out of reach. I let it go and asked the million-dollar question. "Was Billy German?"

Jayne wiped a bit of egg from her lip. "If he was, he never mentioned it."

It wasn't exactly a bragging point. Just as Mr. Smith chose a generic last name, people claimed new nationalities to keep themselves from being labeled the enemy. And who could blame them?

Even the American Asthmatic Association was begging people to stop saying Gesundheit. If we didn't want to respond to sneezes with German words anymore, I doubted we'd want to label the people we liked with them either.

"He didn't have an accent," said Jayne.

"I don't mean German German. I mean, where was his family from?"

Her mouth twittered. She'd been about to say "You met them, remember?" when she realized that the people we met had nothing to do with the boy she'd loved and lost. "He never said. Not the truth anyway."

The rain was picking up outside again, fogging the plate-glass window at the front of the Automat. I swear there was a figure stopped just on the other side of it, looking in at us. Perhaps someone had just paused beneath the awning to keep out of the downpour.

Jayne pushed her plate away. My appetite was still going strong. In fact, I probably could've finished her sandwich and mine without blinking an eye. But out of respect, I stopped eating and dabbed my mouth with my napkin.

"Ready to go home?" I asked.

"I don't care."

The door opened, bringing with it a gust of wind and rain. I looked up to see who would be vying for our table, and I gasped in surprise.

Candy Abbott had just walked in the door.

"Get down," I hissed to Jayne.

"What?"

"Duck down so nobody sees you."

She did as I instructed, sliding down in her chair until only the top of her head showed. "What's going on?"

"Later." I slumped, slipping between the seat and the table. It was too late; we'd been made.

"Rosie? Jayne?" Candy shook her closed umbrella, littering the floor with raindrops.

Jayne regained her full height. I tried to do the same and knocked my noodle on the table. "Candy?" I said.

"What are you doing down there?"

"Looking for my purse." I yanked the strap behind me until the bag fell to the floor. "Here it is."

"Do you mind if I join you?" asked Candy.

"Of course not," said Jayne.

I tried to kick Jayne but hit the table support instead. The salt and pepper shakers danced two inches forward. "Isn't this a funny coincidence," I said. "Twice in one day? What are the odds?"

Candy slid into the chair opposite me, storing her umbrella beneath it. "Oh, this isn't a coincidence. I went by your rooming house, and someone named Ruby Priest said you were headed here for dinner."

I'd have to remember to thank her later. "And so we are," I said. "Everything all right?"

"The thing is . . . I . . . I was hoping I could talk to you, Rosie."

Jayne took the hint and excused herself to use the ladies' room.

"This is rather awkward," she began. What was the use in saying that? Of course it was awkward. How would pointing it out make it less so? "The woman I was with today, that was Mamie Castlegate, Jack Castlegate's mother. Of course you know that, don't you?"

I played with my fingers and nodded.

"I mentioned your name over lunch and she told me about the two of you. She's also the one who told me where you lived." Mamie Castlegate knew where I lived? She must've made a point of learning it to make sure she avoided the neighborhood. "Why didn't you say anything?" asked Candy.

I had no choice but to keep the lie going. There was no reason to admit my culpability when she was still willing to accept the blame. "What was there to say? I didn't realize Jack was the guy you were dating until I saw you with his mother today. And, frankly, I was so shocked, that it seemed easier just to walk away."

Candy accepted the lie. After all, as far as she knew, she was the one with the guilty conscience. "That's what I figured. I just felt awful about the whole thing. I wanted to say I was sorry for foisting the news on you like that. It must've been a hell of a shock."

I forced a smile. "It's fine. Really."

"If I'd had any inkling—any inkling at all—I never would've—"

I cut her off with a wave of my hand. "Don't worry about it. Jack and I are ancient history." I licked my lips. Where was Jayne? "How is he?"

"Not good. He's—"

"Excuse me?" A woman with a cane tried to clear the space between our table and the next, but Candy was blocking her path. Candy backed out of her way, and as the woman passed her, Candy excused herself and announced that she better wash her hands.

As Candy headed toward the ladies' room, Jayne returned from her own sojourn.

"Well?" she asked me.

"Mamie Castlegate spilled the beans."

Jayne sighed and sank into her chair. "At least the truth is out. What did Candy say?"

"That she was sorry to spring the news on me like that."

"And you said?"

"That the past is the past. Jack and I are kaput. End of story."

Jayne stared down her nose at me. "You didn't tell her why we went to the South Pacific?"

"What was the point? She feels bad as it is—she doesn't need to know how much deeper she cut."

Jayne made like she was going to say more, but I didn't give her a chance.

"She doesn't need to know. He's safe, they're in love, and I'm home. There's no reason to make this worse for everyone."

Candy returned and paused to pry a sandwich from behind the glass door. She'd selected turkey on rye as her meal. Jack hated rye. Jayne and I shifted our focus to Billy's letters, pretending this had been the subject of our conversation all along.

"So what's all this?" Candy asked as she sat down. The letters formed an untidy stack. I was about to dismiss them as nothing of her concern, when Jayne piped up.

"Do you remember Billy DeMille?"

Candy's face creased. "Of course I do. He's the pilot you were seeing. I was so sorry to hear he'd been killed."

"Thanks," said Jayne. Her lips rippled, and I knew what was coming next: she was going to tell Candy everything we'd learned about Billy since returning to the States. I wanted to stop her—Candy didn't need to know our business—but before I could, I was distracted by a ring on Candy's left hand.

Had that been there that afternoon?

"So the pages were blank when you found them?" Candy picked up the letters and rifled through them.

Jayne nodded.

"I've heard of this. They call it secret writing. The Germans use it just in case their mail falls into the wrong hands."

I shook myself back into reality. "Doesn't seem like the best ploy," I said. "After all, if people know about secret writing, won't they know that all they have to do is get the paper wet to read what's on the page?"

"It's not that easy," said Candy. "There are specific recipes to make the text show up. What did you use?"

"Cat urine," I said.

"Clever. Ammonia must be the primary component." She suddenly realized what she'd been touching with the same hands she'd been eating with. The page she held fluttered to the table as she scoured her skin with her napkin. "I could translate these for you."

"You know German, too?" I said. Candy had been a code

breaker in Tulagi, spending days poring over Japanese print and radio transmissions in hopes of intercepting information about enemy activity.

"And Italian and Russian."

Bully for her. I knew I should be grateful that there was someone out there who could help us, but I didn't like her butting in like this. What was happening, was happening to Jayne and me. We didn't need Candy's help to get through it. "You've got to be busy," I said. "What with Jack and everything."

She brushed a caraway seed from her lips. "Honestly? I could use a project. I've read so many pulp novels and seen so many movies since I got here that I feel like my brain's turning to mush."

She didn't mean it as an indictment of our lifestyle, but I took it as one all the same.

"So you have no idea who Johnny Levane is?" asked Candy.

Jayne shook her head. "I never heard the name until today."

"What about the aunt? Did Billy ever say anything about her?"

"What aunt?" I asked.

"There's one mentioned in this letter." She picked up her knife and pointed at the text in question. "Johnny refers to a Tante M."

"Auntie Em?" I said. "Like *The Wizard of Oz*?"

Candy nodded. "It could be a code, but I don't think so."

"How long would it take to translate the letters?" asked Jayne.

"Not long. A day, maybe two. Do you have the envelopes? It looks like some of these are missing dates, and the cancellation marks might help us figure out the order they were written in."

Jayne fished them out of her purse. Candy gave up protecting herself from the yellow paper and rifled through the envelopes, presumably matching them to the letters they'd held. As she finished, she paused at the last letter and placed it back on the table. There was an indented bit of text in the center of the note. "This is a Manhattan address. Have you checked it out?"

The address was for a Fräulein *something* at an apartment on the Upper West Side. Unfortunately, the last name hadn't appeared in the great urine caper of 1943. Candy scanned the letter. "Johnny's asking Billy to contact him here. It looks like this is the aunt's address. It wouldn't hurt to pop by there. I'd be happy to go with you."

"Thanks," I said. "But you're already doing more than enough."

CHAPTER 6

The Visitor

"What'd you have to tell her for?" I asked Jayne as we headed home.

"She knew Billy. I thought she could help. Was that dumb?"

What was the matter with me? It was her story to share. I had no claim to it. She could tell the world if she wanted to. "No, of course not. I'm sorry. You're right. Maybe she can help."

Jayne's pace slowed. "You saw the ring, didn't you?"

I thought about playing dumb, but by doing so, that meant Jayne was going to have to break the news, and that certainly wasn't a fair position to put her in. "Yeah. Isn't it great? Candy must be thrilled."

Jayne squeezed up her face. "So you're okay that they're engaged?"

"Why wouldn't I be?"

"I just thought–" She didn't know how to finish the sentence. Who could blame her? "I never asked you how you felt about him being with someone else."

"You were a little preoccupied." The night I'd found out that Jack was with Candy was the same night Billy's plane had been shot down. Jayne's tragedy trumped my own. Jack was alive, after all. What did I have to complain about? "I'm fine. Maybe it's not how I wanted things to turn out, but clearly they're happy."

"It doesn't mean he didn't love you," said Jayne.

"I know." It just meant that he didn't love me anymore.

We hit the sack early that night. Ruby was fast asleep when I returned, and I didn't see any point in disturbing her. For a while I tried to read one of her copies of *Thrilling Love* magazine by the light of the moon, but the task quickly proved impossible when the stories evoked neither thrills nor love. Whether I was tired or not, it was time to go to sleep.

I closed my eyes and tried to drift off. It was still raining, and the sound of the drops hitting the fire escape with a metallic *thwang* made for a pleasant, constant sound. Random images floated through my head. The ring twinkling from Candy's left hand. The cage in the Yorkville basement. Billy's photo. The wet paper slowly revealing its text. Auntie M. Johnny Levane.

Johnny Levane. Why was that name so familiar?

Was he an actor? It was possible, especially if Billy was somehow involved in the theater, but I didn't think that was why it was ringing my bell. The name sounded like a gangster's moniker. Maybe he was a friend of Tony B.'s.

I bolted upright. Tony—of course!

Before we ever left the South Pacific, when Jayne and Tony were still wrestling with their on-again, off-again relationship, a mobster named Johnny Levane had been found dead in a Broadway alley. At the time, we were trying to figure out what the mob's connection was to the Sarah Bernhardt Theatre, and because I had Broadway and gangsters on my mind, I'd held on to the news clipping about Levane's death, thinking it was linked to the mystery we were currently embroiled in. It was in a sense; it turned out that Levane wasn't just any dead mobster. He was a victim of Tony's, a guy who, until that point, I had no evidence was guilty of anything other than bad manners.

Surely it was coincidence. We were in the big city, where nobody was unique unless they changed their name to guarantee it. If Billy had borrowed his name from someone else, was it hard to imagine that Johnny Levane had, too?

There was no hope of going back to sleep now. I quietly dressed in my robe, tiptoed out of the room, and took the stairs two at a time. The lobby was empty.

I could wake Jayne. Ann might not be home, and the two of us could talk this over in the confines of our old room. Maybe there was some booze stashed someplace she'd forgotten to check.

But did I really want to put Jayne wise to this? She didn't know about Tony's connection to Johnny Levane. I'd promised him I'd close my head if he'd do me a favor in return. While I didn't feel any allegiance to Tony now, I wasn't up for piling more bad news on my best pal. The last thing she needed to hear while she was mourning one man, was that the one she used to love was a cold-blooded killer.

I sat on the sofa and tried to read a copy of *Newsweek* that some-one had left sitting around. The issue was a month old; the article that grabbed my interest was about the riots in Harlem. This was what the cabbie had been talking about when he was criticizing Mayor LaGuardia. On August 1, a copper had arrested a black woman for disturbing the peace at the Braddock Hotel in Harlem. A black soldier tried to intervene and get her released and ended up getting shot in the process. A crowd of thousands gathered, wrongly proclaiming that the flatfoot had killed the soldier (he was alive, it turned out) and setting off fires, looting, and paving a massive path of destruction. The riots lasted for two days, leaving several dead and thousands arrested.

The fallout wasn't just the physical damage to Harlem but the lasting suspicion its residents had toward the police and the bias the rest of the Manhattan felt toward people who would demolish their own neighborhood. It was disturbing, to say the least. Now we not only distrusted foreigners, we also viewed the people who made up our own community with similar skepticism—hardly fair, considering these were the same people we'd always marginalized. Even in Tulagi I'd seen it. If you were dark-skinned, you weren't trusted to go into battle side by side with our white soldiers.

I closed the magazine, determined to go to bed, when something grabbed my attention.

Shadows played against the black-out blinds concealing the front parlor windows. Someone was outside. Instinctively, I ducked down and crawled toward the glass. Keeping low, I pushed the sheers open, lifted the blinds, and stared out on the street. The rain had made the glass fog up, making it impossible to see anything but the basic outline of a person standing in the downpour. It was clearly a man, and a large and foreboding one at that. Had our tail in Yorkville been big? I wasn't sure; he never got close enough for me to be able to tell.

I used the sheer to wipe away the steam from the glass. Whoever it was spotted me and waved.

Waved!

I backed away. He'd seen me. Now what?

A faint voice came from the street. Whoever it was, was talking to me.

Was our shadow hoping to lure me outside to finish whatever was started that afternoon? Was this a pervert, hoping to catch me off-guard and show me what was inside his trench coat? Was the urge to show strangers your naughty bits so powerful that you'd wait in the rain for the privilege?

Before that thought was given too much space, the specter said my name.

I pushed open the window and the figure approached me. He tilted his hat until his face was visible.

It was Al.

* * *

Al was a former henchman for Jayne's ex-boyfriend, Tony B. Of course, Al was a lot more than that to Jayne and me. He'd saved our lives and recently gave us the chance to do the same for him. Right before we left for the South Pacific, he'd told me he was going to lie low for a while. He'd managed to tick off both Tony and his cohort in the gangster game, Vinnie Garvaggio. I was able to buy Tony's forgiveness, but I didn't wield any such power over Vinnie, and I knew that if Al hadn't gotten lost, he'd probably gotten dead.

It was nice to see that I'd been wrong about that.

I gestured him to the door and let him in. He was a sopping wet mess from standing in the rain for so long. While it was by no means cold outside, the warmth of summer was passing and autumn gave the air just enough bite to make me shiver at the sight of him.

I was in good company. He was already shaking so much we could've used him to refinish the wood floors.

We stared at each other awkwardly for a moment. And then, before I could second-guess the propriety of the urge, I threw my arms around him and squeezed.

"You're going to get wet," he said.

"Too late. What are you doing here?"

"What do you think? I was looking for you. And Jayne." Her name was almost lost in a coughing fit.

"That sounds good."

"I got something in my throat."

"And apparently it's crawled into your lungs and set up camp."

He coughed into his hand. "It's nothing."

"How'd you know we were home?"

"Home? I didn't know you were gone." He removed his hat and ran his hand through his hair. He'd had it cut recently. It barely reached a half inch in length, making his already large noggin appear monstrous and box-like.

"Didn't Tony tell you we went on tour to the South Pacific?"

His face said it all. He hadn't talked to Tony.

"Where have you been?" I asked.

He coughed again. The sound was deep in his chest. He'd been sick long enough that his skin had an ashen hue. "I enlisted."

You could've knocked me over with a feather. "Seriously?"

"Seriously. It seemed like the safest way to stay out of Tony's reach." It was a brilliant plan, except he didn't need to run from Tony. Pity I hadn't told him that before we left for the South Pacific. "I went through basic and was about to be sent overseas when I got discharged."

I was impressed that he'd been willing to join up to hide out. The military seemed like the one place out of the mob's reach. Of course, Tony had still been able to keep tabs on Jayne, even while we were abroad. And rumor had it that Lucky Luciano had so much pull back in Sicily that our military was dying to sit down and talk strategy with him. But I had to hand it to Al for doing something more than keeping a low profile and praying everyone forgot about him. "What were you discharged for?"

He cleared his throat. It wasn't because of the cough; he was trying to stall. "I was gambling."

"Where's the harm there? The guys in the islands were always playing poker."

"I was winning." And cheating, I guessed by the look on his face. So he'd left the mob but not the racket. "One of the officers didn't appreciate my luck and accused me of stealing from him."

Having rumbled with an officer myself, I knew it was a no-win situation, especially for someone like Al, whose rap sheet meant he'd earned extra scrutiny. "So you just got back?" I said.

"About two weeks ago. Though word on the street is I should've stayed gone."

"What are you talking about?"

"Someone's been making the rounds looking for me. They've been to my ma's house and just about anywhere else I used to haunt."

"Any idea who?"

He searched his pockets for a deck of Lucky Strikes. The package he produced was crumbled, the contents reduced to two gaspers. "Vinnie G."

"How could Vinnie be a problem? He's in the joint."

Al laughed in a sad, sardonic way. "He got out in May, and apparently he's been looking for me ever since."

"I don't understand why he's still after you. Surely enough time has passed."

"Tony got the USDA stamps. I don't know how, but he got 'em, and now he's taken over Vinnie's meat racket."

I suddenly felt sick. While Al had been hired by Tony to get the stamps, he didn't turn them over. Al realized that giving someone the power to pass bad meat wasn't the right thing to do. Unfortunately, Tony ended up with the stamps, thanks to me. That was the price I'd paid to get Tony to agree to leave Al alone. Not that Al knew that. "How'd Tony get the stamps?" I asked.

"Doesn't matter. He got 'em, he picked up the meat racket, and now Vinnie G. has put the curse on me and anyone else who had anything to do with it."

"If Tony is the one benefiting from all this, why doesn't Vinnie go after him?"

Al reddened. I wouldn't have been surprised if a sizzling sound came from his skin. "He's too high up. You can't take out a man like Tony B. So you punish the underlings who did the work for him."

"Vinnie must be squeezed tight to still be mad all these months later."

"Nah. Meat's a small part of his racket. He's still got the theaters, the racetrack, garbage, trucking, and so much pull with the dockworkers they're talking about naming a pier for him."

"If that's the case, then why is the heat still on you?"

"Vinnie's got the law on him now. Someone's got to pay for that."

"Wait—if the cops are watching Vinnie more closely, then how come he's able to keep up with all his businesses?"

"Word is he's got someone doing it for him to keep his hands clean." Al tried to light a cigarette. As his hand touched the lighter, he shook.

"You cold?"

"I'm fine."

"You're not fine."

"I'm fine," he repeated with more conviction.

Arguing with him wasn't going to accomplish anything. Al could be as stubborn as a stripped screw. "Won't Tony help you?"

"You'd think so, wouldn't you? But I've been here two weeks, and every time I call, they tell me he's out."

I didn't like the sound of that. Tony had the stamps. Why would he still be sore at Al? "So if they're keeping watch on your ma's house, where have you been staying the last two weeks?" I asked.

He sparked the lighter, but no flame appeared. "Here and there."

His pants had so many holes they could've passed for fishnets. Even I in my modest means would've burned them a while ago. "On the streets?"

"It's not so bad." He lost his grip on the cigarette and watched it tumble to the floor.

"Why don't you take off again?"

He bent down to retrieve the gasper. "With what money? I ain't got a dime to my name."

"What happened to all your poker winnings?"

"You kidding? They confiscated everything I got at camp."

And I had nothing to offer him. "You can't keep this up, Al. It's going to get cold soon. You'll freeze to death out there."

He didn't say anything. Instead, he tried to light the cigarette again. This time it took. "Where's Jayne?"

"Asleep. I'd wake her for this little reunion, but we're no longer living together."

He took a drag. "You two have a falling out?"

"No, nothing like that." I gave him the quick rundown on the last few months.

"Aw, geez. So this Billy guy died?"

"Yeah. And misrepresented himself. We came home only to find that we no longer had one and that the man she loved wasn't who he claimed to be."

"Does Tony know?"

"Beats me. Not that it matters—she wants nothing to do with him."

Al lost some of the tension in his face. "That's probably for the best." He looked for somewhere to ash his cigarette.

I ducked into the parlor, retrieved a coffee cup from the sideboard, and passed it his way

"It's definitely for the best. Getting rid of him was the smartest thing she's ever done."

The bags beneath his eyes had bags of their own. "He ain't that bad. It's not like he ever stepped out on her."

I tossed him a look that I hoped reminded him of Tony's hundreds of other infractions. What was it about Tony B. that convinced so many people to be loyal to him? I couldn't even get a cat to like me, and I'd never done anything to betray him. "Tell me about Johnny Levane."

Al coughed and waved the smoke away like it was its fault he was sick. "What do you want to dig that up for?"

"If we're going to list Tony's good points, I thought we should dredge up the bad, too."

"I'm not playing."

"I'm not playing, either. I heard the name again recently. It got me curious." A car pulled up to the curb and idled outside the Shaw House. For one terrifying moment I thought it was Vinnie G.'s men, but after a few seconds the driver dimmed his headlights and went on his way.

"There's nothing to tell, Rosie. He was a thug. He crossed Tony. End of story."

"Who was he working for? How did he cross him?"

"That ain't the kind of stuff I know." Hearing Al say that reminded me of the military and how anything I ever wanted to find out about was mysteriously above my pay grade. I didn't push. Al had enough to deal with without me putting more pressure on him.

"When's the last time you ate?" I asked.

"You're not my ma."

"Thank God for small favors. When was it?"

He rolled his eyes. "I had some soup at an Automat about an hour ago."

"Which one?"

"The one on Lex." I knew what Automat soup meant: hot water, catsup, and a little salt. I'd made a free meal at Horn and Hardart myself a time or two. It was amazing how little you could survive on if you didn't have a choice. "Tell Jayne I said hi. And that I'm sorry about Billy." He stepped away from me.

I put my arm on his and he stopped. "Are we going to see you again?"

"I'll stop by when I can." He turned to go. I was suddenly overwhelmed by an urge to make him stay. He needed help, and it was unlikely that anyone else was going to step in and give it to him.

"How about you stop by tomorrow night? I'll make sure Jayne's around. I know she'll want to see you."

His head danced as he weighed the idea. "Maybe I could do that."

"Good. We'll see you then." I poked his bicep. "Be careful in the meantime, all right?"

He smiled or at least tried to. "I always am."

I watched him leave. As I locked the front door and headed inside, the car I'd seen earlier returned to the curb and shut off its engine. If he was here for Al, he was too late.

CHAPTER 7

My Aunt from Ypslanti

Jayne was in the dining room when I went downstairs the next morning. She already had the paper out and was combing the audition notices. That was a good sign at least.

"Anything hopeful?"

"Maybe." She licked a finger and turned the page. Oatmeal was the food of the day. It sat in a large pot on the buffet with unappetizing globs of yellowish orange margarine to be used as a garish garnish.

"I had a visitor last night," I said. "Al popped by." I gave her the lowdown on our meeting, leaving out any mention of Tony in the process. "He's pretty bad off, Jayne. He can't hide out much longer."

"He should leave the city."

"I agree, but he's broke."

"I don't understand why Tony's not helping him."

"I don't think he knows he's back yet." Al must've done something else to upset Tony, something that he hadn't owned up to yet. But what? He'd been in the military since May. If something happened, it had to have happened before then.

Johnny Levane.

That had to be it! I told Tony I knew he was behind Johnny Levane's death when I was trying to buy Al's freedom over that stamp nonsense. Tony was a smart guy; he had to know that the only way I could've found out about Levane was if Al had told me. And that meant I'd managed to underscore that Al was a rat on top of being disloyal.

"Nuts," I said.

"What's wrong?"

At some point I was going to have to share all of this with Jayne, but I just wasn't up to it yet. Normally we didn't keep secrets from each other. Not only was this a big one, I'd been carrying it around for six months now. "Nothing," I said. "I just feel for the guy. Maybe we should put him up somewhere."

Jayne played a melody on the table with her right hand. "With what money?"

"How about Billy's cush?" We had five thousand clams to keep Al safe with.

"That's not our money, Rosie."

"I know, but this is an emergency. Whatever we use, we can pay back. It won't take more than a hundred berries to see him through the month. We owe it to him."

She looked spent from the conversation. She still wasn't sleeping well, that much was obvious. "No," she said. "It's not mine to give away."

I decided not to argue with her. It wasn't my money, and if she wanted to act like it wasn't hers either, that was fine. For now. "Do you want to go by the Manhattan address today? Where Auntie M. lives?"

She lowered her gaze to the newspaper and stared at an ad for girdles like it was the most fascinating thing she'd ever seen. "I don't think so."

"Why not?"

Her attention shifted from girdles to war bonds. "I just don't think it's a good idea."

So this Jayne was back, the one who ran hot and cold without any warning. "Want to tell me why?"

"I told Ann about the letters."

I could feel my lip start to curl the way Ruby's had when I first mentioned Ann. "And?"

"And she said that if the letters are in German, they're bad news."

"Bad news like 'Uncle Adolf died' or bad news like 'We really missed you at the last young Nazis meeting'?"

She frowned. "I think she meant the second thing. Anyway, it got me thinking: Billy kept all this from me for a reason. He wouldn't want me digging it up."

"I don't think he gets to have a say anymore, Jayne. He lied to you, remember? About some very important, very basic facts of his existence."

"He had his reasons. I know he did." She closed the newspaper and set her hands—palms down—atop it. "I just think it would be better to leave all this alone."

"All right."

"I mean it, Rosie. I want to remember him like he was in Tulagi. I don't think I can if we keep dredging up his past."

"Fine by me," I said. "I don't have a horse in this race." I focused on my chow, even though I had plenty more I wanted to say. Like how the Billy in Tulagi ceased to exist the minute Jayne found out that wasn't his real name.

There were three dance auditions that morning. All required more hoofing skills than I had at my disposal, so rather than going along and facing certain rejection, I told Jayne to go without me.

Once she was gone, I decided to pay a visit to our former room.

The door was cracked open, so I walked right in without announcing myself. "Ann?"

She didn't respond. She was sitting beside the radio with a pad of paper and a pen. The dial was tuned to 627 AM, a station that broadcast nothing but pager numbers for taxi drivers who subscribed to the service.

"Ann?"

Her body shifted in such a way that I was positive she'd heard me. Was she ignoring me?

"Ann? Hello?" I clapped my hands to get her attention.

Her head snapped my way. "Oh. What do you want?"

"What are you doing?" I asked. "Did you start driving a hack while we were sleeping?"

She turned the volume off. "I find the background noise comforting. Jayne isn't here."

"I know. I suppose I have you to thank for her change of heart?" She didn't respond, probably because she didn't know what I was talking about. "The letters we found yesterday? She told me she doesn't want to know what they say after all."

She scribbled something on her notepad. "She asked for my advice. I gave it. Is that a crime?"

Maybe she was right. The truth was, Jayne couldn't move on if she kept dwelling on Billy. Forgetting about him was probably the best thing she could do. But I couldn't get over the nagging coincidence of Billy's friend having the same name as the mobster Tony B. gunned down. It felt too important to ignore.

"If he was your boyfriend, wouldn't you want to know who he really was?" I asked her.

"She knows. His name may have changed, but he hasn't."

"You know what I mean: Wouldn't you want to know why he changed his name?"

"No. People are entitled to their secrets."

"Certain secrets, sure, but this isn't exactly lying about your weight, is it?"

She stopped looking at her notepad and turned to me. "What good will her finding out more about him do? Will it change how she felt about him? How she believed he felt about her? Because isn't that what's most important? Right now she has a memory of a sweet boy who loved her enough to ask her to marry him. Why not let her keep that? All this digging around is going to change something and tarnish the one good thing that came out of all she's been through."

God, I hated logic. I hated how it made me seem like the irrational one. And deep down inside, I knew she was right. When I found out that Peaches had been lying to me, it ruined everything. Did I really want to put Jayne through the same thing?

But that was the problem, wasn't it? She was already going through it. She knew he lied. And I know that the first thing I wanted to know when I found out about Peaches' deception was why he'd done it.

"Nothing good is going to come of those letters," said Ann. "You know that and I know that. The secret writing, the German—they all add up to something bad going on."

"Maybe you're right."

She returned to whatever she was writing. "Of course I am."

Would it have killed her to be humble? "Do you mind if I take some of my stuff? The books on the nightstand are mine."

"Be my guest."

I made a beeline to the bedside table. There, beneath the pile, was a yellowing newspaper I'd stuck there all those months before, when I was trying to figure out what the mob was doing on Broadway. The pages I'd saved detailed the death of Johnny Levane, a two-bit thug who only merited a mention at the back of the paper.

I took the newspaper and a few slicks with me and went back to Ruby's room. There, I flipped through the rag until I found the article about the murder. There wasn't much to the story. Just a name, age, and a description of the scene—an alley lined in Levane's

blood after a bullet cut through his chest. There were no witnesses
to the murder. The coppers had described it as mob retaliation and
seemed no more concerned about the death than they were when
the immigrants in Yorkville went after one another, or the darbs in
Harlem. "Let them kill their own," was the philosophy. Who cares
if another criminal is dead?

But somebody had to care, right? Somebody had to know Johnny
Levane. And I was willing to bet it was the aunt whose address
Johnny had included in his letter. She'd be able to confirm that Billy's Johnny and Tony's were one and the same. And maybe, in the
process, I could get enough information about Billy to put Jayne's
mind at ease, if she ever decided she wanted to know more.

I left with the newspaper and the photo of the two men stuffed
in my purse. It was a glum day, the rain from the night before
still lingering in the air, though now it had turned into the sort
of constant drizzle that the South Pacific had been known for. I
got on the subway at Christopher Street, but there were no spare
seats. Plenty of them were taken by men, but instead of offering
me one they kept their eyes fixed out the window. Had Manhattan gotten ruder since we'd been gone? It felt that way. I couldn't
remember the last time a stranger had smiled at me or held open
a door.

"Excuse me," said a woman standing beside me. She had frizzy
hair that the weather was doing no favors. "Are my seams straight?"
One of her hands held on to a strap for balance; the other held a
cage containing two white doves.

I took a look at the backs of her calves and assured her that her
stockings could be used to map out right angles.

"Thanks," she said. As we arrived uptown, the crowd rose and
pushed toward the doors. The frizzy-haired woman with the doves
walked ahead of me. As she jostled forward, she muttered an apology for bumping into the men in front of her. And then something
very peculiar happened: her hand disappeared into one man's
jacket pocket, emerged with his wallet, and quickly deposited it

in the cage. As the woman exited the subway and headed toward the stairs, I stood dumbly watching her. She kept her eyes straight ahead and added an extra sway to her hips.

"Move it, lady," said a man behind me. "Goddamn tourists are always in the way."

I tossed him a sneer over my shoulder. By the time I turned back, the woman was gone. I left the subway and headed topside. There I huddled close to the stem of my umbrella and tried not to let my mood mimic my hair.

The address "Tante M." lived at was an apartment building six blocks off Broadway. It was surprisingly plush for a recent immigrant, if that's what Billy and his family were. I expected to see a doorman at his perch, but he apparently was on a break. Instead, the front door was propped open to allow the gentle fall breeze and the fresh damp air passage into the building. As I stepped into the lobby, I eyeballed the mailbox, looking for a German surname that would point toward the person I sought. Everything looked English to my eyes, but then that shouldn't surprise me. After all, if Billy was using a name that wasn't his own, what was stopping his aunt from doing the same?

"Can I help you?" asked an elderly woman. She was clad all in black and by virtue of her presence seemed to make the lights in the lobby dim. Her face was lined and furrowed, except around her eyes, where the presence of relatively smooth skin made it clear she hadn't smiled since there were sheep in Central Park. In her arms was a small dog that Churchill outweighed by at least ten pounds.

"Um, sure," I said. "I'm trying to track down a relative of a friend, but I'm afraid the rain blurred the name. I know this is the address, but I'm not sure who it is I'm looking for."

"Who is your friend?"

"Billy DeMille," I said. "It's his aunt who lives here. He . . ." I caught my breath in my throat and bit hard at the flesh on the inside of my mouth. Tears propelled themselves to the corners of my eyes. "He's dead," I said. "And before he was killed, he made me promise that I'd tell his beloved aunt in person if anything should happen to him."

"And he didn't tell you her name?" She had the voice of a drill sergeant. Or a nineteenth-century schoolmarm.

"He just called her Auntie M. Well . . . Tante. He was German."

She lifted her head a little, and despite her tiny size, seemed to outgrow me. "There are no Germans in this building."

That's what you think, lady. "She wasn't German. He was a nephew. By marriage. Who liked to refer to everyone by German titles."

"And what did he call you?"

"Kaiser."

The dog moaned. Or growled. I couldn't tell which sound he was going for. "I'm afraid I can't help you. And you cannot loiter in the lobby. It's intended for residents and their guests. Only." Her eyes flickered toward the front door, clearly indicating that it was time for me to leave and for the missing doorman to return.

"Thanks for your help," I said. "But I'm here by permission. I'm just waiting for my friend to meet me down here."

"You have a friend in this building? Why didn't you mention it before?"

"Because you didn't ask."

I was about to invent a complicated lineage for my imaginary pal, when the lobby elevator dinged. The doors opened and a familiar face appeared.

Maureen O'Reilly, Satan's choreographer, saw me and froze.

Maureen choreographed a show Jayne and I had been in right before we left for the South Pacific. I had spent several miserable weeks in her charge after getting put into a corps de ballet neither of my left feet had any right being cast in. She claimed to be Irish, as her name implied, but given her thick Bavarian accent and penchant for Wagner, it was clear something else was afoot. But because no one else made a big deal about it, I hadn't either. If I

could pretend to be a dancer, she was free to pretend to be anything but German.

"Vat are you doink here?" she said as soon as she saw me.

"Looking for you," I said. "See? This is my friend," I told the
woman in black. "So you can beat it."

"Do you know this woman, Miss O'Reilly?" she asked.

"Unfortunately, yes."

With a humph, the lady in black turned tail and disappeared
into the elevator.

"Thanks for that," I told Maureen. "So how's tricks?"

"Much better since you've been out of my hair. How's Jayne?"
While Maureen spent each day wishing for my death, she was, like
everyone else, enamored of my pal.

"She's been better. She's looking for work if you've got any."

She pulled a compact and lipstick out of her purse. "Und you?"

"Know better than to ask."

With a practiced hand, she applied a robust red crème to her
lips. "I thought you two had given up on the theater."

"No, we just decided to take a vacation. Jayne and I have been
touring with the USO."

She snapped the compact shut. "Maybe you should've stayed
touring."

"What's that supposed to mean?"

She underscored her words with the closed tube of lipstick.
"Just maybe dere's a reason de vork has dried up."

"Do you know something?"

"Come now, Rosie. It's not hard to underschtand. Before you
left, you two ticked off de wrong person."

It took a moment for me to parse what she was saying and not
just because of the accent. Vinnie Garvaggio had produced the
show Maureen choreographed. During the production Jayne and
I had discovered he was operating an illegal slaughterhouse in the
theater basement and helped turn him in. Could he be the reason
we weren't working? It made sense. Al said Vinnie wanted revenge

on everyone involved in shutting down his meat business. Surely that included Jayne and me.

"I have no influence," said Maureen.

"Who said you did?"

"I assumed zat vas vy you vere here."

"Then you assumed wrong. I'm trying to find a German woman."

Maureen straightened. "Zere are no Germans here."

"So I've been told. But here's the thing: I've got proof there is one and I need to see her."

"Vy?"

Here we go again. "I was asked by her nephew to deliver a message in person if anything should happen to him."

"So zen vat's the problem?"

"I don't have her name. Only her address. And an initial."

She smiled the same smug little grin that she brought out whenever I screwed up on stage. "Zen I cannot help you." She started to head out the front door.

"Okay, there are no Germans here. I get it. But if you talk to any of your ... er ... Irish pals who reside at this address, could you let them know Billy DeMille was killed in action? If they want details, they can get in touch with me. I live at the George Bernard Shaw House in the Village."

She froze with her back to me. She seemed to wither on the vine, her perfect posture crumbling until I expected her head to rest on her feet.

"Are you okay?" I asked.

"Did *he* find him?"

"Huh?" I said.

"How did he die?"

"His plane was shot down in the South Pacific. He was trying to take out some Japs who'd just blown up one of our ships."

"Ze Japanese killed him?"

"Yeah. He died a hero."

She shuddered ever so slightly. "Did he suffer?" Her voice was so quiet that I had to strain to hear it.

"No," I said.

"Gut. Das ist gut." She took a deep breath, reassembling herself in the process. Before I could say anything else, she pushed open the door and walked out.

CHAPTER 8

The Spy

"Maureen!" I called after her, but she seemed determined to keep moving forward. "I need to talk to you about this. Come on—just give me a minute."

I didn't even get a second. I surrendered my dignity and jogged to keep pace with her.

"Leave me alone," she hissed.

"Come on now—you were Billy's aunt?"

"Vat und who I am is of no concern to you."

"Please talk to me. There's more to the story. Jayne and Billy were engaged. We've been to his apartment in Yorkville. She knows he's not really Billy DeMille, and she needs to know why. She thinks everything he said was a lie now. Her heart's broken."

"Zis is not my problem."

"It's not mine, either, but you don't see me running away from it. Please, tell me what's what. You might not like me, but we both know how you feel about Jayne."

She finally stopped walking. She stared at me, those hard brown eyes of hers passing judgment for things I hadn't even done yet. "Dere is nothink to tell."

"Oh come on now—the guy took a dead man's name. There's got to be a reason for that."

"He vas embarrassed to be German, dat's all."

"Yeah? I'm not too thrilled to be who I am, but you don't see me dodging beneath a fake name." Though, come to think of it, if Jayne and I were being blackballed, it wasn't a bad idea.

"You don't underschtand."

"Then explain it to me."

She sighed heavily. "You might be a lousy dancer, but have you ever been accused of being a bad person just because of vere your family comes from?"

"No."

"Zen you can't underschtand."

"Come on—you know you can't show me the steps once if it's going to sink in. Give me another shot."

She looked heavenward before returning her attention to me. "Do you know about the Alien Registration Act?"

"Sure. Aliens from enemy countries have to register with the government, right?"

"Dat vas de vay it was supposed to vork, but since de var dey make everyone from dat country register, whether legal or not. Those alien cards give the government permission to completely control dere lives. Dey can seize dere property, keep dem from traveling to certain places, prevent dem from getting certain jobs. Dey cannot own guns or radios, ride trains, or board planes."

"Wow. I didn't realize it was so bad."

"Und ven de government views you vith suspicion, everyone else does, too. So Billy did vat he believed he had to do. Zink about it. Vould Jayne have loved him the same vay if he vas Vilhelm from Bavaria?"

I liked to believe she would. Jayne wasn't the kind of person to shun you because of where you were from or how many consonants were in your name. But not everyone was like that. If I'd learned nothing else from our time in the South Pacific, I did realize that we were being taught to hate indiscriminately. All Japanese and Germans were bad. That way, you didn't have to think before you shot them.

I dug into my purse and pulled out the photo. "Who's this in the picture with Billy?"

Surprise showed in her eyes. "That is Johann. Billy's cousin."

"Johann. Did he go by another name, too? Maybe Johnny Levane?"

"Yes."

"Where is he? Could I talk to him?"

She hesitated a moment too long. "He was murdered last spring. Now if you'll excuse me, I must go."

I watched her walk away. So that was it? Billy, like her, wanted freedom from the inconvenience of being German? I was strangely disappointed in this explanation. But it made sense—the secret writing would've been necessary if they wanted to exchange letters in their mother tongue without anyone seeing them. And the name change was just a way of further Americanizing themselves and keeping them above government suspicion.

But then Billy wasn't Maureen. He wasn't saddled by her accent. He assimilated so well that if you'd told us three months before that he was German, we would've called you crazy. And what about the money? How did someone like him end up with five thousand dollars and why did he leave it behind? It almost seemed like everything he abandoned—the clothes, the photo, the trunk—was a way of shedding his old identity and starting anew. But the money wasn't part of that old identity. It was American dough, not German.

And what of Johnny Levane? Had he made a crucial mistake, choosing the name of a man the mob wanted dead, or had he crossed the wrong person in his new identity and ended up a dead mobster rather than a secretive immigrant?

If only I could get into that footlocker. Something important had to be in there.

I walked toward the subway station and tried to push thoughts of Johnny and Billy out of my head. Jayne was on the right track: we needed to forget about all of this and move forward. The temperature had dropped from the rain the night before. Soon we would be adding blankets to our beds and closing the windows at night. I needed to help Al before then and make sure he had shelter. Why had I ever given Tony that stupid Grand Central Station locker key? If I'd kept it to myself, he wouldn't have gotten the USDA stamps. Sure, he would've still been mad at Al, but at least things would be square with Vinnie. And Jayne and I wouldn't be blackballed from ever working in this town again. Of course, if I hadn't given Tony the key, he may have found a way into the locker, if he ever figured out the number. Surely there were locksmiths on the underworld payroll.

Locksmiths?

I stopped in my tracks and looked up and down the street. Sure enough, there was a shop with a giant key for a sign announcing that keys could be engraved and locks could be changed, fast service guaranteed. I marched toward the storefront for Lochanelli's Locksmiths and pushed the door open. A bell tinkled a greeting as I came inside.

"Hiya," I said to the man behind the counter. He had a visor on his head and a jeweler's loupe in his eye. Whatever he was doing required his fullest concentration.

"Can I help you?" he asked.

"I hope so. I have a military trunk. My brother's. They shipped it home with the body but didn't give us the key." I rolled my eyes in mock exasperation. "That's the army for you. Is there maybe a standard key they all use that I could buy?"

"Every lock is different. Otherwise, why lock your trunk when every man around you has a key that could open it?"

Ah, logic—it failed me again.

He removed the loupe and set it on the counter. "I could open it, if you brought it to me."

That wasn't going to happen. There was no way to get the trunk to him and I had a sneaking suspicion that I couldn't afford what he charged to bring him to it. "What about picks? Do you have a set I could buy?"

"I don't sell such things."

Sure he didn't. And I never drank out of boredom. I looked around the shop, hoping another solution would bubble to the surface. He had a racing form on the counter. His horse picks were marked in heavily penciled circles. I knew someone involved in the horse racing business: Vinnie G. In fact, that was where most of his meat used to come from—retired racehorses.

It was worth a try.

"You know, I'm a friend of Vinnie Garvaggio's. He's the one who sent me here."

That got his attention. He removed the visor with shaking hands. "I'll have the money soon. Business has been slow, but I haven't forgotten him. I'll have everything tomorrow, just like I said."

"Relax, I'm not here about your debt. He said you were the kind of guy who'd help a girl out. As I'm sure you know, if you do Vinnie a favor, he'll do one for you."

His hand disappeared from the counter and opened a drawer. Seconds later he emerged with a velvet bag. He lifted its flap and showed me what looked like the torture implements the dentist wielded. "You know how to use these?"

"Of course," I said. How hard could it be? You stuck them in the lock and wiggled them, right?

"And you'll tell Vinnie I helped you?"

"You bet I will. And when he comes here looking for his money, you be sure to let him know what you did for me."

"What's your name, doll?"

I smiled as I took the velvet bag and slid it into my pocketbook. "Ruby Priest."

Instead of heading home, I went to Yorkville. As I passed through the invisible line between our neighborhood and theirs, eyes followed me. I hated how uncomfortable the joint made me. Logically,

I knew that what I was seeing wasn't a desire to harm me but a curiosity and fear that I was there to harm them, but after being told for so long that Germans were the enemy, it was hard not to feel like each person I passed had their sights on me.

They could be Billy, I told myself. Each and every one of them victims of the bias their homeland created against them. If that was in fact what had happened to Billy.

I made it to Billy's former building and knocked on the door to Mr. Smith's apartment. It took ten solid pounds before anyone bothered to respond.

This time it wasn't Mr. Smith.

"*Ja?*" said a woman clad in a flowered housedress. Her thick hair was piled on top of her head and a cigarette dangled from one hand.

"Is Mr. Smith here?"

She turned away from me and said something in German. A voice answered her. She waved me forward, and I passed the threshold into the apartment.

"Who are you?" said a man I hadn't seen before. His English was heavily accented. He wore an undershirt and overly large pants hoisted by a pair of suspenders, one of which had already given up the ghost and dangled, uselessly, around his bloated midsection.

"My name is Rosie Winter. Is Mr. Smith around?"

"He died yesterday."

I couldn't think of how to respond, so all I said was, "Are you sure?"

"Yes. You go now," said the man.

It wasn't a request. The woman took me by the arm and led me back to the front door. By the time I realized that I hadn't gotten what I came for, the door had closed and I was standing in the hallway.

Did I knock again? Was it rude to demand more information when someone had just died?

I decided to take matters into my own hands. I followed the stairs down to the basement and tried the door. It wouldn't budge.

I pulled out the picks and poked at the lock, but it quickly became clear that lock picking was more complicated than I thought. After a few halfhearted attempts, I gave up and admitted defeat.

"The keys are missing," said a voice above me.

I looked up and saw a young woman whose hair fell in a braid across her shoulder. I'd seen her before. She was there the first time we'd come to see Mr. Smith. She lived in the apartment next door to him. "Excuse me?" I asked.

"They were one of the things they took."

"Are you talking about Mr. Smith?"

She nodded. "I am Inge. What is your name?"

"Rosie Winter. What happened to Mr. Smith?" I asked.

She looked behind her to verify that no one else was in the hallway. She came down three steps and paused, her face hidden in the shadows. "He was beaten. The police said he had a heart attack during the quarrel. His wallet is gone. His pocket watch. His keys. Every door to every room in this building can be unlocked with those keys. His brother told us that we will have to pay to have our own locks changed. Can you imagine? We can't afford to do this."

"I'm sorry," I said. This wasn't good. Taking money and jewelry I could understand—that's what thieves did. But keys? That indicated someone wanted to find something in the building. Given what we'd found of Billy's in the basement, it wasn't hard to imagine what prize they were after. "Have you lived here long?"

"Just since June. It is a terrible place, but it is all we can afford."

She wouldn't have known Billy then. "I guess nobody saw the culprit, huh?"

"Saw him? No. But I heard him. I live with my grandfather in the apartment next door."

"What did you hear?" I climbed the steps and met her halfway. Now, close-up, I could see that her face was marred by pimples, so numerous they passed for freckles from a distance.

"They were arguing. Everyone around here argues so you learn to ignore it. But it went on and on. The man kept asking '*Wer sind Sie*' and Smith kept telling him that he didn't know."

"What does that mean?"

She seemed embarrassed, as though she hadn't realized she'd spoken German. "Who are they?"

Were Jayne and I the *who* in question? Or was he asking about someone else?

"My English is good, yes?" said the girl.

"Very good."

"I don't like to speak German. So many around here do, but I think in America we should do as the Americans do."

"That's an admirable idea." I climbed the remaining stairs and attempted to pass her. If it was Jayne and me the man was after, I didn't want to linger any longer than necessary.

"It will be expensive to change the locks," said the woman. "I have been helpful to you?"

"Very." She was blocking my path. I took a step to the left to go around her, but she countered. "You were here the other day? You went downstairs with Mr. Smith?"

Oh, boy. "Yes."

"Maybe then you are who the man was looking for, Rosie Winter. You and your friend."

My blood ran cold. How had she read my mind like that? Or was there more to the conversation that she had overhead?

"I can be quiet," she said. "Like I was that night. If he comes back I can make sure that he never knows what I know."

"And how do I make that happen?"

She held out her hand. I gave her the little bit of coin I had in my purse and left the building.

I rushed home with my head too full for new thought. Who was the man following us? Why was our identity so important to him that he was willing to kill for it? And what clues, if any, had Mr. Smith been able to provide him as to who we were?

Was he following me now?

I stopped just short of the Shaw House. A male figure lingered near the steps, half-hidden in the shadows of the building. He had a hat on his head and a cigarette in his mouth. As he smoked down the gasper, he took a step back and stared at the upper floors of the building.

Oh, God. He'd followed me here. I was the next person destined to die.

I turned and starting walking in the direction I'd come from. I hadn't gone two steps when another figure blocked my path.

I screamed. I couldn't help it.

"Rosie?" It was Tony B., clutching a bouquet of roses in one hand and a cigar in the other.

"Tony. Long time no see." I looked over my shoulder to see what the man by the building was doing. If he shot at me, maybe Tony would be good enough to take the bullet.

"You all right?" he asked. "You look like you've seen a ghost."

I needn't have worried. The man was gone. Tony, for all his faults, had scared him away. "You just startled me, that's all."

"Jayne around?"

If she was, she wasn't going to be too eager to see him. He was dressed to the nines and would've looked like a totally respectable businessman if he didn't have a racing form sticking out of his lapel pocket.

"Jayne's not here. She's at an audition. How'd you know we were home?"

"Grapevine. Tell her I stopped by." He didn't leave the flowers. He turned to go.

"Tony? Al's back in town."

"I know," he said.

"He's in a bad way. Garvaggio's got someone watching all his old haunts. He's living on the streets."

"Good." He headed toward a car parked at the curb.

"Hey!" I said. "What's done is done. I thought you agreed to leave him alone."

"And I did until your boy decided to try and double-cross me."

"It was an accident. He didn't mean to tell me about Johnny Levane."

He turned back toward me and shook the flowers my way. A pink rose bud left the bouquet and tumbled to the ground. "That ain't what I'm talking about. Tell your friend that I know what he's up to. If he thinks he can take me out and solve his problems, he's got another thing coming."

Surely this whole weird day was making me hear things. Al was after Tony? With what as his weapon? Stern words from his mother? "You mean to tell me Al's put the hurt on you?"

"You just pass on my message." He turned to go again.

"Hold on a sec—you can't drop that kind of bombshell and walk away. Whatever is going on between Al and you is a misunder-standing."

"Stay out of it, Rosie. It ain't your business."

Oh, if only I had used that as my mantra that day. "Fine, it's not my business. But Jayne and I are hurting, too. We haven't been able to get work since we got home, and a little bird told me Garvag-gio's behind the ban. Any chance you could ask Vinnie to loosen his hold?"

Tony looked at his hand, wiggling each finger in succession. When he reached his pinky, he examined the gold ring circling it and carefully scratched away something on its surface. "She gonna call me?"

"Jayne? I don't know. She's pretty mad. She found out you had someone tailing her in the South Pacific."

He raised his index finger. "That was for her protection."

I showed him my palms. "I know. And I for one appreciated the gesture, but she felt a little uncomfortable with the idea. I mean you two were broken up." And she was seeing someone else. Who she was planning on marrying. "I can't guarantee she'll call."

"Then maybe I can't guarantee I'll talk to Vinnie." He turned again and made it all the way to his car. Was I really hearing him right? Was he going to let Vinnie continue to blackball us unless Jayne contacted him? When had this become my life?

I followed him, trying very hard to keep my voice calm and measured. "Look, Tony, I appreciate your position, really I do, but it's not my decision to make. If it were, I'd have her call you today. Jayne's got a will of her own, and, frankly, I don't understand why I have to suffer for it. I held up my part of the bargain. Remember? You got the stamps. I kept my silence."

His driver started the ignition. Tony opened the back door and tossed the flowers on the seat.

"I could tell her, you know," I said. "About what you did to—" I looked around and lowered my voice. "Johnny. If I did that, she'd never call you again."

He slid into the backseat. "Then I guess you two better start looking into other careers."

"It must be great being you," I said as he pulled his door shut. "Not a person in the world you need to care about other than yourself."

I don't think he heard me. The car pulled away in a squeal of tires. I returned to the stoop and leaned against the railing, feeling as if I'd just gotten done running a marathon.

"Who was that?"

I hadn't heard anyone else approach. Candy Abbott was in front of me. Who was next? Hitler?

"Jayne's ex-boyfriend."

Candy couldn't have looked more shocked if I'd just said Tony was a walking, talking flounder. "But that man was a mobster."

"What can I tell you? Love is blind. So what are you doing here?"

"I finished the letters."

"That was fast." Somewhere a siren went off. Was it a fire? A robbery? Or had a plane been spotted in the sky above us?

"I had a lot of time on my hands today." She fished the papers from her purse. Each letter was neatly paper-clipped to both its envelope and a typed transcript of its contents. "They're pretty vague."

I led her into the house, and she joined me on the sofa in the parlor. Once we were comfortable, I took the pages from her and scanned the first translation.

Dear Billy,

There is no need to apologize. I understand why you're doing what you're doing. I've thought often of it myself. Maybe if I were a stronger person, I could do so. I hope you are well. I would very much like to see you. I respect that you don't wish to meet face to face at your new apartment, but perhaps we could choose a more neutral place?

Johnny

Dear Billy,

I am concerned that it's been so long since you last wrote. I am hoping that you haven't decided to leave without telling me. I have been thinking long and hard about what you said, and I think you're right. I want to change, too. It's not too late. I'm happy to give it all up and start anew. Will you help me, cousin?

Johnny

Dear Billy,

Two weeks and still no word from you. I'm going crazy wondering what's become of you. I have contacted Tante M., but she swears she hasn't heard from you, either. Action Day is fast upon us, and if I don't hear from you soon, I'll have no choice but to move forward alone. I'm not strong like you. I have no wits, no money to improve myself. Please write to me, cousin. I cannot do this without you. Perhaps you do not find it safe to contact me in Newark? If that is so, write to me in care of Tante M. at 315 West Seventy-seventh Street, Apartment G, Manhattan. She will see to it that your message gets to me.

Johnny

Dear Billy,

Forgive me for defying you, but I have gone by your new apartment in this area called Yorkville. No one there has seen you for months. I am writing in hope that you are still getting your mail and thinking of me, dear cousin. Why did you leave, I ask myself. Did you worry I would betray you? But that is not in my nature. You, if anyone, should know that. I know you say I am not cautious enough, that I don't understand the risks I put myself in. Tante M. has said the same. And maybe you are both right. But I think about the path I have chosen and realize that maybe it is the best thing for me. He is only thinking of our best interests, and so I do what he asks out of gratitude.

Johnny

"There are more of them, but they're all pretty much the same," said Candy. "Every letter is Johnny pleading with Billy to contact him. They stop at the beginning of March."

"He died in March," I said.

Candy's eyebrows tipped toward her nose. "I thought Billy died at the end of June."

"Not Billy—Johnny. Billy's cousin was murdered. That's why the letters stopped."

"How do you know that?"

"I just do." I rifled through the letters, looking not at the translations but at the original German text. Johnny's handwriting was slanted and irregular. You could read the nervousness in his prose, even if the words had no meaning to me.

"Why do you think Billy didn't respond to him?" asked Candy.

"I think he was gone before any of the letters came. By the time Johnny died, Billy had been in the navy long enough to earn his first leave." I focused on the translation of the last letter. "What do you think this means: 'He is only thinking of our best interests, and so I do what he asks out of gratitude.'"

"I had a hard time translating that," said Candy. "I couldn't tell if *he* was a person or a thing, like God."

I returned the letters to their original order and checked again to ensure that we were alone. "I met Tante M. today."

"You found her?"

"Found her? I already knew her. Her name's Maureen O'Reilly. She choreographed the last show Jayne and I were in."

"She's Irish?"

I snorted. "She wishes. She's as German as a Volkswagen. She said Billy's name change was all about protection from German discrimination in the good ol' U.S. of A."

"It's not unheard of."

"Sure, but you knew Billy. There was no way to know he was German. And if you're so worried that the world's going to treat you bad for being a Kraut, why would you rent an apartment in Yorkville?"

"Maybe he had to change his name to go into the military."

It was an interesting idea. Billy might've had a record or a past that would've prevented him from enlisting. His real name may have led back to that. Or maybe his medical history was such that he would've been stamped 4-F and sent on his way. By using the name of a man who already had a military career, he may have been able to avoid that scrutiny, or at least bypass basic training.

But why was Johnny so desperate for his assistance?

My head was hurting. I longed to start the day over with the wisdom to stay out of trouble. And I was desperate to unburden myself. I couldn't tell Jayne anything I'd been up to, so why not Candy? "Something else happened today," I said. I told her about my second visit to Mr. Smith's.

Candy's face reflected the horror I felt. "He's dead?"

"And it's our fault. Whoever killed him was looking for us."

"You can't be sure about that."

"Maybe not, but I'm certain we were followed the first time we went to Yorkville." And just as sure that I'd been followed that afternoon. I felt so sick that I had to bend over. Candy put a reassuring hand on my back, waiting—I'm sure—for an explanation for my green complexion. "I shouldn't have gone back there," I said.

"You were trying to help," said Candy.

"Who? Not Jayne. She told me she didn't want to know."

"But she might one day. You did nothing wrong, Rosie."

"Tell that to Mr. Smith."

"You're looking at this wrong. How would someone know to follow you there? I'll bet whoever this man is visited Mr. Smith long before you came along and told him to let him know if anyone ever came around asking about Billy. It didn't matter if it was you, or the real Billy DeMille's father, or a friend who served with him in Tulagi. If you're guilty of anything, it's bad timing."

I struggled to sit upright. "Thanks." I plucked her careful translations from each of the letters. "I don't want to show these to Jayne."

"Why not?"

"She told me she doesn't want to know, and, frankly, I don't think these letters are going to help her. It's best if I leave all this alone now." I passed the translations to Candy. I couldn't keep them at the Shaw House. I didn't want to risk Jayne finding them. "Would you get rid of them?"

"Of course. If that's what you want." She returned the letters to her purse.

I took in for the first time how weary Candy looked. It wasn't listening to my misadventures alone that had done it.

"You look beat-up. How's Jack doing?" I asked.

"Not good. I know it will take a while to get used to it, but he's just so angry."

"I'd be angry, too, if my CO tried to kill me."

"No, I mean about his leg."

I'd clearly missed a step. "What about his leg?"

She paled. "You mean you don't know? They amputated it right after we returned to the States."

CHAPTER 9

The House That Jack Built

The room became very bright. I leaned against the sofa arm. "What?" I said.

"His leg got infected after he was shot. They amputated it. It's from the knee down, and they're going to fit him with a prosthetic. I told him you won't even be able to tell from the stage. But he's in an awful lot of pain . . ." Candy's voice faded away. I thought I might be sick again. Jack—without his leg?

"I had no idea he was that bad off."

"Why would you?"

Why would I indeed? After all, Candy believed I didn't know Jack had been hurt. I didn't know he was on trial.

Oops. I'd just let my knowledge of that slip, hadn't I?

"Which one was it?" I asked.

"His left one."

I tried to picture it in my mind, but I can't say that I'd ever bothered to commit the uniqueness of Jack's limbs to memory. Instead, my own leg throbbed sympathetically.

"Could you visit him?" she asked.

I thought I'd misheard her. "Why?"

"He needs friends right now, and I'm afraid there aren't very many around. His parents . . ."

Mamie and Clint Castlegate. Admiral Clint Castlegate, U.S. Navy. I doubted he was taking the news well that his son had gone AWOL. As for Mamie, a blousy blonde who thought cocktail hour began when the rooster crowed, the lost limb would somehow become all about her. What would her friends say? How could he ever expect to make anything of himself with only one leg? If she thought he was wasting himself as an actor, what was his value now that he was disabled?

"I know," I told Candy. "I know how they are." The sick feeling wasn't going away. There'd been a playwright I'd known who had a wooden leg and a nasty disposition; he was prone to murdering people who got in the way of his art. I wondered if the absence of his leg made him that way, or if it was simply one of those personal peculiarities that occurred in spite of how many limbs he had. It certainly couldn't have helped. "Is he staying with them?"

"We both are. They insisted on it."

"I'll visit him. Of course I'll visit him."

Candy took my hands in hers. "Thank you," she said. "I can't tell you what this means to me."

I hit the liquor store right after Candy left. By the time Jayne returned from her audition, I was half in the bag.

"How'd it go?" I asked her from my perch on Ruby's bed. Ruby herself was up and out, leaving behind a perfume specter that made me sneeze.

"Are you drunk?" Jayne asked.

"I'm getting there. Care for a tippling?"

"Make it two."

I fixed her a martini while she kicked off her shoes and joined Churchill on the bed. "I'm guessing things didn't go well today," I said.

"Something weird's going on. Every audition I went to, I seemed to be doing fine, until I told them my name. The minute I said it, whatever interest they'd shown vanished."

I emptied my glass and debated making another drink. I was comfortably drunk—Mamie Castlegate drunk. Any more liquor and I'd be approaching the point of no return. "You might be right," I said. "Rumor has it we're being blackballed." I told her about my theory that Vinnie Garvaggio was behind our employment problems.

Jayne pouted at her glass. "I should've known this would come back to haunt us."

"There's good news, though—I found a way around the work ban. A simple way. Virtually painless." My voice was too bright.

"What's that?" She couldn't have sounded more suspicious if she'd asked the question under a bright light in a police interrogation room.

"All you have to do is call Tony."

"How's that going to help things?"

A horrible smell drifted my way. Churchill had broken wind. "I saw him today. He said he can make this whole thing go away if you call him."

She lay back on Ruby's pillows. "I won't be manipulated like that."

"I agree that it's a little unorthodox. But the guy's in love. Can't you just pick up the phone and give him a quick *hiya*?"

She dug an angry elbow into the pillow, narrowly missing the flatulent feline. "That's not how he works, Rosie. Now it's 'Have her call me and I'll make it go away.' But when I actually pick up the horn? It's going to turn into 'Have dinner with me and I'll fix everything.' Or 'Let's go away for the weekend, and then I'll see what I can do.' I won't be blackmailed like that."

I wanted to stomp my feet and demand that she think of me,

me, me, but the new Rosie wasn't like that. She was right—it wasn't fair that he was using her like this. When most guys did something wrong, they tried to make it up to you with good acts. Only a gangster would try to put the squeeze on you.

"Okay. I understand. We'll think of something else." I dribbled what remained of the booze into my glass and finished it in an all-too-brief gulp. "We could start using stage names."

"I can't do that! That's lying."

"No it's not—it's savvy. Half the actresses in this house use made-up monikers."

"But that means ignoring about everything we've done up until this point."

Was that such a bad idea? I'd been in some real dogs in the last year. Wiping my résumé clean could end up being a good career move.

Of course, Jayne had no such affliction. Almost everything she'd been in had turned into gold.

"Just think about it," I said. "In the meantime, maybe Tony will come around on his own."

"Maybe." She snapped her fingers. "I know what I forgot to tell you. Guess who was auditioning with me this afternoon?"

I wasn't in the mood for tales of the famous and infamous. "Cary Grant?"

"Ruby Priest."

I choked on the liquor. Ruby? Auditioning? That was like hearing that FDR had to take the citizen's test. "What was the show?"

Jayne rubbed her eyes. "I've been to so many of them today I'm not sure I remember. Anyway, she tried to hide when I saw her, but it was definitely her."

"Maybe whatever she's in is about to end."

"That's what I thought, and I told this girl standing next to me that Ruby was sure to walk away with one of the leads. And she told me that from what she's heard, Ruby hasn't worked in months."

I blew a raspberry at her. "Impossible."

Jayne held up her hand like she was making a pledge. "It's what she said. Honest. She said the last show Ruby was in was back in June."

I was bewildered. How could Ruby be going without work? She always had jobs. Always. "Did she say why?"

"There wasn't time to. She got called in to see the producers, and that's the last I saw of her."

"Your source has got to have her facts wrong."

"I don't think so," said Jayne. "Has Ruby told you what she's supposedly in right now?"

"Not exactly. But she's gone all the time. She's got to be in something."

"Either that or she doesn't want to run into Belle. And she was awfully nice about taking you in, right?"

It was all starting to come together. Of course that was what was going on. "Right."

"That means she's desperate for money."

I left my roost and approached Ruby's dressing table. A jewelry box sat in the center of it. Not a cigar box repurposed to store her baubles but a wooden box actually designed for the multitudes of gems I'd seen Ruby wear over the years. I lifted the lid and gasped at what I saw. There were a few pairs of earrings—mainly paste and pearls—and a bracelet or two, but otherwise the box looked nearly vacant.

Where were the things gifted to her over the years by her many admirers?

While Jayne took in the shoddy remnants of a box whose contents once rivaled Tiffany's showroom, I went to the wardrobe and opened its doors. Empty hangers played a xylophone tune. The clothes that remained were either too precious to part with or too utilitarian to foist on someone else. Gone were the suits I coveted, the dresses I begged to borrow, the evening gowns she didn't dare be caught in more than once ("Really, Rosie," she once told me, "there's nothing more gauche than repetition.")

I returned to the dressing table and opened the myriad little drawers designed for cosmetics and lingerie. The center-most one contained a stack of numbered tickets, bound together by a pink ribbon.

"Where did it all go?" I asked, even though I had the answer in front of me: Ruby had been lowered to pawning stuff to pay her bills.

Jayne returned to the bed as though she lacked the strength to continue confronting the horror of Ruby's poverty. "So I guess the girl was telling the truth."

I sighed at the ceiling. "I don't know if I want to live in a world where Ruby can't get work."

Jayne picked up Churchill and moved him into the curve of her body. He opened one of his eyes to confirm it was her and not me and went back to sleep. "It's just a dry spell—you know that."

Did I? Jayne and I went through dry spells, but I couldn't imagine Ruby going through one. She was too high-profile for that. "What if it's not?"

"Huh?"

I snapped my fingers. "What if someone told Vinnie that Ruby was our friend and involved in squealing on the slaughterhouse? He might've blackballed her, too."

Jayne combed Churchill's hindquarters, sending out a cloud of loose hair. "Why would he think that?"

"She was in the show. We were with her a lot. At least I was. He might've made an assumption that she helped us turn him in."

Jayne pondered this through her first sip of booze. "If that was the case, she wouldn't have been working in June."

"She could've gotten that gig while Vinnie was in the stir. Then, when it ended, he was out and in control of her fate." I was starting to feel sick. On the one hand, there was something thrilling about knowing we could affect Ruby's future like that. On the other, it was completely unfair that she was being punished when the only role she played was being unfortunately associated with us. Especially when there were plenty of other performers in that show who we'd actually been close to.

"She'll be fine," said Jayne. "Ruby always lands on her feet." She was right. Of course she was right. Ruby was probably already cooking up a scheme to get back on top. "So what'd you do today?"

Oh, nothing much. Just found out that we might be the reason a man in Yorkville is dead and that Tony most likely killed Billy's cousin. Also, Maureen O'Reilly is Billy's aunt. You? "Hit a few casting calls that I was totally inappropriate for. Pity I didn't run into Tony first. It could've saved me a lot of time."

Jayne took in my empty glass and evidence of my last hour of bartending. "Is that why you're getting ossified?"

A sour little laugh escaped me. The days when an encounter with Tony alone could drive me to drink were far behind us. "No, this isn't for Tony. Candy came by."

"Is she done with the letters?"

Had she changed her mind about Billy again? Good God, she was starting to have more faces than Lon Chaney. "I thought you didn't want to see those."

"I don't, but I hate to think she's putting in a lot of work on them."

I couldn't read if she was being honest or not. But then I remembered: I was the liar, not her. "Well, don't worry—I told her to forget about them. The reason she came by was because she wanted to talk about Jack."

"Did you come clean? Is this guilt-drinking?"

"No, this is all for Jack." I tipped my glass until the last precious bit of booze came out. "He lost his leg, Jayne."

She sat in silence as if she was one of the WAC code breakers trying to parse what I really meant to say. As the meaning of my words became apparent, her hand went to her kisser and lingered there. "Oh my God."

"It's funny, but I always thought he could get out of anything. When I found out he was alive, that only bolstered my belief that he was some kind of pulp hero. I assumed he'd come home, heal up, win the trial, and he and Candy would live happily ever after." No. It was me I thought he'd end up with, tossing Candy aside after he realized that we were meant to be together.

At least I used to feel that way.

"That could still happen," said Jayne.

Had she heard my thoughts? Or did I wear them like Maureen's brilliant red lip crème? "Maybe. Anyways, she wants me to visit him. I'm going tonight."

"Drunk?"

I deposited my glass on the side table and filled it with water. "I'll be sober by then. Will you go with me?"

"What kind of friend would I be if I didn't?"

Two hours later I was bathed, dressed in my finest diapers, and so full of coffee you could've used my vibrations to burrow another tunnel through Manhattan. Jayne and I took the subway uptown and hoofed it to Park Avenue. Before the flowers got as pricey as the real estate, I stopped off and bought some red, white, and blue carnations from a street vendor and the latest issue of *Tales of the Terrible*. Jack didn't just share my love of theater; he also shared my passion for the pulps.

As we arrived at the Castlegates' house, a messenger boy on roller skates whizzed past with a package from Macy's. He delivered the parcel two doors down, where a waiting servant had a tip ready for distribution. As the boy on wheels departed to go to his next destination, he narrowly missed colliding with a woman walking three very small dogs on unnecessarily long leashes. These weren't her pets. We were now in a world where people paid others to do their daily drudgery for them.

The war wasn't here; that was the strangest part. Maybe it was present in blackout blinds that hadn't yet been lowered, and meals that were no longer able to ignore the rationing the rest of us were going through, but money seemed to insulate the rich from the anxiety everyone else was suffering. Were they luckier, or were they just better at hiding their fears, having grown so practiced at concealing emotions they found messy and inappropriate? After all, even I had to admit money couldn't make you immune to tragedy. Jack had proven that.

Sometimes I forgot his blood was so blue you could use it to dye navy uniforms. Jack's mother's family had been included in Mrs. Astor's Four Hundred since its original inception and held one of the coveted boxes on the south side of the Met. I knew nothing about society myself, except that they used an exceedingly large amount of silverware when a single fork and knife would just as easily do the job. That's probably why Mamie and I never got on very well; I didn't see the value in the things she couldn't live without.

They weren't thrilled about Jack's chosen vocation. Actors were one step up from vagabonds in his parents' minds. Strangely enough, they weren't too happy with his decision to join the navy, either. It was one of the only things I'd ever agreed with them on. Despite Jack's father's long-heralded navy career, he'd refused to ride his father's coattails to an officer's appointment and instead enlisted, a decision the old man never forgave. Mamie, on the other hand, seemed to view the military with distaste. Maybe she was just aware of how likely it was that her own son might not come back whole.

We arrived at their address just after seven. If memory served, they would still be in their cocktail hour, but not so deep into it that Mamie would forget her manners. I rang the bell and gave Jayne some last-minute instructions.

"No gawking," I said.

She patted her hair and checked her reflection in the door's glass for lipstick on her teeth. "I don't gawk."

"You will when you get inside this house. These people are money, and while it's clear that we're not, we don't need to underscore that any more than necessary. Capeesh?"

She didn't have time to respond. The maid opened the door and looked at us in a way that made it very clear she assumed we were collecting for some charitable society that was beneath the Castlegates. I didn't recognize the girl, though that wasn't surprising. Mamie went through help as fast as she went through gin.

The maid didn't speak. Instead, she raised an eyebrow in a way that asked, Can I help you?

"Could you please let Jack Castlegate know that Rosalind Winter and Jayne Hamilton are here to see him," I said. My enunciation was vaguely British. If I stuck my nose any higher in the air, it was going to brush the doorjamb.

She ushered us into the foyer and, with a sparse gesture, told us to wait. We did as she instructed and watched in silence as she opened a set of pocket doors, glided through them, and closed them behind her.

"Is she a mute?" asked Jayne.

"If she's lucky. Mamie doesn't like the help to talk. She likes them to be seen, not heard."

"I thought that applied to children."

"Not in her case. She doesn't even want to see those."

Jayne gazed around the room. She lasted all of two seconds before gasping, "Will you get a load of this place!"

"I said no gawking."

She pulled her arms into her body lest she be tempted to touch something. "I'm not gawking. I'm appreciating." Even in the foyer, there was much to appreciate. A pair of eighteenth-century debtors' chairs ornately carved with scenes of prison punishment dominated the room. Between them rested a marble table, atop which sat a clock whose pendulum denoted the passing of each second with a click that sounded like money falling. Portraits of Jack's grandparents hung on the wall—oils done by John Singer Sargent, a man whose name I had to look up at the New York Public Library after my first visit to the house. Strangely, learning of the artist's significance did nothing to change my mind about the stiff, ghoulish paintings.

The pocket doors whispered open again; only this time it wasn't the mute maid who passed through them. It was Mamie.

"Rosie. I thought it must be you," she said. The musical tone of her voice was matched by the melodic tinkle of ice in her glass. What I wouldn't have given for a sip of it. "I was so disappointed that I didn't get a chance to talk to you the other day. Candace said she saw you on the street." The way she said it, you would've thought I'd been working the streets, not walking them. "And you've brought flowers," said Mamie. "How . . . quaint." She took them out of my hand and held them at a distance, as though she were afraid that the colors might leak all over her silk blouse. In that house, among all those pretty things, my lousy carnations didn't stand a chance.

"This is Jayne Hamilton," I said, because even if the carnations were dulled by their surroundings, my pal wasn't.

Jayne looked uncertain what to do. Her hand darted out; her knees bent in preparation for a curtsy. In the end, she aborted both movements and merely offered Mamie a tilt of her head. "It's nice to meet you."

Mamie didn't echo the pleasantry. After all, any friend of mine . . . "So I understand you want to see our Jack." Her use of *our* didn't escape me. Jack no longer belonged to me; he was Candy and Mamie's now.

"Candy thought it might be a good idea," I said. "She said he's been having a hard time of it and might enjoy a few visitors."

Mamie clicked her tongue and swirled the ice. "Isn't that sweet of her? I tell you, Jack couldn't have picked a better girl than Candace. So kind, so considerate." *So* not me. "You know they're going to be married."

I kept my expression consistent. I wouldn't give her the joy of watching me break down. "Yes indeed. I couldn't be happier for them."

"We were hoping, of course, for a girl from a good family, but I think Candace's military service speaks for itself." It struck me that while she insisted on calling Candy by her proper name, she'd never done the same to me before. Perhaps Mamie knew that I was too far gone for the use of my formal name to elevate me. "And after everything she did for him on that dreadful island . . . well, it will make the most charming wedding story, don't you think? The *Times* was just fascinated when I told them the tale."

I could see it now: the engagement picture of the two of them taken in the front parlor beside the story telling how nobody Candace Abbott rescued the injured son of one of the most important families in Manhattan. With Candy's luck, they would turn her tale into a movie.

"Have they set a date yet?" asked Jayne.

"We're still working on that. It will probably be a small wedding. Just family, you understand." Translation: we weren't invited. "Jack's up in his room. I'll have Vlasta show you the way."

At the sound of her name, the maid reappeared. "Take them to see Mr. Castlegate," said Mamie. "And do something with these." She passed her the flowers, as though they were a urine sample, and we followed them and the maid into the parlor and up the stairs.

I'd been in Jack's room many times before, but the last thing Mamie Castlegate wanted was to encourage my wandering freely through her house. I was the riffraff, after all, and she would hate to embarrass me by having to pat me down before my departure.

Who was I kidding—she'd kill for the opportunity.

"She seemed nice," said Jayne, as we walked down the upstairs hallway.

"If only you knew," I said.

There were ten rooms on the second floor, each one marked with an iron number lest you get confused about which was yours. Jack was housed in room number ten. I never understood why he ended up in the double digits. He was an only child.

Vlasta knocked twice on the door. Jack grumbled something that she took as an invitation. She turned the knob, pointed us toward the door, and disappeared down the hall in a swish of skirts.

So this was it. After months of worry, grief, jubilation, and shock, I was finally going to come face to face with the man behind it all. I had a similar thought right before I visited Jack in the South Pacific and again the evening he'd been captured. The first time my anticipation was killed by the news that he was dead. The second time my hopes had been dashed when I heard him whispering sweet nothings to Candy.

What would ruin this reunion? A meteor?

CHAPTER 10

Yellow Jack

I took a deep breath and pushed the door open the remaining distance. "You up for visitors?" I said.

Jack's eyes widened with surprise. He was seated on a small couch angled in front of the fireplace, though the fire itself was unlit. Candles flickered in wall sconces. An afghan sat on his lap, hiding the terrible absence I knew would be there. A book lay open next to him, though I was willing to bet that he'd set it aside long before our arrival. "Rosie?"

"And Jayne," I said. My pal made her way into the room while I skirted the wall. I tried to keep my eyes on his face, but they kept wanting to sink to the sofa. If I pretended, I could imagine his leg was merely bent beneath him, the way a child sat so that they were tall enough to reach the table. "Hey there," I said. "Aren't you a sight for sore eyes?"

"You should see the other guy." He smiled. I'm not sure how. "You look great."

"You're too kind." I didn't return the compliment. It would've been too obvious a lie.

Our eyes had remained locked since the moment I'd walked into the room. I was afraid if I didn't free myself from his gaze, I would be lost in those baby blues forever.

"Did you see Mother?" he asked.

"Oh yes. She was charming as always. I'm planning on stealing something, just to give her the satisfaction of being right about me."

He tilted his head and repeated a grin I now realized was as manufactured as the electric wall sconces shaped like candle flames. He turned his attention away from me and repeated the shallow smile. "Hello, Jayne. It was swell of you to come."

"I wouldn't have missed it for the world. We were so glad to hear you were safe," she said.

The lights in the room were dim. I longed to brighten the place up if only because it felt so solemn and funereal. The room was large and filled with carefully chosen pieces of furniture. In addition to the sofa, there were two wingback chairs. The other half of the room was given over to a monstrous bed with the sort of high, carved headboard that seemed designed to make the user feel like a child. There was also a man's chest with an assortment of bottles atop it and a wooden butler where clothes hung ready to be donned by the wearer.

"Why don't you sit?" said Jack. Jayne and I made our way to the wingback chairs. There seemed to be a faint odor of cauterized skin and antiseptic hovering around the room that made my stomach churn. It had to be my imagination, fueled by dozens of hospital visits in the South Pacific. As I sat stiffly, I couldn't figure out what to do with my legs. Whatever position I put them in—crossed, knees pressed together, legs akimbo—seemed like an attempt to draw attention to his infirmity. I know it's ridiculous, but it seemed like every movement I made cried out "Look at Rosie Winter with her two good legs."

"Wow," he said when I'd settled with my ankles primly crossed. "It's swell to see you two. Just swell." I noticed for the first time that he had a glass and decanter by his side. This wasn't the cheap crystal Billy DeMille's parents brought out for a toast, but something heavy and expensive meant to remind the user of the value of each drink he poured. The liquid was almost gone from the bottle. Jack had never been more than a social drinker, a response to his mother's tippling, I'm sure. The sight of him drinking alone affected me. It was one more thing about him that had changed.

I forced myself to set my eyes on anything else. On the end table to the left was a stack of papers. In the dim light it took me a moment to make out what I was seeing. As my eyes adjusted, I realized I was looking at naked women.

My eyes bounced back to Jack. He'd been watching me. As I clutched my metaphorical pearls, he threw his head back and laughed. God, I missed that sound.

"Guess I should've put those away," he said.

"I'm no prude, though I can't imagine Mamie would be happy seeing those lying around."

"She's not allowed in here. And they're not what you think they are."

I picked up the first pamphlet. A woman lay naked and sprawled on her back while a man in a military uniform got to know her better. "No, they're exactly what I think they are."

"It's propaganda," said Jack. "I collected them. Some of them anyway. Half of them came from guys I met who were stationed in Europe."

"I think you're getting your *p* words confused. This is what we here in America call pornography."

He laughed again. "Okay, maybe they're one and the same. When you spend day in and day out in the company of men, what do you think is the first thing you miss?"

I twisted my face like I was thinking hard on the question. "Beer?"

Finally, his smile felt real. We were back to our familiar repartee, lobbing witticisms back and forth like we were playing table tennis. "The Nazis and the Japs dropped these pamphlets from their planes to remind us that instead of being in some foxhole or on a ship, we could be home doing what we love best. And when that didn't work, they started to play really dirty by telling us that because we were here, all those gals back home were finding other ways to entertain themselves."

It was fascinating—one of those aspects of the war I hadn't heard about and certainly hadn't considered. I flipped through the pamphlets and read the broken English narrative describing, in detail, what the pictures were depicting. Some were hand-drawn cartoons. Others were photos. All were meant to destroy morale.

I tried not to linger on each one too long. It's not that looking at them bothered me, but they were doing a fine job pointing out what I was missing out on and *I* didn't have the war as an excuse.

"How're you doing?" asked Jayne.

"I've been better." His good leg stretched, unconsciously, beneath the blanket. I reached the last pamphlet in the stack. A picture of a cartoon blonde in a moment of ecstasy with a foreign soldier was narrated with the text "Gentlemen prefer blondes, but blondes don't like cripples."

I returned the stack to the side table. "You're alive, though," I said. "That's got to count for something."

He cocked his head. "Does it?"

I could see the rage Candy had been talking about bubbling beneath the surface. Jack had always been a man of extremes. Nobody expressed joy more palpably or anger more passionately than an actor who'd been trained to summon those emotions on a moment's notice.

"Of course it does," I said. "God, Jack, we thought you were lost for good."

"Maybe it would've been better if I was."

"How can you possibly say that?"

He shrugged. I wanted to say so much more, about how lost I'd felt when I was told he was dead, how I'd thought that to have any part of him back, no matter how damaged, would've been worth it. But to own up to any of that meant I had to acknowledge why I'd been in the South Pacific in the first place. And I couldn't tell him the truth, not if I hadn't bothered to share it with Candy.

He took a sip of his drink and then examined the liquid remaining in the glass.

"I know Candy is glad to have you home. We all are," I said.

He swirled the liquid around the bottom of the glass. "She said you were over there."

I could feel Jayne's eyes boring a hole in my head, but I refused to look her way. "Jayne and I both were. USO tour. Weird, huh?"

"Yeah." His fingers played a tune on the side table. "Did you get my letters?"

Letters Jack had one of his crewmates send me to let me know he was all right, without explicitly stating so. I'd only gotten one of them; the others were intercepted by the brass when they realized they were about Jack.

"Yeah. I did. One of them anyway. It was pretty clever to use the wrong rank. Was that your idea?" The letter was supposed to hold a clue that it was from Jack; only he assumed I knew a heck of a lot more about the military than I did, including which ranks went with which branch. Someone else had to explain to me that the officer Jack invented in his correspondence couldn't possibly have been in the navy. Perhaps if I'd figured it out sooner, I would've known Jack was in trouble and could've done something about it. At the very least, maybe it could've been me that rescued him instead of Candy.

Oh God, did I really just think that? I was beyond this. That ship had sailed.

Jack held the glass up to the light. "Yeah. I'm surprised you figured it out. I was a little worried it was too obscure, but with the censors reading, I didn't have much choice."

"You know me—I always figure things out eventually. Thanks for that, by the way. It couldn't have been easy getting word out when you were in hiding." Here's what I really wanted to say: *Was I correct to assume you wrote me because you still cared for me? Because that's how I read it. Which is why I went overseas, and why I was confused to discover in the interim you had fallen in love with someone else.*

Instead, I said, "It meant a lot that you wrote to me."

He cocked his head, an old habit that I was relieved hadn't been lost at war. He did it whenever he wanted a new angle on something. What was it about what I had just said that made him crave more information? "I figured it was safer writing to you than my parents. Nobody knew who you were."

So that was it: I was chosen because he'd never bothered to mention me to anyone in the navy. I wasn't a picture in his kit bag, a name on his tongue, an image held in his head as he went off to battle. I was just an ex-girlfriend disconnected enough from him that when he needed to send word home about his safety, he chose me because I was the last person anyone would ever suspect.

Jack scratched at his leg, the one that was only halfway there. "I was hoping you'd let my parents know I was okay."

I wanted to laugh. All these months, all these assumptions, and I was nothing more than a way to pass information on to his family, a family that despised me. How could I have been so naïve? Al was more closely tied to me.

"I tried to," I said. "They're not the easiest people to get hold of. I think your mother pretty much assumes that any contact with me is ill-advised."

"What's done is done."

I couldn't have felt more deflated if he'd opened up my valve and let all my air out. How different the last few months could've been if I hadn't convinced myself that the world revolved around me. Jayne's heart wouldn't be broken. And neither would mine.

Oh, and Mr. Smith might still be alive.

"You got any more of the hooch?" I asked. "I could use a tickle."

He cocked his head toward a cabinet by the fireplace. "There are bottles and glasses in there. Help yourself."

"Jayne?" I said as I got up.

"I'm fine," she said. Behind the cabinet doors was enough booze to supply a clip joint. None of it was to my taste—I prefer my drinks cheap and plentiful—but I dribbled a little bit of vodka into a glass to keep myself busy.

"So what happens now?" asked Jayne.

"Therapy," said Jack. "I get fitted for a leg next week."

"That's exciting," said Jayne.

My back was to them, but I was pretty sure I knew the expression on Jack's face. I downed the vodka and put another finger in the glass.

"What about the trial?" I asked as I returned to my seat. "When does that happen?"

"There's not going to be a trial, Rosie."

That was a relief. At least that ordeal was over and done with. "Oh. So they're dropping the charges against you?"

"Oh no, those are going to stick. I've been dishonorably discharged." He lifted his glass as though this were a thing to toast. "I can't believe Mother didn't tell you. It's her greatest shame. That and her son coming home with only one leg."

Had I heard him right, or was the vodka muddling his message? "What about your commanding officer?"

"He probably has a long career ahead of him if the Japs don't get him first."

"Oh, but I thought . . ." My voice faded as I tried to assemble all the information Peaches had told me. "Never mind. I must've gotten it wrong."

"What?"

"I thought your CO had shot you. Twice. And I was under the impression he'd killed a bunch of guys on a boat with you."

"Who told you that?"

If I told him, that meant I'd have to own up to knowing he was in the South Pacific. "It's just something I heard." Oh, Peaches—had you told me the truth about anything?

Jack smiled at his lap. "Well, at least the rumor mill is accurate."

"Wait—so your CO really was a murderer?"

"Did you think I went AWOL for nothing?"

"Of course not. I just assumed—"

"Look, it's easier this way. I'm lucky I'm not facing a tribunal and jail time. I could be put to death, you know. All he'd have to do is claim that I tried to kill him, and it could be the end of me."

For the second time that night I felt like my brain was scrambling information the minute I'd heard it. "So you're just going to let it go?"

"I don't have a choice here, Rosie. It's not like I was going to go back overseas anyhow. They took care of that for me." His stump wiggled beneath the blanket.

Who was he? What happened to the guy who used to lecture me on the value of art? I left my chair and approached the fireplace. "Of course you have a choice. Men died, Jack. And you could've been one of them. Who's to say this guy isn't going to do that again?"

"Then someone else will have to fight him."

"When did you become so selfish?"

"Rosie," said Jayne, her voice a warning.

"No, Jayne—I really want to know. When did you change?"

"When I lost my leg." The words cut through the air like a hot knife through butter. He scratched at his scalp. "Look, no one believes me."

"There have got to be other men who know." I've met them, I wanted to say.

"And not one of them is willing to face a court-martial of their own. There's a war on, Rosie."

"Don't you think I know that? I was there, Jack." Looking for you. Mourning you when I thought you were lost for good.

He slammed his glass on the end table. "Then you know this is the last thing anyone has time for. No one cares. Thousands of men are going to die in battle. Maybe millions of them. Eight men lost on a boat means nothing in the scheme of things, and my leg means even less. Who's to say we wouldn't all have been killed somewhere else? Maybe he did those men a kindness by putting them out of their misery before something worse happened."

Tears were twinkling in his eyes. I'd never seen him cry before, not in real life anyway. On stage he'd wept, but I'm not sure there'd been tears present to validate the emotion. It was the one bit of actor's trickery he'd never been very good at pulling off.

"You should go," he said.

"Jack—"

"What? I've got one leg, Rosie. One leg. If I didn't have a leg to stand on before, I certainly don't have one now."

It was the kind of exit line only an actor could come up with. And because I respected the effort it took, I obeyed his request and left the room.

Jayne joined me in the hallway a few minutes later. I was too angry to cry. Instead, I paced the rug, hoping to catch it on fire with the speed of my steps.

"He's calmed down," she said.

"Good for him. What did you say to him?"

"That you'd been worried about him. That this was grief talking." She nibbled on her thumbnail. "He has a right to be angry."

"I'm not denying that. It's his being a coward that I can't stomach. Let's go." I led her to the stairs, and we stomped down them side by side. In the sitting room, Mamie awaited us. She wasn't alone. Candy was with her.

"How is he?" asked Candy.

Jayne opened her mouth to respond, but I beat her to it. "Stub-

born. Self-pitying. And a whole lot of other words I'm not at liberty
to say."

"He's fine," said Jayne. She pulled Candy to the side, to continue their conversation away from me. After a few quiet murmur-
ings about Jack's health, Jayne changed the subject and raised her
voice so I could hear her. "I'm glad you're here. Rosie told you not
to worry about translating the letters, right?"

"Right."

Mamie passed Candy a drink and freshened up her own.

"I know it sounds strange," said Jayne, "but I think I'd rather
leave things be."

"Sure," said Candy. "No problem. I didn't even have a chance
to start them yet." She tossed a look my way. Instead of lending
her assistance, I barged back into the conversation they'd already
abandoned.

"Why isn't Jack going before a tribunal?"

Candy was taken aback at the question. "He wouldn't survive it,
Rosie. We're lucky the admiral was able to pull strings."

"His father did this?"

"He would have done more if Jack hadn't been so stubborn,"
said Mamie. "This whole thing could've been swept under the
rug, but Jack insisted on taking the dishonorable discharge." Her
fresh drink had already reached the halfway mark. For her sake, I
hoped there was a hole in her glass. "He's ruined now. But it's his
choice."

Why would he do that? It must've been a way for Jack to punish
himself for not taking a stand. If he wasn't going to go through
with the tribunal, he wasn't willing to have his father clean up his
mess for him, either. This was his way of compromising.

"They would've eaten Jack alive," said Candy. "There were no
witnesses to substantiate what he said was true."

I crossed my arms. "Did anyone try to find any?"

Mamie answered for her. "We can't interrupt the service of a
bunch of men for this. There's a war on."

If one more person said that, I was going to sock them. I turned to Candy. "So you agree with what he's doing?"

"I wish he'd listened to the admiral, but he's home safe. That's all that matters."

My jaw dropped open. Could she really believe that this was the best thing for all concerned? Had I fallen into an alternate reality?

Jayne looped her arm in mine. I think she knew that if I stayed there a moment longer, a slew of regrettable things were going to come out of my mouth. "We have to go," she said. "It was so nice to meet you, Mrs. Castlegate." Jayne steered me toward the pocket doors.

Candy followed behind us, telling Mamie that she would see us out. "Thanks for coming," she said as we reached the foyer. "I'm sure he was glad to see you."

"That's open to interpretation." I started out the door, but something stopped me. I whirled back around and held Candy's gaze.

"Do you believe him?" I asked her.

"What?"

"About his CO and the boat and everything else."

Her left hand wrapped around her neck, her ring glistening like the stone in a choker. "Of course."

"If that's true, you should try to find someone to back up his story."

"It's not what he wants." She ran her hand through her short dirty-blond curls. "He's been through enough. He wants to put this behind him. He's never going to be able to move forward unless he leaves the past in the past."

No, no one else was going to be able to move forward. Jack wasn't going anywhere either way.

CHAPTER 11

Without a Name

"I don't think she believes him," I told Jayne as we hoofed it home from the subway station.

"How can you say that?"

"Because if she did, she would tell him he shouldn't give up. You saw how she was in Tulagi. She fought to keep him safe. She stood up when she thought people were being wronged." We'd seen it firsthand when she took the WAC CO to task for tormenting one of our fellow USO performers, a girl who'd left the military some months before.

"Maybe she's changed. Or maybe she's right and this is what Jack wants."

"Jack doesn't know what he wants. He's so beat down with self-pity that he'd agree to anything just to get everyone to leave him alone."

"Exactly," said Jayne. "And you want to put a guy like that on trial?"

I stopped underneath the awning of a pawnshop. Behind the barred window, wedding rings twinkled beside guns and two-year-old radios. Was Ruby's jewelry in there, waiting for her to earn the cabbage to reclaim it? "There were witnesses. He'd have people to back him up."

"Who?"

"Peaches confirmed it. So did Gris." Gris was the navy cook who Tony B. paid to follow Jayne around while we were in the islands. He was also one of the people who confirmed that Jack had survived the night he'd supposedly gone into the ocean.

Jayne started walking again. "So your witnesses are a guy you know lied to you and an ex-con friend of Tony's? Not exactly the kind of people I'd want vouching for me when my life was on the line."

She had a point.

We stopped at a crosswalk. The wind whipped Jayne's bright blond hair around until it looked like marzipan dribbled on top of her head. "Do you think it's right that I don't want to know about Billy?" she asked.

"Yeah. Absolutely."

"You want to know why I decided that?" I nodded, though I had my suspicions. "I realized that whatever he was doing before I met him has nothing to do with me. He was a different person then."

Literally, I thought. "I think that's smart," I said. "Sometimes it's best to leave the past in the past."

Jayne looked at me as Jack had looked at me earlier, like she was trying to get a new take on a familiar object. "Don't you realize that's what Candy just said? If you think that's the best thing for me, how come you don't see that it might be the best thing for Jack, too?"

I didn't have an answer.

We arrived at the station and found a crowd gathered around the stairs. They were looking downward, but nobody was making a move to travel to the trains.

"What's the holdup?" I asked a man standing near me.

"The line's shut down. There's a body on the tracks."

"It ain't a body," said a guy to the left of him. "It's a dummy dressed up to look like a body."

"Not just like a body," said a woman with a high voice and an even higher hat. "Like a sailor."

What the hell was going on?

"Let's get a cab," said Jayne. Unfortunately, everyone else had the same idea. There wasn't a hack in a hundred miles that hadn't already been hired.

With a heavy sigh, we accepted our fate and began the long walk home.

By the time we made it to the Shaw House, the building was blanketed in black and our dogs were barking so loud we should've been cited for disturbing the peace. Before we reached the stoop, a noise like a fast leak distracted us from our blossoming blisters. Oh God—was it whoever followed me from Yorkville? I wanted to run, but Jayne was already approaching the sound at its source: a shadow near a cluster of garbage cans.

"Al!" she said. She flung herself at him, and he twirled her around the way Billy used to each time they were reunited in the South Pacific. The similarity wasn't lost on her. As she returned to earth, I could see in her face a carefully masked disappointment that the man she'd just embraced wasn't the one she hoped it might be.

Al coughed into his hand in a way that made it clear he'd been hoping to get through this conversation without doing so. It was a horrible, hacking cough, the kind that always signaled a character's upcoming death in a bad melodrama.

"You're hot." Jayne stood on her tippy toes and touched a hand to his cheek. "Are you sick?"

"Naw. It's a warm night."

Except it wasn't. As we walked the four million blocks home, the wind had brought with it a taste of what was to come. It was a night made for closed windows and heirloom quilts. And here was Al still living on the streets.

"Could I talk to you for a second, Jayne?" I said.

"Um, sure." She showed Al her index finger. "Be right back."

I pulled her off to the side. "He looks like hell."

"He's sick, poor fella."

"And homeless. The guy's living on the street, Jayne. He's only going to get sicker."

"He should call Tony," she said.

That old chestnut. "He can't. I talked to Tony. Things aren't so good between the two of them."

"Why?"

I didn't have the energy to lie. "He thinks Al's trying to take him out."

"He thinks Al wants to date him?"

I widened my eyes to encourage her to think logically.

"Oh," she said, as the true meaning of the phrase became apparent. "But Al wouldn't do that."

"Tony disagrees. He wants nothing to do with him." From the other side of the steps, Al lit a cigarette. "Look, we can't just let Al stay on the streets like this. There's got to be something we can do for him." I was hoping that seeing Al would change her stance on Billy's money, and it looked like that was exactly what Jayne was doing. As her gaze shifted from me to him, she rocked from one foot to the other as if she was weighing her options.

"He could stay here," she said.

It was hardly the answer I was looking for. "Be serious."

She leaned toward me and lowered her voice. "I am. We could hide him until he feels better, and maybe by then Tony will have figured out that Al wouldn't hurt him."

I was exhausted from the long walk and not in the mood to fight. Maybe that's why her suggestion didn't seem like such a bad idea. The Shaw House was the one place Al would be guaranteed safe. No men could transgress its locked doors. "Ann will never agree to that."

"I bet she would."

But I didn't want her to. No one else should save Al. He was my responsibility. "No. I'll put him in my room."

"What about Ruby?"

I looked toward the building, trying to picture what Ruby was up to that night. "Let me worry about her."

We returned to Al and presented our plan with the kind of forced smiles that could only indict the idea as a bad one.

"I can't stay in a henhouse," he said.

"It's not permanent. And it's the perfect hiding place," I said. "Besides, I can use the company. Ruby's not the easiest person to room with."

He fought another cough. The wind picked up, and I swear I could feel the heat radiating off his feverish body. "Okay, but only until I'm better. Capeesh?"

"Capeesh," we said.

We told him to return at midnight, when it was safe to assume that Belle and her lackeys would be down for the night and we could sneak him upstairs. To make sure he stayed inside and didn't exacerbate whatever it was he was suffering from, we gave him what little cash we had and told him to grab some chow.

Back at the Shaw House, I went to my room to await Ruby's return. Churchill and I spent a companionable hour as I soaked my feet and went through the p.m. papers. I'd snagged them out of the lobby, worried that if Jayne decided to keep abreast of current events, she might learn about the murder in Yorkville. I needn't have worried. Mr. Smith's murder barely rated a mention. Ernest Smith had been given two column inches at the back of the paper, where the writer described his death as a heart attack brought on by a robbery in progress. The article was placed in almost the exact same position as Johnny Levane's had been. This was where the undesirables went—shoved into the newspaper equivalent of neighborhood ghettos where their comings and goings weren't likely to be noticed by the people who really mattered.

Had Mr. Smith's murderer returned to the East Eighty-sixth Street apartment building yet? He couldn't have known that I would go back there. But then if Candy was right, he hadn't known we would visit the first time, either. He depended on Mr. Smith to keep him apprised of anyone coming by and asking about Billy.

Or did he? If Mr. Smith was the rat, I couldn't see him going out of his way to protect Jayne and me, unless his ignorance angered his killer so much that he lashed out at him. More likely, there was someone else on the culprit's payroll who told him of our visit. Someone who'd been close enough to overhear who we were looking for. Someone like Inge or the old man we'd encountered in the lobby.

But why did our mystery man care if anyone came around asking about Billy? Maybe because he didn't know where Billy was.

What was in the basement may not have interested him as much as the person who'd left those things behind. If Billy and Johnny were resorting to secret writing, it may have been because they didn't want to run the risk of the wrong person finding out where they were. By the time my shadow sussed out where Billy was living, Billy was long gone. And so the murderer paid off someone at the apartment to tell him if anyone came around asking about Billy or trying to get his belongings, hoping that they might lead him to Billy's current whereabouts.

Maybe it was Johnny who had inadvertently led him to Billy's apartment the first time. The "he" Johnny mentioned in his last letter may not have been some all-powerful deity but the person they'd been hiding from. That could've been why Maureen had asked me if "he" had gotten to Billy and why she was relieved when she found out that Billy had died a hero.

But what about Johnny? The mystery man wasn't the one behind his death—Tony was. And he wasn't killed in Newark; he died in a Broadway alley.

It was making my head hurt. Jayne was right—it was best that we left the past in the past. If only I could guarantee that the past wasn't lingering outside the Shaw House because I was stupid enough to give Inge my real name.

I switched my focus from one unpleasant topic to another. How could Candy let Jack ruin his life like that? To say nothing of abandoning the men whose murders he'd witnessed. Part of me wanted to go back to Tulagi to drum up some support for Jack. I'd known two men who'd confirmed his story. No, wait—make that three. There was an injured sailor who went by the name of Whitey. He was the one who'd first told me that Jack might be alive. And while much of the conversation was lost in the concussion I gave myself after passing out, there was one thing I was certain he had said: if it ever came to trial, he'd be happy to speak up for Jack.

Whitey. Whitey what? I didn't think he'd told me. The first time we'd met was at a hospital in Guadalcanal, when he was so sore over the Dear John he'd just gotten from his girl back home that he gave me the cold shoulder. He'd just given me his nickname then. I was sure of it. And that must've been all he'd provided to jog my memory the second time we'd met up.

Gris would know, though. Whitey knew Gris. He was the one who told me Gris had helped Jack.

Once again I was felled by the moniker. Gris was only ever called Gris. The boys had reduced themselves to nicknames that were a shorthand way of reminding people of where they were from, what they did, and what their personalities were like. If Jayne's and my names were keeping us from work, Gris's and Whitey's were doing a grand job of keeping me from finding them.

Of course, there was one person I knew who knew Gris. In fact, he knew him so well, he was able to get Gris to work for him from ten thousand miles away: Tony.

CHAPTER 12

A Bundle of Lies

Ruby came home at eleven. By then I'd worked myself into such a lather over Jack that I'd almost forgotten about Al. Almost.

"Hiya," I said as she came in.

She gave me a perfunctory smile and went straight to her dressing table. "You look like hell."

"You've looked better yourself." I wasn't just poking the bear. She looked wan and tired, just as she had the day before. If Jayne was right, she'd spent her day pounding the pavement, looking for work.

"The subways are shut down. I just walked twenty-two blocks in heels." She kicked off the shoes in question and grimaced as her arches came back to earth. "What happened to you?" she asked me.

Where to begin? There was an overabundance of awfulness to share with her, but as much as I appreciated her asking about me for once, I didn't trust that anything I said in that room would stay there. And the last thing I needed was her telling Jayne about Mr.

Smith, Maureen O'Reilly, and the chance that there was a killer on my tail.

"I found out Jack lost his leg."

The little bit of sardonic wit that Ruby still had left drained away. "I'm sorry. When does he come home?"

"He is home. I ran into his fiancée and she told me what had happened."

"He's engaged?"

"Yeah. Remember the dame who came by here looking for Jayne and me the other night? That's Candy, the bride to be."

"Wow. I didn't know." She sat on the bed so heavily that the springs squealed. "I should've asked you about him, shouldn't I have? He's why you went to the South Pacific."

Another surprise from Ruby Priest. Three months ago I would've bet money that she didn't know where I was much less why I'd gone there, and here she was admonishing herself for not asking me about it sooner.

"She's a nice girl, Candy. Really, they're much better suited for each other." My voice broke. Why had it done that? "But the leg—it's a hard thing to face. I went to see him tonight, and he's so angry about the whole thing. I just wish things had turned out different for him."

She patted my hand primly, like a teacher not wanting to be accused of favoritism. "I'm sure things will get easier."

"Sure, time heals all wounds and all that jazz." But could you call losing a limb a wound? It seemed a bit like calling death a disease.

"He'll start acting again," said Ruby. "That will help."

"I'm not sure that he's comfortable with that idea. He seems to think that without his leg, no one will want him."

She left my side and went to her dressing table. There she unscrewed a jar of cold cream and began slathering it on her face. "There's always radio. He has a fantastic voice. I bet he could make an excellent living doing one of the serials."

"That's true." Her discussion of acting work made a lovely segue into our next uncomfortable topic. "How come you didn't tell me you were out of work?" She didn't respond. Instead, she continued smearing on cream. "Jayne saw you at an audition today."

She sighed heavily, aware that the jig was up. "I figured it wasn't any of your business." I had expected her to lie. Her honesty was reassuring. And devastating. "So do you want to gloat? Rub my face in it?"

"I don't have the energy for that. I made a booze run earlier today. Want a tickle?"

She nodded and I poured her a martini. She took it gratefully, as if she thought it possessed powers mere alcohol couldn't possibly embody. I knew that optimism.

"So how long has it been?" I asked.

She left a smear of white cream on the mouth of the glass. "Three months."

"It's okay, Ruby. We all go through dry spells."

"Maybe you do, but I don't."

Ouch. She'd been nice to me about Jack, I reminded myself. "There's no shame in being unemployed."

She faced the mirror and began wiping the cream from her face. "Of course there's shame in it." Tears bisected the cream faster than she could remove it.

"Does Belle know?" There were rules at the Shaw House. You had to work regularly, and no employment for three months was definitely problematic.

The scent of the face cream awakened something in Churchill. He approached Ruby with his nose lowered in deference. "I did a radio spot six weeks ago. That seemed to placate her."

"Then you are working."

She rolled her eyes at her reflection. "That's not real work."

"You made it sound like it was Jack's last great hope."

She tossed a cream-soaked tissue at the trash can and missed. "That's different—he only has one leg."

I smiled despite myself. There was our girl: only Ruby Priest would think that was an appropriate thing to say.

Ruby finished cleaning her face and took a swallow of her drink. Churchill batted at the moist tissue at her feet. "I suddenly know what it's like to be you, and I hate it."

Strangely, I wasn't insulted. I knew she wasn't out to hurt me. "The work ebbs and flows. You'll be back on top. You'll see."

She shook her head so hard her booze dribbled out of her glass onto the cat. He jumped as the liquid made contact with him, abandoned the tissue, and leaped onto the bed lest this be the beginning of a deluge about to come his way. "It's over for me," she said between tears. "I'm past my prime and everyone knows it. Every audition I've been to has been the same. The minute they know my name, they tell me thank you and send me on my way."

Well, that confirmed something at least: she was definitely facing the same ban Jayne and I were.

"I should just give up acting altogether."

I felt like she'd punched me. I'd said those words before and thought them plenty of other times, but Ruby? She was born to perform. And I don't just mean because of how she drifted through life, always expecting to be the center of attention.

"What about Lawrence?" I asked.

"I'm sure he's loving that my days are numbered. He always said my looks would outlast my talent. Maybe he was right."

I wanted to comfort her, but the task seemed impossible. I never knew Ruby to be so low; in fact, I never knew her to be anything other than smug and self-satisfied. How did you placate a person like that? Where did I put my hands? On her shoulder? On her back? Did I reassure her that she was talented? Did I insult Lawrence just for the sport?

She looked up at me as though she knew I was struggling with what to do. "Do you like me?"

It was such an odd question. She might as well have asked me if I enjoyed a good bowel movement in the morning. "I don't dislike you," I said.

"I think the others dislike me."

"No," I said with more conviction than I felt.

"It's true," she sniffled. "Shocking I know, but people find me arrogant."

"What about Zelda?"

"She didn't even want to live with me." She looked upward, like she was pleading with the heavens. "I've done this to myself. I let success go to my head, and I alienated everyone in the process."

I knew I should tell her the truth about what was going on, but it seemed pointless to do so when I didn't have a solution to our problem yet. And, honestly, I sort of enjoyed seeing this side of Ruby. I was worried that the minute she found out the work ban wasn't her fault, her self-awareness would evaporate. "How are you doing on cash?" I asked.

"I can make it another week. Maybe two."

"Even with me helping out with the rent?"

She nodded.

Oh boy. I needed to fix this little problem, fast. "Do you remember our pal Al?"

"Of course."

"He's in a bit of a pinch. He ticked off the wrong person and managed to become persona non grata. Plus, he's sick—not dying or anything, but I don't think he can take many more nights on the street. I was hoping he could stay here for a few days. He can pay—a hundred clams. Not out of the gate, but I know he's good for it. I don't need a cut—it's all for you."

Ruby finished her drink and placed it on the vanity. "Belle would never allow it."

"I know. It would be on the QT, just like the cat. He'd sleep on the floor, and I'd make sure no one was the wiser."

"Here? In our room?" Her tone made it clear that the idea was as attractive as a hairlip.

"He doesn't have any other options, Ruby. He's a good guy. Trust me on that."

Her gaze narrowed. For whatever reason, she'd decided it was time to be skeptical. "Wasn't he the same guy accused of murder earlier this year?"

"That wasn't what it seemed like. It was pinned on him to keep him out of harm's way. Jail was a safer option than being on the streets."

"Then why doesn't he go back there?"

"To prison? Because he can't, all right?"

"Why doesn't he stay with a friend?"

"He doesn't have any right now. There are men looking for him. They're staking out all of his regular haunts, and he doesn't want to put anyone at risk."

"But apparently you have no such concerns."

Jayne was right. Ruby was never going to agree to this. And why should she? What I was proposing was ludicrous. "Look, I know you don't owe me any favors. And you've certainly done a lot by letting me live with you, but I'm begging you, for Al's sake as well as our own, please let the guy stay here for a few days."

But there was something in the air these days. We were all so desperate that we were agreeing to things that would normally be out of character.

Ruby gestured for me to top off her drink. "All right. A hundred dollars and he pays the rent for the whole month."

CHAPTER 13

Three's a Crowd

I told Ruby to wait upstairs while Jayne and I did the hard work. My pal was waiting for me in the lobby. There was no one else about that I could see, but that didn't mean we could afford to linger.

"We're good to go," I told Jayne.

"Ruby agreed to it?"

"Don't think too hard about it," I said. "Trust me—it'll only make your head hurt."

Al wasn't outside when we opened the door. We whistled into the night, hoping he'd catch our signal, but only the wind replied.

"What if someone found him?" asked Jayne.

It was exactly what I'd been worrying about, though I didn't feel up to giving words to my fear. We stood in silence, the wind howling around us, the smell of fall puncturing the air the way cinnamon foretold the coming of Christmas. He could've changed his mind. Perhaps with a belly full of food and an hour or two in a restaurant, he'd convinced himself that he didn't need our help. Maybe he'd wised up and decided to head out of town.

I was about to share this theory with Jayne when he emerged from the darkness, as quiet as a cat. He limped when he walked. This was new. In fact, for a brief moment I thought it was Jack headed our way, his anger over his injury propelling him forward.

"Where have you been?" asked Jayne.

"Shhhh," he said, the word cut off as he put a finger to his lips. "I'm being followed."

Quickly, we helped him up the steps and into the building. We'd been careful to switch all the parlor lights off, and as we led him through the room and up the stairs, we put a bedspread over his head and shoulders like a cape, in case someone should be watching from the windows.

In retrospect, it was a wise choice on our part.

Just as we reached the first landing, the kitchen door swung open and Belle's voice rang out. "Did you lock the door behind you?"

"Of course," I said, though I was pretty sure my fingers and the lock were virtual strangers. Belle must've suspected the same because she clicked on a lamp and marched to the front door. We took another step.

"Hold it!" she said. The door opened without any effort. "What have I told you girls about safety?"

"That it's important?" I said. I'd tried to start using the new lock, honest, but it was too complicated and my time was too valuable.

"My sister was right. You aren't going to learn until someone gets hurt or something they cherish is stolen. These are dark times."

"And that's a hard lock. I broke a nail the last time I tried to turn it."

"Would you rather be robbed?"

I rolled my eyes. "Fine. We'll be more careful," I said. "Good night." Another step in tandem. Al stumbled as we moved upward. As he regained his footing, a cough escaped him. Try as he might to sound dainty, the sound could've been used to help ships locate the harbor on a foggy night.

"Who is that?" asked Belle.

I looked across Al at Jayne. She took the hint and piped up. "Ruby."

"What on earth is wrong with her?"

"She's . . . uh . . . well . . ."

"Blotto," I said.

"Ruby?" Belle gasped. That was right. Belle thought Ruby was all sunshine and rainbows and that the most immoral thing she ever did was lie about her weight at casting calls (increasing it by two pounds, since why would she need to go in the other direction).

Al let out his best attempt at a feminine moan and slumped forward.

"I don't want to kick the girl when she's down," I said, "But now that we're bunking together, it's become apparent she has problems with the devil's brew. Jayne and I just found her sitting on the curb, a minute from passing out. Who knows what might've happened if we hadn't come along."

"Get her upstairs before the other girls see her. Hurry." Belle pulled her robe closed, as though it wasn't just Ruby's virtue at risk but her own. "And I'll be talking to her about this tomorrow, you can guarantee it."

We got Al safely ensconced in Ruby's room before he was overtaken by another coughing fit. Ruby was on the floor when we entered, rotating her raised legs in a bicycle motion.

"Al, Ruby. Ruby, Al," I said. She stopped her exercise and returned upright. As she stiffly offered him her hand, he became overwhelmed with another coughing fit.

"I can see I made the right decision." She located a handkerchief and wiped her hand clean.

"And how," I said. "If he was out on the streets another night, he'd probably end up with pneumonia."

"And now, we get the pleasure of all of us catching it."

Al hunched over, hell bent on keeping his lungs in his chest.

Ruby retrieved another handkerchief from her vanity drawer and passed it his way. "When can we expect the cash?" she asked.

Al shot me a look. I tried to send a silent message from my brain to his, but apparently that only worked in the pulps.

"What the hell are you talking about?" he asked her.

I burst out laughing. "Oh, Al, you're too much." I put my hand on his arm and squeezed as hard as humanly possible. His flesh didn't yield. "I told her you offered us a hundred dollars."

His tired, runny eyes met my widened ones. Slowly, understanding dawned on him. "A hundred dollars?"

"Yep," I said. "And rent for the whole month."

Now it was Jayne's turn to give me the death glare. *Later,* I mouthed to her.

I was going to have to start writing down my lies. It was the only way I was going to keep anything straight.

"So when can I expect the money?" asked Ruby.

I pinched Al hard on the flesh between his thumb and forefinger. "Soon," he said. "Definitely before I leave."

"Well, good night," Jayne said. "Sleep well, Al."

We bid her good night and watched her leave the room. Al took in the overly girly surroundings and seemed to grow larger and more bulky before my eyes. This was not a space a man could find comfort in. As awkward as Al was, Ruby seemed doubly so. You'd think she'd never seen a man from the way she watched him from across the room. Or maybe she hadn't studied a mobster up-close before and was afraid of what might befall her if she took her eyes off him.

"I was thinking you'd sleep on the floor," I told Al.

"But that's where you sleep," said Ruby.

"I know," I said. "But it's not like there's a lot of other options, right?"

Ruby pulled the top of her blouse closed. She wasn't showing much skin before, and now we'd be lucky to catch a glimpse of her neck. "You can sleep with me," she said.

"Thanks," said Al. "But your bed's pretty small."

"I was speaking to Rosie," said Ruby.

I couldn't have been more shocked if she'd just offered to rub my feet. "Seriously?"

"We don't have much of a choice. We have to do what's appropriate."

My back sang at the prospect of sleeping on a mattress. I wanted to weep with joy.

"That Jim's cat?" asked Al. Churchill lay on the bed, unaware that he would soon be evicted so that I could take his place.

"The one and only. We took him in after Jim died," I said. Jim was a private dick I used to work for. He'd been an associate of Al's as well.

"And then I took him in when Rosie and Jayne went overseas," said Ruby.

Al approached Churchill and scratched him behind the ears. The cat pushed against his touch and purred so loudly that the whole room seemed to vibrate with it. "I forgot about that cat. I always liked him."

"Me too," said Ruby. "Rosie claims he's beastly, but he's always been a doll to me."

"He sprayed your bed the other day," I said.

"Because *you* provoked him."

"Right, I provoked him." I gathered my night things and went into the bathroom to change. When I was done, I made sure the coast was clear and snuck Al in so he could do his business. I began to nod off in the hallway to the sound of running water. When Al finally emerged, he was wrapped in one of my bathrobes, an absurd sight that made it clear that while we matched each other height for height, our other measurements were not in sync.

As we headed back to the room, the limp I'd noticed earlier reemerged.

"What's with the bum pin?" I whispered.

"Like I said, I was followed."

"Sounds more like chased."

"I picked a bad place for dinner."

"What'd you do, dine and dash?"

"Nothing like that. I paid for the eats. But on my way out, I saw one of Garvaggio's men. He made me and I took off. I didn't want to come straight here, just in case, so I went a roundabout way. Someone had a cellar open for their beer delivery and—."

"You tumbled right in."

He grinned. "So how come Ruby thinks I'm giving her a hundred smackers?"

"She's broke and I was desperate. Once I square things up with Garvaggio, she'll be fine."

"Why does she care about Garvaggio?"

"Because apparently he's keeping her from working, too, only she doesn't know it, so don't a breathe a word about it to her. Got it?"

Al was too tired to question the logic of Garvaggio banning Ruby. We left the hallway and entered the room. Ruby was already asleep. She'd left a lamp on with a scarf thrown over the shade to dim it. She'd also prepared Al a pallet of blankets on the floor, including the quilt Churchill had recently sprayed. Al eased into the nest as Churchill leaped off the bed and came to join him.

"You were right. This was a good idea. I can't thank you enough, Rosie," Al whispered.

"You do for me, I do for you. That's the way the world works."

"Still, I'll never forget this."

"Don't worry: I'm sure I'll find occasion to call in an enormous favor one day." I clicked off the lamp, climbed into bed, and rolled onto my side so that my back was to Ruby. For a brief moment, I closed my eyes and imagined that I wasn't in New York but back in Tulagi. Instead of Ruby's room, I had a cave; instead of a grateful Al, it was Jack who was thanking me for saving his life.

Stop it, I told myself. That was the past. This is now. "I saw your former boss today," I said.

"Tony? What'd he want?"

"What does he always want—Jayne."

"And I'm guessing she doesn't want to see him."

"Right you are." I wasn't sure how to broach the next topic, but it had been niggling at me since I'd seen Tony. "He had a message for you. He wants you to back off."

"What am I backing off of?"

I followed the hem of the sheet with my finger. "That's the part that isn't so clear. From the way he was talking, he seems to think you're trying to take him down."

Al laughed and that laugh turned into a cough. "You're kidding me."

"He meant it. Every word."

"You told him he's off the shelf, right?"

"Is he?"

"I wouldn't do that, Rosie. You know that."

I figured that was the case, but I wanted to hear Al say it. Tony was scared for a reason. He'd crossed a lot of people over the past year, and those were just the ones I knew about. If Al wasn't the one threatening him, there were plenty of other heavies who might be hoping to take him out.

Maybe even someone who had known Johnny Levane.

"You ever been to Newark, Al?"

"Sure. Hasn't everyone?"

"Believe it or not, I've avoided it so far. Has Tony been there?"

His voice was muffled. He must've changed positions. "He's from there."

"Really?" I didn't really know much about Tony beyond the bits and pieces Jayne had shared over the years. Truth be told, so much of what she said was colored by her mood toward him at that given moment that I often chose to ignore her.

Al was momentarily lost in a yawn. "Sure, he's Newark born

and raised. Tony was a fighter when he was younger. His pop ran a gym. Why?"

"Johnny Levane was living in Newark before Tony gunned him down."

He made a humming sound as if to say, *Really? How fascinating.*

"I was just wondering how Tony would've known him if he lived all the way out there."

Al didn't respond. He wasn't being rude; he'd fallen fast asleep.

I didn't go to sleep myself. I tried, but not only was Ruby a snorer, she was also a tosser and turner. Every time her body came in contact with me, I jolted awake in a panic. After the fifth time, I got out of bed and went to Jayne's room to see if she was still up. I hit pay dirt. Ann wasn't home yet, and Jayne was lying in bed flipping through an old issue of *Life* with two Lindy dancers on the cover. The couple's faces were exuberant, their limbs so overextended you half-expected to turn the page and find out they weren't human.

"Is Al asleep?" she asked.

"I think he was unconscious before his head hit the pillow."

"Poor guy. We should get him some medicine. And maybe a doctor. That cough's not going away on its own." She sighed heavily.

"What's the matter?"

"I miss dancing."

"It's temporary, Jayne. They can't blackball us forever."

"Why not? It's not like there aren't plenty of other performers to take our spots." She licked a finger and flipped a page.

I fought the urge to tell her to call Tony. After all, he could make this right, couldn't he? "Where's Ann?"

"I'm not sure. I'm guessing she got delayed by the subway stoppage. She had rehearsal tonight." She turned the page again; only this time the paper tore with her effort.

"It hasn't even been a week yet, Jayne. The work will come."

"I need something, you know? The more I sit around, the more I think about Billy."

"I know."

She was getting teary-eyed. How long had it been since she'd last cried? Twenty-four hours? Forty-eight? Or was that the last time *I'd* seen her cry? Who knew what was going on behind closed doors.

I needed to change the subject before both of us were emotional wrecks. My eyes landed on the radio.

"Is Ann still listening to station 627?"

"How do you know about that?"

"I walked in on her doing it. So I take it that's a yes."

"She said it helps her concentrate."

"On what?"

Jayne shrugged. "Memorizing lines, I guess."

I left my spot on the bed that used to be mine and went to the bureau. I opened the drawers that once held my things and stared at Ann's belongings. Underwear. Girdle. Bras. Nylons. Sweaters.

"Rosie," said Jayne.

"What?"

"That's not right, going through her things."

"Why not? We went through Ruby's things, and you didn't seem to have a problem with it."

"That's different. That's . . . Ruby."

On top of the dresser were three cigar boxes stacked one on top of the other. I opened the first and found it filled with earrings. The second held bracelets and rings. The third contained only necklaces. These weren't the paste and pearl pieces that filled out Ruby's reduced wardrobe—these rocks were real.

I turned an open box Jayne's way and mimicked its condition with my mouth. "Did you see this loot?"

"Sure. She said they're family heirlooms," said Jayne.

"Yeah, but whose family? The queen's?" I picked up a bracelet and felt the heft of real precious metals in my hand. "There's something strange about her."

"Like what?"

"I came in here a few days ago. I said her name a couple of times, but she didn't respond."

"Maybe she didn't hear you."

"No, she did. That was what was weird. But it was like she didn't know I was talking to her. What if Ann's not her real name?"

"So what if it's not? You suggested we change ours not so long ago."

That was true. I knew more actresses with fake names than ones who held on to their real monikers. But there was something else that didn't sit right. I returned the boxes to the dresser and went to the nightstand. Inside it were a Bible, a box of stationery, and a stack of subway maps.

And here she was: late coming home on the night someone sabotaged the subways. "Isn't that peculiar?"

"Now what?" said Jayne.

I waved a map at her. She rolled her eyes and showed me her back. "Gee, imagine that—someone in New York with a subway map. You better call the feds and report her."

From the nightstand I went to the closet. Ann had at least two dozen dresses hanging from the side that used to be mine, all beautifully tailored and constructed. On the floor were ten pairs of shoes. They showed a little more wear than the clothes, though they'd clearly been polished to take out the scuffs. On the top shelf rested two hatboxes and several tightly rolled up pieces of paper, bound with string.

"What's this?" I asked as I pulled one out.

"Beats me." Despite her attempts to condemn me, I could tell that Jayne was just as curious as I was.

"You mean to tell me you've lived with the girl for a week and haven't bothered to go through any of her things?"

"I trust her."

I pulled down one of the rolls of paper. It felt like a map or a poster. It was easily three feet long and rolled tightly enough to suggest that it spanned at least as wide.

"Maybe she's an artist?" said Jayne.

"Yeah, a con artist." I scanned the rest of the closet to make sure there weren't any secrets tucked into a shoebox or stashed in the pocket of one of her dresses. Aside from a book of matches and some lint, she was clean. I took one of the rolls back into the room and placed it on her bed while I searched underneath it. She hadn't been quite so thorough in her cleaning as she claimed. Tufts of cat hair danced in the wind provided by my breath. Other than that, the space under the bed was bare.

Jayne removed the string from the tube of paper and carefully unrolled my find. I was expecting stolen artwork, but what she revealed was much more monochromatic than that. The page spanned three feet by four. Pencil squiggles covered the whole of it. At first, it was Greek to me until I realized I was looking at it upside down. We turned it, and it became completely incoherent.

"What is it?" asked Jayne.

"A floor plan maybe." It looked like a blueprint, only not for any kind of building I'd seen before. Numbers littered the page, though it wasn't clear if they were denoting measurements or some other crucial information. "What is she up to?"

"I'm sure it's nothing," said Jayne.

"Then why not ask her?"

"Because she'll know we've been snooping."

"It's your closet, too. And it's not like she hid them very well."

Jayne cocked her head at me in a way that made it clear my suggestion was a stupid one.

"Fine, but I'm telling you, she's up to no good. Better to ask now than find out later." I rolled the paper back up and tied a bow at its center. "Good night," I told Jayne. "Sleep tight." She clicked off her light as I closed the door and murmured her desire for me to have nice dreams.

CHAPTER 14

The Bargain

I didn't. For a long time, I tossed and turned, still uncomfortable with my new sleeping arrangements. Ruby's body temperature jumped to 250 degrees and I found myself desperate to prevent any physical contact with her. Even when I avoided touching her, her body heat continued to radiate toward me, forcing me to hang one leg off the bed and out of the blankets just to keep myself from sweating.

When I finally slept, my dreams were strange and disjointed. I dreamed of Ann affixing wires to dynamite and calmly dismissing my queries about what she was doing. I dreamed of the sailor effigy sprawled across the subway tracks. I dreamed of Mr. Smith, sliced from neck to groin, his vivid red blood staining the already stained rug in his apartment. I dreamed of Jack and Raymond Fielding, the one-legged World War I vet who served as the extent of my prior acquaintance with amputees. In my dream the two men were playing poker. The winner got his leg back. Little did Jack know the game was rigged: it was a right leg that was being offered as the prize. Either way he'd lose.

I awoke with a gasp and once again found myself unable to recognize where I was. Slowly, the day before came back to me, as did a pain in my calf. Ruby had spent most of the night kicking me. I was certain Al was gone, but it turned out he was the quietest sleeper I'd ever roomed with, even with a chest cold. Instead of sawing logs, he purred with each exhale.

I went for the clock. It was only eight. My disturbing dreams were too fresh for me to go back to sleep, so, instead, I went downstairs and enjoyed a solitary breakfast with the newspaper as my companion. The Aqueduct Race Track was opening for the fall. A man in Port Chester had pleaded guilty to illegally selling gas coupons. Al Jolson was returning home after entertaining servicemen in the South Pacific, Brazil, and India. In addition to the subway stoppage, fires had delayed service the night before on the elevated trains at Lexington and Myrtle avenues. I read all of the articles accompanying the el fires, lest it interfere with my own travel plans for the day. The damage was minimal, but the circumstances were suspect. Investigators on the scene found evidence of tampering, and not for the first time, either. Most troubling, the fire started while a large group of servicemen crammed the cars on both lines. One of them was quoted as saying, "We thought we were safe here. Guess we were fools, huh?"

They weren't the only ones. When we left for Tulagi, I remembered feeling astounded that we were at risk of enemy attack the moment our ship left the shore and headed into the open water. But I was realizing that danger wasn't limited to those places where we knew the enemy gathered. Much more frightening were those locations they'd infiltrated without our knowledge, those safe havens that it never occurred to us we'd have to protect. Just because we were on the home front didn't mean the war couldn't one day share our soil.

Spies were everywhere. Maybe even sleeping in my old bed, enjoying a well-deserved rest after creating a night of havoc.

I finished the meal by shoving what edibles I could find into my pockets. That task complete, I returned upstairs and found Al and Ruby starting to stir.

"Nothing for me?" she cooed when she saw what I'd brought for Al.

"I only have two hands."

"Then maybe you should make two trips."

I gave Al his food and showed Ruby my back.

"Flapjacks? Wow. These are great," he said as he scarfed them down. Clearly it was delirium talking. "No wonder you girls stay here. This is A-plus." He was about to say more when the cough returned and interrupted any further conversation. I patiently waited for him to spit phlegm into a napkin before continuing our talk.

"How's the leg?" I asked.

"Stiff. But better."

"And the rest of you?"

"Getting there. The warm room helped."

Ruby left the bed and put on her robe. She stood before the dressing table for a minute, examining any lines that may have sprouted on her face overnight. Once she was done paying heed to the face that demanded a thousand trips, she turned my way and frowned. "Where is he going to . . . *you know* . . . during the day."

I hadn't thought about that. The logistics of having a man in an all-women residence hadn't hit me yet. I searched the room for an answer. There was a washbasin and bowl on the windowsill. From what I could tell it wasn't doing anything but gathering dust. I removed the bowl and showed it to Ruby.

"Are you attached to this?" I asked.

"Why?" she said.

"Why do you think?"

She let out a gasp of disgust.

"Unless you have a better suggestion," I said. "Save your breath."

I passed Al the bowl. "That's your bathroom for the time being. Put it on the fire escape and we'll try to empty it when the coast is clear."

"I gotta stay in here all day?"

"Despite the high cost, this isn't a hotel, Al. If you're seen, you get the gate, and Ruby and I soon follow. Besides, you're sick. And if Vinnie's men were on your tail last night, the last thing you need to do is give them another chance to see you. I'm calling the shots, and for now you're bedridden."

He grumbled again, but I ignored it. There were more urgent things to worry about: someone was knocking on the door.

Ruby looked at me and silently asked what to do.

"It's probably Jayne," I said. I went to the door and opened it a sliver. Zelda smiled from the other side.

"Uh, hi," I said, blocking the view with my body. "It's not a good time."

"I have medicine," she said. "For *you know who.*" The blank look on my face must've told her I wasn't budging. "Jayne told me about your visitor. Here." She shoved a bottle of Hycodan cough syrup through the opening. "Tell him to take two tablespoons every three hours. It'll help with the cough."

"Thanks," I said, and closed the door. "Here," I tossed the bottle to Al and gave him Zelda's instructions. As he twisted the bottle open and downed his first dose, Ruby stared at me with her mouth open.

"Who was that?" she said at last.

"Zelda."

"And how does she know he's here?"

I shrugged. There was no point in getting Jayne in trouble. She had enough to deal with.

"It's going to be all over the house now," said Ruby.

"Relax. Zelda's a good egg."

"No, she's a leaky ship. And if it gets back to Belle, you're taking the fall, not me. And I still expect to get paid."

While it wasn't ideal that Zelda knew Al was there, it was hardly the catastrophe that Ruby was painting. Zelda would tell her roommate, *maybe*, but she wasn't close enough to anyone else in the house to share our secret.

Another knock sounded at the door.

"See?" said Ruby. "She's already told someone else."

I ignored her and opened the door. Belle stared back at me.

I slammed the door and pushed my weight against it. It's Belle, I mouthed to Ruby. To Belle, I said, "Just a second. We're not decent."

While Ruby threw on a robe, I led Al to the wardrobe and shoved him inside. I was halfway to the door when I remembered the cat was also contraband. I scooped him up, took him to the armoire, and handed him to Al.

"Not a peep out of either of you," I warned them. I returned to the door and let Belle in. "Good morning," I said.

"We'll see about that. I need to talk to Ruby. Alone." Her eyes flickered toward the window. "Why is there a basin on the fire escape?"

"Why not?" I said. I grabbed a change of clothes and went to the bathroom. By the time I was done, Belle was gone, and Ruby, Al, and Churchill were restored to their previous positions.

"Everything okay?" I asked.

"Everything is not okay," said Ruby. "Belle just informed me that I have two weeks to either find an acting job or get out."

"But you just did that radio gig. I thought that bought you some time?"

"It did until I showed up here drunk last night. She doesn't like the path I'm headed down."

"Oh."

Ruby crossed her arms. "I take it I have you to thank for this?"

"And me," said Al.

Ruby ignored him. "Great. So not only am I unemployed, now I'm going to be homeless too?"

"Relax," I said. "You'll get work before then. She'll back down."

"You can't promise that."

"And I'm sure giving her a little extra for the month will calm her down. Right, Al?"

He gave me a look that made it clear he didn't want to play along. I widened my eyes, pleading with him to cooperate one last time. "Right," he said. "Maybe I can throw in another ten."

That seemed to do the trick. Ruby gathered her clothes and left the room.

Al shook his head at me. "That dame's got a temper. What are you going to do when two weeks pass and she's still got an empty purse?"

"She'll be working by then. That's all she really cares about." It was clear that fixing things with Vinnie was going to have to be my top priority from here on out. "Where would someone find Vinnie Garvaggio on a lovely fall day like today?"

"That's your plan? Talking to Vinnie?"

"Its ingeniousness is in its simplicity."

"You can't do that."

"The hell I can't, Al. He's got us all by the neck. You're homeless, Jayne's losing her mind, and now Ruby's on the ledge. Frankly, I should've gone to see him before now. So where do I find him?"

"When I said you can't do that, I meant no one knows where he roosts. With the cops on his tail, he's lying low."

"Oh. And I take it he's not in the phone directory?" I ran a comb through my hair, wincing as it snagged on a tangle. Where would someone like Vinnie hang his hat? Brooklyn? Little Italy? Wherever it was, he had to be able to have visitors. After all, even if he was lying low, someone was taking care of business for him.

"If he wasn't going straight, what would he be doing today?" I asked.

Al clearly didn't know the significance of the question. "Visiting his associates and collecting his take."

So someone was doing that for him, going from one concern

to another, picking up Vinnie's protection cash, collecting his vig, making sure he got his take from all the things he was buying and selling. If I could find the person, they would eventually lead back to Vinnie. After all, what was the point of picking up the big guy's cash if you never turned it over to him?

And I knew one place that person was definitely collecting for Vinnie today: Lochanelli's Locksmiths.

Before I took off, I visited my under-the-bed suitcase and borrowed a few of Billy's bills. I felt lousy about it, but I was tailing the mob that day. I had to be prepared. And besides: I fully planned on paying every dime back. Subway service was restored, so I took the train uptown and hoofed it to the purveyor of lock picks who'd so kindly helped me out. I roosted on a bench across the street and sat tight for a long wait.

It was probably good I had thinking time on my hands. After all, even if my plan worked and I found Vinnie G., I didn't have a clue what I was going to say to him.

I played out a variety scenarios as I watched the various skirts and suits who made up the locksmith's clientele. There was more than one man working the floor today—in addition to the fellow with the pony problem, there were two technicians who regularly headed out of the shop to wherever work called them. My target stayed at the counter, assisting men with locked luggage or keys that needed copying. These clients didn't look like the thugs to me. Swarthy, perhaps, but they all seemed to genuinely be there on locksmith-related business. Only one woman came in: since she was clad in a robe with a head full of curlers, it was obvious she'd been locked out nearby and thought it would be easier to come to Lochanelli than to find a phone and call for assistance.

At least, initially there was only one woman. Right about twelve, when I was thinking my time might better be served at a lunch counter, a middle-aged dame sauntered through the door and up to the counter. She had dark curly hair and the kind of body built for childbearing. She wore a no-nonsense day dress and a pair of mid-level heels that foretold a morning of errands to such exotic locales as the butcher and the baker. I was about to dismiss her as another customer in search of a spare key when something stopped me. The guy at the counter kowtowed to her, not like you would for some random frau off the street but as people of importance demanded. He kept his head bent in deference, his hands clasped together as though he was uncertain what protocol dictated he should do with them. Was she someone famous? I didn't think so, though my view wasn't that good. For a moment they exchanged pleasantries, her face frozen with a false smile, his rippling with nerves. Then, he said something she didn't look too happy about. While she was still reeling from whatever bomb he dropped, he removed a small package from beneath the counter and passed it her way. She opened it just enough to count the cabbage inside and give me a view of her take.

Satisfied, she slipped it into her handbag, offered the man a parting remark, and sashayed out the door.

I was almost too stunned to react. Vinnie had a dame working for him? On the one hand, it seemed like a clever way to keep the cops off his tail, but how could he guarantee some moll was trustworthy enough with his business? Besides, how did his associates feel about it? While women were getting all sorts of new job opportunities thanks to the war, the mob didn't strike me as a particularly liberated group.

Before she'd rounded the corner, I gathered my wits and rose to my feet. Keeping a safe distance, I tailed her to three more business stops, where she collected envelopes, transferred them to her sensible but expensive purse, and continued on her way. I was getting weary of her pace, when she paused curbside and a midnight blue Buick Roadmaster glided to her side. She waited for the driver to get out of his perch to open her door and, without a word of thanks, climbed inside.

Nuts. If they were going somewhere by car, there was no way I was going to be able to follow them on foot.

With no choice, I hailed a Yellow and climbed into the waiting backseat. As the Buick slid into early afternoon traffic, I directed the driver to follow the car.

"Seriously?" he said.

"Seriously. And be subtle about it."

It was a good thing I'd hired a hack. Her driver took us on a roundabout trip to Lower Manhattan, finally ending up at New York Harbor. I was worried she was going for a little sightseeing, but her plan was even more maddening than that: both she and her car were boarding the Staten Island Ferry.

"Now where to?" asked the driver.

"This is my stop." I tossed him some coin, fished out a nickel for my ferry fare, and within five minutes claimed a seat on the upper deck of the silvery gray boat.

I didn't see her during the journey, not that I was looking. I was too busy taking in the view as we left Lower Manhattan via the Hudson and passed Brooklyn, with its factory smokestacks, the red sandstone walls of Castle Williams on Governors Island (could such a fortress protect us today?), the dull brick buildings of Ellis Island, and finally the Statue of Liberty standing proud despite the green rash coating her body. No matter how many times I'd ridden the ferry (and at a nickel a pop it was an incredibly affordable entertainment option), I was still amazed by the landscape it offered. This was the New York I'd thought of when I'd been in Tulagi. Not the dirty streets and wasted food and crowded subways but these landmarks of hope, past and present.

At least, they were unchanged—for now.

After thirty minutes we docked at St. George, Staten Island. While the cars idled in a line, awaiting their turn to leave the ferry, I exited by foot and waved forward my second taxi of the day. As thoughts of Billy's diminishing bankroll filled my head, I informed the driver that we'd be following the blue Buick wherever it was going.

Unlike his predecessor, he wasn't amused by the request. A fare was a fare.

The woman and her driver eventually traveled west to New Brighton, an area that had once been a summer resort town but at some point had receded into quiet, residential dwellings. Amidst the humble homes that dotted the streets were pockets of more extravagant Victorian mansions that told of the town's distant past, when Southern planters and wealthy New Yorkers had made this 'burg their town. I expected to see our target pull up to one of these behemoth houses, but when the Roadmaster finally paused, it was to stop at a much more modest abode that faced the harbor along the unfortunately named Kill van Kull.

I asked the cabbie to pass them by and drop me off a block away. The last thing I wanted to do was to alert this dame to my presence.

As I started to walk back toward the house she'd stopped at, Saint Peter's Church bells chimed three times. If this wasn't where Vinnie was hiding out, not only had I blown almost five bucks in cab fare, but I'd also lost almost an entire day.

She was still standing outside the house as I approached, but her attention wasn't directed at me. Two roly-poly boys, the spitting image of Vinnie Garvaggio, were in the front yard playing with a dog that, even from my vantage, I could tell was filthy. Her voice rose into a litany of reasons why the dog had to go. This wasn't the unsolicited advice of a sometime visitor; this was the unquestionable edict of a matriarch who was tired after a long day of work.

One of the miniature Vinnie G.s had the nerve to respond to her. I couldn't hear what he said, but it was obvious he regretted it the minute the words came out of his mouth.

"Vinnie?" she screamed once the boy had said his piece. I paused two houses away, making myself invisible behind a mighty oak. "VINNIE!"

A screen door whined open and Vinnie G., clad only in a bathrobe, padded onto the porch. "What?" He was bigger than I remembered. Zeppelin big. Large enough to take out towns if he was dropped from the air. I'd never seen him outside of an immaculately tailored pinstriped suit before, and I can't say the change in attire was doing him any favors.

"Did you tell them they could keep this dog?"

Despite being three times this woman's size, he looked sheepish. It was clear he wanted to be anywhere but here. "Betty—"

"Don't you Betty me." She approached him and smacked him on the side of the head. While he tended to this injury, she delivered her handbag to his gut. "Here's your cash. No dog. Got it?"

"Sorry, boys," he said to his sons. "You heard your ma."

Ma? So this wasn't some random moll. This was *Mrs.* Garvaggio.

"You collect from everyone on the list?" he asked.

"I look like a moron?" she said. "Of course I collected." Vinnie opened the latch on her purse. Before he could stick his hand inside, she smacked him again. "And so help me God, if you count that money out here, I will beat you black and blue. You want to go back to prison?"

"No."

She scanned the street. "Get inside. And you two," she said to the boys. "I want to see you bathed and changed in fifteen minutes, or I swear to God there'll be no dinner for any of you."

Like a Pied Piper for the Italian and zaftig, Vinnie disappeared inside with the two boys on his heels. The dog, knowing it didn't stand a chance, slinked away to find affection elsewhere. Rather than joining her clan, Betty sat on the porch steps and lit a cigarette she fished out of her pocket.

I was too fascinated to move. I had my preconceptions about mob wives. It was a life I feared Jayne was headed for until she had the good sense to give Tony the gate. Given that I'd met plenty of the younger models destined to one day replace them, I assumed that these women would be old and haggard, fond of wearing black, going to Mass, and making marinara sauce. They were shadows of their former selves, willing to relinquish their own say-so if it meant they could reap the benefits of their husband's lifestyle.

This woman was none of those things.

She was tough, powerful, and completely in control. And maybe, I hoped, she could be an ally.

I stepped away from the tree and, with little thought about what I was about to do, approached her house. I was halfway up the walk before she noticed me. Instead of demanding to know why I was there, she let me continue my approach with a wry smile on her face.

"Hiya," I said. She didn't respond. "Are you Betty Garvaggio?"

"Forget it, doll. Whatever he's told you, it's not going to happen. I could be six feet under and he wouldn't get a divorce. And for the record? I'm doing you a favor. He's no prize."

It slowly dawned on me what she thought I was there for. "Er . . . I'm not . . . I mean Vinnie and I haven't–"

"Then what do you want?"

"Help. From you. I know you're Vinnie's right hand right now and I'm in a fix."

She nodded toward the floor beside her and I took her up on the invitation and joined her on the step. "How'd you find me?"

"I followed you from Manhattan."

She raised an eyebrow. "Impressive. Not even the coppers have done that. So what's your story?"

"My name's Rosie Winter and my friends and I were in a show last spring that Vinnie produced, *Goin' South*."

"I saw it." From her tone, she hadn't thought much of it.

"We haven't been able to get work since. Word on the street is Vinnie thinks we had something to do with his arrest, and so he's blocking us from getting hired. We're getting pretty desperate. If we don't get work soon, we're going to be homeless. And the thing is, we didn't have anything to do with the feds shutting down his meat business. I swear."

She ashed her cigarette into a flower bed. From the butts on the ground, it was clear it wasn't the first time she'd sat here and smoked. "Relax."

And just like that, I did. Like I said, the woman was powerful. "So you'll talk to him?"

"I don't need to. He's not the one who banned you."

He wasn't? "Then who did?"

"Me."

The tension returned. "Wait—what?"

"You know who got Vinnie out of jail?" She pointed a thumb her way. "My family bought him out when it didn't look like there was any hope of him being sprung during this decade. And now he's free on my terms. No more women, or I see to it he serves his time. And don't think I won't."

"That seems . . . fair." But what, I wanted to ask, did that have to do with us?

"While Vinnie knows the rules, some of his old friends haven't been as quick to figure them out, so I thought I better make my message loud and clear. I know he had one of his whores performing in that show of yours. He got her the job special. Only I didn't know for sure which girl it was, and fatso in there ain't talking. So, to be safe, I decided to punish the lot of you to send you a message, just like the one I sent Vinnie. You mess with Betty, you're going to feel it."

I didn't know what to say. She punished everyone? But Zelda was still working, and she'd also been in the show with us. Of course, her work was government-sponsored school shows, one of the few performance domains the mob didn't have a hand in. "I'm impressed. Really," I told Betty. "But doesn't it seem a little unfair to punish all of us? I know the woman you're talking about. She's not even in New York anymore. She went out to Hollywood last spring."

"A girl can't be too cautious. You could be lying to protect someone."

"Trust me, I have no reason to protect her. Her name's Gloria Abatrillo. I can get you an address if you like. Heck, I can get you her headshot."

She dropped the rest of the cigarette into the dirt and rubbed her hands together. "Tell you what: I'm not an unreasonable woman. You do for me, I'll do for you."

I rose to my feet. "Great. Give me a day or two, and I'll have everything you need to find her."

"I don't care about Gloria anymore. That's past history. It's the present I need help with."

"Come again?"

"You followed me today, so clearly you're good at tailing people without being made, right?"

I nodded, reluctantly.

"I spend my days doing his circuit for him while he's supposedly at home, but I got an itch that tells me he's stepping out. I want a name."

"But what if he's not—"

"I want a name," she said, more firmly. "You get me that, I'll see to it that you can work again."

It wasn't the response I wanted, but I had a feeling she was a woman of her word. "And my friends, too?"

"Sure. Tell me who they are and I'll make sure you're all in the clear."

"Jayne Hamilton and Ruby Priest."

Her face darkened. "Not that one."

"Which one?"

"Ruby Priest. I heard today she's going around town dropping Vinnie's name to get favors. You and Jayne I'll help, but that one? She's up to no good. Last I heard she was trying to get her hand on some lock picks."

I asked about Al, but it looked like I was out of luck there. She couldn't deny Vinnie a grudge against the guy who helped Tony B. gain his meat trade. After all, what kind of wife was she?

CHAPTER 15

The Return of the Vagabond

By the time I made it back to the Shaw House, it was after five. I was beat from pounding pavement and starving—I hadn't eaten anything since breakfast. Naturally, that meant my arrival home was going to be delayed by Tony B.

"You give her my message?"

He was sitting on the steps with his shirtsleeves rolled up. It was clear he'd been there for a while, or at least long enough to smoke two cigars and develop a thin layer of sweat on his face. I almost felt sorry for the guy. Almost.

"I told you I would, didn't I?"

"And?"

I leaned against the railing and looked longingly toward the window to Ruby's room. I hoped she was out and I'd get the bed to myself. "She was pretty impressed. Unfortunately, I imagine she won't be so eager to call you when she finds out Vinnie Garvaggio has nothing to do with our not getting work."

He held his arms open. "What are you running your mouth about now?"

"I know who's really behind the work ban, and it's not Vinnie. And that means the only pull you got is keeping your suspenders attached to your pants."

His eyes locked on mine. His peepers were big and jutted out in a such a way that you were convinced he was capable of seeing more than anyone else. "You're the one who said Vinnie was behind it, not me."

"But you didn't exactly deny it, did you?"

"It's not my fault you didn't have your facts straight."

"So here's how this is going to work," I said. "I could go inside and tell Jayne that all you were doing was puffing up your chest, making her even more angry at you, or I could keep my yap shut and you could get back in her good graces by helping out Al."

"Al?"

"Yes, Al." I patted the tops of my thighs, trying to create momentum to keep up this tough dame act. "I talked to him again."

His tone deepened. "You gave him my message?"

"Yeah, but he didn't know what I was talking about. If someone's threatening you, it's not him. I guarantee it. He's in a bad way. He's not going to make it if he has to stay on the streets much longer."

"A likely story."

"I'm serious, Tony."

"You think I'm not?" He reached into his breast pocket and pulled out a small metal cylinder. "You know what that is?"

It was obviously a bullet, but experience told me that ignorance would get me further. "A tiny tube of lip crème?"

"No, it's a slug from a .45. And not just any slug. It hit the door of my car outside Ali Baba's last night." He raised his other hand and demonstrated the distance. "It was this close to hitting me."

"That doesn't mean Al fired it."

He tossed the bullet at me. "Doesn't mean he didn't."

I caught the bullet and closed my palm around it. It was warm to the touch, either from being in Tony's mitt or from the rage that had propelled it the night before. "You're in a dangerous business, Tony. Surely Al's not the only person you've crossed."

"In this world, when you're high up and you upset someone, they let you know you're marked. At the very least, someone talks and clues you in to what's what and that you need to be scared. In this case, no one's talking. I got men all over this city, and no one has heard a peep about a price on my head. That tells me one thing: whoever's after me ain't affiliated."

I still wasn't convinced, but I put the bullet in my pocket, just in case. "What time did this happen?"

"Eleven o'clock."

When Al was supposedly at dinner and being made by Garvaggio's men. Could he have had time to go to Ali Baba's? It was possible. It would've been a good night to try and hit Tony. Especially since Al knew he was going into hiding and wouldn't likely get another chance.

But he would've needed a car to do it. The subways were stopped last night.

Tony slowly rose to his feet. "You can tell Jayne whatever you want to tell her. I ain't doing nothing for that lowlife." He looked to the left, where his driver was leaning against the car, reading a newspaper. With a flick of the wrist, he told the guy to start the engine. As the put-upon chauffeur folded up the *Times*, something just past him caught my eye. There was a man sitting across the street, watching us.

Good lord, was it Mr. Smith's murderer? Was he no longer scared enough of Tony to flee? Or was this whoever was really after Tony?

"You know where he is?" asked Tony.

Tony's voice caught me off-guard. Had he seen the man watching me? "Who?"

"Al."

I kept my expression frozen and resisted the urge to look up at Ruby's window again. "Nope. I have no idea."

He knocked the rail with his knuckles. "If you're smart, you'll keep it that way."

Shows how much he knew. I was going to make sure Al was closer to me—and Jayne—than ever. We needed the protection.

As Tony started toward the car, I remembered that there was something I needed from him. "I have a question for you."

His face darkened and I could tell that he had reached his limit with me.

"Don't worry," I said. "It's not about Al or any of that." I took his place on the steps and smoothed my skirt over my legs. "That guy Gris you were in contact with in the South Pacific, the one following Jayne? I need to reach him."

"Ain't he still there?"

"Yeah, but I need his name. His real name."

"I'd love to help you out, but my memory's not so good." He kicked at a butt someone had discarded on the sidewalk.

"Tony —"

"What? You want a favor after you threaten me?"

And here I thought our conversation had been so amicable. "Okay, maybe I misinterpreted your offer to talk to Vinnie. I won't tell Jayne you knew Vinnie wasn't behind the work ban."

He spit at ground. The concrete quickly devoured the puddle of saliva. "His name's Mike Carlucci."

"Thanks."

Tony pulled a cigar from his pocket and removed the wrapper. "You sweet on him or something?"

"Or something." I rolled my eyes. It must've been nice to live in a world where the only reason a woman had for talking to a man was because of romantic intentions.

As Tony climbed into the car, I looked back toward the man who'd been watching us. He was gone.

Rather than going inside the building, I went to the post office and picked up some V-mail. Over an egg cream at C.O. Bigelow's, I wrote a letter to the man formerly known as Gris, asking him for

Whitey's real name. I kept the letter as vague as possible. Given the reputation I'd made for myself on Tulagi, I didn't want to say anything that might raise the censor's alarm. I dropped the letter in the first box I could find and headed back to the Shaw House. Just as I turned the corner for home, I saw Candy looking up and down the street. My impulse was to turn and run, but it was too late. She'd seen me.

"I was hoping I'd run into you," she said.

"Here I am. What's the crop?"

"It's Jack."

A chill passed through me. Had he caught an infection? Had they taken the other leg? Had he done the unthinkable? "Is he all right?"

"Yes. I mean physically, he's no worse than when you saw him, but emotionally . . . I'm worried, Rosie. I've tried talking to his parents, but they just don't seem to get how depressed he is."

"No. They wouldn't." The awkwardness of the situation was giving me a headache. Now that he was alive and in love with someone else, the fates had decided to punish me by making me his fiancée's confidante. And whose fault was that? Mine, for lying to her in the first place.

"He's convinced everything's over for him. Not only has his military career ended in disgrace, but he seems to think he'll never get another acting job. I just don't know what to do."

How about helping him to gain back the little bit of dignity he left in Tulagi by vindicating him? "There's probably nothing you can do. It's going to take time. He's got to heal."

"He doesn't want to leave his parents' house. He doesn't want to see any of his old friends. He canceled the prosthetic fitting."

"Maybe he's just not ready yet."

"I was hoping you'd go visit him again."

It hadn't been an easy request for her to make. I could see that. But that didn't mean it was any easier for me to volunteer to do what she asked. "I don't think he wants to see me."

"He was better last night. A lot better. Seeing both of you gave him hope."

How much hope could it have been if he was worse off today? Or was what Candy was reading as depression Jack's renewed regret that he hadn't gone to trial? I looked longingly toward the Shaw House. If I'd stopped for a decent meal, maybe I could've avoided this whole messy conversation. "I'll talk to Jayne. We're awfully busy with auditions right now, but maybe we can work something out."

She took one of my hands in hers and squeezed. "Thanks."

For the first time, I noticed how frail Candy had grown. In the South Pacific she was tan, strong, and invincible, but here in the city she had become a very different version of herself. Manhattan could do a number on anyone, but it seemed to have beaten her down. No, it wasn't the city. It was Jack.

"How are you?" I asked.

"What do you mean?"

"What do you think I mean? Never mind what Jack is going through—this can't be easy on you."

She had on a cardigan that was too large. Her hands were lost in the extra length of sleeve. She wrapped her arms around herself and for a moment looked like an inmate at Bellevue. "It's different here," she said. "I don't mean just New York. I've been in big cities before. But just being back. I know that doesn't make any sense."

"I think I know just what you mean," I said.

"Do you?"

I nodded. "I got so used to being in the islands, and I find I want to talk to everyone about what we saw and what we experienced, but no one wants to hear it."

Candy grinned, setting off a dimple near her chin. "Exactly. It's even worse with Jack. He wants to forget that place, but it's not out of my skin yet."

"And the news here," I said. "It seems so removed. I keep trying to pin faces to figures. It almost makes me angry. I don't want all those boys to be forgotten." I was getting emotional. This burden I'd been walking around with since we got home was finally bubbling to the surface. "This place has changed. It's not the home I remember. I feel so helpless here."

Candy's eyes moistened. "Me, too. I keep thinking maybe I should try to volunteer somewhere, just to feel like I'm doing something. But the truth of the matter is, I want to be back in the thick of things. But of course, I can't be."

"Right, Jack needs you."

"No, I mean, I can't because I left the WACs."

"But just temporarily, right?"

A light smile played across her lips. Just before it became mocking, she cut it off. "You don't get how the military works, do you?" I wasn't offended. Even in the South Pacific, I'd felt baffled by how the various divisions operated. "I was discharged, Rosie. I can't go back."

"Ever?"

She shook her head. For the first time I realized the enormity of the sacrifice she'd made. Candy was a good soldier, someone who would've risen through the ranks quickly if she'd wanted to. But she'd abandoned all that to be with a man who didn't even have the courtesy to act like he was happy that she was here with him.

"Sometimes I wonder if I made the right decision. As hard as things were there, they were easier too, you know?" She wiped at the corners of her eyes. "Isn't it crazy that we miss a war?"

It was, although I knew it wasn't about missing the anxiety and loss. What I had there that I didn't have at home was a purpose.

CHAPTER 16

Two for the Show

When I walked into the Shaw House, Jayne was sitting with Zelda in the parlor, flipping through audition notices.

"There you are!" said Jayne as I came in. She was dressed in her usual audition wear—a gray suit with white stripes and a ruffled blouse poking out underneath. At her feet was a bag that I knew contained a leotard, tights, ballet slippers, and anything else she thought she might need. "Where have you been?"

"Just running errands. How's *you know who*?"

"Better," said Zelda. "We checked in on him a little while ago, and he was sleeping like a baby. I think the Hycodan did the trick."

"About that," I said. "I think it goes without saying that Al being here is on the QT, right?"

"Of course," said Zelda.

"I just want to make sure, because Ruby seemed to think that if you knew, everyone would know."

Zelda raised her chin, clearly offended. "I can keep a secret."

I showed her my palms. "I'm not saying you can't. But you haven't told anyone else, right?"

"No," said Zelda. "Of course not."

"And you?" I asked Jayne.

"No one but Zel. Where'd you go to run errands?" asked Jayne.

Were we really back to that topic? "Just here and there."

She looked at my feet, where my pocketbook rested. "For someone who was gone all day, it doesn't look like you got much."

She wasn't going to let this die. And why should she? I'd just learned from Betty that my schemes were going to come back and bite me on the ass. I had to stop the lies from this moment forward.

"Okay, I lied. I went to see Vinnie Garvaggio."

She frowned. "You can do that?"

"You can try. In the end, I chatted with his wife."

Her mouth sank into a pout as I told her my tale of Betty Garvaggio. "She's just as bad as he is. Imagine that—punishing all of us! Like we'd want anything to do with that man."

Although I appreciated Jayne's outrage, I didn't share it. It may have been inconvenient, but I admired the way Betty saw this as an opportunity to get something for herself. She was a woman to be watched, for sure.

"So am I to assume you have an audition?"

"We both do," said Jayne. "Zelda came up with a brilliant way to get us around the ban."

"What's the gig?"

"Lawrence Bentley's new play," said Zelda.

This was their brilliant plan? "You mean the show Ann's in? But it's already in rehearsals."

"The main cast is, but they're looking for lots of other actors. Wives, mothers, girlfriends, sisters. Stage background, really. And given the fact that you two just came off the USO tour, I bet you'd be a shoo-in for something."

"It's a great idea," I said. "But who's funding it?"

"The American Theatre Wing and the USO."

"There's not a dime of mob money backing it, so we don't have to worry about Vinnie G. or his wife," said Jayne.

"Is it full-scale?"

Jayne nodded. "There's just one thing. It's only running for two weeks."

"Yikes."

"But they're thinking of touring. With rehearsals, it should tide us over for a little while. And by the time it closes, maybe you'll have everything taken care of with Betty Garvaggio."

I was torn about participating in it. Zelda was right—we were shoo-ins. And it was the kind of goodwill theater that I enjoyed doing, especially after I'd gotten a taste of it abroad. But being in a show depicting the trials and tribulations of the military didn't sound like the way to get Jayne over Billy.

"The casting call is only until eight," said Jayne.

The look on her face sealed it for me. Of course, we'd do it. Anything was better than sitting around waiting for the sadness to drown her.

We took the subway and hoofed it uptown. On the walk over, I told Jayne about my run-in with Tony. I was hoping she'd focus on the fact that I finally had a way to contact Gris, but all she wanted to hear about was her well-connected ex.

"How is he?" she asked.

"The same. Paranoid. Uncouth. Demanding."

"What's he paranoid about?"

"He still thinks Al's trying to rub him out. That's why he hasn't been too eager to help him. Personally, I think he's gunning for sympathy. He wanted me to know we weren't the only ones in a tough spot; he's in one, too."

"A tough spot he lied about," said Jayne. "How dare he try to force me to call him by blaming everything on Vinnie."

I was tempted to let her continue raging at Tony, but a promise was a promise. "Actually, to be fair, I was the one who originally suggested Vinnie was behind the work ban. He was only offering to help us based on what I told him. I mean, it's not like those two are drinking buddies."

"Oh." It was clear she didn't know how *not* to be mad at Tony. "But still. He could've at least figured out what was really going on before blackmailing me like that." She continued rattling on about all the lousy things Tony had done to her in the past. As much as I wanted to give her an *attagirl*, there were a thousand more important questions bouncing around my head. Who was trying to take Tony out? Who was watching us from across the street? Was Vinnie Garvaggio really stepping out on Betty?

The auditions were being held at the Forty-fourth Street Theater, the venue that sat above the Stage Door Canteen, where Jayne, Zelda, Ruby, and I had briefly volunteered as hostesses the previous spring. The theater was still playing host to *Rosalinda* (a revival of *Die Fledermaus*), which had run much longer than it had any right to and would soon be evicted for Bentley's massive war spectacle. We were hardly the only ones who'd turned up for the audition. A crowd wound its way out of the building and up the street. Men and women—the former in uniform—buzzed with excitement about being in this historic production. Lawrence had ascended while we were out of the country, somehow going from Broadway golden boy to America's poet laureate in people's minds. Given the slop Lawrence had put to paper previously, I doubted this show had earned its praise, but I also knew we were beggars, not choosers.

Potential performers weren't the only ones waiting outside the theater. Newshounds had descended as well, heralding their arrival with steno pads and pencils clutched in their hands. From across the street a photographer trained his camera on us and captured the long line for one of the papers. Reporters called out questions to the crowd, looking for those who had traveled the farthest, who had served in the military the longest, and who thought this show might make them a big star. Up-close, the questions got more serious and the answers were ready-made for the evening papers. "Why do you want to be part of this production?" a man in a brown fedora asked again and again. Lawrence Bentley's recent service had given him a unique viewpoint, the women around us said, helping to produce the grittiest, most touching piece of theater of his career. Finally, someone was going to speak for them, said the men, and if they could help give his words a voice, all the better.

At the doors to the theater, a solemn pair of military police stood watching, like the U.S. version of the guards at Buckingham Palace. As the line made its way through the door, they trained their eyes on each one of us, seeking out a sign that we were up to no good.

"What's with the security?" I asked Jayne.

A man in front of us decided to answer on her behalf. "They're worried we're a target."

"How so?" said Jayne.

Our companion was tall and blond, with the sort of chiseled face that reminded you of ancient sculptures. He had brown eyes that seemed to pick up a hint of green from his uniform. "You know, with all us enlisted men around. It's a hell of lot easier to take out three hundred of us at a theater than it is on a ship. Can't defend ourselves here."

I shivered. So that's how it was now: whether on the elevated trains, the subway, or the stage, nowhere was safe. I looked up at the sky, expecting to see bombs silently descending, but all I got was blue sky interrupted by puffy white clouds.

"Sounds a little paranoid," said Jayne.

"Here's the way I look at it," said the guy. "If someone thinks there's a reason to be concerned, it's 'cause they know a lot more than we do. And, frankly, that's fine by me. It's better to be safe than sorry, right?"

"Right," I said. "Someone tried to set two trains full of men on fire last night, and that wasn't a tenth of the soldiers that are on line right now. If you want to do damage and make a statement, this is the place to do it."

He turned to face forward again. I went to say something to Jayne and realized she was staring at the back of his head.

"He's cute," I whispered.

"Rosie." She swatted me on the arm.

Truth be told, he reminded me of Billy, even if the height and hair color weren't a match. There was something honest and earnest about him. But then, those words hadn't really described Billy, had they? His ability to tell the truth had been a put-on. "I'm just making an observation," I said. "You could do a lot worse."

I'm not sure if the boy in front of us heard me, but the tops of his ears reddened.

As the crowd grew, so did my theory about how this production could be a target. It was great that they were taking precautions by watching those of us who'd turned out for the cattle call, but if you were really clever, you would've infiltrated the theater at a higher level, where you were too important to have your intentions questioned. Then you would be in the perfect position to do damage when no one expected it. If I wanted to wreak havoc, I'd get a job behind the scenes, where sabotage could be as easy as installing the wrong number of screws on a flying piece of scenery. Or better yet, I'd get a lead role and be so demanding that everyone left me alone because they didn't want to have to deal with my diva-like behavior.

Like Ann.

A little jolt went through me. Here was a woman who, according to Zelda, openly voiced her contempt for doing theater and made it clear to anyone who listened that she believed she had a higher purpose. Plus, she was lying about where she was really from and doing some awfully odd things during her spare time at home. Was it really so hard to imagine that her reasons for doing this show weren't exactly artistic?

"Did you ask Ann about those floor plans?" I asked Jayne.

"Nope."

"Are you going to?"

"It's none of my business, Rosie."

It took us an hour to make it into the building and to register with the proctors waiting at a table set up at the lobby. They were dismissing people on sight, thank God, which was helping things move along a little faster than normal. When we arrived at the front of the line, they asked for résumés and photos, then gave us the up and down. We passed the physical attractiveness portion of the audition and were told to wait until we were called into the auditorium. Lawrence was helping with casting, along with the show's director and a number of military personnel. From the look of those who were making it through to this stage, they were looking for apple pie, all-American guys and dolls to fill their stage and sell their show.

We were taken in one at a time. Jayne went in before me, while I nervously paced the floor and prepared myself for seeing Lawrence. She'd worked with him before, to much acclaim, but my most significant interaction with him had come when I ran into him at a wake for another playwright and pretended to flirt with him to get information. That was over six months ago, and Lawrence didn't strike me as the kind of guy who remembered any face other than his own, but I was still worried that that meeting might count against me.

It was impossible to hear what was going on in the auditorium. The doors absorbed all sound and didn't even have the courtesy to have windows I could peer through.

"Next!" the stage manager sang.

Jayne had been ushered out another door, so I had no idea how she'd done. I entered the room, climbed on the stage, and gave them my name.

"Why do you want to be in this show?" asked Lawrence. He was thinner than I remembered him. Paler, too. Whereas once he'd seemed precise and almost effeminate, he'd hardened with time and grown sinewy and conservative in his movements, as if he were saving up his energy in case of an emergency. Had the war changed him? The idea struck me as profoundly sad. I wanted to believe that someone as full of himself as Lawrence Bentley would be unaffected by combat, but here he was showing the wear and tear of even a short period of duty. No wonder Jack was so altered.

"Miss Winter?"

I wasn't an apple polisher by nature. I believed talent should speak for itself and one shouldn't have to pile on praise to get a part. But I needed this job, not just for Jayne's sake but for the chance to see what Ann was up to. "I want to be in this show for a number of reasons. I just returned from a USO tour, and I would love to be part of something that shows the rest of the country what it's really like over there. This is undoubtedly going to be a historic production, and to be part of that history would be an honor. As well, I'm a tremendous fan of yours, Mr. Bentley. I've never had a chance to work with you, though a number of my pals have."

"Ah, so you must be friends with Miss Hamilton?" he asked.

So far, no recognition that he'd met *me* before. "Yes. We were on tour together."

"And you sing and dance in addition to being an actress?"

"Yes."

He scribbled something on a piece of paper. "You understand the roles we're casting are quite small. Chorus parts really. You can't show the impact and size of the war without a large cast, though you'd be little more than stage dressing."

So I'd been told. "I have no problem with that."

"Very good. If you wouldn't mind, we're asking everyone to sing the first eight bars of 'Anchors Away.' Do you know the song?"

I did. It was the navy theme song. We'd sung it repeatedly during the tour in Tulagi, including around the swimming hole the last night Jayne had seen Billy, before he was shot down. "Yes, I do."

A piano thumped to life. I gave the song my all, trying as hard as I could not to remember the last time I'd uttered those plaintive words. Poor Jayne. It had to be an awful experience for her to have to perform this piece.

I came to the end of the selection and stared at the table of men. "Nicely done," said Lawrence. "Anything else, gentlemen?"

They silently concurred that they'd seen all they needed to see. "There will be a simple dance audition in fifteen minutes. Since we seem to like what we see here, we'll ask you to go upstairs and prepare for it with the show's choreographer. Thank you, Miss Winter."

I left through the side door and searched for Jayne. She wasn't waiting for me. The blond guy who'd been in front of us in line was, though. He spied me and stopped whatever silent monologue was playing in his head.

"Looking for your pretty little friend?"

"Yeah."

He pointed to the stairs. "She went up to the dance audition. It's on the second floor."

I started to head that way, then realized I was being rude. I might be a consummate liar, but I didn't want to be completely without social niceties. "How'd you do?" I asked him.

He looked toward the door I'd just exited. "That part went well, but I'm not sure I've got the strength in me to try and dance. I made it all the way up to the rehearsal room, then turned tail and came down here."

"It won't be so bad. They know you guys aren't professional hoofers."

He looked toward the stairs again. "Nope. I don't think I can do it. Staring down a bunch of Krauts is one thing, but dealing with two left feet is quite another."

"I'll put in a good word for you," I said. "What's your name?"

"Private Henry Bankshead, ma'am. What's yours?"

"Rosie Winter."

He frowned. "I know I've heard that name before. Where are you from?"

"New York. Born and raised."

"Huh. Maybe I've seen a show you were in then."

"If you have, you're one of the few. Good luck to you, Private."

"You, too."

I followed signs to the rehearsal room on the second floor and found Jayne and at least twenty other men and women stretching. She beamed when she saw me. Either the song hadn't affected her, or she'd already moved past whatever memories it had brought to the surface.

"You made it!" she said.

"Zelda was right. Apparently, this show is influence-free. How'd things go in there for you?"

"Great. Lawrence said he was glad to see me again. He's changed, you know? I was really surprised by how serious he seemed. And guess what?"

"What?"

She jerked a nod toward the door of the room. A figure was standing there, though I couldn't make out who it was. "Maureen O'Reilly's the choreographer."

Right after we'd arrived at San Francisco, but before we'd completed our journey home, an explosion had killed three men at a West Coast dice factory. Shoddy work conditions were to blame. After years of putting immigrant workers at risk, the owners' luck had finally run out.

I knew how they felt.

Of course, my good luck had abandoned me: Maureen was the one who'd be taking us through part two of the audition. Not only did that guarantee that I wouldn't get a spot in the show, but now Jayne would find out that I'd been to Billy's aunt's house. I changed into a leotard and tights and returned to the rehearsal room. Maureen arrived and I tried to catch her eye to see if I could talk to her, but she failed to look my way. Something seemed off about her. She was usually so confident at work that you thought her choreography was handed to her by God himself, but today she seemed rattled. Her face was pale, and twice I caught her looking toward the closed door as though she expected a ghost to materialize.

Maybe it was the stress of working with such a large cast, especially one that consisted of so few professional dancers (Lord knows, working with me had almost done her in). Or Lawrence himself could be the stressor. Even though he was only a playwright, he could be monomaniacal when it came to his productions, insisting on having a hand in every aspect of the performance. Or maybe I was the one setting her off. After all, I knew her secret. We were equally dangerous to each other.

"Are you okay?" asked Jayne.

At some point, I had started twitching. "Just tired," I said. "It's been a long day."

"It'll all be over soon enough."

Boy, did she have that right.

I bent over and stretched my hamstrings. My knees ached in anticipation of whatever torture Maureen was about to levy on them. Of course, that pain was nowhere near as severe as the fear churning up my stomach acid. Surely she wouldn't say anything to Jayne. Perhaps she'd just refuse to cast us, and I could play it off that the mob must have their mitts in this show after all.

"This show vill be simple in its choreography," Maureen said in that strange German accent of hers. "Vith a cast of three hundred und so many of ze men vithout stage experience, ve can't expect everyone to be prima ballerinas, *ja*?" The crowd tittered. I relaxed. A little. "Usually, I use a dance captain, but because dis show is so important to so many, I have decided to employ no one but myself." She clapped her hands together. "On your feet." While the pianist played a medley of military pieces, she walked us through the choreography. It was certainly easier than what she'd thrown at us when Jayne and I were in the corps de ballet she was leading for *Goin' South*, but it was hardly simple. The steps came in rapid succession, and while you would've thought an old gal like her

didn't have it in her, she executed each maneuver perfectly, with
the energy of a woman half her age. She was nicer than I remembered; rather than just showing us the dance once and expecting
us to get it, she repeated it three times, calling out the steps as she
performed them.

Jayne was flawless as always, making it look so easy that I almost
convinced myself that I could do it. But my nerves were making
my feet disagreeable, sending them to the left when everyone else
was going to the right, and vice versa. I knocked elbows with ill-
tempered dancers twice before I remembered to correct myself. By
the time we went through the routine for the official audition, I
had most of it down. Most of it.

"Zat is all," said Maureen. "Zank you, ladies und gentlemen.
Casting lists vill be posted tomorrow."

I had a sinking feeling that I'd blown it. No, I knew I'd blown
it. I should've trusted my instincts and convinced Jayne that this
wasn't the gig for us. Then she never would've seen Maureen and I
could've maintained a little of my dignity.

"Miss Vinter, Miss Hamilton—a vord." Maureen's voice rose
above the chatter as our group shuffled out of the room and a new
crew entered to take its place. I decided to pretend like I hadn't
heard her. I grabbed Jayne's arm and headed toward the exit.

"Rosie," said Jayne. "She wants to talk to us."

"I don't want to talk to her."

"Why not?"

"Because she's going to praise you and bury me, just like she
always does. I know I screwed up. I don't need her to point that
out to me."

"You're being silly." She took me by the wrist and tried to pull
me back into the room.

Desperation blurred the lines around me until it seemed like I
was looking at everything through a haze of fog. "Please, Jayne—
let's not talk to her. I'm feeling low as it is." She wasn't going to
relent. I needed to drag out bigger guns. "Candy wants me to visit

Jack again and between that and this, well I just can't—" Before I
could articulate what it was that I couldn't do, Maureen crossed the
room and joined us.

"Didn't you hear me call you?" she said.

"Sorry," I said. "It's noisy in here."

Jayne greeted her with an embrace. "It's so good to see you
again, Maureen."

"You, too, Jayne. I can see your trip didn't cause you to lose any
skill."

Jayne's brows tipped toward her nose. I knew what she was
thinking: How did Maureen know we'd been abroad?

"We better go," I said. "We have another audition bright and
early in the morning."

"Zat won't be necessary," said Maureen. "I am casting both of
you."

"Seriously?" said Jayne.

"You have more zan earned your place, Jayne. As for you, Rosie?
You vere not so bad, but not so good, either. Since you cannot get
other vork, I cast you out of pity. Dere vill be enough dancers to
hide your flaws." I was hoping that was it. I started to turn to begin
my exit, when Maureen opened her mouth again. "Maybe you come
to my house, Jayne."

"What?" she said.

"Maybe you come for lunch tomorrow. I vould like to catch up
vith you."

"Don't we have that thing tomorrow?" I said.

"What thing?" said Jayne.

It was like watching a truck barreling toward a stray dog from
a locked second-story window. I couldn't do anything to stop it; all
I could do was pray that either the truck or the dog had enough
sense to get out of the way.

"Never mind. I must've gotten my dates confused," I said. I tried
to silently plead with Maureen, but she didn't seem to catch the
hint.

"Dere is so much I vant to tell you. Let's say one o'clock? Rosie can give you de address." With that, she turned and went toward the next group of dancers. Jayne and I left the room and entered the stairwell.

"How do you know where she lives?" she asked.

Indeed, how did I? "I ran into her once. Her apartment's not far from here."

"How come you never mentioned it?"

"I didn't tell you what I had for breakfast, either. I didn't think it was important."

She wasn't done with the questions. "What do you think she wants to talk to me about?"

I was feeling so warm that I was getting dizzy. I had to come clean and tell Jayne everything. And I would. Just as soon I could catch my breath. "Maybe she wants to hear about the USO tour."

"How'd she know about that anyway?"

"I told her about it. When I ran into her. Near her apartment."

"So this happened recently?" Was she putting two and two together?

"Yeah, just a day or two ago. With Al and everything, I must've forgotten to mention it to you."

"Did she tell you about Lawrence's show?"

"Nope. Which just goes to show you that the woman was not eager to work with me again."

She mulled over my answer. She'd been testing me, and, fortunately, it looked like I had passed.

"You know, if you're uncomfortable, you don't have to go," I said.

"Why would I be uncomfortable?"

I motioned for her to move forward, that I didn't want to have this conversation in the theater. We hurried out of the building and onto the street. Already a line was forming of men hoping to get into the Stage Door Canteen. The sun had set and that, plus the dimmed streetlights, turned Forty-fourth Street into an avenue of shadows.

"Well?" said Jayne.

"She's German," I whispered.

The shock on Jayne's face couldn't have been more real if she'd just licked a light socket. "Are you sure?"

It took everything in me not to laugh. Had she really not picked up on the accent? Or was Jayne naïve enough that she took everyone at face value? No wonder Ann didn't mind living with her; she was the perfect dupe. "Positive. What if she wants to talk to you about Nazi propaganda or something?"

"She wouldn't do that."

"She might. It could be why she cast me. She figures if she scratches my back, I'll scratch hers."

"That's ridiculous."

I was getting desperate. "She slipped me some literature when I ran into her on the street. Pro-Bund stuff."

That got her attention. Her eyes grew as big as fifty-cent pieces. To passersby, she must've looked like little orphan Annie.

"And while I hate to worry about these things, if word about her gets out and someone sees you visiting her outside of rehearsal, they might assume you're guilty by association."

Jayne nodded gravely. "Then I guess I better not go."

CHAPTER 17

A Love Scandal

To celebrate getting work, we picked up enough take-out Chinese for ourselves and Al and headed home. When we arrived, Al was reclining on the bed, reading an issue of *Photoplay*, with Rita Hayworth on the cover. The sight was so incongruous that I fought a laugh. What was next? Cold cream on his face and a box of chocolates at his side?

"We brought chow," I said. He bent the corner of the magazine, to mark an article about the demise of Rita and Victor Mature's relationship, and set it aside. "Busy day?"

He shrugged and took the cardboard containers of food we offered him.

"How's the cough?" asked Jayne.

"Better. I think in another day or two, I'll be jake." As we ate, he regaled us with tales of fictional characters who'd kept him company that day. Unfortunately, he'd begun to confuse the storylines of Nick Carter, Archie Andrews, and Kitty Foyle, leaving Archie to solve a murder, Nick to deal with the travails of being a woman, and Kitty navigating the challenges of high school. It was clear that if Al was locked up much longer, he was no longer going to be able to discern between what was real and what wasn't.

Later, after dinner was eaten and Jayne had returned to her own room, I gave him the scoop on our new jobs and my visit with Tony.

"I can't believe you threatened him," he said.

"Believe me, it wasn't easy."

"He's never going to help you with Vinnie now."

"Turns out he's not our problem." I told him about Betty. As I finished my tale, I dumped our food containers in the trash and watched as Churchill circled the can, looking for a leftover morsel to devour.

"You know, I'd heard rumors about her, but I just assumed it wasn't true. He sure picked a good one, eh?"

"Yeah, she's a treasure all right. So how do I find out who Vinnie's stepping out with?"

"You don't. The only thing worse than a woman scorned is a man who knows he's been squealed on."

And Vinnie wasn't just any man; he was a mobster who we already knew had a predilection for revenge. "I don't have a choice, Al. We need to work and Betty holds the reins."

"To *your* future, sure."

I'd forgotten about him. "Actually, the way I see it, this is going to fix your problem, too. If Vinnie is stepping out on her, he's going to end up either back in the pen or in the East River. What you need to worry about is Tony. He said someone tried to shoot him last night."

"So?"

"He thinks it was you." I fished the bullet out of my purse and tossed it his way. "Look familiar?"

He eyed the slug. "Nope. You put him straight, right?"

Before I could answer, Ruby came in the room, making it impossible to continue the conversation.

I glanced at the clock. It was almost eleven. "Where have you been?" I asked.

She slung her pocketbook onto the vanity, setting off a rattle of bottles. "Where do you think? Pounding the pavement."

Al cracked open a fortune cookie and shoved the whole thing—paper free—into his mouth. The crisp cookie seemed to echo in the room, although I have to imagine it was only the tension that made it seem that way.

"Do you have to do that?" Ruby said to him.

"Do what?" he asked through a mouthful of cookie.

"Chew so loudly."

"How else am I going to eat?"

Poor Al wasn't schooled in that high-strung breed of woman who could be irritated by you breathing, if her day had gone wrong. I tried to draw the focus away from him.

"Have any luck?"

She plucked a pair of rhinestone clip-ons from her lobes and tossed them into her jewelry box. "What do you think?"

Al unwrapped another cookie and bit into it.

"Seriously, could you chew that any louder?" barked Ruby.

Al removed the cookie from his mouth and returned it to the bag, a long line of spittle momentarily connecting the confection with his mouth. Ruby surveyed the room. My clothes were piled on the floor. Her magazines had been stacked on the bed, the same bed that Al now occupied.

She picked up the stack of slicks in a huff and slammed them on her nightstand. "Might I remind you that you're both guests in this room? I would appreciate it if you didn't use my things without my permission."

Al slid off the bed and onto the floor. He looked completely diminished but not surprised. I had a feeling what I was witnessing wasn't new to him. Ruby was one of many women—including his ma—who harangued him on a regular basis.

"Easy," I said. "He's bored. He's got nothing to do all day."

Ruby took a deep breath, closed her eyes, and put her index fingers to her temples. As she exhaled, her eyes opened. "I'm sorry. I could really use some good news right now."

"Jayne and Rosie got jobs," said Al.

I shot him a look that did a fine job castrating him further.

"Well, bully for you," said Ruby.

"Actually, this might be an opportunity for you, too," I said. "We're doing Lawrence's show. It's only guaranteed for two weeks, but the press on it is going to be huge."

"You're doing that military thing? Why on earth would you want to be part of that? Most of the women's roles are furniture." She crushed the contents of the trash can with her foot to keep it from overflowing. "Besides, two weeks hardly makes it worth my time." She flung the clothes over the back of her dressing table chair. Her body was stiff, her mood foul. "How was he?"

"Lawrence? There wasn't time for chitchat. And it's not like I know him that well, but he seemed . . . different. I was a little shocked, to tell you the truth. The last time I saw the guy he was so full of himself I expected the button on his pants to burst."

Ruby smiled at that. "That's how he was the last time I saw him, too. Changed. So much more . . . serious."

"I guess the war will do that to you."

Ruby dismissed me with a wave. "Oh please—it's not like he saw any action. Lawrence was more protected than Hitler."

I was starting to see why their relationship had ended. If this was how much empathy Ruby showed him when he came home from his tour of duty, it was no wonder he gave her the gate. "When's the last time you talked to him?"

She shrugged. "I don't know. This summer, I guess."

"Still, it's a good thing he's doing. From what we saw at the audition today, the soldiers seem to think it's high time someone gave them a voice."

She rolled her eyes. "Oh, it's a brilliant move on his part. I just question why any self-respecting performer would want to be part of it."

"Because maybe we want to be part of something that isn't self-serving for once."

Ruby smiled at me. "Then why on earth are you an actress?"

* * *

Ruby went to take a bath, leaving Al and me to entertain ourselves. Cabin fever hadn't just extended to his conversational topics. His body was constantly moving with a sort of nervous, fidgety energy that ignited anxiety in me. He was driving me crazy, but I knew it wasn't fair to call him out for it. In his place, I would've been off the shelf, too.

"He won't hire her, you know," he told me as I shuffled a deck of cards for the first of many games of gin rummy.

"Who won't hire who?"

"That Lawrence guy you was talking about. He won't hire Ruby. That's why she won't audition."

"How do you know that?"

"We talk when you're not here. When they broke up, he told her she was never supportive of anything he did, and she told him that's because he's a hack writer."

I sorted my cards by suit. "Ouch."

"So now, she ain't got a prayer of working for him, unless she apologizes, get it?" He beat my hand without blinking an eye. "Unless she comes up with something else he wants."

"Like what?"

He collected the deck and started to shuffle it. "Beats me. It just seems to me she needs to be more valuable to him than he is to her."

I snorted. "That's going to be hard. He's already got more press than he can handle. He doesn't need Ruby Priest to sell tickets. No one does."

He was taking much too much time shuffling the cards. While I appreciated his thoroughness, it was completely unnecessary when neither of us had anything to wager.

Power. That's what Al needed, too. If he was ever going to get back in Tony's good graces, he needed to give Tony something he wanted. But what? Tony already had the stamps and Vinnie's meat business. Perhaps plain old peace of mind would do. If someone was gunning for Tony—and the evidence made it clear something was going on—then the best way for Al to redeem himself was to prove he was innocent and hand Tony the real culprit.

Al finally dealt my hand. "She don't want me here."

"Relax. She's in a foul mood. It'll pass."

He shook his head, silently letting me know that he didn't believe me. "How's Jayne?" he asked.

My cards were lousy. "You saw her before."

"I know. That's why I'm asking."

"She might be back on the Billy trail, thanks to me." I told him about Maureen.

"You got to come clean with her."

"It's too late for that. I've told too many lies."

"That's not your fault. You're just good at your job."

I smacked my hand over my cards and collected them. "What the deuce does that mean?"

"You know—you're a good actress."

It was nice to get a compliment, especially one from a guy who wasn't known to see theater willingly, but I wasn't thrilled with the way he'd framed it. "Acting isn't lying, Al."

"You say potato, I say potato," he said, not varying the pronunciation of the word.

We'd had this conversation before. When I'd first met him, Al had minimized my profession to the pithy "you pretend to be other people."

I discarded a card and pulled one from the deck.

"There's nothing to be offended about," said Al. "You fake stuff—feeling things, hearing things, how you talk. It's all a lie."

"But the audience is in on it," I said. "It's not deception."

"It is if you make 'em cry, too."

He was starting to make my head hurt. Was he right? Was my whole life a lie? "Look, this isn't about what I do for a living. Whether that's a lie or not, what I'm doing to Jayne right now isn't right."

"So change it. Get her in on it."

"I can't." I longed to explain it further, but I didn't know how. I wanted so badly to protect Jayne—it's all I'd wanted to do since we left the South Pacific—and yet at every turn I'd managed to screw things up with my good intentions. When she took care of me, she made it look so effortless, probably because she was a good person. Which led me to believe that maybe I wasn't. "Besides, I'm safe for now."

"But how long is that going to last? She's going to be at rehearsal every day. Even if she doesn't show for lunch tomorrow, this German broad is bound to say something."

I hadn't thought of that. Of course, that was my problem these days: I couldn't think far enough ahead to see how lousy each of my schemes was proving to be. "I'll deal with it if and when I need to."

"And if Maureen doesn't say anything to her, you're just going to let it go?"

"That's my plan."

"So you're going to let her walk away thinking this guy was a saint?" asked Al.

"Is that so wrong? We don't know for sure that he wasn't. I don't see the harm in letting her think the guy was a good egg. It's a lot better than the alternative."

"Which is?"

"I don't know yet, but I'm pretty sure it's not good."

As Al predicted, my luck didn't last. By morning Jayne had changed her mind and decided that going to Maureen's was the right thing to do. While she put the finishing touches on her face, I waited with Ann in the parlor, praying something would intervene to postpone our trip.

"Why'd she change her mind?" I asked.

"You'd have to ask her." Ann picked up a copy of *Movie Show* from the coffee table and idly flipped through it. Rita Hayworth was on the cover, posing with a turkey that was too big for its pan. Good God, that woman was everywhere these days. What I wouldn't give for that kind of press. "I hear you're going to be in Lawrence Bentley's show," said Ann, when the silence grew too long to be comfortable.

"That we are." I tried to read her expression. She didn't seem too happy with the prospect. I'd like to say it was my participation that bothered her, but in a cast of three hundred, it's not like we'd be bumping elbows regularly.

"It's a little beneath you, isn't it?" said Ann.

"We need work. They need bodies. Now's no time to have standards. Besides, it's a good cause, right? A lot of serviceman are going to see the show, to say nothing of the ones who are participating in it."

"Maybe," she said. What did that mean? Maybe it would have a lot of impact, or maybe the show would never get beyond opening night?

I shook the thought out of my head. Did I really believe Ann was a spy sent to sabotage the subways, the show, and anything else she could get her hands on? It was a ridiculous theory. And yet —

"I'm not sure it's the right thing for Jayne," said Ann. "All those soldiers are going to make it awfully hard for her to move on."

Was this genuine concern for Jayne's psychological well-being, or was she trying to protect her new friend from whatever was about to happen at the Forty-fourth Street Theater?

"There's no avoiding the war," I said. "Sometimes the best way to heal is to face your demons head-on."

"The script is weak," said Ann. "Even Bentley knows it. I see it on his face every time we speak one of his wooden lines. He'll get the audience, but the show's going to be a disaster, and some brave critic is going to have the courage to say it in print."

Before I could respond, Jayne joined us and began to recite her rationale for going to see Maureen after all: just because Maureen was German didn't mean she was a bad person. "It's only right that I give her a chance," said Jayne. "She doesn't speak for her whole country."

I felt like a fool as she rattled on with her reasoning. Of course, I knew that. I'd helped keep a Japanese soldier from being killed in the South Pacific because I knew one's government and military did not speak for the people as a whole. But because of my stupid fib, I'd turned myself into a racist, and I was forced to continue that charade unless I wanted to come clean. Which I didn't. Not in front of Ann.

"She gave me propaganda," I said.

"What did it say?" asked Ann. She wasn't just asking to be polite. I swear, heat was coming off her body. And who could blame her? I was acting like an idiot.

"I don't know," I told her. "It was in German."

"Then how do you know it was pro-Nazi?"

"Because there were pictures. Naked pictures. Of American women with German soldiers."

Ann turned to Jayne and addressed her as if I was no longer there. "You're right to talk to her about this. She needs a chance to defend herself."

Jayne nodded solemnly. "Will you go with me?"

"Of course," said Ann.

That did it. I might have been nationalistic, a habitual liar, and an occasional thief, but I was not going to be made second banana on top of it all. "Hold on—I'm the one Maureen gave the stuff to, so I should be the one to confront her."

"She has a point," said Jayne. "It would be easy for Maureen to deny everything if Rosie wasn't there."

Great. Not only were we visiting Maureen, but now I got the chance to accuse her of imaginary crimes. "Why don't we do it tomorrow after rehearsal?" I said.

"Because she expects me today," said Jayne. "It would be rude to just not show up."

Ann was watching me with the kind of care Churchill gave to pigeons roosting on the fire escape. I thought through my potential tactics, but all my possible ploys—playing sick, etc.—would give Ann an opening to go alone with Jayne. And I couldn't stand the thought of everything unraveling without me being there to defend myself.

I think Ann sensed this. She gave me a studied look that seemed to suggest that it was my move. "You don't need to go with us," I said. "Jayne and I can do this alone."

"I know you can," she said. "But I want to."

CHAPTER 18

Dead End

As we walked to the Christopher Street station, my mind filled with what was about to come to pass: Jayne was going to find out that Maureen was Billy's aunt. She was going to learn that the other man in the photograph—Johnny Levane—was dead. Hopefully, that would be everything, and my involvement in all of this would never come up.

Hopefully.

Despite my best attempts at dawdling, we arrived ten minutes early. Once again, the doorman wasn't there. I buzzed Maureen's apartment number from the alcove and waited for a response. Nothing.

"She not here," I said. "I guess we should go."

Jayne blocked me with her body. "We're early. She told me one o'clock."

Ann gave me that look again, the one that indicted me for the things she didn't even know I'd done.

"Why don't we wait in the lobby?" she suggested. "It would be more comfortable."

"You go ahead," I said. "I want to get some fresh air."

I lingered outside the front of the building, hoping I could catch Maureen and talk to her before she entered. Given how little she liked me, I doubted she would just agree to deceive Jayne for my benefit. If push came to shove, I could remind her that Lawrence Bentley didn't know her history and might not be too happy to learn he had a German working on his show.

Yeah, that was a great idea. Threaten her—that would endear me to her.

"Back again?" The woman in black who'd greeted me on my first visit appeared on the front stoop. She had her dog in one arm, a shopping bag in the other.

"Miss me?" I said.

"And who are you seeing today?"

"Maureen O'Reilly."

She clucked her tongue. I couldn't tell if it was an admonishment of me or Maureen. "Are you sure she wants to see you?"

"There are some people who look forward to the chance."

"Somehow I doubt that." She collected her mail, walked past me, and entered the building. I watched warily as she passed Jayne and Ann, but unlike me she didn't give them the third.

I willed the hands on my watch to move faster. Please let this be the first time in her life that Maureen is late, I prayed. Let there be an accident or a choreographic emergency that prevents her from showing up.

"Rosie?" said Jayne. "We think we should go up to her apartment. Maybe her buzzer's not working."

I joined them, and the three of us took the elevator up to the third floor and walked the hall until we reached apartment 312.

"This is awfully nice," said Jayne.

"I know. Good neighborhood. Great building. I don't know what the interiors are like, but I'm willing to bet they're a sight better than the Shaw House." I was babbling, but I couldn't help myself. Nerves had taken their hold and refused to let go.

"How does she afford something like this?" asked Jayne.

"She's a Broadway choreographer. Surely that pays okay."

Jayne looked up at the ceiling, where a chandelier cast its warm brilliance on the hall. "Maybe we need to get out of acting."

"If this is what causes you to change careers, I'm going to be very disappointed in you."

"Why?" said Ann.

"Huh?" I said.

"What's so bad about leaving acting?"

I waited to see if she was joking. She wasn't. "We love it for one. Don't you?"

Ann shrugged. "It seems to me that we're capable of a lot more. At least, I know I am."

So this was what Zelda had been talking about when she described Ann's nonchalant opinion of acting. If she was a spy, it didn't seem advisable to dog the very occupation you were pretending you belonged in, but who was I to judge the ways of those in espionage?

"What would you rather be doing?" I asked.

"Something that requires my brain would be nice."

She wasn't just hinky—she was rude. "So Jayne and I are idiots?"

"I didn't say that. I said I feel like theater doesn't challenge *me* intellectually. Perhaps you disagree. I'm sure there are things I enjoy that would bore you stiff."

Actually, I expected quite the opposite. I had a feeling that whatever Ann was really up to would excite me to death.

We knocked on Maureen's door and waited. There was no sound from within. My wristwatch said it was one o'clock on the nose. As the second hand began its journey around the face, I prayed in time to its jerky movements. *Please don't come home. Please don't come home. Please don't come home.*

"You did tell her you would meet her here, right?" asked Ann.

Jayne confirmed that she had. "Are you sure this is where she lives?" Ann asked me.

"Of course," I said, though I was cursing myself for not even thinking about taking them to the wrong address. I could've blamed my poorly developed, theater-loving brain for the error. I moved from Maureen's door to two Victorian chairs sitting by a window at the end of the hall. They were awkward things, designed for decoration not comfort, but I was tired of hovering in the hallway.

Another five minutes passed. The elevator dinged open and a portly man waddled his way to apartment 315. If he noticed us, he didn't show it.

"Maybe there was a problem at the theater," I said.

"They're not rehearsing today," said Ann. "Otherwise, I would be there."

Ah yes. My tiny actress brain had failed again. "Still, they might've called her in. You know how Lawrence is. He might've had a brainstorm overnight that demanded she rechoreograph the whole thing from top to tail."

"That's true," said Jayne. "I wouldn't put it past him."

My optimism was growing. We might escape this day without Maureen telling Jayne anything. Then I could grab her before rehearsal and beg her not to tell her any more than she'd already told me. Jayne was too heartbroken to take bad news, I'd say. Any more might push her over the edge.

"Why don't we go?" I said. "I'm tired of waiting and I hate to leave *you know who* alone all day again."

"You don't need to be secretive," said Ann. "I know about Al."

I shot Jayne a look. Was there anything she hadn't told Ann?

"We should leave a note," said Jayne. "I don't want her to think we didn't show."

"Why? She didn't," I said.

"It's rude, Rosie." Jayne dug into her handbag and produced a pencil, so gnawed it looked like a woodcarving. "Do you have paper?"

I passed her my pocketbook. "It's doubtful, but you can check if you want." She rummaged thorough my belongings and pulled out some subway tokens, a hairpin, and eighty-six cents in change.

"What's this?"

Oh, and the lock picks I'd stupidly kept in my purse since the day Mr. Smith was murdered.

"Just something I found," I said.

Ann came over to inspect the object. "Those look like lock picks."

"Really? Can't say I would know myself. How come you do?"

She didn't fall into my poorly thought out, poorly laid trap. "I've seen pictures before. Where did you get these?"

Indeed, where did I get them? "I found them on the subway the other day."

"Amazing what you'll find there," said Ann.

Jayne returned the picks to me, and I restored my purse to its previous state. Rather than accepting that the plan to leave a note had been aborted, Jayne marched over to apartment 315 and knocked on the door. The Waddler opened it, clearly shocked to find he had a visitor, to say nothing of his surprise that she was an attractive one. Jayne asked him for paper. While her voice was notoriously high and squeaky, his was so low that I couldn't hear it over the beating of my heart. Clearly it wasn't just my proximity to him that was the problem. Jayne leaned in until only an inch stood between her and the stranger and seemed to struggle to make sense of what he said.

"Oh, that would be wonderful. If you're sure it's okay?" She spoke a little too loudly, as though he were deaf or foreign, which I don't think he was. Perhaps she was just trying to compensate for his poor projection. He disappeared into his apartment, and Jayne waved us over.

"What's the wire?" I asked.

"He's the super. He says he's got to go into Maureen's apartment to fix a clogged sink. If we like, we can leave a note while he's in there."

He returned with the kind of key ring prison guards carried in films about women gone bad and spent the next four years trying to figure out which key went to her door. Finally, a click sounded, indicating he'd made the right choice. He pushed open the door and gestured us in.

It turned out we didn't need to leave a note. Maureen was home. And dead.

Jayne screamed as soon as she saw the body. Ann gasped and turned away. I was a little slower to react. The whole scene seemed so surreal, so theatrical that I had to get my bearings first.

Maureen was on the floor with her feet pointed toward the door. Her blouse had been pulled partially over her head, probably as a way of blindfolding her while the murderer did his deed. She'd been stabbed in the back—literally. Red hatch marks bisected her pale, still flesh.

Finally, it hit me. I started to feel woozy.

"Is she dead?" asked Jayne. Then more loudly, "IS SHE DEAD?" My pal was shaking me. Her hands squeezed my upper arms, and she looked like a child caught in a nightmare who desperately needed me to rouse her from sleep.

The super was still behind us. His mouth was moving, but his voice was so quiet and Jayne was so loud that I couldn't hear what he was saying.

Ann noticed the problem, too. "Calm down," she told Jayne. "It's all right."

But that wasn't working. Jayne wasn't seeing Maureen on the floor; she was seeing Billy. Her voice rose, becoming increasingly frantic. "Who would do this? Why? Why?" She was shaking and shivering, even though the room was, to my mind, much too warm.

"Everything will be okay," said Ann. She embraced Jayne and rubbed her upper arms.

With the room finally silent, I could hear the superintendent's voice. "The police. I'll call the police," he said.

With that bit of wisdom delivered, he left the room. Jayne wrestled herself free from Ann and once again approached the body. "Maybe she's not dead. Maybe she's just hurt," she said. She kept talking, the ideas getting increasingly absurd. Maybe she was sleeping. Maybe it was a game designed to punish us for being early. And if she's alive, maybe Billy is, too. Maybe, maybe, maybe. . .

Without thinking, I slapped her.

"What did you do that for?" said Ann.

"She's in shock," I said. My hand tingled. I'd left an imprint on Jayne's face.

"What on earth is going on in here?" Black Dress was at the door, with her small dog in her arms. Both of their faces wore the same, stern expression.

"Maureen is . . . it looks like someone . . ." I couldn't get the words out. Jayne backed into the wall with her hand clasped against her injured cheek. She was in shock, not that Maureen had died but that I had hit her. Why had I done that? I was no better than Tony.

Black Dress marched into the room and removed an umbrella from its stand by the door. As though she were about to participate in a duel, she poked Maureen in the side with it. The body didn't respond to the intrusion. "She's dead."

"Thanks," I said, "but I think we already figured that out."

The coppers arrived ten minutes later. Since my luck had run out before the day began, I wasn't surprised to discover that I knew the flatfoot assigned to the case. It was Lieutenant Schmidt, the same guy who'd mislabeled my boss's death a suicide six months before. Although I'd ultimately helped unravel the truth behind his demise, Schmidt had never given me my due, or an apology. And judging from the look on his face as he entered the room and discovered me near yet another corpse, he wasn't planning on remedying that any time soon.

"Well, well, well—Miss Rosie Winter. We meet again."

My teeth involuntarily gritted. "It sure looks that way."

"Who's the stiff?"

A great question, and one that I wished I knew the answer to. Sure, she was Maureen O'Reilly, but that was about as accurate as saying the guy Jayne was engaged to was Billy DeMille.

Fortunately, Black Dress decided to speak for me. "Her name was Maureen O'Reilly."

"And you're . . . ?" asked Schmidt.

"A neighbor." She ran her hand over the scruffy hound's head. "She was also a German."

I gawked at Black Dress. "How do you know that?"

"Please. The accent. The music. Besides, she confided in me."

Schmidt's eyebrow went up. He'd gained weight since I last saw him. While before he'd been as big as a planet, he was now headed toward becoming his own solar system. "What did she confide in you, Miss—?"

"Goldstein. Frieda Goldstein. Miss O'Reilly and I became friends over the years. She would watch Buttons for me when I visited my son." At the sound of his name, Buttons cocked his ear. "About a year ago, she told me she was actually a German citizen living here illegally."

I gawked at the woman; I couldn't help it. Would it have killed her to tell me this the first time we met?

"And why did she tell you that?" asked Schmidt.

"There had been a number of ne'er-do-wells hanging around the building. One of them was particularly gruff and made it clear that he didn't care for my"—she cleared her throat—"religion. I was mortified, and that's when she confessed to me that she was living here illegally and that some of these young men were kin of hers who had tracked her down, much to her dismay. She wanted me to know that she didn't share their views." She had to be talking about Billy and Johnny.

"Did you ever see these men again?" asked Schmidt.

"I don't know. They all look alike to me at that age."

Schmidt scribbled in his pad. If memory served, it was just as likely to contain a grocery list as actual information about this case.

"Anything else you can remember about them? Names?"

Oh, God. Here it comes. Even with Maureen dead, I wasn't safe. *Please don't let her remember their names,* I prayed.

Frieda put a finger to her mouth. "I'd have to think on it. It was an awfully long time ago."

I silently let out a long slow breath. I was safe.

He flicked his pencil toward Jayne, Ann, and me. "And how do you three fit into the scheme of things?"

"Maureen just cast us in a show. She was a choreographer," I said.

"So this was some kind of audition?"

"No. That was yesterday. We were just coming by for a visit today. To catch up. We did a show with her back in March, so we were kind of . . . friends." I didn't clarify Ann's involvement. I preferred to pretend she wasn't there.

"That's not how she treated you when you came by the other day," said Frieda.

"We played this kind of game," I said. "She'd act like she hated me and vice versa."

"So there was tension between the two of you?" asked Schmidt.

"Most definitely," said Frieda. "I saw you chase her down the block."

"There was no chasing. I mean, yes, I ran after her, but that was because I forgot to ask her something. And she definitely liked Jayne. Right, Jayne?"

Jayne glared at me. "I thought you said you ran into her on the street."

"I did. And then she invited me inside. I was hoping she'd have a lead on work, but she wasn't exactly open to the idea of casting me again."

"Then why did she cast you?"

How had things gotten to this point? My attempts to protect Jayne had spiraled into this mess of lies and deceit. I had been trying to do the right thing, really I had.

"You heard her at the audition—she felt sorry for me," I said.

"But why?"

My heart thumped again in my chest. I would have to tell Jayne everything. But not now. Not in front of Schmidt. "She knew I couldn't get other work."

"So when was the last time you saw Miss O'Reilly?" asked Schmidt.

"Yesterday," I said. "That's when she invited us to lunch."

Another mark on his notepad.

"Billy!" said Frieda. We all jumped, expecting to see that someone had entered the room. "The nephews. One of them was named Billy."

I felt weak at the knees. Surely Jayne wouldn't make the connection. There were a million Billys in the world.

"Are you sure?" asked Schmidt.

"Absolutely. Let's see, his last name wasn't German . . . it's on the tip of my tongue . . ."

No, my brain screamed. It's not on the tip of your tongue. It's not anywhere near you.

"No, I don't think I can remember it," she said.

For the second time, I exhaled until my knees felt weak. My victory was short-lived. The Waddler had joined us and took over where Frieda's memory had failed. "DeMille," he whispered. "He said his last name was DeMille."

CHAPTER 19

Ladies Don't Lie

We finished with Schmidt an hour later. The Waddler vouched for Jayne, Ann, and me, and Frieda helped verify when she'd seen us arrive, so technically we weren't suspects. At least not to Schmidt. I can't say that Jayne considered me innocent at that moment.

"Did you know that Maureen was Billy's aunt?" she asked as we left the building.

I wanted to say no. It was in my nature to keep lying. But the co-incidence would've been too big for Jayne to swallow, and then everything I'd ever said to her would be called into question. "Yes," I said.

We'd walked an entire block before she spoke to me again. "I don't understand why you didn't tell me."

"You told me you didn't want to know anymore, remember?"

"But this . . . this is huge. I would've wanted to know about this."

From a shop window, a stark sign in red, white, and blue announced WARNING ALIENS and went on to describe what would happen if those here illegally applied for military positions. Maureen must have passed that sign everyday. "How was I supposed to know?" I told Jayne. "You've been through a lot. I didn't want to take a chance that I'd make it worse."

She ignored my rationale. She didn't want emotions; she wanted facts. "So her address was the one in the letter?"

"Yeah."

"And you came to see her, even though I told you I didn't want to."

It was funny how shabby my reasoning became under someone else's scrutiny. Was I delusional, or was everyone else off their nut? "I thought you might want to know one day, and I was afraid if I didn't go see her now, the chance might be lost." I didn't bother to point out that I'd actually been right about that. "I was hoping she could tell me why Billy changed his name."

"And did she?"

I shook my head. "Not really. She said he was German—like she was—and that they both did it to avoid harassment."

"That could be the truth, couldn't it?" Yes, my brain screamed. Tell her that's all there is to the story. Let her believe exactly what Maureen wanted her to believe. But I couldn't. Maureen was dead now, and I had to believe her death was related to Billy and Johnny and Mr. Smith. And if Maureen was dead, there was a very good chance Jayne and I also were in danger.

Plus, the optimism in her voice was killing me. She deserved the truth. I had to give it to her.

"There's more," I said. "I went back to Yorkville. I thought I could get into the footlocker."

She nodded; things were coming together for her. "That's why you had the lock picks. What was in it?"

We paused underneath an awning near an A&P. I didn't want this conversation to carry where anyone else might hear it. It was bad enough that Ann was there, silently lording over my lies like a judge waiting to render her verdict. "I don't know. I couldn't get into the basement. Mr. Smith's keys were missing."

The A&P window display was an exhibit on how to make all those foods rationing had limited out of other items you might have in your pantry. Want apple pie but can't remember the last time you saw the fruit? Make a mock version out of Ritz crackers! "Maybe he's found the keys by now," said Jayne. "Let's go over there."

"That might be kind of hard," I said. "Because he's dead."

Poor Mr. Smith's fate came tumbling out of me, as did my fear that I had been followed home, while Jayne watched me in numb silence. I couldn't look at Ann. Who knew what she was thinking of me right then?

Jayne's face grew progressively redder. I'd seen her mad before—Tony could bring out the worst in her—but this was beyond my previous experience. I wouldn't have been surprised if steam came out of her ears, like a cartoon character.

"What else have you been keeping from me?" she asked.

I'd made it this far. I might as well tell her everything. "Candy translated the letters."

"But I told her not to."

There was no point in getting Candy in trouble, too. "I know, but she did them right away. Before you'd decided you didn't want her to."

Her eyes were tearing up, but it wasn't grief that was doing it. Clearly, this was rage working its magic. "I want them."

"I told her to get rid of them."

"YOU . . . DID . . . WHAT?!" She grabbed my arm and started pulling me uptown.

"Where are we going?"

"Where do you think? We're going to Jack's. Even if she did throw them out, I want to know what those letters said."

"Jayne—"

She raised her index finger and shoved it in my face. "No. No more excuses."

"I didn't want to make excuses. I wanted to apologize."

The crowd around us split to make their way past us. "I'm not that fragile, Rosie."

"Then you haven't seen what I've seen the last few months. Look: the more I dig, the less I like what I find. Two people have been murdered in the last week, and there's a good chance that that's only a sample of what's to come. If we pursue this—if that's what you really want to do—you have to consider the fact that you may not like what you find out about Billy."

"I have considered that."

"Okay then. I'll do whatever you want to do."

Her answer was to keep dragging me uptown. Ann caught up with us and began talking furiously with Jayne. At first, their words were lost to me, but soon it became clear that Jayne was wondering if it might be useful to go back and talk to Frieda Goldstein about what else she might know. To my surprise, Ann advised her against it.

"I don't trust that woman," she told Jayne. "After all, she's a Jew."

We arrived at Jack's parents' house and rang the bell. Vlasta greeted us with a tight grin that told of a day that hadn't been going well so far.

"Remember us?" I said.

She nodded, briefly, to acknowledge that we were familiar.

"We were hoping to see Candy Abbott. Is she here?"

Wordlessly, she stepped aside and gestured us into the foyer. She did the same disappearing act as before, silently slipping between the pocket doors. I braced myself for the arrival of Mamie. Surely one didn't pass the threshold of her house without seeing the grande dame.

"Rosie? Jayne? What a nice surprise," said Candy. Her eyes landed on Ann.

"I'm Jayne's roommate," she said, by way of introduction. *And her new best friend,* I silently added.

"How lovely to meet you. Why don't you come in?"

"We can't stay," I said.

"Do you still have the letters?" asked Jayne.

Candy looked at me to confirm that it was okay. I wished she hadn't. Jayne's rage didn't need the fuel.

"They're mine," said Jayne.

"Of course. Yes, I still have them," said Candy. We followed her into the parlor and sat while she went upstairs to retrieve the correspondence. A radio was playing somewhere on the first floor. It sounded like the Yankee game. Was the admiral home, or had Jack finally descended the stairs and joined the living?

"Here," said Candy when she'd returned. She handed Jayne the neatly assembled packets. "Why don't I get us something to drink?" She rang a small silver bell resting on a side table until Vlasta appeared at her side. "Could we have some tea, Vlasta? And maybe some sandwiches, if there are any left." The whole scene made me incredibly uncomfortable. It wasn't just being waited on by someone who probably made more in a year than I did that made me cringe; Candy was asserting control in the house, assuming her rightful place as the heir's wife.

"That's not necessary," I said.

"No, let me. I've been desperate for company. Jayne, why don't you go into the courtyard? That way you can read the letters in peace and let me know if you have any questions."

Jayne turned to Ann. "Would you come with me?"

Ann nodded and my heart broke a little. It wasn't just that I'd betrayed her trust; Jayne found it necessary to replace me completely.

Jayne and Ann moved to other end of the room, where French doors opened into a paved garden. There, in the pale afternoon light, she sat with her back to us and pored over the last link we had to Billy.

"They slipped my mind," said Candy. "I forgot they were still in my purse."

"It's fine," I said. "She deserves to see them."

"So what's new?"

"You mean other than this? Jayne and I got work." There was a time when I would've used a plural pronoun, not her name. But I'd lost that right, just as I'd lost it with Jack. She and I were no longer a "we." Now there was Jayne. And me. And Ann.

"Really? What's the show?" asked Candy.

Candy could be my new best friend. We could giggle over cocktails about the people we knew and the places we'd been and hold each other when the stuff of daily living got to be too much. But "best friend" wasn't just a role; it was a person, and that person was sitting outside hating me.

I brushed the thought aside and concentrated on Candy's question. "It's this new tribute to the armed forces called *Military Men*. It's only a two-week gig, and the parts aren't much more than stage dressing, but the show's kind of a big deal. It opens in a week."

"I think I read about it. Is this the piece that has all the enlisted men in it?"

"Yeah. Three hundred of them. It'll be like being back on Tulagi, only without the mosquitoes." Or the death.

Vlasta arrived with the refreshments on a silver tray. In addition to tea and cookies, there were tiny triangle-shaped sandwiches with their crusts removed. Candy thanked her and waited until she'd left the room before saying anything else.

"Ann seems nice," she said.

Sure, if you liked anti-Semites. "I don't know her very well."

"Where's she from?"

"New Jersey, I think." I glanced back at Jayne. Ann huddled next to her and periodically pointed at a letter and whispered something in a voice as quiet as a hummingbird wing. What was she saying? Was she pointing out all the things I should've told Jayne?

"No, I mean before then," said Candy. "I thought I caught a hint of an accent."

I shrugged. "If she's from somewhere else, she's not spilling."

I longed to tell Candy that I thought she was up to something, but I knew that my motive was questionable. It wasn't because I cared one way or the other anymore, I just wanted someone rational to team up with me in my dislike. Someone other than Ruby.

"How's Jack?" I asked.

Even though we'd been speaking in quiet voices, she lowered hers further. "The same. Maybe worse. I can't tell anymore."

"I heard the game in the other room."

She poured a cup of tea for me and passed it my way. "The admiral's home. He offered to take Jack to see the game in person, but there was no way he was going to do that. He couldn't even get him to come downstairs to listen to it in the same room."

"What about the prosthetic? Did he reschedule his appointment?" I dropped two sugar cubes into the murky brown liquid.

"Now Jack's saying it's silly to be fitted for one. Everyone knows he doesn't have a leg, so why pretend otherwise?"

Because it would improve his mobility and give him one less excuse to stay upstairs moping in his room?

I knew I should offer to go upstairs and say hello, but with the state Jayne had put me in, the last thing I could face was Jack.

"It's not a good day to see him," Candy said, as though she'd read my mind and wanted to give me an excuse so I wouldn't have to manufacture my own. "He's been drinking since noon."

God, that sounded nice. Good, drunk, oblivion. And yet as tempting as it was to fall half in the bag, the fact that Jack was doing it alone was beyond troubling. "Is that such a good idea?" I said.

"He's in a lot of pain. He says it helps. And, frankly, I don't feel right lecturing him about the one thing that's giving him relief." Candy looked anxiously toward Jayne. Her back was rigid, making it impossible to read what she was thinking. "So what's going on here? How'd she find out about the translations?"

I scooted closer to Candy. "I told her about them."

"Good for you."

"I didn't do it by choice. She found out I'd been to see Billy's aunt and demanded I tell her what else I'd been keeping from her."

Candy claimed a cookie and nibbled the edge of it. "How'd she find that out?"

"Maureen was the choreographer of *Military Men.*"

"Ah." Candy nodded. "But why did you say 'was'?"

"We found her body two hours ago. She'd been stabbed to death."

"Wow." She picked up a cup of tea and placed it in both of her hands, as though she needed the heat to warm them. "No offense, Rosie, but I would've led with that news." It was the first glimpse I'd seen of the Candy I knew back in the islands, the one with the sense of humor who was always ready with a wry quip or a shoulder to cry on. The girl who could've been a good friend, if she hadn't chosen to love the man I'd traveled across the world to find.

"Sorry," I said. "I'm kind of trying to forget about it."

"So who do they think did it?"

I shrugged, wanting to leave it at that, when Jayne reentered the room. "It could be the guy who wrote the letters, right?" she said.

"What?" I said.

"The killer. It could be Johnny Levane."

"Doubtful," said Candy. "Johnny's dead."

Jayne took a tentative step toward us. "How do you know that?"

"Rosie told me." And there it was, the last secret. The worst secret. Come to light.

"How do you know he's dead, Rosie?" said Jayne.

Because Tony killed him. "Actually, you know, too. Remember last spring when I held on to that article about the guy who was zotzed in the Broadway alley? That was Johnny Levane."

"Are you sure it's the same guy?"

I tried very hard to keep my voice steady, to give her no hint that there was anything else I was keeping from her. "Maureen confirmed it."

"Oh." Jayne's eyes dropped to the letters again. "Then I guess my next stop is New Jersey."

Jayne was silent most of the journey home. As the subway rumbled toward its destination, alternating between light and dark, I struggled to come up with a way to get her to talk to me. But the task seemed insurmountable. By the time we arrived at the Christopher Street station, I assumed that she wasn't going to be speaking to me ever again. In retrospect, that might've been preferable.

"What else have you kept from me?"

I wanted Ann to leave, but she insisted on hovering over us. "Nothing," I said. "That's everything."

"I never would've done that to you, you know."

"No, I don't know that. Right after I thought Jack died, I think you would've done anything to protect me from suffering anymore. I was only doing the same." The streets were so dark. Alone, I would've been terrified to walk them, but in the company I was in, I would've been grateful to be mugged just for the distraction.

"You don't have to worry anymore," said Jayne. "I can handle this."

"I know you can. I shouldn't have treated you like you were a child." I longed to touch her, but it felt like I'd given up that right as well. "We have a dark night coming up. We could go to Newark then."

"I'm going to New Jersey alone, Rosie."

Ann linked her arm in Jayne's. "I'll go with you."

"No. Thanks for the offer, Ann, but I don't need you."

I was relieved she'd refused her help. Even though it meant that I hadn't just destroyed her faith in me; I'd ruined her faith in everyone. "You can't do that," I said. "Someone killed Maureen and Mr. Smith. That can't be a coincidence, Jayne."

"He doesn't know who I am. I'll be perfectly safe."

"They know who *I* am. Or they might anyway. And if they know me, it's not hard to know you. Please, let me go with you," I said.

"No. I'm doing this on my own from here on out."

"Jayne, you can't. More to the point, you shouldn't."

She sighed and shook her head. "You don't understand. You don't get a say in this anymore."

CHAPTER 20

The Temperamental Journey

Jayne didn't go to New Jersey right away. Rehearsals took up too much time to make a jaunt to Newark. It only took a day before there was a new choreographer assigned to the show. He was suitably morose at our first meeting, referring to Maureen's death as "sudden and unexpected" but giving no indication that it was unnatural. As far as anyone else in the cast knew, it was a heart attack that felled her. Even the newspapers were cryptically hush-hush about what had happened. The issue of her ethnicity was never brought up, and eventually I realized that was the reason for all this secrecy. The police didn't want a panic. If a German woman, here illegally, had been murdered, that opened up the possibility that there were other Germans hiding on the fringe, too. Our public imagination was already wild with stories of saboteurs. They didn't want to run the risk of people eyeballing their neighbors and accusing them of something.

People like me.

"Here's the script," said Lawrence Bentley at our first rehearsal. "I have made ten copies available so that those of you in the chorus may read it on your own time, should you so choose." What a guy: ten scripts to share among three hundred people. That wasn't the paper shortage talking; that was greed. "I trust that if you read it, you will respect that it is for your eyes only. I am sharing a secret with you that I must insist you keep."

I was first in line to check out one of the precious, mammoth scripts. As soon as it was in my clutches, I took my place in the audience. All three hundred members of the cast were present, filling the seats the way an audience eventually would. At least, I hoped they would. There was nothing more embarrassing than giving a performance when the cast outnumbered the ticket sales.

But then this was a war show with a cast of hundreds of military personnel. There was no way it wouldn't sell.

Lawrence walked the stage as he talked about the production. The set was only half-constructed, but its most important element was already in place: a revolving platform that would allow the scenes to rapidly change. While one vignette was going on, the stagehands would be loading the props and set pieces on to the other half of the platform. The transition between scenes would involve nothing more than a motor turning the platform 180 degrees.

I flipped through the script out of boredom while Lawrence rattled on about how much must be accomplished in the next week with the bulk of the cast: costume fittings, completion of the set, testing the revolve, and, of course, instruction in the songs and limited dance moves. I was expecting the script to be amazing, though past experience with Lawrence's work should have taught me otherwise. I guess I assumed that if a man could be so changed by war, so could his writing. But the pap I looked at on the page was the same dialogue I'd seen in his other "great" works. His characters were wooden and idealized, his rhetoric so nationalistic he could've used stars to dot his *i*'s and bars to cross his *t*'s. Most offensively, the version of the war he showed wasn't what Jayne and I had witnessed firsthand. Oh some of the camaraderie was there, but when he tried to touch on the fear, the boredom, the way racism casually became a part of everyday life, he missed the mark again and again. I was embarrassed for him, more so because I knew his audience would eat it up as authentic. Surely the real military men in the show wouldn't let this go. I looked into the crowd, at the chiseled faces of our men in blue, khaki, and white, but none of them reflected my own hesitance. If they'd read the script, the thrill of doing theater rather than fighting war blinded them to its flaws. Or maybe they were just wiser than me and accepted that art would never be an accurate reflection of the real world, no matter how much we tried to make it so.

"This is terrible," I whispered to Jayne. "I wonder if he even talked to other soldiers when he was abroad."

Jayne made a gesture intended to shush me and kept her attention directed at the stage, where Bentley was talking about taking the show on tour if things went well with the New York run. It wasn't that she was particularly interested in touring; Jayne was, predictably, still giving me the cold shoulder.

I looked around the auditorium, hoping to find someone else to commiserate with. The blond soldier we'd met the day of the audition—Henry Bankshead—was sitting just behind me. As our eyes met, he held up a copy of the script that he'd checked out. Noting our shared taste in reading material, he clucked his tongue.

"Bad, huh?" I whispered.

"I wouldn't use it for toilet paper," he whispered back.

I grinned at my lap. At least I wasn't alone in my opinion.

As Lawrence's lecture came to an end, I gathered up my things and headed toward the door. Jayne was already gone, having decided she'd rather go home alone than in my company. As I followed the crowd, Henry fell in step beside me.

"So I see you went through the dance audition after all," I said.

He gave me an aw-shucks grin and moved his foot like he was

kicking a rock. "It seemed foolish not to. Chance of a lifetime and all that."

"You regret it now that you've read the script?"

"Naw, I'm just grateful I don't have any lines. You finish it?" He tucked his copy of the script beneath his arm.

"I'm not sure I want to. No wonder he only made ten copies."

"Still, a job's a job." He looked over the sea of heads working their way out of the auditorium. "Where's your friend?"

"Jayne? Already left, I guess."

"She sore at you?"

"Is it that obvious?"

"Sorry, ain't none of my business."

"No, it's fine. I did something stupid, and now I'm paying for it. She has every right to be mad."

"She doesn't strike me as the kind to hold a grudge."

"You'd be surprised."

At last we made it into the lobby. Henry still stuck by my side, and I was starting to feel weird about it. Was this just a conversation we were having, or was he flirting with me?

"How 'bout some dinner?" he said. He jerked a nod toward a group of privates lingering near the box office.

"I thought you boys would be heading downstairs to the Stage Door Canteen."

"After a day of rehearsal, I think the last thing any of us wants to do is dance for our supper. What do you say?"

Oh boy—he *was* flirting. "That's a swell idea, Henry, but I got to be honest with you: I'm only up for food, nothing else."

He frowned. "Oh, I didn't mean anything by it. Honest."

"Okay."

"I mean you're a swell girl and all, but you're not my type."

I raised an eyebrow. He wasn't my type, either, but who wants to be discounted like that? "And just what is your type?"

"Small, blonde, sweet."

So that was his game: butter up the best friend to win the

affection of the girl he really wants. If only he knew it was Ann he should be kowtowing to, not me. "Gee, I can't imagine where you'd find a girl like that." In the end, I decided to join him. It was a better option than going home and being ignored. We went to Schrafft's and shared a table with six other guys in the show, where I held court telling them about life as an actor, and they filled me in on what I was missing in the battlefield. For the first time since I'd been home, I felt at peace. They reminded me so much of the boys in Tulagi, and even though I knew half their tales were made up to impress, it felt important to sit there and lend them my ear.

As they began to leave one by one, Henry changed the topic from what was happening over there to the bombshell with the bright blonde hair. "She seeing someone?"

"Not at the moment. But she is getting over someone."

"He must be pretty special."

I almost told him about Billy, but something stopped me. Instead, it was Tony I named, describing the on-again, off-again nature of their relationship as though it had ended three days ago, not over three months before. Over a piece of pie, I poured out the story of their relationship and my belief that she deserved so much more. He listened in silence, his expression deepening minute by minute. While he seemed like a simple country bumpkin before, something stripped away as I told him about Tony B. Maybe it was fear. No one wants to know that competition for the girl you like packs a pistol.

"Wow. Sounds like he's not over her yet."

"No, but she's over him. That I can guarantee you." I realized that in omitting Billy, I was also omitting how wounded Jayne was. "But she's hurt. And a little gun-shy. Anyways, now might not be the best time to ask her out, especially if you're only in town for a short while."

He nodded solemnly. "No, she needs time. A heart doesn't heal quickly."

* * *

The next morning I got up intending to have a heart to heart with Jayne about why I'd done what I'd done. Instead of finding her in the dining room, I found Ann.

"Oh," I said, trying not to look disappointed. "What are you doing up at this hour?"

"Couldn't sleep," she said in a strange, halting way. Was Candy right? Did she have a hint of an accent?

"Me, too." I tried to read in Ann's face what Jayne had been telling her the last two days, but she was a master at keeping her emotions concealed. "So is Jayne joining you for breakfast?"

"No, she's already gone."

"Gone where?"

She shrugged and focused on putting margarine on her toast. Whoever had added the yellow dye to the stuff to make it look more like butter hadn't done a very good job. It was a shade too bright, making it hard to look directly at it.

I decided I would get nowhere by asking her questions, so I changed tactics. I snapped my fingers. "Right, she's headed for New Jersey today. I forgot about that."

"She told you?" Her eyebrow underscored the question, while her face confirmed that my guess had been correct.

At least that mystery was solved. Now I just needed to correctly guess the answers to any other questions I might have and I was home free. "She might be mad at me, but I am still her best friend. I wish she'd let me go with her, though."

"Me, too," said Ann.

"But no go, huh? She can be stubborn when she's got her mind set on something. I hope she finds what she's looking for." I paused, inviting her to comment. Instead, she took a bite of toast and chewed it much longer than should've been necessary. "Hopefully, it's just like Maureen told me, and all this name-change business was nothing more than a way for Billy to distance himself from his homeland. I can't imagine feeling that way, you know? Like you have to disguise who you are. It must've been really hard for him to deceive so many people."

She swallowed, and for a moment I was worried she would dig into another bite before responding to me. Fortunately, the bread was dry enough to necessitate a sip of coffee before she could proceed. "If he thought he was in danger, it was probably an easy decision to make. And if you're in trouble, you certainly wouldn't want to put anyone else at risk by sharing the truth with them."

That was a dimension to this whole thing that I hadn't considered: Billy wasn't necessarily lying for the sake of lying; he was protecting Jayne and anyone else he came in contact with. I hoped Ann had told her that. "But here's what I don't understand," I said. "What would he have to protect himself from?"

Another bite of toast. Given how laboriously she was chewing it, I was starting to think I'd rather skip breakfast than suffer through all that work for such little flavor. "The Alien Registration Act is pretty invasive. He may not have wanted to be under that kind of scrutiny."

"Yeah, but that's just an inconvenience, not a reason to change your whole identity."

"Maybe not to you." She was echoing Maureen's words that day I went to visit her. How could I ever understand what any of them were going through? I was an American, in my own country. The only thing I was ever looked down on for was my gender.

I expected our conversation was done. I cut a small piece of bread for myself and applied a thin layer of margarine, planning to take it and a second piece upstairs to share with Al. Before I could gather our meal, Ann spoke again. "There are other reasons. Perhaps he was hiding from someone."

"Like who?"

"Family? Billy and his cousin may have come to America thinking they would be safer here. When they found out they weren't, Billy decided to change his name and go his separate way, assuming they'd be better off apart than together." Her left thumb itched at the base of her ring finger.

"Maybe," I said. It certainly made sense. Billy was willing to tell Johnny where he was living and what his plan was, but he didn't want his cousin to visit, clearly because he was concerned someone might follow him there. And when it came time to leave, he didn't let Johnny know he was going. "I'm scared for her," I said. "Two people are dead. I don't want her to be next."

"Why do you only say two?"

"Billy wasn't exactly murdered. Trust me on this: we know the Japanese were behind that one."

"I mean by my count there've been three murders: Mr. Smith, Maureen, and Johnny."

I didn't realize how obviously I'd drawn a line between what happened to Johnny and everyone else. "Oh, well he died six months ago."

"That doesn't mean it couldn't be the same person who killed him."

I concentrated on buttering my bread. "I guess you're right."

She stared at me for a moment and I knew she was trying to figure out why I was still lying. Instead of giving her a reason, I got up and left the room.

CHAPTER 21

Follow Me

I needed to do something useful that day, something that wouldn't get me in any further trouble with Jayne. I decided the best use of my time would be to track down Vinnie Garvaggio and see if I could get an angle on his new mistress—if one existed—for Betty. While I couldn't expect Jayne to forgive me overnight, I had a feeling her attitude toward me might improve if I at least secured our freedom from future blacklisting.

While Al was hardly a fan of my scheme, he was easily persuaded to pony up Vinnie's potential location in exchange for my running a few errands for him, one of which involved buying him underwear. It was amazing what a man would do for a clean pair of shorts.

"What day is today?" he asked.

"Sunday."

"Then he's at church. Try Saint Patrick's; I hear he's a fan of

Cardinal Spellman's. He takes his ma to Mass in Manhattan and then out to lunch every Sunday, rain or shine. It's a good show for the feds. Makes him look like a respectable citizen."

"Won't Betty be with him?"

"Word is she can't stand the mother-in-law, so she worships closer to home." It was hard to picture Vinnie Garvaggio as a mama's boy. Harder still to imagine the woman who had birthed him. I'd just assumed she hadn't lived through the experience. "If Mass is already out, try Giradeli's. I hear he likes to get a table by the window."

"With all due respect, Al, the last place I'm going to find Vinnie with his mistress is at lunch with his mother."

Al poked me in the noggin with his index finger. "It's where he's going to go *after* lunch. After spending the morning with his ma telling him how to live his life, he ain't going to want to go home to Betty. If there's another dame on his menu, he's going to head over to her place."

"You can't be serious that this big-time mob boss is being be-rated by his mother."

"He's Italian, Catholic, and recently sprung from the joint. Trust me, his morning is going to be very unpleasant."

I sat in front of Rockefeller Center and stared across the street at Saint Patrick's Cathedral for an hour, waiting for services to end. I wasn't a churchgoing gal; the closest I got to religion was acci-dentally hearing one of the thrice-weekly concerts of sacred organ music at Grand Central. As I looked on the magnificent church, though, I thought I could feel some of the power others sought within its doors radiating off its tan stone and marble edifice. Maybe it was the building itself that inspired awe, in the same way the Empire State Building still managed to seem like a marvel, even though it was practically empty until the war started. You wanted to believe something that large was more than a mere building.

Al was right. For all of Vinnie's moral inconsistencies, he was a creature of habit, especially when it came to his mother. At eleven o'clock on the dot the two of them exited Saint Patrick's arm in arm. It wasn't affection that kept Vinnie clinging to the stooped, frail old woman but a desire to keep her from toppling over. She was tiny, even if she hadn't been next to her obese son. One of his meaty thighs exceeded the circumference of her waist; his arms were thicker than the tiny pins that propelled her. But despite the differences between them, she possessed a power I didn't normally attribute to the elderly. As they came down the church steps and onto the sidewalk, she rattled in a deep voice about all the wrongs that had recently been committed against her. When Vinnie tried to interrupt her to offer words of encouragement, she smacked his arm with a noise that carried all the way to me and barked that she wasn't done yet. Vinnie zipped his lip, and a look took hold of his face that I was pretty sure meant he was somewhere else mentally, hoping to make it through this morning on the strength of his imagination.

Al was right. If I had to spend a couple of hours listening to that, the last thing I'd want is to go straight home to my fishwife.

I blended into the church crowd and kept twenty feet behind Vinnie and Mrs. Garvaggio as they slowly made their way up the block to the restaurant that was their Sunday lunch tradition. As Al had predicted, they took a table at the front of the room, near the large glass window that faced the sidewalk. I stayed outside on a park bench and tried to look like I was reading the morning papers while I watched the two as if they were a zoo exhibit. Vinnie, the consummate gentleman, pulled out his mother's chair and slid a cardigan across her shoulders to keep her warm. Once settled into his own seat, he pulled out a cigar and went to light it, only to receive another slap on the arm. I couldn't hear what his mother said, but the message was clear: don't you dare smoke that disgusting thing in my presence.

It was a shame Betty and she didn't get on; they had a lot in common.

I longed to be inside with them, but there was no way I could afford to eat at a joint like that. The platters of food were heavy with homemade cavatelli, meatballs, a rich red sauce, and wedges of bread bespeckled with parsley. They washed down the chow with large glasses of red wine that captured the sun. Vinnie ate with vigor, hoping I'm sure to end the meal as quickly as possible. His mother picked at her food as she continued talking, so busy relaying whatever it was she needed to tell him that, to my eyes, her mouth never stopped moving.

Forty-five minutes later, the meal was completed. A car pulled up to the curb as they exited the building. Vinnie opened the door, helped his mother into the backseat, and bid her farewell with a kiss. As the car pulled away, his relief was palpable. He removed a handkerchief from his coat pocket and wiped at his brow. Then he deposited his cigar into his mouth, lit up, and took a long inhale that brought a smile to his face.

I had to feel for the guy. With both Betty and his ma browbeating him, he was constantly under siege. Normal mob violence had to feel like a vacation.

I expected him to turn up the block and walk away, but, instead, he joined me on the bench. I stiffened as his weight caused my seat to elevate. I was surprised I didn't go flying into the air, like a cartoon cat after a rhinoceros joined it on a seesaw.

I lifted the newspaper slightly to make sure my face wasn't visible. I doubted he would remember me, but I didn't want to take any chances.

"How's things?" he said. Was he talking to me? Had he recognized me? I lowered the paper just enough to see his face. "When will I learn not to ask her 'How's things'?" He was talking to himself. He shook his head and looked at his watch. So he wasn't just pausing on this bench; he was waiting for someone. "What time you got, doll?" he asked me.

"Twelve ten," I said through the paper. He thumped his fingers on the bench beside him. Even their movement was enough to make the bench vibrate. I cleared my throat and turned the page. Would his mistress get here already, so I get a slant and go underwear shopping for Al?

"When will people understand my time is valuable? Sheesh."

I pitied the woman coming to liaison with him. She clearly didn't realize that the clock was ticking. After all, Betty would be expecting Vinnie home soon.

His conversation stopped as he devoted his attention to devouring the cigar. Glaciers formed, shifted, and melted when at last he stood. "About time," he said.

"I'm so sorry. I went to the wrong restaurant," said a female voice.

"Where do you want to do this?"

"I know a place just around the corner that would be perfect."

"Lead the way."

I waited until I was certain that the two of them had their backs to me. Then I lowered the paper and set my gaze on Vinnie's competition.

She was tall and leggy, with a head full of frizzy hair. She handled heels like she'd been in them her whole life. Vinnie walked beside her like a favorite uncle; he kept his arms—and hands—to himself. Perhaps there was no room for error in this neighborhood. If you were stepping out on your wife, you better do it behind closed doors.

I decided to follow them to see if I could see the puss to match the stems. It didn't take long. They paused at an intersection, and Vinnie's companion turned to check her reflection as she passed a shop window. Her features seemed vaguely familiar. She was pretty but not overly so, certainly not such a looker that you'd risk your wife's ire to be seen with her. As she continued checking herself out in the glass, she turned to see the backs of her calves, where her seams zigzagged up the middle of her legs. She was one of the few women in New York who still had access to stockings. Had Vinnie gotten them for her? She took a second to straighten her seams, then proceeded across the street.

That's when I realized I had seen her before: that was the dame with the doves from the subway, the one whose sticky fingers had walked away with at least one man's wallet. But what was she doing with Vinnie?

I didn't bother to find out. Instead, I headed toward home to pick up Al's necessaries. The whole journey I tried to put together what I'd seen. Could it be a coincidence that the same petty thief I watched in action just a few days before was meeting up with Vinnie? Was this like a Dickens tale, and he had a marauding band of pickpockets working for him, not poor children but women dressed to the nines? Or had his bad taste in women simply brought him in contact with a broad who'd likely take him for all he was worth?

Since it was Sunday, I didn't have a lot of options for underwear shopping. I ended up on the Lower East Side on Hester Street, where the pavement market was doing booming business as housewives battled the crowds to stock up for the week. The sidewalk was thick with vendors hawking dresses, produce, jewelry, toys, and baked goods still hot from the oven. They were collecting things too: tin, fats, stockings, and anything else they thought the war might have use for. I found an old woman hovering over a cardboard box full of men's shorts and haggled with her—me in English, her in Yiddish—to get the price to my liking. Al hadn't told me his size, and so I had to guess at it with my hands. I end up with two pairs of shorts that set me back a quarter and a bagel I ate on the journey home.

I made it back to Shaw House just before five. I was exhausted from hoofing it everywhere and no longer able to ignore the pangs of hunger that the bread had only temporarily quelled. I'd picked up some deli for Al and me, and a little extra in case we could persuade Jayne to join us. If I was anything, I was an optimist.

As I entered the building, my mailbox caught my eye. Now that Jayne and I were residents again, we'd been given a single box to share. I was so out of the habit of looking at it that I hadn't both-

ered to check the door for days. A letter was waiting for me. No,
two letters were.

I ripped them open and sat on the parlor sofa.

Dear Rosie,

    I got your letter. Whitey's real name is Greg Buchanan. Rather
than putting you in touch with him, I think it would be faster if I
gave him your address and told him what's what.
    Tell Tony hey.

Gris

I eagerly exchanged Gris's brief note for the next letter, expecting to see that it was from Whitey. I was wrong.

Dear Rosie,

    It's taken me a while to get up the courage to write to you. I
hope you're still living at the same address. I know I'm probably
the last person you're expecting to hear from after all this time, but
I couldn't live with myself if I didn't write this letter. I know you
believe I betrayed you by giving up Jack's hiding place and you're
probably right, but there were a lot of factors involved that I don't
think I can explain to you in writing. Just believe me that I thought
I was doing the right thing for Jack—and you—at the time. Since
that day, not a moment has gone by that I haven't thought of you.
I'm not sure I deserved a second chance, and I'm pretty certain that
I've done nothing to earn a third, but if you could see it in your
heart to forgive me, I would be eternally grateful.

Peaches

I crumbled the letter to keep myself from reading it a second
time. Why now? I hadn't spoken to Peaches since July. Why the

need to unburden himself three months later? Had he gotten wind that I was trying to find a witness for Jack and thought the best way to stop that was to butter me up?

I tore the letter into multiple pieces and dumped it into a waste-basket. Peaches didn't deserve an answer, and he certainly hadn't earned the right to ruin another day for me.

I went up to Ruby's room and found Al sitting enraptured in front of the radio listening to some sudsy drama that had him reaching for a handkerchief.

"I got chow. And underwear," I announced, when the program came to its end. I kicked Churchill off the bed and spread out my offerings.

"You bring something for Ruby?"

"Er, no. But I did bring something for Jayne. Has she been by?"

He stacked salami on a piece of rye and dug a knife into a pot of mustard. "Nope."

That wasn't good. Things may not have gone very smoothly in Newark. I hated to think she was alone in her room dwelling on whatever new things she'd learned about Billy.

"I'll be back," I said. I crossed the hall and knocked on her door. After a moment, a voice invited me to enter.

Naturally, it wasn't Jayne. Ann was lying on her bed, flipping through *Scene Magazine*. For someone who reviled theater, she was sure fond of reading about it.

"Hiya," I said. "Jayne around?"

"She's not back yet."

"Oh." I wasn't sure how often the trains ran to Newark, so it wasn't inconceivable that she was still there. If she had even gone there. "When she does get home, will you let her know I popped by?"

All I got in response was the turn of a page. From the back of the slick, a fresh-faced young woman advised me that if I didn't hide my zipper placards, I ran the risk of turning off whichever young man I was trying to turn on.

I rejoined Al. "She's not back yet."

"You worried?"

That hadn't occurred to me. "Should I be?"

He shrugged. "Newark can be a rough town, more so for a dame going solo."

It was amazing how my opinions had changed in a year's time. I used to buy into the idea that a woman needed an escort wherever she went, but as the men vanished to fight in the war, I'd started thinking Jayne and I could take care of ourselves. I hated to think I'd been delusional.

"She's tough," I said. "She just came back from a war zone."

"Tough there ain't tough here."

She would be home soon, and all this would be moot. Al plucked two pieces of bread and some more salami from my offerings and set them aside.

"Midnight snack?" I asked.

"I figured Ruby might be hungry later."

I raised an eyebrow. "What's with all these considerations for Ruby? Is she making noise?"

"She brought me lunch; I thought I'd return the favor." He took a bite of his sandwich and chased a stubborn scrap of lettuce into his mouth. "She seemed kind of low today, 'bout still being out of work."

In all the flurry over Jayne and me securing our own employment, I'd neglected to come up with a solution for Ruby. And what would that be? She burned bridges with Lawrence, so casting her in his show was out of the question. She could survive on radio work, but she didn't want to. And thanks to me dropping her name at the locksmith's, making peace with Betty was out of the question. Maybe Zelda could get her work in a school tour.

"Can't you help her?" said Al.

"I'm trying." I made myself a cheese sandwich and coated it with mayonnaise.

"She asked me about the money again," said Al.

"What did you tell her?"

"What could I say? I gave her the same song and dance that she'd have it hand before I left. But she needs it now. I can tell."

"I know." I had to come clean with her. But now wasn't the time for that. Until Al was out and safely stashed somewhere else, I needed her to believe that she was invested in his safety. Otherwise, there was nothing to stop her from giving him the boot.

"How'd things go with Vinnie?" asked Al.

"Good. He was exactly where you said he would be."

"You catch him with his hand in the cookie jar?"

"Yes and no. I caught him with a dame, but they didn't look too friendly." I took a bite of my sandwich, but the waxy cheese did little to encourage me to keep eating.

"They were out in the open. You never know who's watching."

"That's what I was thinking, too, but it still seems . . . weird. I've seen this Hershey bar before. I watched her lift some guy's wallet on the subway the other day."

"Charming," he said through a mouthful of food. "You think she's playing him?"

"Maybe."

"Serves him right."

We finished eating, and I went through the odious task of emptying Al's temporary toilet and bringing him sufficient water to clean himself up and shave. Ruby arrived just as I was finishing, as though she'd been waiting until she knew she wouldn't be asked to help.

"We got food for you," said Al.

"Thank you," she said.

She removed her hat and gloves and sat stiffly on her vanity chair. I could see what Al was talking about. The day had worn her hard; a thousand unkindnesses creased her skin and left her makeup splotchy.

"How'd it go?" asked Al.

"Oh, you know," she said. Her eyes were wet. She picked up her sandwich and looked at it as though it wasn't bread and meat but two sponges with flypaper between them.

"You ever think about Hollywood?" said Al. "I bet you'd be the biggest star around."

Ruby smiled weakly. I hadn't seen such unconvincing acting since Joan Crawford tried to play pious in *Susan and God*. "I'm sure I'm too old. Who would want me?"

"You're twenty-five," I said as I unwrapped a pickle swathed in wax paper. "Don't go buying a plot yet."

Al ignored me and plowed forward with his praise of Ruby Priest. "You're a knockout. Better than half the women they're using now."

The tension was slowly starting to leave Ruby. After a day of being told no everywhere she went, she was being given something she desperately needed: hope.

"It's a thought anyway," she said before finally picking up her sandwich and taking a bite.

The three of us passed the bulk of the evening in quiet companionship. We played a few hands of poker, rewarding the winner with peanuts, then traded slicks back and forth while sharing pithy comments about the material they held. Al was fascinated by the stuff aimed at women. He'd never considered how complicated it was to be a dame, how many rules there were for what we wore, where we went, and who we saw.

"I don't get it," he said again and again. "Why do you put up with this stuff? Painting your faces, wearing girdles—it's dumb."

"Tell it to the rest of the men, would you?" I said.

"And what's this nonsense about changing what you have? Fake bosoms, fake eyelashes, fake hair color. We don't need all that."

I laughed and scanned an article on how to make my nail lacquer last longer. "We wouldn't do it if you didn't like it."

"You don't do it, do you, Ruby?" he said.

Before she could respond, I dissolved into hysterics. When I finally caught my breath, I asked him, "Are you off your nut?"

"What? She's a natural beauty."

I expected Ruby to claim that Al was right: all she possessed was what nature had given her, despite what the bottles atop her vanity implied, but she was enjoying a rare brush with honesty. "Some of us do more than others," she said, the implication being that I should be doing much more. "But Rosie's right. If a woman's attractive, it's doubtful it's because she was born that way."

He wasn't buying it. "What about Jayne?"

The grin spread to Ruby's eyes. "She's a platinum blonde, Al. Hair doesn't come that color."

"Really?"

"Yes, really," I piped up. His mention of Jayne reminded me that I hadn't checked on her for a while. Could she have made it up the stairs without our hearing her? "I'll be back," I told them.

As Ruby schooled Al on things only her hairdresser was privy to, I once again crossed the hall and knocked on Ann's door. She invited me to enter, though her voice made it clear she wasn't pleased by the interruption.

"She's still not back," she said before I could get out the question.

The clock on the bedside table said 10:30.

"Thanks," I said, and then I closed her door.

At midnight, we snuck Al into the bathroom and sat guard in the hallway while he performed his constitutional. The house was blissfully quiet, granting him an entire half hour of uninterrupted time. I expected Ruby to declare she was off to bed and to leave me alone on my watch, but she stayed with me, the two of us sitting side by side in the hall.

"You don't have to wait," I said.

"I don't mind."

I kind of did. With Ruby there, I felt forced to talk, when I wanted to ruminate on where Jayne was. "I know this is awfully inconvenient, having him stay here for so long." She hummed a response that didn't seem to deny how inconvenient the arrangement was. "I'm working on getting him out of here."

She wrapped her arms around her knees. "Doesn't he have family he can stay with? Or a girlfriend?"

"Family? Just an elderly mother with a foul temper. I think prison would be more enticing. And Al hasn't had a girlfriend for months." In fact, Al and I had officially met on a blind date orchestrated by Jayne and Tony. His love life, like his professional life, hadn't exactly been flourishing.

"Do you think he could give me an advance on the money?" said Ruby.

"His cash is pretty tied up right now. He's good for it, though."

At a quarter to one, we sneaked him back into the room, and with a yawn, he said he was down for the night. I was too wired to sleep, so I told them I'd go downstairs and wait for Jayne.

Night turned into morning. I dozed on and off despite my best efforts to remain awake. Jayne never appeared.

"What are you doing down here?" I awoke with a start at the sound of Belle's voice. She was standing over me with a look of concern on her face. "Did you and Ruby have a fight?"

"No. I must've fallen asleep down here."

"Don't let it happen again. You have a room for a reason."

I assured her it was a one-time deal and went upstairs. It was just after eight. Al was still flat on his back, wheezing away, with Churchill on his chest. Ruby was sprawled across her bed, leaving no room for me. I tried to push her limbs over to her side, but they had grown so heavy we could've used them to hold up the ceiling. I was considering the wisdom of lying on top of her until she moved of her own volition when the phone began to ring. In a panic, I dashed out of the room and answered it on the fourth ring.

"Shaw House," I said, out of breath.

"Rosie Winter, please."

Oh, God—it was about Jayne. This was some nurse calling to tell me she was in a hospital. What if she'd been shot like she had in Tulagi? Or worse, what if she was dead?

"This is she."

"Hi, Rosie. I didn't recognize your voice. It's Candy."

Slowly, I exhaled. "Little early for a call, isn't it?"

"Oh, I'm sorry. I wasn't thinking. How's Jayne?"

"Your guess is as good as mine. She went to Newark and no one's heard from her since."

"Wow. I'm sure she's fine." There was silence as she contemplated how ineffective that assurance was. "How about we get together for breakfast? My treat."

I thumped my fingers on the marble phone table. A free meal sounded attractive, as did a sympathetic ear. And if I left the Shaw House, Jayne was bound to turn up. But did I really want to depend on Candy Abbott to get me through this?

"Are you there, Rosie?"

"Yeah, breakfast would be great," I said. "Just tell me where."

CHAPTER 22

Before Breakfast

She invited me to the Plaza Hotel, a place I'd passed a thousand times but never dared to enter. She met me in the lobby, where the outfit I'd carefully chosen magically turned scuffed and thread-bare. I expected the red-clad doorman to ask me my purpose or to suggest that I use the service entrance in the future, but fortunately Candy's swift arrival robbed him of the opportunity to treat me as an interloper.

"Have you been here before?" she gushed as the host took us to our table.

"Loads of times," I said, as I tried very hard not to gawk. All around us were women who had so much money society had gifted them with multiple chins. Ice and oyster fruit dangled around their necks and from their ears, dazzling like the chandeliers that twin-kled above us. On their hands were gloves that had been altered so that the third finger had extra room to accommodate their enormous rings. Even though it was temperate outside, furs adorned shoulders and slinked across backs, begging to be petted. I resisted the urge as we were ushered to our table.

A waiter arrived before my derriere met its seat. He helped me the rest of the way into the chair, just in case I came from one of those places where sitting on furniture wasn't a common skill. For a brief moment, I was disappointed we weren't at the Waldorf. Legend had it the waiters there were obligated to tell their customers that there was absolutely nothing they couldn't serve you, and I was dying to test that claim.

"Good morning, ladies," said the waiter in an accent that might've been French. I had a feeling it was as manufactured as the gilt on the tabletops. "May I offer you a libation?"

I wanted a martini, but I asked for coffee and Candy got the same. Even before it landed on the table, I could tell it was real. The Plaza wasn't serving chicory, or if it was, it was a better form of the stuff than I was used to. Once we'd gotten it into our systems and ordered some chow, Candy leaned back in her chair and looked at me expectantly.

"I'm so glad you could come out."

"It was swell of you to ask."

"I'm just so alone here. Jack's family has been swell, but it's hard to talk to them, and I desperately need to talk to someone."

I felt ambushed. Here I was, hoping to talk about Jayne, and, instead, I was going to spend my morning hearing more details about Candy and Jack's relationship.

"I think he blames me," she said.

"For what?"

"His leg." Her eyes were rheumy. I felt in my pocket for a handkerchief and passed it her way. "He thinks it's my fault that he lost it."

"He said that?"

"Not exactly, but I can tell he's thinking it. I was sneaking him antibiotics. I knew the infection was bad, but I couldn't get enough medicine to stave it off."

I'd been there for that conversation in Tulagi, eavesdropping on the scene between them while envy ate a hole in my heart. "You did the best you could. You saved his life, Candy."

"But that's the thing; I think he's starting to wish I hadn't. I just don't know what to do anymore."

I hated being put in this position, but I also knew that if there was anyone who could give her advice on the whims of Jack Castlegate, it was me. "He's just feeling sorry for himself right now. It'll pass. He'll find a purpose again, and he'll be back to normal in no time."

"Are you sure?"

"Of course I am." The fact was, the few times I'd seen Jack down in the past were small potatoes compared to this. I had no idea if he'd recover from something as major as losing a leg, though there was one thing I was pretty sure would give him back his fire: getting his day in court.

"I've been having a heck of a time myself," I said, hoping she'd catch the swerve. "Jayne's been gone a day. I'm worried that something's happened to her."

Candy's forehead crinkled with concern. "Maybe she didn't find what she needed, so she decided to stay until she did."

"Where? And with what money? We're both flat right now."

"I'm sure she's fine, Rosie."

I shook my head. "Everyone keeps saying that, but I'm not buying it." An idea that had been lurking in the depths of my noodle finally made it to the surface. "Maybe I should go there?"

"Newark? That seems awfully silly. What probably happened is she got there and decided that she wanted some time away from everything. If she's as angry as you said, is it really so hard to think that she might have holed up in some Jersey hotel to give herself time to calm down?"

She'd done it before. One night, earlier that year, someone had threatened her out on the street. The guy had done a number on her—bashed in her lip, given her a black eye. Instead of coming home, she'd stayed at a flophouse hoping her face would heal so she wouldn't have to explain what had happened.

"She might do something like that," I said.

"Or maybe she actually made contact with one of Billy's relatives and is sitting down with them right now, trading stories." That seemed much less likely. And dangerously naïve. What we knew of Billy's real family was that at least two members of it had been murdered. "Give her another day," says Candy. "When's your next rehearsal?"

"This afternoon."

"Ten to one she'll show up for it. And if she doesn't . . ."

Then I was calling in the cavalry.

"How's that going anyway?" asked Candy.

"The show? So far, so good, I guess. The script is a dog, but it pays cold hard cash, so what's to complain about?"

"It's getting a lot of ink. I saw another article about it in yesterday's *Times.*"

"Lawrence Bentley is a master of self-promotion. He always has been."

"It's a pretty easy hit, though, isn't it? All those servicemen on stage—of course people are going to want to support them."

"Oh, it'll sell out all right." Our food arrived. As the silver domes were removed from the plates, a heavenly scent arose into the air and momentarily paralyzed me. I shook off the stupor and dug into a pile of lyonnaise potatoes. "The men are definitely the best part of the show," I said. "I wish they'd take Lawrence to task for the lousy script, but I'm pretty that'll never happen."

I was talking with my mouth full, but I didn't care. Never had I eaten anything quite this delectable, not at the officer's mess, not on the boat to the South Pacific. Military food, even the stuff made for the higher-ups, had nothing on rich people food.

"I have an idea," said Candy.

I was too busy gorging to notice the shift that had happened at the table.

"I think you're right about what you said, about Jack needing a purpose again."

Was she finally coming around about the trial? I hoped so. It would be a lot easier to convince Jack to fight if I had Candy on my side. And if she needed to believe the idea was hers, so be it. I wasn't greedy.

"So how can we do that?" I asked.

"By getting him into Lawrence Bentley's show."

The food lost its flavor. "You want to do what now?"

Candy mapped out her plan with her fork. "Get Jack a role in the show. Think about it, Rosie: he's an injured vet and an actor. Lawrence would be nuts not to use him."

I returned my cutlery to the table. "Yeah, but who's to say Jack's going to want to do it?"

"I know we can convince him."

We? When had we become a team? "I don't know, Candy. The script is pretty set. Lawrence isn't exactly the kind of guy to take casting and story advice from someone like me."

"What about Jayne? She's worked with him before, right?"

And he liked her. A lot. But that didn't mean she had any critical weight. "Trust me, she holds as much sway as I do. Plus, in case you forgot, she's missing right now."

"There's got to be someone you know who he'd listen to."

There was all right, but like a marionette, she came attached to all kinds of strings.

I agreed to look into the idea but didn't promise Candy anything. The truth was, it wasn't a terrible plan. Getting Jack on stage again was bound to help him get through this period of self-pity, and if Lawrence wrote him something meaty, it could do unbelievable things for Jack's career and Bentley's show. Having a talented actor who served in the military was boon enough, but to have one who lost a leg in the war show the true face of the sacrifices we were making would be electric. I got chills just picturing it.

By the time I returned to the Shaw House, I was completely sold on the idea.

"Any idea when Ruby's coming back?" I asked Al. He was listening to the radio again and seemed irritated that I was interrupting whatever program he'd been investing himself in.

"She went to get her hair done."

Great. Who knows when she'd be back from that. "Any sign of Jayne?"

This time I only got a shake of the head.

"Thanks," I said. "You've been a big help."

I went to Ann's room, but the sound behind the door made it clear she was still unconscious. I couldn't tell if she was alone in there or if Jayne was finally home and sleeping off her adventure, and the unyielding doorknob made it clear I wasn't going to be able to find out this information any time soon.

I returned to Ruby's room and lazed about with Al, until it was time for rehearsal. I went to the theater alone and divided my time between practicing dance steps and searching for Jayne. She never showed.

I was hoping to catch up with Ann and travel home with her, but she left the theater before I did. When I arrived home, I found Al asleep with a copy of *Captain Midnight* open across his chest. Rather than waking him to get the update on Jayne, I knocked on Ann's door and received her standard, tentative invitation to enter.

"Still not home," she said as soon as she saw it was me. "But she called."

My heart stopped. "You talked to her?"

"Nope. She rang during rehearsal. Doris Newcomer took the message." She passed me a slip of paper. In an unrecognizable hand, someone had written, "Ann: Jayne called, said to say she's fine. Doris."

"That's it? When is she coming back? What did she find?"

Ann pointed at the note. "You know what I know."

No, she knew more than I did. After all, Jayne had left the message for her, not me.

Just like the night before, Al fell asleep long before I did. I stayed in the room for a while, reading *Double Indemnity* and trying not to think about murder in real life. Why would someone have killed Maureen? Sure, she was a vicious choreographer and, apparently, a reluctant relative, but those weren't reasons to off someone. Of course, we didn't know anything about her, beyond the nationality she so carelessly cloaked. She could've had a dozen relationships with potentially murderous people and I'd have no way of knowing about them.

Somehow, I doubted that was the case. She struck me as the kind of person to keep to herself, if for no other reason than because she didn't want to elicit anyone's curiosity. Perhaps Frieda Goldstein would know more about her. She certainly seemed eager to spill details about Maureen once she was dead.

I resumed my roost in the parlor. I lost myself for a few hours in the tale of a woman who hired an insurance investigator to help her kill her husband. My eyes were starting to grow heavy when the door opened and Ruby appeared.

I didn't bother to hide my disappointment. It's not like she would've cared one way or another.

"Still no Jayne?" she asked.

"Still no Jayne. Where have you been?"

"Making a fool of myself, if you must know." Her hair reflected the dim light in the parlor the way a clean floor served as a mirror. A long, lazy strand fell across her face á la Veronica Lake.

"How'd you do that?"

She shrugged out of her jacket, catching the sleeve on her bracelet. I watched her struggle to free herself for a moment, then gave in and helped her detach the snag. "I went to Sardi's hoping if I put in a little face-time someone might take pity on me."

"I take it that didn't work?"

"I'm not even cut out for the casting couch anymore." She was beyond the point of tears. In fact, she'd grown so bitter I could taste it in the air, like coffee.

"Maybe you should take a break from auditioning for a while."

"No. I'm not done yet. I've still got another way out of this."

"I've got something that might cheer you up." I pulled a wad of bills out of my robe pocket and passed them her way. I'd decided that if I was going to broach the subject of Lawrence's play, I'd better sweeten her up with a little cash first. Provided, naturally, by Billy DeMille.

"What's this?"

"A down payment. From Al. He was able to get access to some cash today."

She counted the bills, and with a smile, slid them into her purse.

"When's the last time you talked to Lawrence?" I asked.

"Months ago. Didn't we already have this conversation?"

"I'm going somewhere different with it this time. Would you be willing to talk to him?"

"I'm not going to beg him for work." I waited for her to admit that he wouldn't give it to her if she did, but apparently that information was for Al's ears only.

"I'm not suggesting that you do. You already made it perfectly clear what you think of his new show."

Her eyes narrowed. "Then what do you want?"

I had to be careful how I sold this to her. It had to seem like her idea, or she would never make it happen. "I'm worried about his show, Ruby. I finally got a look at the script and the writing seems awfully . . . ungenuine."

"How is that surprising?"

She spoke the truth. "The show could be great. It's such a powerful concept, after all. But it's missing something."

"Let me guess—you in a bigger part?"

"Haha. No, I've thought about this long and hard. He's integrated all these soldier's voices, but he doesn't have a single vet on stage. That's the perspective the show needs."

Her fingers fluttered near her lips while she pondered this. "It's an interesting idea. Of course, it's a lot easier getting a bunch of real soldiers onstage playing themselves than it is to get an actor skilled enough to walk among them and show their aftermath. Plus, could you imagine the uproar if the only professional actor up there was one who hadn't seen combat?"

"I guess that could be a problem. It's a pity he couldn't find someone who served their time and knew their way around the stage. I'm sure Lawrence already dismissed the idea." I feigned a yawn, like the impossibility of the idea had worn me out. "Forget I said anything. I'm heading up."

I turned and started toward the stairs. I hadn't made it to the first landing when she stopped me. "What about Jack?"

"What about him?" I said.

"He's a talented actor and a disabled veteran. Hello?"

I smacked myself on the forehead. "I can't believe I didn't think of him." I let my enthusiasm die almost as quickly as it appeared. "Of course, I doubt he'd be willing to do it. There's no way we could ever get him to audition. Candy can't even get him to leave the house."

"I bet Jack would consider the idea if Lawrence came to him and suggested it."

"Do you think Lawrence would do that?"

"It's hard to say. If I proposed it to him, probably not, but if he thought the idea was his, I'm sure he could be quite enthusiastic about it."

They really were cut from the same cloth, weren't they?

"Do you think you could do that?" I said.

"I've done it before." She tapped a nail against a tooth. "And if I can help him improve his show, he might be willing to let bygones be bygones." A smile snaked across her mouth. I half expected to hear it rattle. "Let me work on it," she said.

CHAPTER 23

Her Family Tree:

Morning came and went and still no Jayne. I was reluctant to do anything. If she didn't show up to rehearsal again, I would have cause to panic, but right now I hadn't earned that right.

At least, that's what I told myself.

I bid Al farewell and headed uptown. I stopped at Maureen's building and lingered in the lobby, hoping Frieda would show. She must've sensed my presence because ten minutes after my arrival both she and her little dog were staring me down.

"What do you want now?"

"To talk to you," I said. "Heard any more from the coppers?"

"What business is it of yours?"

"I'm a friend of Maureen's. I want to know what happened to her."

"You didn't look like a friend the day you came to see her." She started to leave, and then seemed to second-guess herself. "No, I haven't heard from the police. And I'm sure I won't."

"How do you figure that?"

"She's German. Why do they care if one of them is gone?"

"But you care, don't you?"

"She was always nice to me. Kraut, Jap, or Wop, it didn't matter."

I was starting to like this broad. "How well did you know Maureen?"

"Well enough. She always gave me free tickets to whatever show she was working on."

"How long did you know her before she admitted she was German?"

"Not long—the accent was a dead giveaway. And even if I'd had my doubts, they would've vanished the minute her nephew showed up."

"You said that more than one nephew visited her, right?"

"That's correct."

"Was Billy the one who gave you a hard time? Or the other one?"

Her fingers pinched the air as if she was trying to pluck something from it. "I don't remember." She stroked Button's head. "Whoever he was, he was very ill tempered. Called me *Juden,* like it was something dirty. She seemed scared of him."

That sort of racist language was so contrary to everything we knew about Billy. Maybe Johnny was the one with the odd politics and the bad temper. "What did he look like?"

"Very young. Very German."

I wasn't sure I knew what that meant anymore. When I thought of Germans, I thought of blond, blue-eyed men with lantern jaws and broad shoulders. But that wasn't who Billy was, and while Maureen was sturdy enough to tend fields and milk cows, it was her accent that betrayed her, not her appearance.

"How often did the mean nephew come by?"

"I just remember the one time. She was surprised that he showed up, didn't think he knew where she lived."

But according to the letters, both men knew where their aunt lived. In fact, Johnny had encouraged Billy to contact him at her address. "Did you stick around for their conversation?"

"No. After he . . . after what he called me, I left."

She didn't strike me as the kind of woman to walk away and wash her hands of the whole thing. I would bet my left arm she'd lingered in the hallway and eavesdropped. "But you heard some of their conversation, right?"

She raised her head to show me the question was an affront. "They were speaking in German."

Of course they were. "Did you ask her about the conversation after he left?"

"She didn't want to talk about it. She apologized for how he talked to me, and that was that."

Except it wasn't that. I could read this woman faster than a dime novel. "What else?" I said.

"There were red marks on her neck. They looked like finger-prints."

"He tried to strangle her?"

"Maybe. I don't know."

"How long ago was this?"

She stared at the ceiling. "Last fall, maybe? I'm not sure. I remember the weather was nice enough to have the windows open. That was how I could hear them."

Last fall Billy would've already been in the military. But why would Johnny threaten his aunt? Could Frieda be confused about the relationship between Maureen and the man she saw? Could it have been someone other than Johnny? Or was I wrong that our Johnny was the man Tony murdered? Was it possible that Billy's cousin was still alive?

And if Johnny was the one who killed Maureen, why did he come see her this week? Had Jayne and my visit to Billy's prompted it? Was he still trying to track down where Billy was? Perhaps her death was a snap reaction after she told him Billy was dead.

I shivered. I now had Maureen's blood on my hands, too. "What else did you know about Maureen?"

"They were performers. Her whole family was involved in theater. Most of them were actors, except Maureen, of course."

"Her nephews, too?"

"I would assume so. That was how she made it sound. The family did quite well for themselves in Germany."

Billy an actor? No wonder he was drawn to Jayne. And no wonder he had no problems picking up an American accent and passing it as his own. "Did you tell the police all this?"

She waved me off. "Of course. They don't care. Let them tend to their own is what that Schmidt said. It's a German name, you know—Schmidt—and yet here he is discounting the whole race."

"That's Lieutenant Schmidt for you," I said. "The man just doesn't understand irony."

Jayne didn't show up for rehearsal again. I combed the crowd for her, my heart skipping a beat at the sight of each blond head, but every time it proved to be someone else. Fortunately, there were so many of us that no one noticed her absence. Except me and Henry Bankshead.

"Where's Jayne?" he asked me. "I didn't see her yesterday, either."

"She went to Newark."

"She back together with the boyfriend?"

"No, it's nothing like that. She went to visit family."

He fell back into line, and I watched as the lead actors came into the auditorium. Ann held her head high as she climbed on the stage. She didn't speak to the other performers. While the rest of them bumped elbows and flapped gums, she flipped through her script and stared into space. I had to fight the urge to track her eyes. What was she looking at? Stage rigging she could damage? Places to hide explosives? Or something even more nefarious?

For four hours we were herded like cattle. There was even less to our role than I had originally imagined. The boys enjoyed it, though. Being in a real theater, rehearsing for a real play, had to be loads more entertaining than waiting to go into battle. Their humor was infectious; try as I might to brood over Jayne's plight, I found myself smiling as they cracked jokes about which foot to lead with, whose voice was the most off-key, and how it was they could do so little and still get paid for it.

As rehearsal came to an end, I noticed we had an observer in the room: Ruby had joined us.

"Hey," I said as I went to gather my things to go home. My brief foray into high spirits plummeted. Why was she here? Had something happened to Jayne? "This is a nice surprise."

"Is it?" she said. "You knew I was coming." I raised an eyebrow, inviting her to go on. She led me out of the theater and onto Forty-fourth Street. "I went to see Lawrence this afternoon and told him my idea. Of course, I let him think it was his idea."

"Of course."

"I told him that you were rooming with me and had left the script lying around. I read it in an hour and spent all evening trying to figure out why it didn't work, when it hit me: the brutality of war was missing." As she told the story, she enacted it. It wasn't hard to understand why Lawrence had bought it hook, line, and sinker. For all of Ruby's superficiality, she was a marvelous actress. "He was thrilled that I'd finally taken an interest in his work. Rather than being insulted by my criticism, he suggested that it lacked the veteran's perspective. He said he knew the show was missing something, but he hadn't been able to articulate what it was until I showed up."

"That's great." So one thing in my life was going right. That was something to hold on to.

"Naturally, he was worried about getting a veteran who could play the part adequately."

"But you told him about Jack, right?"

Ruby nodded. "Oh yes. He remembered him, of course. He saw

his Hamlet years ago. When I told him what had happened to him, he was practically shaking, he was so excited."

Only Lawrence Bentley could view an amputated limb as an opportunity.

"He said that the scene had to be more than a mere monologue, though. It would be a homecoming: a young wife seeing for the first time the damage the war did to her husband. Of course, he needed the right actress to play the wife." How did I know Ruby would go to get Jack a job and end up getting one for herself? "He sat down at the typewriter and started writing immediately. We tossed scene ideas back and forth, though the piece practically wrote itself. By the time he was done, we were both crying."

"And?" I said, between gritted teeth.

"He insisted we call Jack right then. And so we did."

I suddenly knew how this story was going to turn out. She hadn't come to gloat; she needed someone to blame.

Ruby's features hardened. "He hung up on us."

"Maybe it was a bad connection."

"Oh, we called him back. Two more times. And each time he did it again. Until finally we gave up. I humiliated myself," said Ruby.

"It's a good idea."

"If it can't be executed properly, it's nothing. And now Lawrence is convinced that without Jack, he can't make it work."

I stopped walking. "The whole show?"

She smacked me on the upper arm. "Of course not the whole show." I tried not to show my relief. "*My* scene. This is exactly the break I've been waiting for. I need this."

"It's one little scene in a show with a cast of hundreds."

"It's all I have left." She was tearing up. "My career is over, Rosie."

We were starting to attract looks from passersby. I sheltered Ruby with my body, forcing her to hug the shop line. "You know that's not true."

"No, it is. I peaked too early and now I have nothing."

"This is a phase, that's all. A month from now, you won't even remember that there was a time when you weren't getting work. Besides: you despise Lawrence."

"But I don't." She sobbed. "He was right—I should've been more supportive of him."

Oh God, not this again. I found a handkerchief in my purse and passed it her way. "Okay, fine—what do you want me to do?"

"Talk to Jack. Convince him to do the show."

I would rather have hacked off my own leg. "I don't think I can, Ruby."

"I'll go with you. I'll show him the pages. When he reads them, I know he'll understand that he has to do this."

I agreed, not because I thought we would accomplish what Ruby wanted but because I owed it to her to do *something* to help her out.

We headed over to the Castlegates straightaway. Ruby was still emotional, but I had high hopes some fresh air and a little bit of legging it would bring her back to herself. The truth was, I didn't want her to come with me, but it was apparent that she wasn't going to give me an option. And besides, if I went without her and failed in my mission, she'd find a way to pin the failure on her absence. This way, she could at least see what we were up against.

"Park Avenue? Nice," she said, as we rounded the corner to Jack's parents' house. I'd never thought of Ruby as someone easily impressed. I just assumed she's been to every address, kept company with every sort of dignitary. But her wide eyes told a different story. She may have tasted this life, but she'd never had a substantial drink. And that, more than anything, was what she was craving. "Is he still engaged?" she asked.

I rolled my eyes. "Yes, Ruby."

We knocked and waited the requisite fifteen seconds before Vlasta greeted us. She seemed surprised to see me with a new face in tow, and I half-expected her to ask where my little blond friend was. After all, Jayne and I were a matched set. Or so I used to think. And what about Jayne? Was she missing my presence wherever she was or relishing the break?

"Hiya," I told Vlasta. "This is my friend, Ruby Priest. We were hoping to see Jack."

She motioned us into the foyer, then put out her palm to make it clear that we were to stay put while she inquired about whether or not our presence was welcome.

"Does she talk?" asked Ruby.

"Not so far."

She nodded, and I knew she was taking it all in as a character study. Ruby had impersonated a Polish maid at one point to get access to an otherwise off-limits apartment. If she'd met Vlasta before, she might've done a better job at it.

"You know, I never asked you: Why did you and Jack break up?" she said.

"Where to begin? He enlisted, I got mad, he thought I wasn't being supportive, just like his parents."

Ruby swallowed a laugh. "Amazing how much he and Lawrence have in common. I was told I was selfish for wanting him to stay home."

"From what you told me, it's not like Lawrence was seeing much action anyway."

"He's a coward at heart. I knew he wouldn't do well over there. He's precisely the sort of man whose personality would get him killed. But when I tried to explain that to him, he took it as a personal slight."

That sounded about right. Lawrence was the kind of fellow who enlisted on a bet or after a drinking binge. He wanted to add "soldier" to his résumé because it increased his authenticity as a writer, and he couldn't stand the idea of anyone questioning his playing that role with the sort of vigor I played sweet and demure.

"Are you still in love with Jack?" she asked me.

I wasn't prepared for the question, but that didn't stop me from answering it right away. "No," I said. "Absolutely not."

Mamie emerged from the parlor, her half-drained cocktail in hand. "What an unexpected surprise," she said, in a tone that made it clear that I was as welcome a visitor as a mole newly sprouted on her chin.

"I apologize for coming without calling first, but we wanted to talk to Jack as soon as possible."

Mamie didn't move. She was not impressed by my rationalization.

Ruby elbowed me and extended her arm toward Mamie. "I'm Ruby Priest." She fluttered her lashes and extended her vowels. Mamie ate it up like it was crème brûlée.

"How nice to meet you, dear. Wait a minute—I know you, don't I?"

"I don't know why you would," said Ruby.

Mamie tapped the air with her finger. "Aren't you an actress?"

"I've done a little theater. And radio. And a few print ads here and there."

"Of course! You were brilliant in *Goin' South*. We saw you in it last spring."

It took everything in me not to shout that I'd been in that show, too.

"And you also did some of that Bentley fellow's shows, didn't you?"

Ruby nodded, a blush coloring her face a flattering rose. How did she do that? If I tried to redden on command, I would've looked like a clown.

"That's what we wanted to talk to Jack about," said Ruby. Her eyes glanced toward the sitting room.

"How terribly rude of me. Please, won't you come in and make yourself at home? I'll have Vlasta make us some cocktails."

I assumed the invitation didn't include me, but I followed them into the room anyway. There, while gagging down gin, I listened to Ruby sell my plan, as though it were her plan, with such conviction that Mamie Castlegate believed *she* had conceived of the idea herself right at that moment.

"It's perfect," she declared with a rattle of ice. "He needs something like this."

"I tried talking to him on the phone this afternoon and he seemed . . . unconvinced," said Ruby.

"Really? I'm shocked." Mamie's eyes skirted me before returning to Ruby. "And you're the one who talked to him? Not her?"

I finished the gin, aftertaste be damned.

"No, it was me. And Lawrence," said Ruby. "I asked Rosie along tonight because I thought, with her and Jack's history, she might be more persuasive."

Mamie raised a penciled eyebrow. "Do you really think that's wise?"

"I figure it was worth a try."

"He's just had his pain pill, so he's going to be as agreeable as he gets these days. Don't keep him up long, though. He has his physical therapy tomorrow. He berated that poor girl to tears the last time."

Vlasta took us upstairs. I stopped her before she knocked on Jack's door and let her know we could proceed without her. Ruby was about to open the door when I put my hand on hers.

"Give me some time alone with him first," I said.

"Why on earth would I do that?"

"Because he already said no once to you. Trust me—this isn't going to go well if we both go in there guns-a-blazing."

She reluctantly agreed. In the dim light of the hallway, she surveyed her chipped nail varnish. I took a deep breath and knocked on Jack's door. He didn't respond, but then I didn't expect him to. He was beyond the point of pleasantries.

Fortunately, he was also beyond the point of locking doors. I opened his up and found him sitting by the fireplace, reading Lloyd Douglas's *The Robe*.

"Hiya," I said.

He barely offered me a glance in return. His own evening cocktail sat at half-mast at his side. I wondered if his doctor knew what he was washing his pills down with each night.

But then Candy said this was to be expected, right? Who was I to judge—I had two good legs.

"So things didn't go so well on my last visit," I said.

He turned a page and his finger traced a line of text he pretended he was reading.

"I'm sorry about what I said. I meant it, but I'm sorry if it hurt you."

Still no look my way. This was worse than a staring contest. I took my seat in the chair I'd previously christened as mine. The propaganda ads were still on the table. It looked like some new ones had been added to the mix.

"I see your collection has grown."

He peered over the top of the book. "A friend sent them a few days ago."

"Don't you wonder who the girls who posed for these are?" I said as I flipped through the pictures. "I mean, do you think they knew what they were being used for?"

"As long as they got paid, I'm sure they didn't care."

I shook my head as I surveyed one scantily-clad body after another. A series of them were completely nude. "Still, it would be hard to know you were being used to defeat the enemy, especially if they're not *your* enemy."

He didn't answer me. He wasn't in the mood for philosophical conversation. The same nude woman was depicted over and over again. Lying with her back to the camera. Sitting in a bubble-filled tub. They looked like movie stills, not posed photos. In fact, the model looked awfully familiar.

The last picture clearly showed her face. Ann. There was no doubt it was her. She was lying nude, her face a picture of manufactured ecstasy, as the text warned the viewer that if he stayed away too long because of the war, his wife might find other ways to entertain herself.

Spy, anti-Semite, and star of propaganda? What the hell was she up to?

"Can I borrow these?" I asked.

"Why?"

"Honestly? They look like a friend of mine, and it would be delicious to razz her about it."

"Do what you want. I don't care."

And he didn't. His voice was monotone, his actions so sparse you would think he was trying to survive on a limited number of calories each day. Was this what he had been like when he was hiding on Tulagi? "I'm not used to seeing you so defeated, Jack."

"You're not used to seeing me with only one leg, either."

"Technically, you've still got half a leg there." I regretted it the minute I said it. The old Jack could laugh at anything, but even he might've considered it too soon for humor.

"And your point is?"

"Maybe it's not so bad." I left my seat and approached the fire-place, wishing I had something to do with my hands. I should've brought my drink upstairs. "I can't pretend to know what you're going through. It must be awful. Worse than awful. And I know it doesn't help to sit here and remind you that things could be worse. But you've got a choice to make. Either you spend the rest of your days in this room letting the bitterness eat you alive or you move forward, changed, and see what you can make of all this."

He finally looked away from the book. "And what do you propose I make of it?"

I sat on the chair to the right of him. "A career, for one. I know you've been gone for a while, but there's not a lot of young actors to choose from anymore. Any director would be thrilled to work with you."

He came to life for a moment. Just in small degrees, but I could see the old fire stoking beneath the surface. "Have you really forgotten what this business is like? Come on, Rosie—don't be naïve. You've been at enough casting calls to know that all it takes is the wrong hair color for someone to pass you over." He pointed at his stump. "This isn't going to win me any friends."

"You don't know that. Lawrence Bentley is dying to work with you."

He slumped against the couch. "So that's what this is about. Let me guess: Candy put you up to this."

Just saying her name made her part of the conversation. I didn't want her there. This was between Jack and me. "She doesn't know I'm here."

"But this was her idea, wasn't it?"

"Actually, it was mine." I may have made a pledge not to lie to Jayne anymore, but I'd made no such promises to anyone else. "I'm in Bentley's show. Jayne and I both are. They're just chorus parts, but we read the script. For a man who served overseas, Lawrence Bentley wouldn't know the real war if it walked in here and awarded him the purple heart. The play is facile, juvenile, and offensive in ways that I didn't think were possible. And the worst part is, he's got all of these servicemen agreeing to perform in it who are so tickled over the idea of being onstage that they can't see how awful the piece is. Oh, it will succeed—don't get me wrong. This thing's going to sell out and add double matinees to handle the overflow. It'll probably tour, too, and that's the real crime, because he's going to take his sanitized vision of the war and pass it around until everyone believes that's what's happening over there."

"Why do you care?"

"Because I was there, Jack. I heard the bombs, I saw the carnage, I walked through hospital wards where the smell of rotting wounds was so bad you couldn't get it out of your head for days. I lost friends when ships were sunk and planes were downed, baby-faced boys who were so goddamned thrilled to get in on the action that they forgot that it meant they might die. I was a civilian and I still know what war is. It offends me to my very bones that a man who served can be so ignorant about the experience." I was surprised by my outburst. Oh, I could improvise with the best of them, but what shocked me was that I meant it.

"So what? You parade the one-legged vet across the stage and that somehow makes the war real?"

"No. It would take a lot more than that." I tossed him the script I'd brought along. It landed with a thud beside his leg. "Read this. You'll see what I'm talking about. He's got ideas—maybe some good ones, I don't know—about how to work you in. But I'm betting if you read this thing, you can come up with a better one. He knows the show needs you. He's convinced of it. You hold the power here. You tell him what you want your role to be, and I guarantee he'll make sure that's exactly what you get."

He picked up the script and folded it into a tube. "And if I don't do it?"

"Then you don't do it. Just read it and think about it. Please."

I stood up and turned to go. Ruby was going to be furious that I hadn't let her be part of the conversation, but I knew Jack. That was what killed me—as changed as he was, I still knew him.

"Why were you there, Rosie?" he asked.

I paused and watched him over my shoulder. "Where?"

"Tulagi."

I was so thrown off by the question that tears leaped to my eyes. What was wrong with me? "I went where the tour took me."

He traced the rim of his glass with his fingertip. "Did you ever wonder if I was there?"

I receded into the shadows, hoping he couldn't see how emotional the topic made me. "Sure. I mean I knew you were in the South Pacific. It's only natural that I wondered if you'd been on any of the islands I visited."

The finger tapped the tabletop—once, twice. He was trying to build momentum for something. "Did you ever think about looking for me?"

There were so many answers I could've chosen in that moment. I wanted to tell him the truth, but after Candy had worked so hard to protect him only to find herself holding the blame for what happened to him, it didn't seem right to let him know what my role had been. So what if I'd gone over there? I hadn't saved him.

"There was no reason to," I said. "I'd already been told that you were dead."

CHAPTER 24

Our American Cousin

I was wrong about Ruby being mad at me. It turned out she thought I'd played the whole thing off brilliantly.

"You put him in control. That was so much better than bullying him into it."

"I told you—I know him."

As we walked home from the Christopher Street station, she rambled on and on about how perfectly this was going to work out. Try as I might, I couldn't catch her excitement. My mind was still with Jack, wondering how he'd taken my parting words.

"Hello? Rosie?" said Ruby, as we rounded the corner for home.

"What'd you say?" I asked.

"I said, Should Lawrence call him tomorrow?"

"No. Wait for him to call Lawrence."

"But what if he doesn't?"

"He will," I said. "Trust me on that." Jack would spend the night reading the script. He'd take copious notes about everything that was wrong with it and possible fixes for each and every scene. He wouldn't go to sleep until dawn, and then he'd sleep heavy and long, roused when Vlasta was sent into the room to make sure he was still breathing. Only then would he call Lawrence Bentley, his tone so calm and in control that you would swear he had three legs rather than one and a half.

And while he did that, I'd find Jayne.

When we arrived at the house, the man was standing in front of the building again. I grabbed Ruby and pulled her back with me.

"What?!"

I shushed her with my hand. "That man. He's been here before. I think he's been following me." Oh, God—was this it? Was I going to die now? Had he found Jayne, done her in, and then come looking for me? "Let's go to Schrafft's," I told Ruby. "I'll buy you dinner."

"I want to go inside. I'm tired."

"But—"

"You're being silly, Rosie." She shook free of my touch and marched over to the building. Rather than going right inside, she stopped in front of the man, looked him in the eye, and asked, "What do you want? My friend says you've been following her."

"I'm looking for a woman." His voice was deep, his accent distinctly Queens.

"Then you're in the wrong neighborhood. Try Tony Pastor's Girlie Show. I hear some of those dames will give you more than a dance for a dime." She looked at me over her shoulder. "Come on, Rosie."

Without another word, Ruby marched into the building. I started after her, but our gentleman caller wasn't done with us yet. "Excuse me," he said as I passed him. "I'm with the FBI. I'm looking for this woman." He handed me a photo. It was Ann, no question about it. "She's called Heidi von Stromburg. Do you know her?"

So now I could add lying about her name to her list of crimes. And if Von Stromburg wasn't a Teutonic moniker, I was a monkey's uncle. "Yeah, I know her."

"Is she here?"

What an interesting day this was turning into. After weeks of feeling like I was the bad guy, I finally had the chance to put Ann in her place. "I couldn't tell you. She's in a show at the Forty-fourth Street theater. You can find her there most days."

He smiled, showing me a mouth that was missing all but the most essential of teeth. It seemed strange for a G-man, but who was I to judge? "Thanks," he said.

"Don't mention it."

Upstairs, we made drinks and Ruby relayed our meeting with Jack to Al. "She was brilliant, Al," she told him. I should've been happy for the compliment, especially considering the source, but there were too many things to worry about for celebration.

Al knew what was bothering me. How couldn't he? "Jayne's still not home," he said.

"How do you know?"

"Her roommate came by." So Ann *was* home. Pity I hadn't invited the fed to come inside and wait for her.

"You talked to Ann?" asked Ruby. Her face was a parody of horror. "She'll tell everyone you're here."

"Relax," I said. "Jayne told her days ago. So what did she want?"

"Just to let you know Jayne hadn't shown up."

For the first time in my life I lost my taste for booze. "It's been three days. I'm going out there."

"To Newark?" Al shook his head. "I don't think that's such a good idea. You don't know what's there."

"No, but I know who's there—Jayne. Something's wrong, Al. She missed two rehearsals. The girl I know doesn't do that. She's in trouble."

"She left a message," said Al.

"Over a day ago. And we don't know what shape she was in

when she left it. She could've had a gun to her head. Maybe she wasn't even the person who called."

"I'm going with you," said Al.

"No way. New Jersey is mob heaven. You'd be spotted before we stepped off the train."

That damped his fire. "Come on now—you can't go alone."

"Why not?" I said. "Jayne did."

"And look how good that turned out."

But we didn't know how it turned out yet. That was the problem.

I debated all night whether or not I was overreacting. What if Jayne was fine and just taking time to herself? How would she feel if I showed up and demanded she come home? But something didn't sit right with me. Every time we'd been to one of the locations Billy or his relatives lived at, someone died shortly thereafter. I couldn't take the chance that Jayne might be next.

I got up at eight and scavenged for breakfast in the dining room. I devoured dry toast and jam, washed it down with some weak coffee, and scanned the morning papers. There'd been a mysterious package found at Grand Central Station. Upon removing it, the porter had heard ticking noises coming from inside. Fearing it contained a bomb, the police had cordoned off the area where it was discovered. After twenty-four hours of ticking and no explosion, some brave rookie unwrapped the package and discovered an alarm clock.

Third Wake-Up Call for New York Transit, read the headline.

I went back up to the room and grabbed my purse, the original letters, and more of Billy's cush to fund my trip. I'd intended to take the photo of Johnny and Billy as well, but when I returned to its hiding place, it was gone. Jayne had been there before me.

I was headed back to the lobby when a voice stopped me. "Are you going to Newark?"

I looked toward the stairs and found Ann waiting for me. Black circles underscored her eyes. "What business is it of yours?"

"I'm her friend, too."

What was I doing? This was no time for a battle. "Yeah, I'm going. I should've gone days ago."

"I want to go with you."

"Don't you have rehearsal?" I asked.

She arched an eyebrow. "Don't you?"

"I have no lines. I'm one of three hundred. The only person who's going to miss me is the guy whose feet I keep stepping on."

"I'll call in sick," said Ann.

"I can go alone."

"I'm sure you can, but I'm not doing this for you."

There was no point in arguing with her. Even if I said no, it was a free country. She could climb on the train and get off at the same stop, and I couldn't say one word about it. And besides; if she was in Newark with me, whatever she was planning at the Forth-fourth Street theater was at least momentarily delayed. Perhaps I could use this trip to find out what she was really up to before the feds got their mitts on her.

We took the subway uptown and boarded a train bound for Newark at Penn Station. Neither of us was up for talking, so I spent much of the ride going through the letters we'd found with Billy's belongings. Jayne had apparently taken the translations with her, so all I had was the original German, which I squinted at as though I'd suddenly gained the power to read the foreign tongue.

"Are those the letters?" asked Ann.

"Yeah." I pointed to the return address on the top note. "This is where we're going."

She took the letter from me and stared at it. She wasn't looking at it the way I had—she was actually reading it.

"You read German?" I asked.

She quickly looked up. "No."

Sure, Heidi von Stromburg. Whatever you say.

I longed to whip the photos of her out of my purse and demand an explanation, but I knew it wasn't the right time. Once we knew Jayne was safe, I'd take care of her.

"So Jack's your ex-boyfriend?" she said.

"What?"

"The man whose house we went to."

Ah, so this was her game. I brought up a topic she didn't like, so she did the same to me. "It's his parents' house. And yes, we used to date."

"Jayne said he lost his leg."

I loved that word *lost* when it came to permanent physical change. You lost your sight, your hearing, your limbs—all of which implied you could one day get them back, if you just looked in the right place. And what of lost love? Would it be hiding there, too?

"It was amputated from the knee down," I said.

"And you're friends with his fiancée?"

That curious way she had of speaking suddenly grated on me. It was like she was thinking half of the conversation and only uttering aloud the conclusion she'd reached, which wasn't the part that interested me the most. "Sort of."

"That's big of you. Of both of you. I'm not sure I could be friendly with a woman who was going to marry someone I used to love."

The pictures sang to me from their hiding place. *Soon*, I told them. *Soon*. "What can I say? I'm a big girl."

We were silent for the rest of the trip.

We hailed a hack at the station and asked the driver to take us to the address on Johnny's letter. The town seemed dingy and un-kempt, the trees not bearing their blazing foliage like their cousins in Central Park so much as wilting into a sea of gray and dingy brown leaves. There was a smell in the air that wafted through the open cab window—something sour and rotten that made me wonder if we hadn't just rolled over the body of someone's long dead dog or cat.

We followed the route to South Orange and passed a large

cemetery lost in the shadows of ancient trees. We passed the
courthouse and a park, and then the Passaic River loomed before
us like a black licorice ribbon. At last we came to our destination
and the car groaned to a stop. Ann insisted on paying the driver.
While she tipped him, I stood idly by, feeling as if I had no purpose.

Johnny's address was a two-story gray A-frame house that
leaned, perilously, to the right. A porch hung off the front of it,
though its supports had been replaced by two-by-fours that looked
like they would soon need an upgrade. The stairs and floor were
half-rotten. Where there weren't holes, there was trash—cigarette
wrappers, beer bottles, crushed cans that should've been assembled
for a scrap drive but instead were spending their final days here,
helping no one. We climbed the porch slowly, mindful that each
step could send us plummeting to whatever horrors lay beneath
it. The glass on the front door had a spider web of cracks fanning
through it. Something had been thrown at it at some point, but not
hard enough to shatter. Small favor, that.

Two black mailboxes hung one on top of the other. Names
scrawled in pen and tacked up with yellowing tape declared who
the current residents were.

I took a chance and tried the door. It opened with ease.

"Now what?" Ann asked.

"We see if anyone's living here. If they are, we ask them about
Johnny Levane."

"And they're just going to tell us what they know?"

For a spy, she sure didn't seem to know how to get information
out of people. Maybe that's why they'd sent her here: she wasn't
very good at her job, but in a place unprepared for an enemy attack,
she'd do just fine.

"Just follow my lead," I said. "I'll probably come up with some out-
landish lie to get what we need. When I do, you follow suit. Got it?"

She nodded, though for the first time since we'd set out on this
trip, I could see worry in her eyes. I tried to not let it get to me.

The foyer was bisected by a rickety staircase. On the main floor were three doors, each marked with a number. From what I could see, there were three more doors on the second floor. I stood outside each of the first-floor apartments and listened for signs of life. Somewhere in the distance, a radio played. The tune sounded foreign, but it could've been that the closed doors were muffling the words.

I pointed toward the staircase, and Ann followed me upward. The music was louder here, the lyrics definitely German. My heart skipped a beat. Please let Jayne be here, I prayed. Please let her be safe. I knocked on the door and then took a step back and waited.

Someone muttered something from inside the apartment. The music was silenced. Footsteps rained across the floor like anvils falling from the sky. Metal skittered on metal until, at last, the door opened.

"What?" said a woman who couldn't have been more than five feet tall. A hump rose out of her back, forcing her to bend forward. She wore a dirty pink housedress whose neckline gave us too generous a view of her cleavage. Her breasts hung free and unencumbered.

"Good morning," I said. "I'm looking for my friend, Jayne Hamilton. I'm wondering if she might've been by here in the last day or two."

She looked at me dumbly; her mouth opened and a string of spittle threatened to connect it with the floor. I thought she might be deaf, so I started to repeat the question, but with a roll of her eyes she cut me off and said something in German.

I should've brought a picture. At least then I could've shown her who Jayne was and mimed what I wanted. Better yet, I should've brought Candy.

"Guten Morgan, Fräulein," said a voice behind me. I whirled around to see who had joined us, only to discover it was Ann speaking. She continued in German for a minute, gesturing, un-

doubtedly for my benefit, as she asked after Jayne. The woman's face brightened as the conversation continued. It didn't look like she got to talk to many people in her native tongue.

"Sendete Hans Sie?" she said in reply, one eyebrow raised in a manner that I could only describe as suspicious.

"Nein," said Ann. *"Wir sind Freunde von Johann's Vetter Wilhelm."*

The eyebrow relaxed. She gestured us forward and into her apartment. The main room was tiny—only about eight by five feet. A settee dominated the space, along with the radio we had heard earlier. She gestured for us to take a seat on the sofa and closed the door. I searched the room, hoping to find a sign of Jayne. There was one door leading off the main room and a small kitchen area, but from what I could see, the woman was alone.

She spoke to Ann in rapid-fire German. I ached to understand what she was saying. What if Ann hadn't explained things right? What if she frightened the woman and she refused to tell us where Jayne was? So far, though, there was no indication that the situation was anything but amicable. In fact, as the woman spoke, she retreated into the kitchen area and put on a kettle for tea.

When there was a pause in the conversation, Ann leaned toward me and translated. "Jayne was here," she said. "Two days ago. She showed Mrs. Gottlieb—that's her name—a photo of Billy and Johnny, and while she recognized Johnny, she didn't know what Jayne wanted. She ended up drawing her a map to Montgomery Hall, a place where she thought there might be people who could help Jayne."

In other words: English speakers. "So that's where we need to go," I said.

Ann shook her head. "Not yet. There's something she wants to show us. She said that when Johnny died, there were things left in his room. A man called Hans came by and asked to retrieve them, but she didn't like the look of him, so she told him she'd sold everything."

"Who's Hans?" I said.

"Your guess is as good as mine. But she wants us to know what was there."

I didn't understand. So the guy left behind some clothes and photos or something? Who cared? How was that going to help find Jayne? "All right," I said, reluctantly. "But then it's straight to Montgomery Hall."

Johnny's room had been on the first floor. Like Billy's, however, his possessions had been removed to the basement. That wasn't the only similarity. Just like his cousin, Johnny had left behind a locked trunk.

The basement was small and primitive. There were no divided sections for tenants down here. Rather, things were stored wherever they fit, whether they were related to one another or not. The concrete foundation had cracked in several places and then shifted, creating a dangerously uneven surface the old woman carefully navigated. It wasn't hard to imagine that in another year or two the entire house would topple over.

She paused at the building's south wall and pulled the cord to the overhead light to better illuminate the find. There sat a trunk exactly like Billy's, right down to the water damage that puckered its sides.

"Billy had one, too," I told Ann. "But we never found a key."

She said something to Mrs. Gottlieb, which I assumed was a translation of what I'd said. The woman muttered something, then turned and rummaged through a stack of precariously stacked boxes. She identified the one she wanted and carefully removed it from the center of the pile.

"She doesn't have a key, either," said Ann. "She said this is the rest of what he left."

I took the box from Mrs. Gottlieb and sat on the trunk to open it.

Inside were a small German Bible, a razor, and a photograph. I removed the framed picture so I could better see it. It was similar to the photo Billy had, the one of Johnny and him sitting on the stage. It looked like it had been taken just before or after the other shot.

Mrs. Gottlieb said something else. As she spoke, she wrung her hands, clearly articulating that she was uncomfortable with whatever she was saying. When she finished whatever it was she confessed, Ann responded in a gentle voice that I could tell was intended to reassure the old woman that she had done nothing wrong.

"There were clothes, too," said Ann. "She gave those to her son and his friends. I told her that was fine. It was very nice for her to hold on to what she found."

I wondered if there was money in Johnny's stash of diapers. If so, shame on young master Gottlieb for not taking better care of his ma.

A loud ringing interrupted the solitude of the basement. It was the phone. Mrs. Gottlieb gave us her apologies and rushed upstairs.

"So nothing new?" asked Ann.

"Not that I can tell. If only we could get into that trunk."

"Don't you have lock picks?"

I'd forgotten about those. "Yeah, but I don't have a clue how to use them."

She held out her hand.

"Seriously? How do you—"

She cut me off with a shake of her head. "I just do."

I fished out the picks and handed them to her in their velvet bag. She opened the case, found what she was looking for, and inserted the thin metal tools into the lock. All it took was a couple of sharp movements and we heard a click.

"Voila," said Ann. She lifted the lid. What was inside made us gasp.

Guns. Artillery. And some sort of material that looked like pounds of butter but which I was willing to bet was a kind of explosive. There were also floor plans lying flat against one side of the trunk to keep them from curling and maps lying against the other. I pulled an envelope from the top and was about to snatch the other papers when Ann grabbed my arm and pulled me away. "What the deuce?" I said.

"The trunk could be rigged. At the very least, the things inside it might be unstable. This whole place could go up, the three of us with it."

I took a step away from the trunk and begged my heart to beat a little more quietly. Mrs. Gottlieb stomped down the steps so loudly that I was surprised the clamor didn't trigger explosives a continent away.

Ann went to her and whispered something. The old woman stared at the trunk and put her hand to her neck. She was clearly in shock. All these months, she had no idea there was a bomb in her basement. And judging from the scratches on the lock, she'd probably banged on the trunk a time or two trying to open it herself.

Ann pulled her toward the stairs, and the two engaged in an extended conversation. I wished they would go somewhere else to talk, somewhere where there wasn't enough artillery to turn New Jersey into an island.

"Danke," said Ann, as the woman's words came to end. *"Wir tun, was vir können."*

Mrs. Gottlieb grabbed her hands and echoed her thanks, her eyes starting to tear up.

Slowly, because it was the only way to keep our feet quiet, we climbed back upstairs. I don't think I breathed again until we were outside.

In unison, we exhaled and sat on the porch steps. "Well?" I said.

"She thinks Johnny was a saboteur."

"A spy?" And that meant Billy was one, too. Two German boys sent here to wreak havoc. But neither of them had done what they'd been enlisted to do. Johnny I could understand—he'd been killed before he could act. But what about Billy? Had he joined the navy, hoping to do something bigger and more destructive, or had he changed his mind and escaped into the military as a way of putting his past behind him? "What was with all the gratitude at the end?" I asked.

"I told her we'd get rid of the trunk."

CHAPTER 25

The Prodigal Husband

Mrs. Gottlieb had given Ann directions to Montgomery Hall, which was only a few blocks away. It was still early, and since I was willing to bet the place was a bar, we kept our pace leisurely. Even the most hardened drinkers rarely started before noon.

As we walked, I opened the envelope and pulled out its contents. It was a typewritten page, presumably a list, though it was hard to tell for sure since it was also in German.

"Any ideas?" I asked Ann.

She took the paper and quickly parsed it. "It's a list of potential targets. Bridges, train stations, subways. Any place where servicemen gather. 'Avoid military bases,'" she read. "'Instead, seek out those places where large groups of soldiers may go for their evening entertainment. Bars. Dance halls. Theaters. Movie houses. Remember: the more soldiers you can target at once, the better.'"

"Oh God." I felt sick. It wasn't hard to imagine that what had been happening in Manhattan was related to this. The el fires, the subway stoppages, the package at the train station—these could all have been test runs for something bigger.

The possibility hadn't escaped Ann. "If Billy and Johnny are dead, there must be others out there. I wonder how many."

I knew of at least one more.

"So you speak and read German?" I said, after it became apparent that Ann wasn't going to acknowledge any of what had just happened.

"A little."

That was all she was going to give me. "And you know how to pick locks."

"I've always been mechanically inclined."

"And you don't like Jews."

"What are you getting at, Rosie?"

"That before we go looking for spies, maybe we should take a closer look at you."

She stumbled over a crack in the sidewalk. "You have saboteurs on the brain."

"Can you blame me? You're clearly not American. You're hiding floor plans in your closet, and Ann isn't your real name."

"You were in my closet?"

"I was getting something for Jayne. And don't change the subject. Why do I get the feeling that if we dig enough, we're going to find your own trunk full of explosives hidden in the Shaw House basement?"

"You're paranoid."

"Oh yeah?" I opened my pocketbook and fumbled through the contents until I arrived at the propaganda card bearing her picture. "Then how do you explain this?"

The sun was bright enough that for a moment I don't think she saw what I was offering her. Gradually, the image became clear. As it did, her eyes and mouth widened, until I was a little worried they'd been stretched beyond their capacity. "Where did you get that?"

"It doesn't matter. You know what it is, right? Enemy propaganda. The Germans put this out to upset our soldiers so they'd do worse in battle."

She took it from me and turned it over, looking for a sign of where it had come from. "Who else has seen it?"

"Here? The two of us. Over there? Who knows how many thousands of men."

Her hand reached behind her, looking for something to steady herself with. There wasn't anything handy. Once she realized that the only thing she could depend on for support was me, her knees gave way, and she buckled and fell to the ground.

"Ann?" I said, after a couple of minutes had passed. "Are you all right?"

She shook her head and continued staring at the picture. "How dare he?"

I crouched beside her. "Who are you talking about?"

"My husband."

It wasn't quite the revelation I'd been looking for. "You're married?"

She scratched at her empty ring finger. "I was. I don't know what I am now."

"You're really going to have to explain yourself."

She took a deep breath and stared up at the sky. "You're right. I'm not American. I'm Austrian. I was married to a powerful man there, so powerful he used to dine with Hitler, Goering, and Goebbels. I didn't like the changes I saw in him, so one day I left and came to America. As soon as I got here, I changed my name to make certain he could never find me."

"You expect me to believe that?"

"Is it any more far-fetched than your belief that I'm a saboteur?"

She had a point.

And the secretiveness, the accent, the lush wardrobe and jewelry collection certainly pointed to the life she described. Why had I been so quick to accuse her of something nefarious? Was it because the evidence had really been there, or because Jayne liked her and that was reason enough for me to suspect her?

But if she was innocent and on the run, who was the guy I'd talked to outside the Shaw House? He certainly wasn't FBI.

"Oh no," I murmured.

"What?"

"Er . . . nothing. So how did he get the pictures?"

"They're movie stills."

I'd been right about that. "You were in movies?"

She smiled sadly and nodded. "Yes. This one was called *Nadya's Loves* and caused quite a scandal back home. I appeared nude in it. Heinrich was furious with me. I suppose this was his way of enacting revenge. A sick little joke, huh?"

"Very. What do you think he'd do if he found you?"

"At best? Make me go home. At worst? Kill me. But that's not going to happen. I've been cautious."

That's what she thought. "What about the floor plans we found in the closet? What's that all about?"

She rolled her eyes. "They're not floor plans. They're schematics. It's for a device that jams radio frequencies."

I rose up on my haunches. "For what—to prevent us from contacting our ships?"

She let out a laugh that sounded like a squawk. "Are you mad? No, I was hoping to sell it to one of the big networks. Eventually. It still needs some refining. It's to keep higher-wattage stations from interfering with lower-wattage signals."

Even though we weren't moving, I was having a hard time following her. "So you stole these schematics from somebody?"

"Of course not. I invented this myself."

So that was why she listened to static, why she spent so many hours in front of the radio. "You invented something?"

"Not every actress is an idiot, you know." I wished I could count myself among them. "It was one of the reasons I left. I didn't want

Heinrich using what I created to help the Nazis. It was bad enough that *he* was helping them. He didn't have to make me complicit." She smacked the photo. "And yet he still found a way, didn't he?" She put her fingers to the corners of her eyes to stop her tears. "No, I won't let him win. He can punish me all he wants, but at least he hasn't found me."

Oh boy. "Yeah, about that. There's been some guy hanging around the Shaw House asking about you. And I kind of maybe let it slip that you live there." I prepared myself for a hit. If she'd punched me right then, I can't say I would've blamed her.

"You told him where I was?"

"He said he was with the FBI. And it's not like your behavior hasn't been a little suspicious."

She wobbled and I worried she was going to pass out. "Oh God. I can't go back there. He'll kill me if he finds me."

"He won't find you. I won't let him."

"How can you promise me that?"

"I've hidden someone from the mob for two weeks. If that doesn't speak to my skills, nothing will. Get up," I said, rising to my own feet. "Let's focus on Jayne for now. Once we find her, I'll fix things for you. Got it?"

We finished our journey to Montgomery Hall. It was going on eleven thirty and the doors were already open for business. It was part social hall, part bar. During the noon hour, workingmen came in for a shot, a beer, and some lunch. It was obviously not the kind of place most women broached during the daytime, which I thought might work to our advantage. We weren't hoping to blend in; we were hoping to find someone who was still standing out.

We entered the large, dark space and mapped out the territory. Pool tables took up part of the room, a dance floor and bandstand the other. A long bar with stools in front of it lined one wall; behind it dirty mirrors struggled to make the space seem twice as large. The air was a mix of floor cleaner, cigarette smoke, and bacon grease. A sign on the wall posted rules for Minutemen meetings. I wasn't sure if it was a relic of the revolutionary war or something else entirely.

We went to the bar, where a middle-aged man was spit-shining glasses, which I had to imagine were cleaner before he started his work. Even though I was sure he'd seen us arrive, he continued his task without acknowledging us. I would've been perturbed, but I was grateful for the respite. After the scene with Ann, I wasn't ready for another ugly confrontation quite yet.

"Excuse me," I said, when enough time had passed for his silence to go from rude to weird. "We were wondering if you could help us."

"What you need?" he asked in a gruff, vaguely Slavic voice. It was obvious his English wasn't steady, so I forgave him for the long drawn-out silence.

"We're looking for a friend," I said, even as I realized that the "we" in this question had become an "I." Ann had wandered off. "She's a small blond woman named Jayne Hamilton. She would've been here two nights ago maybe."

If he recognized the description, he didn't show it. He stared at me for a moment, and I realized that he hadn't understood a word I'd said. He held up a finger in the international sign for "just a minute" and disappeared into the back. I was starting to think he was dodging me when he reemerged with a second man in tow. This guy had twenty years on him and maybe two-hundred pounds. He was huge, but he was also familiar, though I couldn't place why.

"I'm Sal Balducci. What can I do for you?" He had a cigar in his mouth, which he removed long enough for the introduction before reinstalling it between his lips.

"I'm Rosie Winter. I'm looking for a friend of mine. A little blond woman about yay high." I demonstrated with my hand. "Her name's Jayne Hamilton."

"Tony's Jayne?" he said.

I wouldn't have been more surprised if he'd named her shoe size. "Yeah. I mean she was. They're not together anymore."

"No kidding? I'm Tony's uncle Sal."

So that was why he looked so familiar. "Have you seen her?"

"Not if she was here two nights ago, doll. I was in the city for the big A's opening."

"Oh."

"I think Adam was tending bar. He should be stumbling in here around two. You want to wait?"

"Sure. That'd be swell."

He nodded and ashed his cigar into a heavy crystal dish. "How come you think Jayne was here?"

I wasn't sure how much to tell him. After all, this was Tony's uncle. But at the same time, if Tony B. could keep tabs on us while we were in the South Pacific, maybe this guy would have the skills necessary to find her in Newark. I laid out my story from top to tail, leaving nothing out. As soon as I got to Johnny Levane's role, Sal got tense, so tense he bit his cigar right in half.

"I know 'im," he said, after I commented on his reaction. "Worthless scum who got what was coming to him. You drink?"

"Only when I'm thirsty."

"You thirsty?"

"Like a dog in the desert."

He poured me a whiskey, straight up. Even though it wasn't my drink of choice, and despite the early hour, I drank it down. I figured I'd earned it. "So why do you say he got what was coming to him?"

"They're Nazis, the lot of them. That's why."

I was glad Ann wasn't there. No doubt this statement would've triggered a second breakdown.

"The whole family are members of the Nazi party?" I asked.

"I can't speak to the great-greats, but the ones I met sure were. Back in '39 Tony and me and the other Minutemen ran them out of town, but that Johnny was a slick one. He came here a few years later pretending to be as American as you and me, but we figured out what was up."

"Wait a second—who are the Minutemen?"

"It's like a protection society here in Newark. A bunch of us fel-

lows got together when Bund members started messing with the
Jewish businesses. We became their protection."

"So it was like a mob thing? Helping out the Jews?"

He laughed and relit his cigar. "Mob, fighters, bootleggers—you
name it. This was Bund headquarters." He raised his arms to in-
dicate the building. "They used to call this whole block Hitler's
park. A bunch of us guys from the third ward bought it after we
ran those sons of bitches out. That's back when Tony was boxing,
so he was our best man—wasn't afraid to tangle with no one. That
kid grew courage the way the rest of us grew hair. Everyone was
afraid of him. He had a real talent for beating a man within an inch
of his life."

I tried to picture it. Tony was a boxer before he was the gangster
we'd grown to dread? And he made it his mission to protect New
Jersey Jews? How come Jayne hadn't mentioned that? It almost
made him . . . likable.

"Why the desire to help the Jews?" I asked.

"Why not? Who said it wouldn't one day be us the Krauts were
tangling with?"

It was funny how you could find good in the last place you'd
expect to see it. "So how did you figure out what was going on
with Johnny?"

He nodded and poured himself a finger in a dirty glass. "When
he got here, he started rooming at Gottlieb's place. She's the one
who told us he wasn't American. Oma Gottlieb is one dependable
broad. She didn't like the way the Bund was ruining it for the rest
of the Krauts, so every time anyone showed up in town smelling
like brautwurst, she went out of her way to make sure they were
on the up and up. Next thing you know, she's calling me, saying
he's getting weird letters in the mail—blank pieces of paper with no
return addresses."

"She was stealing his mail?"

"Not stealing. Looking. So one day Hans Richter comes back
to town."

"Who's Hans Richter?"

He raised an eyebrow. "You mean you don't know?" I shook my head. "Nastiest son of a bitch I ever met. Cousin of Johnny's, or so the story went. Tony took care of his pops years before and he wasn't too happy about it. Anyhow, he starts lurking around town, asking after Johnny."

"And you realized they knew each other?"

"And we asked Tony to come home and make sure Johnny knew we knew it, too, only by then the kid had cleared out. But he wasn't so good with the cleanup. He left behind all kinds of notes detailing plans to blow up train stations, bridges, theaters—you name it, he was gonna wreak it. And these weren't his plans. They came from the big boys back in Berlin."

"Yeah, I've seen some of the notes. He was a saboteur," I said.

He nodded. "So we go through his stuff and get a name and an address: some guy named Wilhelm living in Yorkville. So we figure that's where Johnny must be heading. Tony puts out the word on the street and our little problem gets taken care of."

I knew how that problem had been dealt with. "What about this Wilhelm guy? Did Tony take care of him too?"

"He'd cleared out of the apartment months before Tony had a chance. The landlord in Yorkville said he split in the night."

"And Hans?"

"Showed up once, trying to get into the Johnny's apartment, but Gottlieb put a stop to that fast. We ain't seen his ugly mug since."

I hoped that was the case, but I was starting to think that while Hans hadn't reappeared in Newark, he'd been in Manhattan, trying to find out where Billy was and stalking the women who'd visited his apartment. And when one of those women went to Newark, he followed her all the way there.

Ann finally emerged, her face scrubbed of makeup and showing every sign that she'd spent the last twenty minutes crying herself dry in the bathroom. She joined us, and Sal, sensing that the gal could use a little pick-me-up, poured her a drink. She drained it in a single gulp.

Once she'd composed herself, I caught her up to speed and then shared my theory with her and Sal.

"Why would Hans follow Jayne here?" said Ann. "It sounds like everyone in Newark has his number."

She was right. This was the last place Hans would willingly go. If he'd gotten his mitts on Jayne, it had to be *after* she left here.

A bell tinkled, indicating that someone had entered the bar. An older man with gray hair at his temples came in with a newspaper resting in the crook of his arm. As he passed the coatrack, he put his fedora on top. "Set me up, Sal. I've had a hell of a morning." He started when he saw us. "Afternoon, ladies."

"Adam, these are friends of Tony's girl, Jayne. They're wondering if you've seen her around."

He broke into a grin. "I've seen her all right. Couldn't miss that little spitfire if you tried."

"So she was here?" I asked.

"Yeah, two nights ago, asking about Johnny Levane. She sat at the bar, tossed a few back with me, and I told her all about those no-goodniks. I don't know what's what, but she didn't take it too well. I never seen someone her size drink like that. There was no way I was putting her on a train back to the city, so I put her in the backroom to sleep it off."

That was that—Jayne knew about Johnny and Tony. "Where is she?"

"I called Tony to come get her. Figured he could handle her a lot better than I could."

"So she's with him?" I asked.

"Last I checked."

I shared a look with Ann. I didn't know whether to laugh or cry. All these nights, all this worrying, and she was shacked up with Tony somewhere. "You have a number for him?"

He gestured me around the bar to where a phone sat by the bottles of booze. "I'll do you one better. I'll dial."

After two quick rings, a voice came on the line. I asked to speak to Jayne, and my message was relayed to a number of male speakers. After an eternity, her sleepy voice came on the line. "Hello?"

"So you're alive."

"Rosie?"

"The one and only."

"Did you get my message?"

"Ann did. Two days ago."

"I called this morning, too. Where are you?"

"In Newark. At Sal's bar."

"Oh." Her voice was small, like she was waiting for me to throw an ing-bing. I wasn't going to give her one.

"Ann and I wanted to make sure you're safe," I said.

"I am. Tony's given me a quiet place to gather my thoughts."

"Good." She was silent for a beat. In the pause I thought I could hear a thousand things: the clinking of dice . . . ice clattering in a glass . . . a faucet on full blast . . . a radio playing "In the Mood." What I couldn't hear was how learning about Johnny and Billy had affected her these last two days. But I knew it was there in the silences.

"I'll be home tomorrow," she said.

"Good," I whispered. "We miss you."

CHAPTER 26

The Awful Truth

Sal made us lunch, and over a delicious feast of bar food we told Adam and him about Ann's problems. There was a method to my madness: I knew Ann couldn't go back to the Shaw House, and I couldn't think of a safer place for her to stay than with kin of Tony's. After all, they'd run the Nazis out of Newark. How hard would it be to keep away an Austrian and his lackeys?

But they surprised me. For two men who'd been hospitable since our arrival, they didn't leap at the chance to hide out a woman on the run.

"We could pay," I said. How much of Billy's money was left? It wasn't going to last forever, not with the way I was spending it. And no matter how much I claimed I'd repay every cent, there was no way I was going to be able to afford to.

But Ann was in this fix because of me. I had to help her.

"How much?" asked Sal.

"Five bucks a day. But you've got to feed her for that and give her a place to take a bath." It was highway robbery. For three dollars a day she could stay at the Barbizon and have a private shower. But the Barbizon didn't provide the security that Sal and Adam could.

The two men looked at each other. "That could work," said Sal.

"She could stay here for a few days," said Adam. "There's a cot in the back, where Jayne slept, and a shower downstairs."

"Or Gottlieb might take her in," said Sal. "She could use the dough."

"About that," I said. "What would you two charge to remove some explosives from her basement?"

"What are we talking?" asked Sal.

"Your guess is good as mine. They're explosives. They blow things up. Maybe a lot of things."

"This we'll do for free," said Adam. "Who knows when we might be able to get our hands on something like that again."

So all was well that ended well. Ann was safe from her ex, Gottlieb was free of the trunk, and Jayne was safe and sound with Tony.

Oh, and I'd just given the mob enough explosives to blow up the city, should they choose to do so.

"And then what?" said Ann.

"Huh?" I said.

"I stay in Newark for a few days, and then where do I go?"

I pulled an idea out of the air. "How about Hollywood? And once you get settled, I'll send you your schematics and anything else you need."

"I don't know anyone there."

"You don't need to. Lockheed is there—you can talk to them about your radio thing. You'll have a pick of acting jobs. And I'll give you a few names." I grabbed a matchbook and scribbled down three monikers that were safe for her to look up. Vinnie Garvaggio's ex-girlfriend Gloria was out there now. And so were Violet

Lancaster and Kay Thorpe, two dames that owed me a hell of a favor after certain events in Tulagi.

"Call them," I told Ann. "Tell them you know Jayne and me and you also know everything we know. If you say it right, they'll bend over backward for you. Trust me."

I got Ann settled into her new living quarters, and then Sal drove me to the station. By the time I got home, it was dark. As I approached the Shaw House, the man who'd claimed he was FBI popped out of the shadows and stopped me in his path.

"You seen Heidi?"

"No. Did you try the theater like I told you?"

"Yeah, she was a no-show today."

"Then I can't help you."

I started past him. He grabbed my arm and stopped me. "Did you tip her off?"

I rolled my eyes. "Yeah. Because even though I can't stand the dame, and I'm the one who told you she was here, I thought I'd help her out. Now buzz off before I change my mind and tell her you're on her tail." The front door to the house flew open, and Ruby came down the stairs.

"There you are!"

"I missed you, too," I said. "What's up?"

"Vinnie Garvaggio's men were here today looking for Al."

"What?"

Her voice rose an octave. This wasn't Ruby overreacting; she was genuinely hysterical. "They refused to leave until Belle threatened to call the cops."

A pain shot across my forehead. I should've been here to keep him safe. If I hadn't gone to Newark, I could've helped him. "Where is he now?"

"Same place he's always been. But he can't stay here. If they've been here once, they'll be back again."

I paused at the mailboxes and retrieved my loot. I had V-mail waiting for me. "How on earth did they find out he was here?"

Something changed in Ruby's face. "I'm not sure. But from the way they were talking, it was clear that whoever told them was someone they trusted."

As I followed her upstairs, her words continued ringing in my head. Ruby had been behaving very erratically lately, one minute demanding to know when she was getting paid and the next insisting Al stay. Did she know something? It was possible she'd put two and two together and figured out that if Jayne and I were having trouble getting work, too, it might be for some common reason. Clearly Al had said something to her about Vinnie being after him. She may have realized that if Vinnie was behind the work ban, all she had to do was give him Al to get in his good graces. After all, she told me she had a way around her unemployment before our little scheme with Lawrence had materialized. Perhaps this was what she was referring to.

"Did you find Jayne?" she asked.

"Yeah, she's safe. The whole thing was a big misunderstanding." Right before we reached her room, I stopped her. "What did you mean the other day when you said you knew how to get yourself work?"

"Huh?"

"The other night when I talked to you about Lawrence's script. You said you still had a plan."

"Oh that. I figured I'd move to Hollywood or maybe Chicago."

"With what money?"

"Al said he'd help me out."

Could it be true? Could the down-on-his-luck mobster who stared daggers at me every time I invented another sum of money to give to Ruby really have started bribing her on his own? I couldn't see it. Al felt bad for Ruby. He wouldn't willingly string her along.

"You know, don't you?" I said.

"Know what?"

"About Vinnie Garvaggio."

"I know he's after Al."

"Cut the crap, Ruby. Vinnie Garvaggio—he produced *Goin' South*." No recognition. "Fat guy, fond of cigars and pinstripes."

"That's the same guy? What about him?"

"He's the reason you're not working. The reason why all of us weren't working." While she sat there continuing to play dumb, I told her about the meat racket, Al's role, and why the three of us had been hard-up for jobs. I didn't bother to mention Betty Garvaggio. Or the fact that I'd made things worse by dropping Ruby's name when it was more convenient to use than my own.

"You knew this all along?" she snapped.

"Don't tell me you didn't. You called Garvaggio and told him where Al was, didn't you?"

"Are you goofy? I just told you I didn't know who Garvaggio was beyond his connection to Al. And might I remind you, I'm the reason he's still safe."

"So?"

"Wow." She looked away, as though she was hoping to find the words she wanted to say lingering just to the left of her. "I really thought things had changed between us. You came home so different from the South Pacific. I convinced myself the new you was capable of being a friend."

"Me changed? You're the one who climbed on the cross and became a martyr. I'm the same person I always was."

"If you say so." She put her hand on her doorknob and turned back to me. "I didn't tell Vinnie, Rosie. Believe it or not, I like Al, even if you lied to get him to stay here. And even more amazingly, I'm pretty sure he likes me."

I stared at her for a moment, wondering when it was that the world had gone topsy-turvy. I used to be a good person who told the truth and helped my friends. I didn't steal; I didn't scheme; I didn't relish other people's misfortune. Had the war changed me, or was this the course I'd always been set for?

* * *

I left Ruby and went down to the lobby with my mail in hand.
There on the sofa I opened the letter, half-expecting to see another
plea for forgiveness from Peaches.

The letter was from Whitey. You could've knocked me over with
a feather.

Dear Rosie,

*Gris passed your message on to me. Of course I remember what I
told you I'd do for you-know-who (can't be too cautious, you know).
And yes, my word is good. I'll do whatever I can to help you. I have
leave coming up at the end of the year. You say the word, and I'll
show up wherever I'm needed to help him out.*

The letter closed with his contact information in the States. I
could send details there, he said, and he'd make sure his folks sent
them on. And I wouldn't have to worry about writing in code.

I wanted to call Jack then and there, but I knew it was too late.
I'd show him the letter the next day at rehearsal.

At ten thirty a car pulled up out front, and voices sounded outside the building. I went to the front window and peeked around
the blackout blinds. It was a mob car, long and sleek, sitting at the
curb. Jayne was home!

I went to the door to greet her, but another figure appeared.
Vinnie Garvaggio's frizzy-haired girlfriend opened the front door,
entered the foyer, and started at the sight of me.

"Oh, hi," she said.

"Hiya," I said back.

"I don't believe we've met. I'm Doris Newcomer."

This was Doris, the former magician's assistant Zelda was rooming with? "I'm Rosie Winter."

"Right. I've been hoping our paths would cross. Zelda talks
about you all the time."

I looked over her shoulder and watched as the car pulled away.

I knew that car. It was the same one that had idled at the curb the first night Al came to see me. "Take any wallets lately?"

"Excuse me?"

"I saw you on the subway last week picking pockets. I guess you were looking for money to give to the church."

She flashed me her pearly whites. "I think you have me confused with someone else."

"And then, two days ago, I saw you meeting up with Vinnie Garvaggio outside Giradeli's."

"I'm not sure where you're going with—"

"Neither am I, but let me take a shot in the dark. Zelda said the work dried up after your boss accused you of stealing. So what? You lift a few wallets, and when that's not enough to keep you flush, you decide to use the one piece of useful information Zelda let slip and offer to sell it to Vinnie Garvaggio. You told him Al was here, didn't you?"

Her careful attempt to plead ignorance faded away. "You're good. I heard you use to work for a private dick."

"I'll bet Vinnie wasn't too happy when his men couldn't get in here today."

She tucked her frizzy red hair behind her ears. "I may have had to offer something else to make the price worth his time."

"You do know he's married, right?"

"I know it, but I think he's forgotten." She pushed past me. "It's been swell meeting you, Rosie, but I'm beat. Let's catch up another time, okay?"

"Absolutely," I said. "I can't wait."

I fell asleep on the parlor sofa and woke up to the sound of the door opening. This time it was exactly who I was hoping it would be.

Jayne looked great. For the first time in months, she was well rested. Even though her face was scrubbed clean, her natural color was back, making it look like she'd spent hours in the makeup chair. "You weren't waiting up for me, were you?"

"Not exactly. Ruby and I had a tiff, and I thought I should spend some time down here while she cooled off."

She lowered an overnight bag to the floor. "What happened?"

"I underestimated her."

She gave me a wry little smile. "You're making a habit of that."

"So I'm starting to realize."

She joined me on the couch and kicked off her shoes. She had a new dress on, no doubt a gift from Tony.

"How's Tony?"

Her smile brightened. "Okay."

"And you?"

"I'm all right."

"So Adam told you about Johnny and Billy?"

She nodded.

"And Tony?" Another nod. "How are you doing with all this?"

"I don't know. Billy and Johnny—they were bad people, weren't they?"

"Johnny maybe, but I'm not so sure about Billy. You read the letters. It sounds to me that Billy backed out of whatever Hans wanted them to do. Leaving everything in Yorkville, joining the navy—these were his ways of making a fresh start. Away from the reach of his family." Johnny may have wanted to do the same, but we'll never know for sure. "So how'd Tony react to the news that you were engaged to Johnny's cousin?"

She intertwined her fingers. "I didn't exactly tell him."

"No?"

The irony of her lying to Tony after raging at me for doing the same wasn't lost on her. "I almost did. There he was, telling me everything about his life back in Newark, but I felt like it might make things worse for him. If I told him that Billy and I were engaged, I had to tell him that the Billy I knew was a good person. And if I did that, then maybe he'd think Johnny—"

"Didn't deserve to die." I wanted to chime in that my own rationales for lying had been equally complicated, but it didn't seem like the time. "So why did you tell him you were in Newark?"

"I said I was trying to find out what happened to Maureen."

Poor Maureen. First, she gets murdered because of us, and now she was a convenient distraction to drag out when we didn't want someone to know our true motivations.

"I got some things from Johnny's apartment," I said. "Some of Billy's letters and another copy of the photograph of Johnny and him. I thought you might want them."

"Thanks. Is Ann upstairs?"

"Not exactly. She's gone." I caught her up to speed on everything that had happened to Ann, including my ratting her out. "I told Sal and Adam we'd pay for her upkeep, but I don't exactly have the cash."

"It's okay. We'll use Billy's money."

"About that—I kind of already have been." Since confessions seemed to be the order of the day, I told her about the money I'd been pilfering to help Ruby, tail Betty, travel to Newark, and pay for the other incidentals that had cropped up in the last week. She wasn't mad. Now that she knew the money was Billy's payment for being a saboteur, she no longer felt like she needed to protect it. But I still felt like a louse.

"Don't worry about it, Rosie. Give Ruby whatever else you promised her, and tell Al we'll put him up at a hotel until the heat dies down." There she was, fixing all the messes I'd made without breaking a sweat. "Anything else you need to tell me?"

"I'm sorry that I can't touch anything without screwing it up."

"What are you talking about?"

All my rationales for my behavior over the last few weeks came pouring out of me. "When Billy died, all I wanted to do was to help you, the way you'd helped me. But for some reason I couldn't stomach the idea of someone else helping you, too. No matter what I do, it becomes about me, doesn't it? I can't do anything that isn't completely selfish."

She rubbed my back. How could she stand to touch me? "I don't think that's true."

"How couldn't it be? Look how much of a mess I've made of things."

She screwed up her face as she thought hard on the question. I expected her to reach the same conclusion I had—there was no other way to interpret my behavior—but she didn't. "I probably would've felt the same way in your shoes. Anyone would've. Of course, you didn't want someone else to step in and help me. After all, look what happened with Jack."

"Wow." Why couldn't I have seen it? I wanted to save Jayne and Al because I hadn't been able to save Jack. And because I'd convinced myself that if I didn't, I'd lose them just like I lost him.

"You don't have to worry anymore. I'm not going anywhere, Rosie."

"I know."

She squeezed my hand. "Do you really know that?"

I thought for a long time before responding. We could never fully trust that we were safe. There would always be dangers lurking outside, threatening to destroy us. But, for the moment, I truly believed the beast was at bay. "I do now."

I went to Ruby's room, hoping to apologize to her for my accusations, but she and Al were both asleep when I arrived. I spent the night on the edge of her bed, figuring my discomfort was penance for the way I'd treated her. Jayne and I went to rehearsal early the next day to kowtow for our absences. It turned out to be unnecessary. Henry, our soldier friend, seemed to be the only one who missed us. Being two of three hundred meant that we weren't just irrelevant when we were on stage—we were ignored off it, too.

Of course, who had time to worry about us when, for the second day in a row, the female lead was a no show?

The second he realized Ann wasn't there, Lawrence berated the stage manager at a volume better suited for the gladiator ring. Even though they'd left the room for their conversation, the timbre of his words shook the auditorium walls.

A few months before I might've tried to weasel my way into Ann's part. But while my faith had been restored in the show, I didn't think I wanted the responsibility of being up front and center. There was something so reassuring about being part of the anonymous chorus, where I was one of many whose voices and movements would work together to create a whole. There would be other chances for me to shine, but for right now I wanted to stay where I was.

I grabbed Ruby and pulled her to the side.

"Look, I know you're still sore at me, and you have every reason to be, but I think you should know Ann left town and she's not coming back. If I were you, I'd find a quiet place to break the news to Lawrence and perhaps suggest that there's no reason why your newly created character couldn't also step into Ann's role. The beauty of his thinly written female parts is that they're virtually interchangeable."

Ruby's mouth dropped open as she considered the idea. Then she followed the sounds of Lawrence's unraveling and disappeared. We didn't see her again for almost an hour. When she returned, Lawrence calmly announced a last-minute casting change that made Ruby his new female lead.

She was back, thank God.

Of course, she wasn't the only one. Jack was there, too. After a painful rehearsal of the chorus parts, Lawrence introduced the new scene he had added to the play and let Jack and Ruby take the stage.

Ruby was right—it was a good scene. An actor's scene. Full of meaty dialogue and silent subtext-filled looks, their brief ten minutes on stage became the heart of the show. Surrounded by all those moments of tomfoolery embodied by the other serviceman, Jack's starkly realistic portrayal of a vet who comes home to show his wife what he couldn't bear to write to her about made you realize that all the inconveniences we were facing on the home front were nothing compared to what these men were sacrificing on our behalf. And Ruby, who'd wrongly guessed a few weeks before that her talent had left her, was in full bloom here. At once grief-stricken and self-centered, she took you to that painful moment when a young wife realizes all her dreams for the future have to change in such a way that you felt like you were living it. As I watched the distance between them diminish, as they shifted from strangers to renewed lovers, I was overcome with emotion. When had Jack gotten so damn talented?

After rehearsal ended, I told Jayne I'd meet her at home and went off in search of Jack. He hobbled by on a pair of crutches, traveling with a cluster of other sailors. I called out to him, and he stopped and turned my way.

"Can I talk to you for a minute?" I said.

He shrugged, which I took as agreement. His new friends murmured their good-byes and continued on their way.

"You were great in rehearsal," I said.

"You saw that?"

"Everyone did. It's exactly what the show needed."

"I suppose I have you to thank for that."

"Ruby actually. She's the one who convinced Lawrence."

"But you're the one who convinced her."

I didn't admit my culpability. "Shall we sit?"

"Fine by me."

We planted ourselves on a bench facing the road. Whitey's letter was in my pocketbook and I was itching to pull it out and hand it to Jack, but it felt like it was too soon. For the first time since he'd come home, he looked satisfied. I didn't want to ruin that for him.

"So what did you want to talk about?" he asked.

"Just wanted to see how you are."

"I thought we already established that."

"So we have." I tried to come up with another topic, one that had nothing to do with his going AWOL, but my mind was a blank. I leaped to my feet. "I'll hail you a hack."

He looked up and down the road. There was color in his face for the first time since I'd seen him Stateside. "I don't want to go yet. This feels good."

"The fall sun?"

"All of it. The weather. The job. The company. I really do thank you for your persistence."

I sank back onto the bench. "Making you the first person to ever thank me for such a thing."

"You do have a way of overstepping your bounds."

"So I'm learning."

He stared at the buildings in front of us. The sun was setting and putting on a spectacular show, painting the skyscraper glass a thousand shades of pink. It wasn't an island sunset, but it was extraordinary in its own way. Maybe better. "I really missed this city. Sometimes it feels like New York is the only great city left. London's in ruins. Paris is occupied. Only Manhattan stands proud and sturdy."

I thought of the view I'd witnessed on the way to Staten Island. Would that be all that was left of New York one day? "Do you think the war will ever reach here?"

He shook his head. "No. They'll try. Maybe they're trying now. But I think we're safe."

I wasn't so certain. After all, Hans was still out there. And he was the only one we knew about.

He turned until he was facing me head-on. "I'm surprised you didn't step in for Ann."

"Ruby's a much better choice. Trust me. And I like being in the chorus. Even if I never get noticed, I'm proud to be part of it. Wasn't that always your argument: do theater you're proud of?"

"Something like that." His eyes never left mine. The way he was looking at me was making me uncomfortable.

"For the record, you were right before—it was Candy's idea for you to do the show. I figure I should give credit where credit is due."

"She thinks I blame her."

"Do you?"

Finally, he broke the gaze. "Of course not. I blame myself for getting in this stupid position to begin with. If I'd kept my mouth shut, I'd be in such a different place right now."

"Like maybe a watery grave in the South Pacific?" The rush-hour foot traffic picked up its pace. "When did you first meet her?"

"Candy?" I nodded. "January, I guess." January. When I was first trying to muster the courage to write to him and tell him how I felt. Only by then, he'd already moved on. What a fool I'd been. "I couldn't stand her at first. She and those friends of hers—they thought they ruled the island. But when I told her I was in trouble, she rallied right away. Came up with a hiding place, and when she knew they were going to try to flush me out, she came up with a plan." He pulled a cigarette out of his pocket and lit it. "Who told you I was dead?"

I don't know why, but I didn't want to tell him about Peaches. He didn't need to know that I'd moved on, too. I wanted him to stew on the idea that he was the one who'd betrayed me. "I got a letter," I said.

"That must've been hard."

I looked away from him, worried that if I didn't, I might start to cry. "So what exactly happened with your CO? I've never gotten the full story. I don't even know the guy's name."

Jack exhaled a perfect smoke ring. It was a party trick of his. He could send loops into loops, each as distinct and fluffy as a cloud. "His name is Captain Franklin Ascott, but most of us called him the old sonofabitch."

I froze. Ascott. That was Peaches' last name. "Was he from Georgia?"

"Yes, ma'am," he said in a perfect imitation of a Southern drawl. "How'd you know?"

"Lucky guess."

"One of the pilots on our tub was his son. Kid got hell for that, believe you me. Especially since he was getting all the plum assignments. Of course, it wasn't his fault the old sonofabitch was unfair. It was in his nature, just like his hatred of anyone who wasn't as white as the driven snow. God he hated the Italians and the Jews. And if you had a drop of Mexican or black in you, you were done as far as he was concerned. One night a group of us were sent on a boat to one of the islands off Guadalcanal—recon of sorts. We were looking for missing men, floating bodies, what have you. It was a rotten mission. Most of us were handpicked because we'd been mouthing off on the ship. I just wanted to get through the night and get off that little boat. This guy Jimmy starts giving the captain trouble about how he picked his crew. I didn't hear it all, and honestly it doesn't matter what the guy said, because there weren't enough words to make what happened to him all right."

"What happened?"

"The old sonofabitch shot him. Point-blank. Right in the head. And then he tossed his body overboard." He paused, as though Jimmy needed a moment of silence. "The men went nuts. He knew he had a mutiny on his hands. And so he told them that they could either forget what they'd just seen or join Jimmy in the big drink. And one by one, he picked them off, even the fellows who promised they wouldn't say a word."

I hadn't breathed in almost a minute. "How did you survive?"

He shook his head, a faint smile playing across his lips. "How else? I talked my way out of it. I convinced him he needed a witness. That if he came back the only man alive, no one was going to believe his story. But if I was there to corroborate, they just might buy it." He ashed his cigarette on the ground. "And I did. We came up with this wild tale of an ambush by a couple of Japs. We even fired a few shots in the hull to make it look like they'd pursued us. But I couldn't let it rest. The men who hadn't gone with us wouldn't have believed a story like that. And I respected them too much to lie to them."

"So he found out you told them the truth?"

"No. I was careful. But he still came after me. He knew a witness was dangerous no matter which side I claimed to be on. We were on Tulagi then. I was a wreck. I couldn't sleep. I couldn't eat.

All I could think about were those dead men. And so I went to the infirmary, hoping they'd give me something to make my mind stop running. They let me stay the night. Not a soul was with me." I could picture the scene. I'd been in that infirmary. Jayne had recuperated there. Gilda DeVane had breathed her last breath within its walls. "He shot me when I was lying down, half asleep. I heard the bone shatter."

"Oh, God."

"To this day, I don't know how I got away. I guess I had youth on my side. Even with my leg ruined, I knew those jungles better than he did." He didn't have to tell the rest of the story. Candy had found him shelter, had helped him heal, and then when word had gotten out that he might still be alive, a few loyal men from his own crew helped stage his death by claiming he'd dived into the ocean and met his fate in the shark-filled waters.

I gave the story the silence it deserved. "How do you think they found you?"

He laughed. "Oh, I know how they found me. It was Ascott's son who led them there."

"So he really was as bad as his father." At least I had confirmation now.

"No," said Jack. "He saved me."

I shook my head, as though it were the echo in my noggin that made me mishear him. "What do you mean?"

"Word had gotten back to the old sonofabitch that I was alive. He was going to flush me out and kill me. If Peaches—that's what we called his son—hadn't gotten there first and placed me under arrest, I'd be dead."

Was it possible? Peaches hadn't arrested Jack because he was jealous of my feelings for him; he'd arrested him to protect him from his own father. And how did I reward him? By refusing to talk to him ever again.

"Are you all right?" asked Jack.

"It's just an upsetting story, that's all."

"Try living through it."

I tried to shake Peaches out of my head. If I was going tell Jack about Whitey, I had to do it now. "If there was someone to corroborate your story, would you go after Ascott?"

"There isn't anyone. It's my word against his."

"But there were other men there that night. The night you ran into the jungle."

He cocked his head at me. "How do you know that?"

"It was a small island, Jack. People talked. If one of them was willing to speak up for you, would you be willing to take on the old sonofabitch then?"

"You're never going to find anyone willing to do that."

I passed him the letter. "You're wrong. I already have."

He unfurled the page and read it. When he was done, he carefully refolded it and then stared at the closed letter. A car horn shrieked its warning, followed by a cabbie shouting an expletive. "I don't understand. Where did you get this?"

"This guy Whitey was part of your crew, Jack. He told me he'd do anything to help you."

"When?"

I tapped the page with my hand. "Now. In this letter."

He cocked his head to the left. "No. You've talked to him before."

I hadn't thought this through. There was no way to explain how I'd met Whitey, how he'd come to tell me that he'd do anything for Jack.

"I mentioned your name. That's all," I said.

"Sure, I bet it is." He stubbed out the cigarette on the bench and awkwardly rose. "I should get home. You know Mamie."

"That I do." I hailed a taxi and helped him into the backseat. Once he pulled away, I sat back on the bench and stayed there until the sun finished sinking behind the buildings.

CHAPTER 27

The Last Enemy

I walked the whole way home. I needed the distance to sort out my thoughts. I finally understood why Peaches had lied to me about Jack, why he'd changed crews, why he'd helped smoke him out in the end. There was a sense of family loyalty driving him and repelling him at the same time. It had to be hell being told one tale by the men you served with and another by a commanding officer whose blood ran in your veins. Who do you believe—the man you've known your whole life or the ones who couldn't stop snickering when they found out you were the captain's son?

What price had he paid when he'd decided that helping Jack was more important than being loyal to his father?

Yet . . . if you were born of someone evil, someone full of hate, wasn't there a chance that you carried that bile, too? I liked to think we each came into this world with a fair shake, but just like Billy's nationality made me question him, I had to wonder precisely how innocent Peaches really could be. He did the right thing this time, but would that always be the case?

But, then, was it always the case with me?

A group of young women were gathered outside Whelan's drugstore. They were disassembling a table that had been set up during daylight hours. I paused to read the sign that had announced their purpose:

WRITE A SOLDIER. BE A PEN PAL. MAKE A DIFFERENCE IN THE WAR.

"Excuse me," I said to a girl in a plaid skirt. "Do you have V-mail?"

"We sure do." She pulled a piece out of a box and passed it my way.

"Any chance I could borrow a pen, too?"

She removed one from her lapel pocket. There, in near darkness, I scribbled a note.

Dear Peaches,

  I know now. Everything. And I forgive you, even if there is nothing to forgive you for. Can you forgive me?

Rosie

I still knew his address by heart. I dropped the letter in a mailbox and continued on my way home, so lifted by my actions that I felt like I was flying.

Jayne and I stayed up late that night talking and drinking in our old room.

"So guess who asked me out today," she said when I'd finished my tale of Jack and Peaches.

"Tony?"

"Ha ha. No that sweet little private in the show with us. Henry Bankshead."

So much for taking my advice and giving her time. "What'd you tell him?"

"I said sure."

I shook my head like there was water trapped in my ears. "Did you or did you not just reconcile with Tony?"

"He helped me out, but nobody made any promises. I don't think I want to be anyone's girl for a while."

I don't know why, but that made me sad. Maybe it was learning about Tony's past that had changed him for me. He wasn't just a mobster anymore and that meant I couldn't dismiss him out of hand as a bad idea. And there was something to be said for his persistence. The minute Jack was out of sight, he'd found someone new and gave them his heart. Even with Jayne thousands of miles away, Tony hadn't been willing to give up on her.

Jayne noticed the shift in my mood. "I thought you'd be glad that I wasn't repeating the same mistakes."

"I don't know that I completely believe Tony's a mistake."

"I don't just want to be some moll," said Jayne.

"You were never a moll."

"I dated a gangster. What would you call me?"

"Misguided. Prone to living dangerously. I think Tony has to be married to someone else for you to be a moll. And for all of his many, many faults, I actually think he intends to put a ring on your finger one of these days."

"He already has."

"You know what I mean. Not some piece of ice that's intended to make up for his stupidity. He loves you. I really believe that."

"Yeah? Maybe one of these days that'll be enough." For all the confessions I'd made in the past twenty-four hours, there were lots of things Jayne had never explained. Not that she needed to, but it had to be hard to discover that neither Billy nor Tony were who they claimed to be. That was the kind of knowledge that might put you off men for life.

And perhaps she was right that being with Tony was just repeating past mistakes. It's not like marriage to a mobster had worked out so grand for Betty Garvaggio.

"So when's the big date?" I asked.

"Tomorrow after rehearsal."

I suddenly remembered that I hadn't exactly been straight with dear old Henry. "Did you tell him about Billy?"

"No. I don't think I want to. If I want to move forward, I've got to stop thinking about the past."

Not so with me. After all, with Ann gone, I could now move back into my old digs, and Jayne and I could return to our normal lives. As she readied my bed, I crept into Ruby's room, intending to gather my things. She hadn't said anything to me since rehearsal, and it didn't escape my notice that she was pointedly ignoring me as I pulled my suitcase out from under the bed.

"Where's Al?"

She jerked a nod toward the bathroom.

"I'm sorry," I said.

"Oh, really? For what?" She fluttered her lashes in the worst parody of innocence since Capone was put on trial.

"I know you didn't squeal on Al. And I know you've helped him a lot more than I have." I tossed a few loose things into the case and snapped it shut. "You did me a good turn by letting me stay here, Ruby. I shouldn't have lied to you about Vinnie."

She stared at me for a moment, and I thought that would be the end of the conversation—just silence delivered to make me wonder what she was really thinking. But Ruby had changed. "Your apology is accepted. So, is Ann gone for good?"

"From New York, definitely."

"Thank God for small favors."

"She was more complicated than you might think. All that bluster about being too good for acting—there was a reason behind it."

She put aside the script she'd been memorizing and sat up. "There's never a good reason for putting down what other people cherish."

I'd have to remind her that she said that. "Al's welcome to bunk with Jayne and me. I know you must be dying to get your privacy back."

"Actually, I think it would be better if he stayed here. After all, Belle knows you two regularly hide contraband. I, on the other hand, follow the rules. She has no reason to come into my room without an invitation."

She had a point, I guess. "So you've squared things with Belle?"

"Now that I have a job and have promised her I've given up the devil's brew, things are fine between us."

"We'll move Al to a hotel as soon as the show opens. Jayne said she's happy to pony up the cash. Here." I passed her a small wad of bills that Jayne had been kind enough to give me. "It's one month's rent and a hundred clams for your trouble. A promise is a promise."

She raised an eyebrow and pushed the money back toward me. "Keep your cabbage, Rosie. Once I'm back, you're going to need it a lot more than I am."

That first night back in our room was pure heaven. I slept deeper and longer than I had in months and woke up with a smug little smile planted on my face. So this was home. Why had it taken so long to get here?

The next day at rehearsal, the new additions to the cast made me increasingly hopeful that the show had more bite than I'd given Lawrence credit for. For once in my life I wasn't jealous of those whose parts were bigger than mine. I was happy to be in the chorus and enjoying the newfound camaraderie with the men I'd gone to dinner with, including Henry Bankshead. I began to see the possibility of making Manhattan more like Tulagi. We didn't have to travel thousands of miles to make a difference. We could do it right here, just by spending time with these boys before they shipped off to their next location.

After rehearsal, Jayne left with Henry for their date. He was a nervous, jittery mess, and I didn't hold out much hope for their evening together. Oh, they'd have fun, Jayne being Jayne, but he seemed to have a lot more invested in the event than she did, based on his careful attention to grooming alone.

I journeyed home by myself, expecting to find Tony waiting outside the Shaw House, demanding to know where Jayne was, or the fake G-man inquiring once again about Ann. Or maybe even Hans Richter, ready to finish whatever he had started. But there was no one there . . . except Jack.

"Hiya," I said as he approached. How had he gotten here before me? We'd left the theater at the same time.

He seemed to read my mind. "I took a cab. I tried to catch up with you."

"Is everything okay?"

"Yes. I just wanted to tell you that I wrote to Whitey."

"For real?"

He nodded. "I've decided to go forward with the trial."

"Good for you." Reflexively, I went to touch him, but it suddenly occurred to me that it wouldn't be appropriate. Instead of resting a hand on his arm, I closed my fist and gave him a gentle punch.

"Easy, Jake LaMotta. I've only got one leg, remember?"

I smiled at his joke. "How'd Candy take the news?"

"She's supportive. I think she knows I'm up for a battle."

"And your parents?"

"Don't know yet. I want to get my ducks in a row before I break the news to them." He cleared his throat and ran his finger along the inside of his shirt collar. "I can't thank you enough, Rosie. For the job, for tracking down Whitey. You really went to bat for me."

"It was nothing. Really."

"Still, you've been a good friend at a time when I don't know that I really deserved it." His eyes burned into mine. If I hadn't already accepted that he was Candy's, if I wasn't holding out hope that Peaches and I could still work things out, I'm not sure what I would've been thinking at that moment. As it was, I just wanted him to leave before things got any more uncomfortable. "I–"

I didn't want to know what he was going to say next. Whatever it was would disappoint me. "Really, don't mention it," I said. "Someday, maybe you'll do the same for me."

He nodded deeply, acknowledging my silent request to leave the past in the past. "I know this is a lot to ask, but will you come?"

"To the trial? I guess. I mean sure, if you need me to."

"Good. I think it's exactly what I need." He looked up the street. The dimmed lights made the road seem like it was awash in water. "I should go."

"Need help getting a cab?"

He tapped his crutch. "No thanks. I'm getting pretty good getting around on my own."

I went into the parlor and stood at the window, watching him as he walked away. He was right—he was doing a fine job on his own.

Jayne got home just after midnight. I was still up, reading a copy of *Photoplay* Ann had left behind and slowly draining a cocktail I'd used as my evening's entertainment.

"How'd it go?" I asked her as she came in. She looked exhausted but happy. They must've gone dancing. An evening of rug cutting always did that to her.

"It was nice. He was nice."

"Good. Are you going to see him again?"

"I don't know yet. Maybe. If he wants to see me again." She kicked off her shoes and dropped onto her bed.

"I can't imagine why he wouldn't."

She didn't respond. We both were asleep within the hour. When we awoke in the morning, it was with the knowledge that it was the day of our final rehearsal. It would be a crazy afternoon of last-minute costume fittings, lighting adjustments, and scenery repairs that was bound to run until late in the evening. Inevitably, things would go terribly wrong, convincing us that the show was on a crash course to disaster.

I tried to look forward to the predictable chaos as Jayne and I enjoyed breakfast and the morning papers. But real disaster lurked on the front page and demanded I pay heed: PLOT UNCOVERED TO PLANT EXPLOSIVES AT STAGE DOOR CANTEEN.

"Did you see this?" I asked Jayne. She shook her head and joined me at my side of the table. Together, we read about how the police had unraveled a plan to plant bombs in the basement of the Forty-fourth Street theater, where the USO's popular nightclub was filled every night with visiting servicemen. What the article didn't say was when the plan had been discovered. Was this something they were made aware of last week? Last month? Or had it occurred much earlier than that, and only now that the danger was long past did the government allow the press to cover it?

"Could you imagine?" said Jayne. "They could've killed hundreds of men at once."

It wasn't clear who "they" were. The article made vague reference to the other spies on trial in New York and New Jersey but never came out and said they were the ones behind the plot. They could've been the masterminds, but then so could've Hans Richter or any number of nameless, faceless spies who hadn't yet been captured.

"The suspect is currently in custody," concluded the article. "But authorities believe coconspirators may still be at large."

We set the paper and our breakfast aside. Neither of us had any appetite left.

At eleven we joined Ruby and headed out for our last rehearsal. Before we could make it out of the building, Tony appeared and asked Jayne if he could talk to her.

"I've got rehearsal."

"It won't take long. If you want, I could give you a ride to the theater so you won't be late."

"Okay," she said, her voice strong and steady. "I guess I can do that."

Ruby and I left them to their business and hurried on our way.

Jayne didn't need to worry about being late. When we arrived, the theater was in a state of chaos. News of the plot in the basement had spread fast and created two new problems: increased theater security and worry that the general public might be too scared to set foot in the theater. None of us could get in the building right away. Instead, we were subjected to a rigorous up and down by an army of MPs stationed at the door. They were hardest on the men, especially those fellows who had the misfortune to possess features that made them look foreign. While the women passed through with very little scrutiny, these soldiers who were willing to risk their lives for our country were subjected to insulting questions about their reasons for doing the show, their family's nationality, and their allegiance to Roosevelt.

The whole thing left a terrible taste in my mouth.

"Rosie!" While I was waiting in line, I heard a male voice calling my name. Henry Bankshead was ten feet away, his features turned sickly by the green of his army fatigues. At his feet was a large duffle bag that was packed so tightly its zipper strained.

I left the line and approached him. "What's with the getup?"

"I got my orders this morning."

"Seriously?"

He shrugged. "I know—rotten timing. I was hoping they'd give me more time with the show and all, but apparently the war aces everything."

"Do you know where you're going?"

He looked nervously toward the MPs. "I'm not sure that I'm allowed to say. Anyways, I was hoping I could talk to Jayne."

"She got held up at home."

"Nuts."

"I'm sure she'll be here soon."

"I don't think I can wait. I wasn't supposed to stop by here to begin with, but I couldn't stand the thought of taking off without saying good-bye." He fished an envelope out of his pocket and passed it to me. "Would you give her this?"

"Of course."

"And maybe, if it's not too much trouble, could you give me an address where I could write her?"

"Absolutely." I scribbled her contact information on a piece of paper and passed it to him.

"I have one more favor to ask. It's kind of a big one."

"I'm not kissing her good-bye for you."

He blushed and looked away. "No, nothing like that. We were talking last night about opening-night traditions. You know gifts and flowers and things. I got her something. I was wondering if you might hide it in the dressing room and give it to her tomorrow night, if she's not too sore at me for taking off."

"Sure, Henry. I'd be happy to."

He unzipped the duffle and pulled out a rumpled cardboard box with a bow circling its center. "It's kind of heavy."

I bowed under its weight. What did he have in there? Iron filings?

"It's a book," he said. "I didn't have time to shop, but I thought she might like it. I told her last night about how my ma used to read to me from it when I was small."

"Are you sure you want to give up something like that?" I asked. "It sounds pretty personal."

"She's had a hard time lately. I figure she could use a few fairy tales in her life. And besides . . ." His voice faded away. That was okay—I didn't want to hear what came next, especially if it had anything to do with the possibility that he wouldn't need the book anymore because he wasn't coming back. A horn honked somewhere. "I gotta go," he said. "Thanks a million, Rosie."

"Anytime."

"And break a leg tomorrow night."

A half hour later we were finally in the theater. I went up to the dressing room to get in my costume and stash Jayne's present. My timing couldn't have been better: she arrived five minutes later.

"So," I said, hoping that was all the prompt she needed to spill about Tony. But her lips were sealed tight. The conversation was either too upsetting to repeat or too private to share. "Henry asked me to give you this." I passed her the envelope. As she read it, her face slowly sank into a frown.

"He's gone?"

"For now. But he'll be back." They were weak, poorly chosen words. Words she'd used to reassure me about Jack. Words I'd said when she was worried about Billy. They were no more real than a fairy tale.

A tear formed in the corner of her eye and started its slow journey. "I know it was only one date, but I felt good again, you know? Like maybe things wouldn't always go wrong. I even told Tony . . ."

"Told Tony what?"

"Never mind. It's not important."

"Don't assume the worst, Jayne. He might be fine."

"But he might not be. That's the problem."

Between her mood and the anxiety hanging over the theater, rehearsal was a miserable affair. Bentley frequently interrupted the action with reports of canceled reservations. We weren't allowed to go home until almost midnight. Even if there were only ten people in the audience the next night, Lawrence wanted the show to be perfect.

Jayne, Ruby, and I took a hack home and silently climbed up to our respective rooms. Even being in my own bed couldn't take away the sour taste the day had left behind.

I slept like the dead and didn't dream.

In the morning I woke up bound and determined to make this day go better than the one before. The first thing I was going to do was unpack my things. I was back in my own room, after all. There was no reason to continue living out of a suitcase. As I restored my belongings to their previous positions, I found the box of things I'd rescued from Mrs. Gottlieb's basement.

I looked toward Jayne, who was lying in bed reading a comic. Should I give her the things I'd saved for her now or wait a few months, when the memory of everything that had happened was less raw?

"What is it?" she asked me.

The decision had been made. "I'm not sure if you still want this," I told her. "But these are the things Johnny left behind."

She closed the comic and claimed the box. Slowly, as though she feared she might find a body part inside, she removed the lid. Out came the letters, the shaving cup, the Bible, and the photo. She stared at each item as though she were trying to remember it for posterity, then picked up the loot and dumped it in the trash.

"What are you doing?" I asked.

"I threw out the other stuff last week. I don't want anything out there that would tie Billy to his past. Just in case."

"That seems smart."

"Do you think this stuff will burn?" she asked.

"Don't know. The cup and the frame might be a problem."

She plucked the photo from the pile, pried open the back of Johnny's frame, and removed the picture from it. She was about to return it to the wastebasket when she stopped and frowned. "Hey."

"What?"

"The photo's folded." She showed me the flap that had been facing the rear of the frame. There was a third man in the photo, the one whose foot had been on the edge of Billy's copy. "It's Hans, isn't it?"

I gestured for her to come closer to the window and we stared down at this new visage. I couldn't say if it was Hans or not, but I did know one thing for sure: the guy in the photo was a dead ringer for Private Henry Bankshead.

CHAPTER 28

Let's Face It!

It wasn't hard to put together what was going on. Henry was Hans. Hans was a saboteur. He and his cousins were sent here to do whatever they could to thwart the Americans and injure their morale. What better way to do that than to disrupt a performance involving hundreds of enlisted men? And what could be easier than pretending to be an enlisted man yourself in order to get cast? Especially if you came from a family of actors.

"Maureen must've seen him," said Jayne.

Of course. The day we'd auditioned, she'd looked upset and distracted. Henry had told me he'd been scared away from the dance audition, but it wasn't because he didn't know how to dance. He realized the choreographer was his aunt. And if he had any hope of infiltrating the show, he had to get rid of her. That's why he killed her—not because of us or Johnny or Billy. That was all just a terrible coincidence.

"At least he's gone," said Jayne. "The increased security at the theater must've spooked him."

Thank God for small favors. If the article hadn't been in the paper, who knows what Hans may have had planned for tonight. As a member of the cast he would've had access to anywhere in the—

"Oh, God."

"What's the matter?" asked Jayne.

"He gave me a package for you yesterday. He asked me to hide it in the dressing room to give it to you tonight."

"So you . . ."

"Did exactly what he asked. He made me his patsy."

We were out the door in two minutes.

The guards were still stationed at the theater doors. We hadn't even finished our story before they had left their post and headed toward the dressing room. The package was still there, still intact. As we watched from the curb, a dozen police cars arrived and the box was whisked away.

I don't think either of us breathed for a half hour.

The MPs advised us to stay put until we were told otherwise. We passed the time in a coffee shop across the street. Two hours passed. Three. Four. I was stretched so thin you could've played a violin sonata on me. If the cops set the bomb off, could we hear it from here? How powerful was it? Would it have just felled the theater, or was the entire city at risk? How ironic that after all these weeks of worrying about Manhattan being a target and accusing Ann of being a spy, I was the one who unknowingly put us at risk. Would they arrest me as an accessory? What about Jayne? Would our remaining days be spent in the bing surrounded by hardened women who were so intimidated by what we'd done that they deferred to us at every turn?

Who would play us in the movie?

Just as we were about to start our fifth hour of waiting for disaster, a siren warned that that the police were approaching. Only these weren't standard black and whites that pulled to the curb.

These were G-men cars—slick, black, anonymous vehicles to match the slick black suits the occupants wore. The coppers pulled to the curb and, after a quick exchange with the MPs, headed our way.

"Thanks for waiting, ladies," said the man in charge. He was all angles, from his wide shoulders to his chiseled jaw. He had to be FBI or CIA, or maybe a member of one of those more mysterious organizations set up specifically to deal with wartime crime.

"Were you able to disarm the bomb?" I asked.

"It wasn't necessary." He gestured to one of the blue-clad officers who'd accompanied him. The copper produced a book and passed it his way. "This was what was inside the box."

It was a copy of *Grimm's Fairy Tales* in the original German.

"That's it?" I said.

"That's it." He returned the book to the flatfoot. "Of course, given what you've told us, it doesn't mean that there isn't a bomb in the building. Just that this isn't it."

"So what are you going to do?" asked Jayne. Arrest us, I thought, for wasting everyone's time.

"Sweep the building. Comb every inch, just in case. You dames have uncovered something big, and it's obvious Hans was using this book to send us a message."

Yeah, I thought, there are no happy endings. I looked at my wristwatch. We were four hours to curtain. "How are you going to search the building when the show opens tonight?"

"Not tonight, sister," he said. "No one's going near that theater until we're certain it's secure. Now tell me everything you know about Hans Richter and his cousins Wilhelm and Johann."

They whisked us away to a nondescript federal building. There, over rapidly cooling cups of joe, we gave our statement as a wire recorder captured every nuance for some poor stenographer to transcribe later. There was no way to keep Billy out of it, though we both made it clear that, as far as we knew, he'd never done anything wrong. I still had the target list and Johnny's German letters in my handbag, so I surrendered them to the feds, along with the photo of the three men that Jayne had uncovered that morning. There were a few details we didn't share. Like the five thousand dollars we'd squirreled away or how I'd given the mob a trunk full of guns and bomb-making materials in exchange for their help.

"So, as far as you know, Wilhelm's belongings are still in the basement of the Yorkville rooming house?" asked our interrogator. I nodded. "And what about Johann's? Is it still in"—he consulted his notes—"Irma Gottlieb's house in Newark?"

"Gosh, I don't know," I said. "I guess it must be, unless Hans came back and got it."

By the time we got home, it was almost midnight. The feds dropped us off in front of the Shaw House and took off as soon as our feet met the pavement. Our safety was not their number-one concern; Hans Richter was.

For a moment, Jayne and stood on the street and stared at each other. Then, because exhaustion and stress had worn us both to nubs, we began to laugh hysterically. How had all of this happened? Less than a month ago we were two girls on our way home from a USO tour, and now we were key witnesses in a plot against the United States.

"Shhhhhh . . ." said Jayne just as our laughter was approaching epic proportions. Everyone must be asleep. The house was cloaked in darkness, every light either turned off or blocked from our view by the blackout blinds.

I caught my breath and let the laughter die in my throat. "Boy, is Lawrence going to be upset," I said. "That show isn't opening anytime soon."

"Lawrence? What about Ruby?" said Jayne. "She's never going to forgive us for this."

I wondered if I could ask the feds not to mention our role in what happened, just to be safe.

"I still don't understand why he left me the book," said Jayne.

"Maybe he actually *was* sweet on you."

She made a face. "What if it was a distraction?"

"Huh?"

"What if he was worried we'd put two and two together and that once the Stage Door Canteen plot got out, there'd be too much security around for him to do whatever he intended to do. So he leaves the book, knowing that the feds will jump on it, giving him time to escape." Boy she was smart. And why I was surprised? Did I think if I acknowledged her intelligence I had to question my own?

"If that's the case, I hope wherever he lands is some place far, far away from here."

We tiptoed up the stairs and into the foyer. While Jayne fumbled with her keys, I tried the interior door. It was unlocked.

The parlor was pitch black. I stumbled to the side table to turn on the lamp, but it wasn't there. Had someone rearranged the furniture again? Before I could explore the terrain, a lamp clicked on from across the room, illuminating the space and our company: Hans Richter.

Jayne and I froze. He had a gun in his hand and it was pointed right at us.

"It's about time," he said. "I've been waiting for you for several hours. I assumed the show would be out by now." The country bumpkin accent was gone. In its place was something vaguely European, though after years of suppressing his German intonation, he had, like Billy, almost eliminated it entirely.

"The show didn't happen," I said. "When the feds found out you were lurking around, they thought it best to shut us down just in case you left any surprises lying around the theater."

"So you put it together, did you?"

I crossed my arms. I hoped it made me look tough, but the truth was I did it to keep myself from shaking. "It wasn't that hard. Johann had a picture of the three of you together."

"He always was sentimental," he said. "And now the police and government are tied up searching a theater that isn't even a target. Doesn't sound like a very good use of their time."

"They're also looking for you."

The left side of his mouth quirked into a smile. "Yes, but not here."

"Not yet." I was fully committed to keeping this verbal sparring going, but Jayne had no such desires.

"Why didn't you blow up the theater?" she asked.

The gun was so shiny that it reflected the entire room. "I thought about it. And up until a few days ago I probably would've gone through with it, but then the plot at the Stage Door Canteen was uncovered and the opportunity was lost. Fortunately, my time here wasn't a complete waste. Thanks to Rosie I got two things I've been waiting a long time for."

I turned to Hans. "What are you talking about?"

"Don't play dumb, Rosie. It doesn't become you. The trips to Yorkville, the visit to my aunt, Jayne's jaunt to Newark—it's obvious you two were trying to flush Billy out. So where is he?" He turned until the gun was pointed at Jayne alone. There were two of her now: the one beside me and the one reflected in the revolver.

"He's dead," she said.

"Don't lie."

"It's not a lie. He enlisted last year. He was shot down in the South Pacific in July."

A normal person might've shown emotion at the news his cousin was dead. But Hans was hardly a normal person. The smile spread across his lips, and he let out a chuckle so menacing I was afraid it would suck all the air from the room. "Of all the things for him to do, of all the places for him to end up. He thought he was being clever, didn't he? Enlisting. And look what it got him—dead."

"He changed his mind," said Jayne. "He didn't want to be like you."

"He was a coward. He could've been set for life you know. He would've been a hero."

"You should go," I said. "You got what you came for—you know where Billy is now."

"But that's not all I came for. It's a relief to know Billy won't be a problem, but I have an old score to settle." He glanced at his watch. "One that should be arriving any minute now."

"What are you talking about?" said Jayne.

He said I'd given him two things he'd been waiting a long time for. Two? And that's when it came to me: Sal and Adam had told me everything I needed to know about what Hans was up to, but I was too wrapped up in my own theories to put it together. "Tony. You want revenge on Tony, don't you? You're the one who's been gunning for him."

"Why?" asked Jayne. "Because of Johnny?"

"That idiot?" said Hans. "Tony did me a favor. He was going to be a traitor just like Wilhelm."

"No, this is about something else," I said. "Tony ran Hans and the rest of the Nazis out of Newark. He killed his father. He's been hoping to take him out ever since."

Hans nodded to acknowledge that I spoke the truth. "And I'd given up thinking I'd ever be able to pull it off until Rosie told me that Tony and you had recently broken up, Jayne. Thanks to her, I got exactly what I wanted."

"What's that?" she asked.

He smiled again. "Bait." A car door closed outside the building. "Look at that—right on time. I wouldn't have thought a mobster would be punctual. That speaks well of you, Jayne. He cares about you enough not to dally." He jerked the gun upward. "Let him in, Rosie. But let's make this perfectly clear: if you tip him off to my presence, your friend will die. Understood?"

"Understood," I said.

Hans took hold of Jayne's arm and pulled her to the side of the room, so Tony wouldn't see her when he first entered the building. I went to the foyer and found Tony on the front stoop, pacing. With a quick look back at Hans and Jayne, I took a deep breath and opened the door.

"Come on in," I said.

"Is Jayne okay? I got her message."

"Yeah, she wants to talk is all." *Please read my mind*, I begged. *You can be a perceptive guy. Don't let those powers fail you now.*

"At midnight?"

"What Jayne wants, Jayne wants." I turned and Tony followed me back into the building. Once we were both inside, I struggled with the lock until it clicked into place.

"She change her mind about things?"

"You'll have to talk to her, Tony."

He looked nervously around the room, seeing everything but the two figures hidden in his blind spot. "You sure this is a good idea? What about your housemother?"

"She sleeps like the dead." *Stop talking*, I begged. *Don't make me say anything else to lead you on.* Tony rounded the corner. Before he had time to respond, a shot fired.

It missed Tony by an inch. His years of boxing had taught him to be fast and nimble, even if his lifestyle since didn't regularly call upon those skills. As he gathered himself together, he called out Hans's name like a war cry that had been taught to him since his tribe's founding.

"RICHTER!"

Hans seemed surprised that he'd missed with the first shot. Rather than immediately taking a second, he stared at the iron as though he couldn't believe the gun had failed him. Jayne sensed his distraction, wrenched herself free, and slammed her elbow into Hans's stomach. The gun went flying. Tony yelled at Jayne to run while I tried to find a spot out of the line of fire. Upstairs, chaos broke loose as the sound of gunfire wrenched everyone from sleep. A rush of women appeared on the upstairs landing, wanting to diagnose the cause of the commotion. The sight of the two sparring men and the revolver on the ground set off squeals of panic and sent those who had left their rooms back into them. Someone hollered for everyone to lock their doors.

"Get Jayne out of here, Rosie," roared Tony. I snagged her

blouse and pulled her behind the sofa. For a moment, time slowed down. Tony had the gun, then Hans, then Tony again. I grabbed Jayne's arm, crawled to the kitchen door, and pulled her through it with me. Together, we barred the entrace with the pastry table and braced our bodies against it. Another shot fired, but we were blind to who was giving and who was receiving. A woman screamed. Footsteps sounded as someone ran to the front door. Whoever it was couldn't get it open, though; the new lock wasn't budging. Abandoning that option, they slammed against the kitchen door, setting our teeth to rattle, but it, too, wouldn't move. The footsteps moved away, faster and faster. Without thinking, I pushed the table from the door and peeked out of the kitchen just in time to see Hans running across the parlor and up the stairs. He was looking for another way out.

"Tony!" Jayne shrieked. He was on the floor lying in a pool of blood. His skin was the color of newsprint. She pushed past me and ran to him, the bright flush of her face making it all too apparent that his minutes were numbered. Upstairs, Hans tried one door after another, only to find that everyone had locked themselves into their rooms. Everyone except Ruby.

He made it through her door, and a primal scream let me know that Al had been waiting for him. I couldn't see the ruckus, but I could hear the slam of bodies as Al let Hans know exactly what he thought about his shooting his former employer.

I took the steps two at a time and grabbed the phone. As I requested a meat wagon and the police, I watched Hans free himself from Al's grasp and leap out the window and onto the fire escape. He landed with a boom and his body quickly disappeared as he lowered the ladder. Al wasn't done with him yet, though. He climbed after him, picked up his pee basin, and threw it downward. He had no trouble hitting his target. I ran into the room just in time to see Al climb down to the street, where an unconscious Hans lay in puddle of blood and urine.

* * *

By the time the coppers arrived, there wasn't much left of Hans Richter. Oh, he was still alive, but between Al's beat down and the damage done by the washbasin, the man was barely hanging on by a thread. He was taken to the same hospital as Tony, though it was unlikely he would survive.

Tony, on the other hand, was rallying, thank God.

"I can't believe I almost lost you," Jayne told him again and again from her place by his bedside. She refused to leave him, even after stern words from the nurses. She wasn't going to take a chance this time. She'd lost one man she loved; she couldn't bear to lose another.

"Relax, sweetheart. I'll be fine," said Tony. He tried to look strong, but the color was still gone from his face. It was disturbing seeing him so fragile. I'd always considered him, like Jack, immortal.

Maybe that's why I didn't want to leave him, either. I hadn't been vigilant when Billy died. His safety had been the furthest thing from my mind. By sitting through the night with Jayne, I hoped to right that wrong. I'd make sure Tony pulled through this. If I had to donate my own blood, I'd make it happen.

"Rosie," he said to me after Jayne had fallen asleep. "You know where Al is?"

"Yeah."

"You let him know he's back in the fold. Whatever he wants, from here on out, I'm taking care of. Including Vinnie G." He winced as the pain in his chest momentarily reignited. "And you tell him I'm sorry."

"I will. I promise." I poured him a glass of water and fished out one of the white pain pills the night nurse had left for him. "Why'd he do it, Tony? Hans could've gotten away scot-free. Why'd he come back for you?"

He took a pill and chased it with the water. "Ain't no logic in hate."

By morning, the doctors were confident that Tony was going to make it. I offered to get Jayne some clean diapers and went back to the Shaw House to catch some quality Zs. Reinvigorated by my nap and refreshed by a shower, I decided to pay a quick visit to Ruby's room to pass on Tony's message. I knocked on her door, but no one answered. I could hear Ruby wheezing behind it, though, still sleeping off the evening's adventures. Was Al asleep, too? Probably so, but I figured that Tony's message was the kind of news he wouldn't mind waking up for. I still had my key from my brief stay, so I opened the door and peeked inside. Al was asleep all right. In Ruby's bed. With Ruby still in it.

Although they were both fully clothed, they were wrapped in each other's arms in a way that could only be described as familiar. I couldn't stop myself from smiling at the sight. When had this happened? And how had I missed it?

Ruby's eyes opened, and she offered me a stern frown. I was about to apologize for interrupting when she put a finger to her lips and gestured for me to close my head. I nodded my understanding and started toward the door. I was almost there when she snapped her fingers to get my attention.

What? I mouthed.

Key, she mouthed back, then pointed at the dresser, where she wanted me to leave it.

I did so, then left in a fit of giggles.

Ruby might've had a man because of me, but I still owed her. That meant I had to pay a visit to Betty Garvaggio.

I met her at Giradeli's on a Tuesday afternoon. I figured if she was paying, I might as well choose a joint I'd been dying to dine at.

"My mother-in-law loves this place," she groused as we took our seats. She waited until we'd ordered to get down to business. "So? You have a name?"

"Doris Newcomer. She's a former magician's assistant currently taking up space at the Shaw House." I passed her the photo I'd plucked off the foyer wall.

She sneered down at the freckled face. "I wouldn't have pegged her as Vinnie's type."

"She's got nice stems. And sticky fingers." I told her about her subway habit. "So are we settled?"

She nodded, folded the photo in half, and stuck it in her pocketbook. "Consider yourself among the employable." She paused and removed a compact from her purse. With a heavy hand, she applied that blood-red lipstick she was so fond off.

"Thanks for the chow, Betty. And for the stay of execution. If you need anything else in the future, just let me know." I started to leave, but my feet seemed unwilling to work. What had my lying gotten me? Nothing good so far. One by one each falsehood had come back to bite me on the backside. "Look," I said to Betty. "Ruby's not the one going around dropping Vinnie's name. I am."

"Huh?"

I took my seat and prepared myself for humiliation. "Sometimes I need information and I don't want anyone to know it's me who's asking for it, and so I give a false moniker. And because she and I have a bit of history, nine times out of ten, the name I give is Ruby's."

Betty laughed, a deep wondrous sound that vibrated through the floor. "Seriously?"

"I'm not proud. And I'm not regularly dropping Vinnie's name, either. I needed some lock picks, and I took a chance after I saw the shop owner had a racing form. I would've said Tony B.'s name, but I thought Vinnie's carried more weight, no pun intended. If you want to keep me from working, I understand, but it's not fair to Ruby. She might need a few lessons in deportment, but she's not the one you should be sore at."

Betty leaned back in her chair, a glass of red wine in her hand. I wished I could read her mind. She was so much more complex than I'd ever imagined. And so much more terrifying. "Okay, she's off the hook."

"Really?"

"And you are, too. Though there's a good chance I might need these skills of yours in the future. Understood?"

"Understood."

"Now get out of here before I change my—"

I was through the door before she could finish her sentence.

As I came home that afternoon, my stomach full of food paid for with someone else's dime, I mused on how lucky I'd been to survive all my stupid schemes. Jayne and I were friends again; she was ready to move forward with her life. I'd fixed things for Ruby, and Tony and Al were copasetic. Thanks to Billy, we had enough money to see us through the end of the year if the work wasn't there. And Jack had hope and an upcoming shot at justice. I might have been the luckiest person alive to have made it through these horrible few weeks without doing any permanent damage.

"Hi, Rosie."

Candy was waiting for me on the steps of the Shaw House. Maybe it was the wind, but her voice sounded cold to my ears.

"Hiya yourself," I said. "Longtime no see."

She didn't respond in kind. I wasn't imagining it—something about her was changed.

"Everything all right?" I asked.

"I'm not sure how to say this, so I'm just going to come out with it: Why did you lie to me?"

I wasn't prepared for this. "What are you talking about?"

"You went to Tulagi to find him. Why didn't you tell me that?"

My breath caught in my chest. Who had squealed? Jayne in a fit of rage over everything I'd withheld about Billy? Ann? Or was it Ruby who'd accidentally let it slip? "Where'd you get that idea from?" I asked.

"I put it together on my own. I'm right, aren't I?" I was about to deny it when she showed me her hand—her left hand. The one with the engagement ring on it. "Please, Rosie. Stop. Your story hasn't been straight since day one. It wasn't until Jack told me that you'd tracked down a witness that I realized how much you'd been keeping from me. I just don't understand why you didn't come clean."

I was at a loss for words, but I scooped some up anyway. "I'm not sure. It just seemed easier. I mean, how could you and I be friends if you knew why I was there?"

"And how can we be friends after you lied about it?" She absentmindedly played with her ring. "I've tried to figure out what was going through your head. I want to believe that in some convoluted way you were trying to keep me from being hurt the same way you were trying to protect Jayne from the truth about Billy, but I just can't make the story work. There are too many things that don't fit. When you're solving code, sometimes the easiest message is the one you overlook the fastest because you can't accept that it could be so simple. I think that's what happened here." She took a deep breath. "You're still in love with him."

"I'm not," I said.

She shook her head. Tears twinkled in her eyes. "And even after all of that, you can't stop lying to me."

Tony spent a week in the hospital with Jayne at his side the entire time. Much to everyone's amazement, Hans Richter survived his injuries. Until the night of his transfer to prison. When the guards arrived to escort him out of the hospital, they found him hanging from a noose made out of medical tubing, a feat considered quite extraordinary given his injuries and the enormous amount of security that had been stationed outside his door. He'd been dead at least an hour before they discovered him.

Ruby never spoke to me about what I'd seen in her room, nor did I broach the subject beyond asking her to tell Al to get in touch with Tony. Al moved out the next day, but it's certainly not the last time we've seen him at the Shaw House. For better or worse, he's under Ruby Priest's spell.

After the theater was determined to be bomb-free, *Military Men* opened a week late. The first few audiences were pretty thin, but once the reviews started to appear, the numbers picked up. Ruby won raves for her performance, but it was Jack Castlegate who the critics hailed as the real standout. In fact, his praise has been so loud, rumor has it Hollywood is interested in talking to him about starring in a film version of Lawrence's script.

Doris Newcomer was nabbed by the Port Authority police after a woman pointed her out as the purse snatcher who'd stolen her pocketbook as they were exiting the subway. Three other passengers, all Italian immigrants, also came forward with tales of missing wallets. A stack of them were discovered inside a birdcage Doris was toting around. And to add insult to injury, someone in her rooming house reported missing a portion of the cash she'd inherited when her fiancé died. There was no proof that Doris took it, but the circumstances were such that Belle decided it would be best if she found other living arrangements. She hasn't gone to trial yet, but it's not looking good for her. The woman she mugged is married to a high-level gangster with a great attorney.

Speaking of that gangster, no one's heard a peep out of Vinnie G. for weeks.

As for me, I'm keeping my nose clean, sticking to the truth, and slowly coming to accept that I can't rescue everyone. I'm also finally reveling in being home in the slightly changed city that I love. As optimistic as I'm trying to be, I know winter is on the horizon. I can taste it in the night air. And with its bitter chill comes Jack's approaching trial, the one I promised him I'd be at.

For now, though, I'm going to enjoy what the fall has to offer.

Dear Rosie,

Forgiveness is yours. And so is my heart if you'll still have it. I'll be on the West Coast for Christmas. I know it's a million miles from New York, but if there's any way you could swing it, I would love to see you.

Peaches